ICY
LITTLE
PREY

A PARANORMAL SHIFTERS
REVERSE HAREM ROMANCE NOVEL

M.K. KATE

Cover Design by Meredith Hale & Cover Background Photo by @brand169230094

Cover Typography © Bookin' It Designs

Book Interior Graphic Illustrations by Canva, Inc. @andrias-adinata, @raytas, @sketchify, and @eduardocv3

M. K. Kate - https://mkkate.weebly.com

Ebook ASIN: B0DM4PBWMR

Ebook ISBN: 9798224353736

Paperback KDP ISBN: 9798301122699

❊ Created with Vellum

For the reader who wants some hot arctic shifters this holiday season & for the reader who wants to see a cold-hearted Grinch melt just for her

ALSO BY M. K. KATE

Out Now

PRETTY LITTLE PREY: A Smutty Paranormal Shifters
Reverse Harem Romance Novel

ICY LITTLE PREY: A Spicy Holiday Reverse Harem Winter
Shifters Paranormal Romance Novel

Coming Soon

SUCCUBUS LESSONS: A Scorching Incubi Paranormal
Reverse Harem Romance Novel

Prophecy

*Hearts of ice
will melt in snow
for the one woman
they burn to know.
But Arctic shifters are known
for their frigid hearts.
And hares are known to run.*

—*Ye Ole Wise Seer, aka "The Hag," aka "Start listening to my
prophecies, dammit!"*

PROLOGUE

*I*sa's mother used to tell her the tale about the rabbit's foot.

How, once those with power heard of the token of luck, they hunted and removed the paws from the speedy creatures every chance they got.

Once rabbits were known to have a use, that became all they were known for. All they were good for.

"Never let them know what you are," her mother would whisper to Isa every night as she grew up in the harsh Arctic tundra, far from civilization and other Arctic shifters or even humans—for a reason.

Her mother told her, "If they ever find out what you are, that will be all you are good for."

But Isa had been young and naïve, only knowing survival in the tundra.

Never knowing society or relationships. Never knowing that, inside some, there was a selfishness and a cruelness she could have never fathomed.

Isa had not known what hare shifters were known for in the shifter world—especially the females.

Hare shifter females experienced mating hormones at the drop of a hat once they were of mating age. Meanwhile, other prey shifters—lambs, mice, fawns—only went into heat after prolonged exposure to predators as a defense mechanism of *"Please don't kill me. Have sex with me instead!"*

The stereotype was: *One touch and a hare will melt into a puddle of horny need.*

When they went into heat, their lustful bodies overwhelmed their minds, and they emitted sensual airborne chemicals that drove the male shifters mad with lust.

After one inhale of a prey's scent whilst in heat, the alpha males' cocks would swell, their pupils would dilate and grow into huge black circles, and their lips would curl back in an animalistic, primal growl. They would fuck the female hard and relentlessly. And she would... love every second of it. Until her heat ended, and she was left satisfied.

Female hare shifters were known in the shifter world as "Fuck Bunnies."

Only good for one thing; their libidos and ability to move their hips at lightning speed. It created an infamous "lure" for alphas to "try them out."

But as a child, Isa could have never imagined that being a female prey shifter meant that the male predators—werewolves, bear shifters, dragon shifters, etc.—would hunt her, desire her as a rare trophy, and as a toy for their own pleasure.

At too young an age, Isa lost her mother to sickness.

Not yet ten years old, Isa wandered the icy terrain alone for days. Until she was found, shivering and half frozen. She welcomed the new shelter—regardless of how odd its traditions seemed at first.

"You were lucky to be found and adopted by our tribe," said the leader of the cult that found her. "No longer will you be at risk of being hunted. You no longer need to fear being the dinner of an Arctic predator shifter. We will teach you a new way to be valuable to the alphas."

He smiled, and Isa would never forget the way his curled lips gave her chills. "You will be protected because you will have valuable skills," he promised.

If Isa had absorbed her mother's mistrust of every stranger, if she had accepted her mother's teachings to believe everyone was out to get her, Isa might have never ended up in a cult, raised by a leader, calling himself "The Redeemer."

She might have never ended up brainwashed to believe she was only good for providing pleasure and joy as a "pet" to powerful predator shifters.

How would she have ever guessed at that age that the

leader who offered her safety and food intended to sell her off to the highest bidder once she was of mating age?

CHAPTER 1

"*D*amn, Isa, the bow looks perfect. Stop fooling with it," Isa's closest friend, Blanche, told her.

A nervous laugh rang in Isa's throat as she finally lowered her hands and clasped them behind her back. "Sorry, I just...I just want to look perfect."

Blanche rolled her eyes at Isa's overachiever nature. "You want to be adopted that bad?"

"Don't you?" Isa shot back with a huge, dreamy smile. "To bring joy and pleasure to a Master—it's what we were made for."

Blanche frowned at that, which always confused Isa. Granted, Blanche had only been in the tribe for a few years. Isa had been there from age ten. Now, at twenty-two years old, Isa finally qualified for adoption. She finally had the chance to put all her tribe's teachings to work and pursue her life purpose: *to provide pleasure.*

And what better timing to be adopted than right before the holidays?

She practically vibrated with excitement. Isa loved Christmas. Christmas movies had been a pivotal part of her training growing up. Every year, her tribe played *A Christmas Carol,* and her favorite—*The Grinch.*

She may have never experienced a Christmas tree, gift giving, eggnog, or hot chocolate, but those movies were her look into the outside world. Outside of the uncivilized Arctic tundra, where the tribe habited.

In her classes, her teachers reinforced how Santa only gave gifts to the good and obedient. They highlighted how even if the main male character was grumpy, the plot of the holiday stories focused on bringing him joy and reminding him of the world's pleasures.

Isa's classes started as *"you must pleasure and please to survive."* Now, she had graduated to *"I receive pleasure when I give pleasure."*

Each night, she was the perfect student. She always did her homework. Alone in her room, she would remove her clothing, lay on the bed, and grind the heel of her hand between her legs as she repeated her teacher's mantras:

Giving pleasure gives me pleasure.

Good pets revel in making their masters feel good.

Good girls feel so good when they give their masters pleasure.

I am a good girl, and I feel so good.

I will do whatever my master wants.

I will always kneel for master and present my mouth for his pleasure—

"Oh Gods, your eyes are all dazed and glassy again," Blanche commented, pulling Isa out of the short daydream of finally pleasuring a master. "You're getting closer and closer to your first heat cycle."

"Teacher Ryson says I could go into heat in a matter of weeks," Isa replied. "He says that he thinks I will get adopted soon because of it."

After all, if Isa went through her heat *before* she was properly adopted by someone, she could end up in a sexual fever, ready to crawl to any random alpha shifter's doorstep and beg him to fuck her.

The whole point of being adopted was that her master was assured by her tribe that she was pure.

It was said that virgin prey shifters were rare, so the tribe viewed Isa as unique. Special. She was often referred to by the tribe's leader as "the perfect pet." Her people-pleasing, overachiever body hummed whenever he said that.

I must be adopted this year, she thought to herself.

Blanche pressed her lips into a thin line and analyzed Isa's face for a moment in silence. "What happens if you don't like the man who adopts you?"

Blinking, Isa's expression melted into one of complete bafflement. Isa's mouth said words without her thinking, as if they were a triggered response, "Pets love their masters."

"Predator shifters are known to be selfish assholes," Blanche whispered, knowing better than to be over-heard when describing predators while they stood in the hallway. "What if you're adopted by someone cruel?"

"No one can be cruel if they are provided enough joy and pleasure," Isa said in a *stop-being-so-silly-Blanche* tone. "My master will love me, and I will love him."

Even if her new master was a sadistic, cold-hearted wolf or a Polaris bear with blood on his hands, she would warm him like her very own Grinch.

Because love and pleasure and joy could melt any icy man. Right?

"*J* am so proud of all of you," the leader of the tribe—called the Redeemer—said to the line of women who had reached maturation age and stood in beautiful gowns and makeup, waiting to be perused and picked by visiting alphas. "Remember, wolves, foxes, Polaris bears—those predator shifters all have one thing in common. They wish to dominate, and they enjoy pleasure."

The ceremony was set up in his "throne room," which was as obnoxiously decorated as could be assumed when a white man with too much money lived in an igloo palace and deemed himself a cult leader. But naïve Isa thought it was beautiful, considering it was all she knew.

Blue lights were set around the room to reflect and make the ice walls appear to glow like auroras. Isa missed those majestic Northern lights—their beauty stained some of the few memories she still retained of roaming the Arctic terrain with her mother.

Ever since she had been "saved" by the tribe, she had been kept inside, unable to see the sun or the magical rays and dynamic flickers of blue and purple light across the sky.

Females aren't safe outside without their master.

On top of a lifted stage at the front of the throne room—because the Redeemer had to be higher than everyone else—sat a single, red velvet monarch throne chair with button-tufted accents and a regal high back. The ceiling was an ice-carved dome, typical of a tribe of Arctic shifters living in the middle of nowhere in the frozen tundra. A chandelier of icicles dripped down in the center.

Holding sharp, frozen spears, ice sculptures of the

Redeemer stood in two rows on either side of the room, meant to intimidate any who approached the throne.

The Redeemer gestured to the line of women. "Some prey shifters are taken off the streets by force and expected to perform for their new masters—and some of them don't even know the proper way to pleasure. But thanks to your lessons, you've learned to be good, submissive pets for the men who will buy—adopt you."

Isa wanted to be adopted. She wanted to finally see the outside world, laugh, ice skate, and wrap Christmas gifts for the people she loved who loved her. There was a sense of loneliness in Isa ever since her mother passed. Her tribe liked her; she was a great student, but... *I cannot wait to be loved.*

"Now, what do good pets say when their mouths aren't otherwise occupied?"

"Yes, master," the women replied in unison, their voices taking on a monotone as their eyes glazed over.

The pleasure conditioning was no joke.

The Redeemer chuckled lightly and cooed, "Very good pets."

Isa's breath caught in her throat as those words caressed her ears. As if an invisible hand rubbed between her legs, she felt it like a real touch. Her nipples stiffened behind her red dress. She grew slick between her legs.

Good pet.

It was wild how only a few words could ignite her entire body.

In classes, she had worn her headphones like the others, listening to the mantras play at a soft, melodic volume as her hands explored her body. After all, the teachers welcomed the women to explore their pleasure when they thought about serving their future masters.

While listening in class, Isa watched as the teacher projected images of other female prey shifters being good girls for their masters. Images of them on their knees. Images of strong, masculine fingers dominantly wrapped around their necks.

The sexual images soaked into Isa's subconsciousness as she touched herself.

Good pets give pleasure. Good girls feel pleasure when their masters do. The mantras ran through her mind after the Redeemer's words floated through the chilled air of the throne room. Isa's hands bunched in front of her as she subtly rocked herself against them.

Gods, she could not wait to finally touch and be touched by her future master.

Someone to love me and hold me and protect me. Someone who will smile at me like I am his favorite gift he has ever received. Someone to ride to multiple violently powerful orgasms and then sweetly cuddle. Wasn't that what everyone wanted?

The doors to the throne room burst open, and

everyone turned their heads to see who had walked into the ceremony early.

"I would like your finest sex slave, please," a feminine voice called out from the entrance. A cloaked figure, the voice's owner, grew closer and closer. Abruptly, the mystery woman slid several feet and did a twirl like the ice skaters Isa saw in Christmas movies. She shook her head at the Redeemer and waved a disapproving finger at him. "You really should look into carpet flooring."

"Who are you, female, who dares to interrupt the auction?" the Redeemer asked in a booming voice that seemed to have no affect on the intruder.

The cloaked woman stepped forward, close enough now for Isa to see slightly under the cloak hood. Under the shadow of the fabric, black beady eyes gleamed, and a wrinkled mouth grinned crazily. "Did you not hear me? I've got an alpha with an attitude problem who needs an emotional support animal. I'm here for one of your sex slaves."

The Redeemer glanced at the tribe females up for adoption and cleared his throat. "We do not deal in 'sex slaves.' These are pleasure pets—"

"Whatever vocabulary floats your culty little boat," the woman said. "I am here for her." Her arm swung out; one finger stretched and pointed directly at Isa.

Isa's jaw dropped. *Here for me?*

The Redeemer rubbed a hand over his chin and smirked. "I doubt you have the funds to buy her. She is the cream of the crop. Best pet available. A virgin—and she will be in heat in a matter of weeks, if not sooner. I already have *several* very high bids for her."

Suddenly, the cloaked woman appeared right in front of Isa. She stared down at her. Her beady eyes appeared haunted and...abnormally wise.

"Ah, yes. You are the one who will end the war once we get all that brainwashing out of your pretty head," the cloaked woman told Isa, quiet enough for the others not to hear. "Ice Princess, ready to melt your king?"

Meanwhile, the Redeemer made a flabbergasted noise. "How did you move so fast—"

"I believe six million dollars will beat out all competitors," the cloaked woman said, turning back around to address him.

The Redeemer continued to gape.

"Now, I haven't got all day. We have a long drive ahead of us. Do you prefer cash or card?"

It happened quickly. One second, Isa stood in line with the others; the next, she was being ushered out of the compound—her home for eleven years—with an old, cloaked woman.

The Redeemer handed the cloaked woman a brief-case along with a receipt. "This case contains a complimentary week's worth of treats."

If Isa had been in hare-shifted form, her ears would have perked up at that. She loved getting treats. The little, light blue pills were as good as gold stars. Only good girls got treats. And if she went too long without getting one...pain.

Not that she needed any convincing to be a good pet. Treats were just... They were nice. She frowned at the thought. *Will my new master get more treats once the case runs out?*

"A list of certain trigger behavior words can also be found on the back of the receipt. She has never been touched—pure ripe product—yet, she has learned all the ways to give and receive pleasure through visual demonstration—"

The woman threw back her cloak hood and revealed the wrinkled face and wild black beady eyes of the most famous Seer in the world of paranormals.

Those dark eyes flashed bright white light as she said in a grave voice, "Once they find out what you did to her, you will die a very graphically violent death."

The Redeemer's eyes widened like Isa had never seen before. "Excuse me?"

"We really must be going." The cloaked woman grabbed Isa's arm and pulled her toward the large, bright red Arctic truck, which was poorly parked at an odd angle, just outside the ice walls of the compound. "Ta-ta!" The Seer waved.

CHAPTER 2

*I*sa jolted awake. How had she even fallen asleep? She had been far too excited to meet her new master.

Did the woman bespell me? Isa had heard only a little about witches and the rest of the paranormal world.

Isa's body violently bounced around, held only by a thin black seatbelt in the passenger seat of the large, Arctic truck speeding over hills of snow. The comically large tires kicked up airborne snow behind them.

"There you go!" the strange old woman cheered beside her as she drove like a maniac. "The smelling salts worked."

"Gods, what *is* that?" Isa cringed and swatted away whatever the woman held to Isa's nose. The black substance flung out of her hand and landed in the snow somewhere behind them. At the speed the old woman drove, within seconds, the object was a mere dot in the blizzard.

"Coal. Because you've been a naughty girl." The cloaked old woman winked and cackled. "Haha." The next instant, she grew deadly serious. "Or maybe future-you is the naughty one. Your future keeps blurring; it's quite frustrating."

She could see the future? Was that why she had said such an odd thing to the Redeemer when her eyes flashed white? *Once they find out what you did to her, you will die a very graphically violent death.* The Redeemer had done nothing *to* Isa. Her tribe helped shape her into a valuable prey. A perfect pet.

Isa had heard rumors of fortune tellers, but witches never visited the Arctic. "You are a Seer?"

"*The* Seer. My name is Hag. *The* Hag. H-A-G. Heckle A God. Have A-lot-of Guesses. Hurt A Guy's ego. Hag." She laughed crazily again; the piercing pitch hurt Isa's ears.

Unease rose in Isa with each second she spent with Hag.

"Oh!" Hag slapped a hand to her forehead, and the steering wheel jerked left, driving them over huge, bumpy clumps of snow. "That's right," she exclaimed. "You've lived in a cult for most of your life. Hardly know anything. You're like Buddy the Elf about to head to New York."

Hag grinned chaotically, and her eyes flashed a terrifying silver-white. "Darling, I am the Seer to the royals. Heard of them? The ultimate alphas of all shifters? The biggest bad that ever existed? Leading members of the paranormal council—the most powerful beings on the earth."

Isa blinked at her.

"Well, I had a vision where your interests align with theirs."

"When will I get to meet my master?"

Hag sighed. "One track mind. I don't blame you; you've got a cult-brainwashed mind, after all."

Isa rubbed at her eyes, feeling more overwhelmed by the minute. She was supposed to be adopted by a handsome alpha, not a crazed Seer.

Hag added, "You have been selected—by me, yay!—to fulfill a prey and predator relationship quota. You see, someone I may or may not owe a debt to needs more powerful predator shifters to be mated to prey shifters. If you hadn't been living under a cult igloo all these years, you'd know about the uprising rumors after the biggest and baddest King of the Shifters married a prey —a lamb shifter." Hag abruptly turned the steering wheel, and Isa's body jerked to the side. Hag sped up, pushing her foot fully on the gas.

Isa frantically gripped the safety handle but said nothing about the dangerous speed. A people pleaser at her core, she was taught to never question the actions of others. "Can you tell me about my new master?"

"I know you are approaching your first heat and all, but you need to learn that there are more important things happening than dick. Though I will tell you, your new 'master' has got *plenty*. Thing freaking swings when he walks."

Hag winked, taking her eyes off the landscape and swerving the truck again. "Anyway, I wasn't done giving context! Many alpha predator men don't like the idea of bowing to a prey queen, and it's my job to ensure the future where Queen Luna stays in power."

"I don't understand," Isa said.

"Ugh, yeah, once the drugs from the cult food wear off in your system, you might be a little more interested in this." Hag added, "The first way to get people to accept a prey queen is to have other predator and prey relationships start popping up. Especially the toughest, most you-do-not-wish-to-rage-war-against-him type of guys."

The Hag grinned. "And did you know that male Arctic shifters are the coldest, most feared monsters around? You will be their queen. Cause the alpha I'm driving to you right now...is the king of the Arctic shifters. Used to be the Arctic's underworld mafia lord before they gave him an official crown."

Isa froze. Not even the jolting, bumpy ride moved Isa as she stared at Hag.

Speechless, Isa sat stiffly for a moment of complete silence. A queen to all Arctic shifters? Including predators of immense strength and speed such as Arctic wolves and Polaris bears?

"Impossible. Arctic predator shifters would never accept a prey queen. We are not meant to rule. We are pets to provide our master pleasure. I could never rule —"

"Not with that attitude!" Hag bounced the AT up over a massive snowy hill. "Which is why we need to *change* the attitude. I can get you to be queen of the Arctic shifters."

Why would Isa want to be a queen when she could be an obedient pet? "That doesn't sound like something I would want."

"Tell me that again in a week when all the cult-y obedience drugs are out of your system." Hag turned to her once more while manning the steering wheel. "I am going to tell you your future, Ice Princess. Are you ready?"

Hag's eyes flashed silvery-white again as she spoke in a spooky, dramatic voice. "Hearts of ice will melt in snow, for the one woman they burn to know. So, grab onto the mistletoe, or the Arctic alphas will surely go. In a dress the color of merlot, if she cannot thaw his heart, he will freeze hers. If she does not fill him with holiday cheer, she will take her last breath and shed her last tear."

Isa stared at Hag. Stared for a while. "What?" Isa finally asked. Was she supposed to remember all that?

"It's your prophecy. I will give you to the alpha king of the Arctic shifters; you will make that Grinch enjoy Christmas again and melt his heart. He will marry you, and no one will question a prey queen's rule without questioning the coldest man in the paranormal world. Or you don't grow the Grinch's heart, and you die."

Make him *"enjoy Christmas?"* Did her future master not like Isa's favorite holiday? *How sad.*

Isa frowned, a question nibbling at her brain. "Why would the king of the Arctic shifters marry a pet? Prey are meant for pleasure, not for power." It made no sense to her.

Hag took both hands off the steering wheel to rub them together with excitement. "Because I'm going to give you a charm to make him think you're his mate."

*J*sa fiddled with the bracelet Hag gave her. The charm would trick the King of the Arctic shifters into thinking she was his mate. *This feels... wrong.* Good pets did not lie.

Isa nervously bit her lip, bit at the inside of her cheek, and bit her fingernails. She was just meant to be a pet. She wanted her master to love her, not through spells or witchcraft.

I want to bring him joy and pleasure, so he loves me.

It did not help that Hag told her just as they drove through tall, black metal gates, guarded by ten heavily armed men in fur-lined winter coats, *"Now, remember, if you cannot warm him and fill the king's heart with holiday cheer, you will die out in the cold."*

It sounded as if Isa was to be married or murdered.

"Oh, mustn't forget," the Hag tsked as she fastened a collar around Isa's neck. "It even has a cute little bell," the Seer cheered. "His first instinct will be that you were sent by the royals to spy on him, and he will...not treat you well. Try to convince him that you are an innocent pet."

Isa's heart wrang itself. Was her master that suspicious of strangers? "I *am* an innocent pet."

"Those are the brainwashing-cult drugs talking."

The Hag drove Isa past fields of snow to the largest gothic mansion Isa could imagine. The tribe's compound was a large igloo in comparison. This was...

The mansion featured a baroque black-walled exterior and metal detailing. The dark gabled roofing, all sharp edges and various triangular peaks, astounded her. Snow sprinkled over the estate, but the frozen water refused to fully cover the dominating black.

Soft, golden light glowed through the arched glass windows. Even the smoke wafting from the chimneys appeared blacker than normal.

The Arctic king's "castle" surprised Isa. Was it

symbolic of him? Extravagant wealth and eerie taste? She wanted to learn everything about him. What made him smile? Why didn't he like Christmas? What aroused him? Where did he most like to be kissed?

"Guess what his favorite color is," the Seer joked as they approached the black estate. "Matches his heart."

As they grew closer to the hauntingly magnificent gothic castle, Isa again saw a line of menacing guards, all over six feet tall. Isa knew they were predator shifters from their size and evident muscular builds. Arctic wolves? Bears?

Many guards. Was there danger there? *My master will protect me.*

Hag pointed to the entrance as she parked the vehicle in the circular driveway. "There we go. Are you ready?"

"Will my master be waiting for me? Would he prefer I kneel when he meets me? Will the guards let us inside?"

"*Now* you ask questions."

"How will we get inside?"

"I'm *The* Hag," the Seer reminded her.

"Right. Yes. *The* Hag. Of course." Isa rolled her eyes.

"Look at you, getting a little sassy," the Seer laughed. "I like it."

CHAPTER 3

"*They what?*" King of the Arctic shifters and Russian mafia overlord Nicolas Sokolov shouted at his most trusted friend and advisor. "How did they get in?"

Known as the coldest mother fucker around, Nic constantly wore a scowl and an accompaniment of head-to-toe black. Today, the Arctic werewolf king sported a tight black turtleneck that covered the tattoos and physical scars he got tired of receiving stares over.

He was the kind of man who radiated vicious power. The man who did not blink when firing a pistol or when being actively tortured.

And two strangers—two *women*—had just pranced into his heavily guarded castle and demanded hot chocolate and an audience with the king.

"The guards let them in," Wyn, Nic's oldest friend and only still-employed advisor, replied.

Wyn never let his feathers get ruffled. *Damn him*, Nic thought jealously.

As an Arctic wolf shifter, Nic had no feathers to get ruffled; yet, there was constantly something driving him up the wall in the last few years of being king of all Arctic shifters. Something about finally getting a crown he had originally been shunned for, whilst losing most of his family members, did that to a person.

"Why the hell would my guards let two strange women into my compound?" Frustrated, Nic continued on with his bad attitude, shoving a hand through his long, glossy, silver-white blond hair.

As a cool, collected, and utterly wise Noctu owl shifter, Wyn pushed his black-framed glasses up on his nose and said, "One of them is The Hag." Wyn stressed calmly, using his talk-to-his-king-like-he's-a-five-year-old voice. "*The* Hag."

"What did I say about using that tone with me?" Nic grumbled. "I'm your king."

"Stop having a toddler temper tantrum, and I will." Wyn smirked in his costly and well-tailored suit. "If *The* Hag has come to talk to you, you must listen. Her fortunes... Nic, she is quite possibly the one immortal you wish *least* to piss off."

"So, the guards heard she was the royal Seer, and

they let her walk right in? We need to talk with them about letting riffraff in."

"Are you guys talking about me behind my back again?" Alban, an Arctic fox shifter and the final member of their little friendship trio, entered Nic's study. He strode to the dark wooden bar and poured himself a vodka. "Or are you talking about the new visitors requesting an audience with the king?"

Nic glared at Alban for interrupting, but the fox shifter shrugged.

Alban had gotten used to a constantly glaring Nic over the last two years. His old friend had…changed. Losing his brother and stepping into his new role as the Arctic king was hard on Nicolas. Nic was used to underworld dealings and delivering punishments to those who broke his laws. Now, he had to be…above board.

Wyn sighed. "The Hag—"

"I know that's her name, but it still feels rude calling her that," Alban commented, stretching out in his "FOXY Mother F*cker" T-shirt.

Compared to Nic and Wyn, Alban stood out as the Americanized member of their trio, lacking his Russian accent since he came back from several years in the States, fraternizing with Alaskan humans.

"The Hag should not be kept waiting. The guards took her to the parlor. Are you going to go greet her, or should I?" Wyn asked, his nose wrinkling under his black-rimmed glasses to display his apparent vexation.

"I would remind you that I am your advisor—not your servant or butler."

"When you go greet the Seer, can you bring back better vodka?" Alban asked, throwing himself onto the black velvet lounge chair in the grand office and leisurely laying back as if the jobless fox shifter had a long, hard day of more than just drinking and making snide comments.

Grinding his teeth, Wyn stated, "Nic, I will go *politely* greet the *immensely powerful* guest. Join me within five minutes."

"*Ooooooo*," Alban cooed over his glass of clear, potent alcohol. "He's so scary when he gets passive-aggressive."

*W*alking down the left side of the stately U-shaped staircase and toward the parlor, Wyn shook his head at the attitudes of his two closest friends. Both of them were stuck in ruts. One of anger and the other of avoidance.

Wyn understood that Nic had never been raised for political power. He understood why Nic was vexed and paranoid at each turn of his reign—because other Arctic wolves and Polaris bear shifters threatened to over-throw him any day now.

However, the Hag visiting was of massive importance. What if she had a prophecy about Nic?

I do all the damn work around here, Wyn thought to himself as he opened the double doors to the parlor. Wyn stroked a hand down his suit jacket and said, "Hag, so good of you to visit—"

He cut off.

Because Wyn's gaze collided with the palest blue-gray eyes he had ever seen. Dark lashes framed the reflective, icy ocean irises.

The beautiful feminine eyes were narrowed on him yet seemed so wide and innocent and big as she stared at Wyn. The woman had a cute little nose and plush pink lips that pursed as she analyzed him. She sported round, blushing cheeks that a grandparent would fall to their aching knees and beg to pinch.

She also wore a questionable sparkly red collar with a gold-colored bell on it and a *very* revealing red silk gown.

But the most heart-stopping feature of the woman was her icy white-blond hair. A trait of Arctic shifters.

"An Arctic prey?" Wyn muttered his question softly as if he feared full volume would scare the woman standing beside the infamous Seer.

A prey was likely to go into heat around predator shifters. "You brought an Arctic prey to a predator compound?" Wyn asked again; this time, his cool and collected state crumbled. "Are you *crazy?*"

"Only on Tuesdays," Hag replied. "What day is it again?"

Silent and contemplative in her collar, the female prey reminded him of a wallflower that could over-power a room. Her scent... *Sheer heaven.*

She smelled like one of the few flowers that grew in the Arctic. Purple saxifrage with bristly edges. Wyn had always considered it one of the greatest beauties of his icy home. After all, it grew colorfully amid its bleak and desolate surroundings.

I want to know her, he thought to himself.

This intrigue, this spark of interest, was new. Para-normals said Noctu owl shifters were the first to grow tired of immortal life because their brains never slept. *But I am far from bored now,* Wyn thought, feeling his chest move up and down with sudden inhalations. *That succulent scent.*

Wyn tried to shake the distracting thoughts away even as his body grew unfamiliarly warm. "You brought a beautiful, defenseless prey shifter to a compound of predator thugs who haven't been around women in months? What if she goes into heat? Do you know the kind of chaos she could bring here?"

Hag turned to the icy blonde and stated, "I don't know about you, but I stopped listening at 'defenseless.'"

"I got stuck at the word 'beautiful,'" the stunning pale woman shot back in a voice of jingling bells. Harmonic and hypnotic.

She shifted and wrung her hands nervously in front of herself. The movement rang her little bell on her collar, and she blushed at the sound.

"Where is the king?" Hag asked him.

The Arctic female's curious gaze on Wyn swung over to Hag. She blinked in confusion. Had she thought Wyn was the king, there to greet them? Was her curiosity and blush meant for Nic, then? Why did that hurt Wyn's chest?

"Why did you bring her here?" Wyn asked, risking pissing off a powerful Seer by questioning her actions.

Wyn, a cold man who believed in hard facts and numbers, never *felt* things. Not immediately. Not without data. But the more he inched forward in curiosity and breathed in the Arctic blonde's scent, the more he felt he knew her.

He swore he saw the cogs of her brain spinning at lightning speed, taking in every detail around her. Eyes like magnifiers, she analyzed everything. Just like Wyn.

Did she search for a threat or an advantage? He would have assumed she was being vigilant and maybe anxious about her new situation. However, an excited wonder sparkled in her eyes as if, no matter what happened, she might find some joy in it.

What an odd creature. "Where did you find her?" Wyn asked another question.

As a Noctu, his curious nature led him to become one of the most knowledgeable beings in the paranormal world. Now, his brain was shooting off questions, one after another.

Must know her. A subject unstudied. A destined mystery to be uncovered.

As he inched closer, he noticed her pupils were as big as saucers. His body shot forward, eating up the space between them so he could get a closer look. He cupped a hand over her nape. His fingers brushed her cheek as he demanded answers. "Why is she drugged?" Something clamored inside him like a silent rage.

Noctu were known for being slow and calculated. Yet, for the first time in his life, Wyn was overcome with emotion.

"What drug is it? What does it do?" Wyn asked his questions at lightning speed. He clutched her closer, fisting some of her hair. "Who the fuck drugged you, little *tsvetok?*" Flower.

Her lips parted, and a soft, pink blush colored her pale cheeks. Her bottom lip displayed a slight tremble. Instead of speaking or reacting in any expected manner, she licked her lips and looked at Wyn like she wanted to lick him.

Gods, he could scent her wetness. He aroused her? Was she that close to her heat cycle? *She smells like pure pleasure.* It drove him—the virginal man who once equated sex to a tedious, unnecessary act—crazy.

Suddenly, her arms were wrapped around him as she gave him a friendly hug—something new to Wyn. Arctic shifters did not *trust* enough to hug. Her front pressed to his; the embrace took his breath away.

"I thought I'd help you get the vodka—" Alban stumbled into the parlor and stopped, frozen, at the sight of the collared woman hugging Wyn. The female prey let go of Wyn and smiled at Alban, waving in excited greeting.

A prickle of unease and jealousy settled in the back of Wyn's throat at how Alban stared at the female Arctic shifter.

"Oh boy," the Seer commented through an evil grin. "I did not foresee this."

CHAPTER 4

*I*sa watched in awe and confusion and lust—because *hello there, fast-approaching heat*—as the most attractive men she had ever seen stood in front of her, staring intensely. She had always wondered what it would be like to have multiple masters. *Think of all the pleasure I could give.*

The two men were a fascinating dichotomy. A juxtaposition. Chaos and order. Impulse and restraint. Fire and ice.

One of the men had a crooked smile, gray sweatpants, a T-shirt that read "FOXY Mother F*cker," and an air of havoc about him. Yet, he sported a buzz cut like a loyal and obedient soldier in someone's war. Add the "foxy" T-shirt to his slanted, mischievous eyes, and she wondered if he was an Arctic fox shifter.

"Why the hell is she in a collar?" Buzz Cut, aka possible fox shifter, asked the Hag.

"Because she is a gift," Hag replied as if it were obvious.

Isa nervously smiled at the men. As far as she could tell, they were not the king. Not her master. *Disappointingly.*

Still, she learned to always be polite to predator shifters. *Good girls smile.* A slight painful pang shot through her side at that thought, and she barely hid her internal frown.

Maybe it was the beginning of her withdrawal. She would need to earn one of her treats soon. She glanced over at the briefcase Hag had sitting beside her feet. *What could I do to earn a treat?*

"A gift?" the other man—not Buzz Cut—repeated. The man who had asked her who drugged her as if he planned to filet any of her enemies.

He had long white-blond hair that chopped off right at his chin. Broad shoulders, plush lips, and long limbs— he was *tall.* Six four? Maybe mid-thirties. A crisp suit— had to be worth thousands—fit him perfectly as if his tailor was as obsessed with the man's perfectly proportioned body as Isa now was.

He wore black-framed glasses and looked like a villainous, billionaire hacker brainiac with a knack for trouble and possible danger. A desire for control.

She could see it. The imaginary image of him

undoing his tie and whipping off his belt—debating which to tie her up with first. The fantasy of him snapping his fingers and commanding her to strip. To kneel. To be a good girl for him, tell him what he wanted to know, and he would reward her. She shivered.

I want to make him smile and moan and earn a treat.

"Don't mind her. Her eyes glaze over every once in a while due to how close to maturation she is," Hag explained on Isa's behalf as Isa attempted to hide her drool over the perfect male specimens.

The man in the glasses blew out an alarmed breath. "Maturation?" That meant her heat cycle could be triggered any day soon.

Hag added as an aside to Isa, "Also, hun, because I foresee getting tired of you calling them Buzz Cut and Glasses in your head, Buzz Cut's name is Alban, and Glasses is Wyn."

Could Hag read minds, too?

"Maturation as in a Zayka hare shifter? A sex bunny?" Buzz Cut—Alban—asked, exasperated at the prospect of her species. "They're rare as fuck."

Isa's lips curled down at the edges. How much longer until her master made an appearance?

"She is a gift for *whom*?" the long-haired, glasses-wearing Arctic shifter, Wyn, asked.

"A gift for the Arctic king, of course."

That detail made Wyn appear a little...disappointed.

Did he not think she was a worthy pet for the king? *I will prove him wrong.*

Alban ran a hand over his mouth and jaw before his lips cracked into a false smile. "Like an emotional support animal for Nic? Genius. Guy has been a real asshole lately. Could use a sex bunny to raise his spirits."

The long-haired shifter, Wyn, thumped Alban on the back of the head. "She is not a damn sex slave," Wyn growled.

Sex slave. That was what Hag had called her and the other females at the adoption ceremony. Isa was a pet, not a slave. Isa...wanted to be submissive. To bring someone joy was her life's purpose.

How could there be something wrong with that?

Alban faked a wince and rubbed at a section of his head. Sucking in a dramatic breath, Alban exasperated to the broad-shouldered man named Wyn, "I was just joking. You know that."

"Stop cracking jokes because of your own trauma," Wyn told Alban.

Alban blinked and shot back, "Well, damn."

Wyn turned to the Seer. "Hag, you cannot simply 'gift' a person," he said. "If she does not wish to be here, we cannot keep her here."

"Oh, she is here of her own free will," Hag said.

Isa nodded hastily. She did not care for Hag's plan and bespelled bracelet, but Isa wanted a master to please. She wanted a home. She wanted...love.

Alban commented, "To stay here, she has gotta be able to survive a cold Russian winter and an even colder-hearted werewolf."

"She is capable of much," the Hag replied cryptically. Even Isa wished to know what she meant by it.

If the Arctic king was such a cold-hearted man, how would she fill him with the Christmas spirit and get him to love her? Hag expected him to *marry* her.

Or I die.

"*Why* offer this gift?" Wyn asked.

"Don't you think your temperamental king deserves a gift for the winter holiday?"

"Hell yeah, he has been a real grump," Alban remarked.

"He has been...going through a rough time," Wyn rephrased his blunt friend's words. Were they friends? They were such opposites.

"Well," Hag said. "Just like Santa, I know when he's been bad or good, and he has been a real Grinch. She is here to Cindy Lou Who him. You know, make his heart grow three sizes bigger. Make him better understand the meaning of Christmas. Prevent him from starting a war—"

"War?" Wyn jumped in, clearly wanting more details from Hag. Hastily pushing his glasses higher up on his nose, Wyn asked, "Have you seen something? Invaders from the North? South? Something we should know—"

"What *the fuck* is this?" a booming voice sounded by the doorway of the parlor.

The voice pierced and shook the room, quieting Wyn, Alban, and the Hag. The dominating tone licked up Isa's back shoulder, feeling palpable.

Isa turned to look, and the little bell at her collar chimed at the movement.

When she saw him...

Her breathing stopped. Her lungs quit. The scowl she had worn dropped to the pristine marble floor.

Had there ever been a more magnificent face? The utter vicious power he exuded had Isa in a chokehold.

A black turtleneck stretched over broad, muscular shoulders. Crisp, silvery-white hair was cut short on the sides of his head but hung in lengthy waves at the top. A dusting of facial hair and a ruthless, grim expression painted the picture of this man as rough and uncaring.

Deadly and sexy. Deadly sexy. His plump Cupid's bow lips pouted into a firmly pressed line as he took in the scene around him. His chin had a cleft in the middle that Isa wanted to flick her tongue against.

Is this...him? Could she be lucky enough to have such a strikingly sexy master to love and cherish and seek passionate pleasure in?

When his gaze locked onto Isa's, she felt as if she fell down an eternal rabbit hole in his eyes.

Down.

Down.

He had one pale, stunning blue eye and one deep, dark brown. The contrast was hypnotic. Entrancing. Like he was a balance between dark and light.

The icy blue eye whispered romantic promises. It widened and penetrated her with its intensity. It preached desire and devotion.

Meanwhile, the dark brown eye laser-beamed her with despise and disgust.

The man whom Isa assumed to be the Arctic king—due to the raw aura of powerful darkness invisibly swirling around him—grated, "What the fuck is an Arctic prey doing in my house?"

*N*ic was pissed. Not simmering; seething. His whole body was a lit flare burning red hot. Surely, everyone in the room could see it, could see him as a walking and talking S.O.S.

His mood for the last two years was a resounding call for help.

And now a fucking *prey* shifter stood in his home? After everything his family had been through due to a prey shifter?

"Hello, Grinchy," Hag said. "This here is a gift from

the Queen and Kings of the Shifters. Not only is Isa an emotional support animal, but she is your mate."

Mate? She was Nic's fated mate—his one perfect match for his entire immortality? *Impossible.*

"*Mate?*" Wyn cursed.

"Holy shit," Alban contributed his pivotal thoughts.

Meanwhile, Nic replied simply, "No."

Hag blinked. "*No?*"

"You're lying," Nic shot back at the Seer, not daring to glance at the beautiful prey shifter. "Now tell the truth, and you will leave here with your limbs attached. Understand me, witch, I don't stand for tricks."

Wyn's expression silently screamed at Nic, "*THE ONE PERSON I TOLD YOU NOT TO PISS OFF.*"

"She is your mate, Arctic king," Hag deadpanned. "Protest and deny all you want. Once you breathe in her scent, your cock will go as rock hard as the icy cliff your castle is built on."

The little Arctic prey female—Isa, Hag had called her —gasped at that.

Nic's hands fisted at his sides as he glared at the women from the doorway, not wishing to enter and accept this new situation. "Lies. I would never be unlucky enough to be mated to a prey."

Not. Fucking. Possible. Not after what happened to his brother.

Wyn made a warning sound in the back of his throat,

but what shook Nic was the facial expression on the pretty, platinum blonde in the alluring, shiny red dress.

Isa's expression dropped into one of...hurt.

Nic frowned and rubbed a hand over where his chest panged from seeing the sudden disappointment in her eyes. Noticing what he did, he clenched his hand into a fist and dropped it to his side.

She cannot be my mate. Mates were given to those who fate favored. *When has fate ever done anything but fuck me over?*

"Why would I lie about gifting you your mate?" Hag asked.

Nic smirked and crossed his arms. He leaned sideways against the doorway, maintaining distance from the enticing Arctic prey. "Because the royals know about the uprising rumors. Because they want regional kings to marry prey queens to 'unite.' Until less and less paranormals view prey shifters as beneath humans. Am I close?"

Hag's eyes flashed silver-white as a haunting expression lit her face. "Why don't you stop acting like a coward, come into the room, and scent your mate for yourself? Worried you'll get an erection in front of your friends?"

Nic gaped at the crazed Seer. "Fuck you. She is not my mate."

"You haven't slept with a woman since you became king," Hag told everyone, staring at Nic like the most annoying know-it-all to exist. "In fact, you've never —"

"*Hag*," Nic warned.

"You think I can't see you, rolling around in your bedsheets at night, reaching out for a mate you wish you had?"

"More lies," Nic exclaimed defensively.

"I'm basically Santa—I see all. Including the masturbation."

"Shut your fucking mouth."

"Nic," Wyn scolded loudly from where he stood *right* next to the Arctic prey. Why was Wyn standing so close to her, dammit? "Do not curse out *the royal's* seer," Wyn stressed.

"I'll do what I fucking want, thanks."

"You really are an asshole," the beautiful blonde, Isa, murmured softly.

She had not intended anyone to hear, but the men were predator shifters with supernatural hearing. She might as well have spoken at full volume.

Tension prickled up Nic's spine as his arms uncrossed and fell back to his sides. "What—" He stepped further into the room. "—did you just say?"

Though he asked, he knew the answer. But would she repeat it?

She bit her lip and glanced at Hag as if the Arctic female worried what she might do next could lead her down the wrong path.

Nic did not know which path was worse for her: honestly insulting him or meekly taking it back.

"I said..." The Arctic female licked her lips and pushed her shoulders back. In a surprising turn of events, the prey shifter held her chin high. Her gaze collided full-on with his, and she stated, "Your friends are right. You really are an asshole. But don't worry, I can fix you."

CHAPTER 5

*I*sa held her breath as the Arctic king, the man who had her heartbeat racing, stalked toward her. Step by step, his dominating presence filled up the entire room.

Even though his stride was a flawless, menacing pace that dripped with potential threat, the Arctic king—looking like a sexy mafia lord—walked with a slight limp on his left leg. It was barely noticeable. Hardly perceptible.

But Isa noticed and frowned.

The limp did not affect how he moved with deadly precision. It was not a new development. He had lived with the limp. Had he gotten hurt at a young age? Would he like for her to massage it? One of her classes focused on the art of massage.

When the Arctic king let out a low, loud growl, Isa

looked up from how his dark pants encased muscular thighs. The king glowered at Isa, his eyes spewing anger and...vulnerability.

He doesn't like that I noticed the limp, she realized.

Blinking and swallowing and trying to remind herself that Hag told her the Arctic king was notorious for being a heartless killer, Isa quickly said, "I—I didn't mean it?"

She wanted to please her master—what the heck had possessed her to call him an asshole? Maybe because everyone else had done it before her, and she wanted to please them?

Can't please everyone.

The king paused in his approach to her and smirked. "You 'didn't mean' it?" He quirked a disbelieving eyebrow. "I think you did, little prey—" He choked on the air as if finally inhaling while close to her.

He sucked in a sharp breath, eyes widening and looking at her in such an accusatory manner that one might think she leaped forward and stabbed him. He coughed once. Twice. Hacking out the air he breathed like it personally offended him.

She moved forward, her instinct to help him, but he stepped back.

"What..." He shook his head emphatically, plush lips parting. He rubbed a fist over his chest and appeared to have trouble swallowing.

"What's happening?" Had he ingested poison or

something? Isa moved closer to him again, wanting to help. He was only a few steps away; she took two toward him. This time, he closed the distance between them instantly.

Lurching toward her, he grabbed her by her nape, fingers secured around her throat as he exclaimed, "What the fuck are you doing to me?"

Hag snickered from behind Isa. "I told you; she is your mate, Saint Nic." Hag cackled some more.

Isa could do nothing but try to breathe through his solid—but not tight—grip. What would happen if the king realized her bracelet was charmed to make him only *think* she was his mate?

I have to make him love me before that happens.

The king's scrunched expression depicted nothing but disgust and disbelief. But the emotions behind his eyes looked as if he fought an internal war of hope and utter disappointment.

"No…it's a spell," he said.

Uh oh. He really guessed it right away.

The king added, using an accusatory tone toward Hag, "You did something."

Hag tsked, "I'm not the one making your cock swell like a boulder balloon."

For a moment, no one in the room breathed.

Then, the fox shifter, Alban, tipped his head back and laughed. "*BOULDER balloon.*"

"Very mature," the long-haired Arctic shifter in the

professional suit, Wyn, commented dryly at Alban's reaction.

Isa glanced down at where the king's arm stretched between their bodies while he held her by the throat. Her gaze fell to the front crotch of his black pants, and sure enough... Bulged. Big, *big* bulge.

So, the bracelet doesn't make him love me; it just makes his body think I'm his mate and get turned on by me. Isa tried to hide her disappointment. *I want my master to desire me because I'm me, not due to a spell.*

But also...that *bulge.*

Good girls get on their knees when their masters are hard, a lustful voice whispered in her head as she licked her lips and stood on shaky legs. The overwhelming lust...

"It's true, man," Alban said, amused. He did not speak to the king like a subordinate; he spoke as if they were friends. "No whiskey dick for you. You are rock-hard right now. Does she smell that good?"

Alban moved forward as if to get closer to Isa for a sniff, but Wyn yanked him back. "Damn, bro, I'm not going to *fuck* her," Alban joked after being halted. "I mean, unless she asks nicely, or compliments me, or breathes in my direction."

"Fucking. Shut. Up," the king growled out, chilling the entire room and threatening to give everyone frostbite from his voice alone. It acted like a harsh gust of Arctic wind, slicing through any scrap of clothing and numbing the bones.

"I've heard rumors that the first scenting of a mate can cause a werewolf to go mad," Hag commented. "Where the years of pent-up cum just build and build— I think the erection won't go down until you claim her."

"Stop. Talking," Nic grated.

"This should be good news, right?" Alban asked warily to his king. "You've found your mate, dude."

"It's some kind of trick," the king grated.

Isa let herself breathe in his scent as well. He smelled like mulled wine. Orange, cinnamon, cloves… The drink only mated pets were allowed to partake in, according to Isa's tribe, because the beverage led to "adult situations." Whispered dirty promises and passionate embraces.

"You smell good, too," she whispered.

If she breathed in too much of his scent, would she become drunk off of it? The fruity, spiced oxygen already had a blush forming across the tops of her cheeks and her nose. Her body tingled with each breath so close to him.

The unsatisfied horniness she constantly felt roared to life as her nipples tightened into little sensitive peaks.

My master is hard, and I haven't touched him yet.

"Fuck," the king cursed as he stared at her. Stared *through* her, light and dark irises burning. "Stop getting turned on," he told her.

Isa's blush deepened, and her mouth hung open in

horrified embarrassment. He could *smell* how turned on she was by him? And he did not like it?

"Don't you want your mate to be attracted to you?" Hag inquired.

The king *still* held Isa by the throat.

I see what Hag means about him needing the holiday spirit. The king needed every Christmas movie lesson there was to learn.

She *wanted* to help him—not just because her life depended on it. She wanted to bring joy and pleasure and prove what a good pet she was.

And for the first time, she was free from the confines of her tribe. She was finally in the outside world. She had never had a traditional Christmas; she had only ever watched holiday movies on repeat, during the coldest months of the year.

I'll finally get to bake snowflake-shaped sugar cookies, and build a gingerbread house, and decorate a tree, and have amazing oral sex under mistletoe, she realized, taking another breath of his mulled wine scent and growing excited. *I'll finally get to touch a man, feel his body moving with mine, and put all my lessons to the test.*

Her smile flashed over her face before she could stop it. *Giddiness* sparkled inside her.

The king exhaled shakily as he questioned, "And now you *smile?*" Apparently, her expression added to his disbelief and suspicion.

But her smile only spread like some kind of uncontrollable force. *I just have to help my master enjoy Christmas and show him all the pleasures of having me as his pet.* She had little interest in the political play the Hag worked in the background.

I will make my master orgasm so hard, he will lose the ability to scowl. The smile stretched into an even wider grin.

"Damn, look at that smile," Alban commented in a different voice than before. This time, he sounded raw and genuine and slightly entranced. Not tipsy and jokey.

Shaking himself, Alban added in his original jesting tone, "Are you smiling cause you heard rumors of the Arctic king's big cock, bunny?"

"She *is* nearing her heat," the Seer informed the men.

The king finally released his fingers from Isa's throat but pressed them to the bottom of her chin. He forced her gaze to meet his and stared into her, transfixing her with his unique light and dark eyes.

"You gonna kiss your mate or what?" Alban asked.

The king ripped his fingers from her face and stepped back, taking his mouthwatering scent away with him. "She is *not* my mate," he said darkly. Definitively.

Isa fiddled with the charmed bracelet, mentally begging it to work better.

"She will sleep outside with the dogs tonight," the king said.

Wyn coughed; his pale eyebrows shot up in shock.

"*What?*" Alban asked, again sounding less like a comedic relief when he gaped at his king.

"Nic," Wyn warned.

"My mate would be able to survive out in the cold," the king shot back, striding toward the room's exit, his back to all of them.

"Even the strongest Arctic shifters shouldn't sleep out there. The weather is—"

"Dude, she'll freeze to death," Alban said, cutting off Wyn's lengthy explanation.

At the doorway, the Arctic king turned his head just enough to say over his shoulder, "If she does not survive the night, she is not my mate."

CHAPTER 6

"*F*uck," Nic exhaled roughly as his hand furiously stroked his cock. The erection wouldn't go down, just like the Hag crazily stated.

Would he really stay this hard until he claimed her?

I keep trying to fucking come.

In the privacy of his study, he gritted his teeth and tightened his fist around his dick. The grip shot pleasure down his stiff spine—*but not enough.*

"Goddamn it." He slammed his left hand onto his desk and jerked himself with his right. Forehead beading with sweat, he panted and thrust into his hand.

I want her. He didn't want to admit it. He bit his inner cheek until he tasted blood, then he bit harder. *I cannot afford to want her.*

Beautiful, stunning woman.

Surely, he could orgasm without her. He didn't even

know her, and one whiff had him harder than he had ever been, pre-cum leaking from his length at the thought of kissing down her throat.

It has to be a spell.

Those familiar tingles at the base of his spine and his full, heavy balls informed him that he was close to coming. Yet...nothing. He just kept getting hornier for her.

Fuck, masturbating was just damaging his resolve.

Must stay away from her. The erection had to die down eventually.

Bursting through the doors of the king's study, Wyn glowered at Nic like never before. "Are you going to make her go through trials to prove herself?" Wyn bit out each word to his king, "Do not fucking do this."

Alban trailed in after Wyn and stutter-stepped when he saw his king's trousers were hanging at his knees. "Are you...jerking off right now?"

Nic growled a deadly animalistic sound as he pulled his underwear back up over his massive, throbbing erection. "The prey shifter's scent is plaguing me," the king replied.

Alban snorted. "Oh yeah, it's plaguing you really *hard.*"

"Stop looking at my cock," Nic told him.

"Sorry, I've just never seen you exhibit any evidence of being a warm-blooded male before. This is shocking. I'm shocked."

"Let her come back inside," Wyn told his king. "She is out there, freezing, while you play with yourself."

Meanwhile, Alban slipped his phone out. "Bro, you've never taken any interest in women. Should I take a picture to memorialize that monster in your trousers or what?"

Wyn looked ready to whack Alban in the back of the head. Nic shared his advisor's sentiment.

Nic replied to Wyn's concerns, "She is an Arctic shifter. She is not going to freeze. And if she does, then it wasn't meant to be," Nic said, as if he could take or leave his mate. His cock screamed at him for relief.

"A leader does not torture others the way he was tortured," Wyn stated in a very *"Be better, you idiot"* tone.

Nic bared his teeth in anger. His closest friend and confidante should have known better than to bring up the past. "If *I* didn't die out there, then she will be fine—"

"She is a *prey*," Wyn reminded him. "Not a predator shifter. Not born with the strength and speed. Not truly made for the harshest of conditions. A snowstorm is coming."

"Prey are herbivores, right? She probably eats lettuce or something," Alban helpfully added. "Lettuce doesn't keep a girl warm in the Arctic."

"She. Will. Freeze."

"Then, she isn't my mate."

For the first time, the eternally calm, collected, nerdy, and detached Wyn *broke* in front of the two men.

His impassive neutrality fell to the floor with a silent, clamorous *clang*. His composure and poise shattered like a thin pane of ice.

Wyn stole the glass of scotch from Nic's desk and threw it against the wall. Shards of broken glass scattered across the floor.

"You *selfish* motherfucking asshole," Wyn snapped. "I swear to the gods, if you let her sleep out there all night…"

Alban's jaw hit the floor.

Even Nic's constantly narrowed, angry eyes opened wide at Wyn's display of emotion. "You'll what? What will you do to me, *Noctu*?" the king challenged, stressing Wyn's species for a reason.

Nic was an Arctic wolf shifter; his strength and speed were fearsome. Noctu owl shifters were known for their brains.

"You *know* why she cannot be my mate," Nic said darkly.

Wyn bristled and almost had the gall to look at his king with pity. "You are different from your brother. His fate would not be yours—"

"She is *not* mine," Nic said adamantly.

"Do you truly believe that, or do you simply not wish to end up like him?"

Nic glowered but said nothing.

"What if she *is* your mate, and you let her freeze to death? You will lose your chance at happiness."

Nic replied smoothly, "Since when have I coveted happiness? Sounds like an unwanted distraction."

"Is this how you plan to rule for the rest of your life? With bitterness?"

"Haven't you heard?" Nic quirked an eyebrow and slapped his chest with feigned masculine pride. "I'm the heartless king."

"Oh damn, should I get that on some business cards?" Alban asked.

Wyn snorted. "Oh, you were never heartless, Nic. No matter how much you wished you were. Even as the underworld boogie man with constant blood on your hands, the one everyone feared at their doorstep, you would have never banished a prey female out in the snow to freeze. There are lines we do not cross."

"Maybe it's time I drew a new line for myself," Nic shot back and poured himself a second glass of scotch. "Maybe this is the new me. I have no interest in a mate, and I will do everything to keep the power I *rightfully* deserve. A prey mate threatens that power."

"If you let her die because of this warped imitation of your asshole father where you think power and being feared are all that matter, I will *help* them overthrow you," Wyn promised darkly and spun around to leave Nic's office.

"Where are you going?" Nic asked.

"I'm going to go keep her *warm*."

"...nd now I'm here. So, yeah, it has been a wild day," Isa told the dogs that growled viciously at her from inside the small, enclosed kennel-shack twenty feet from the castle.

She added, "Did I mention that I hate being trapped in small spaces? When I was first taking my lessons, if I didn't understand a topic fast enough, they would put me in this cage and leave me there for a day."

She sighed. "It was impossible to sleep, and my stomach would always growl so loud by the time they let me out. It did teach me to take my studies seriously, but...I don't like cages. Maybe it's a prey hare thing. Are any of you particularly against cages and being kept in here?" she asked the big, gray East European shepherds who took up the other half of the shed.

More ferocious growls.

"It would be a lot easier if you liked me so we could cuddle," Isa remarked. "Cause over here, all alone, I am quite cold."

An understatement. Her teeth chattered. Her skin *stung*. The small shed, where the dogs were kept, at least protected her from some of the strong gusts of Arctic wind, but the ground she sat on was so cold that any part of her that touched it went numb.

"Maybe he didn't fully understand how cold it was when he sent me out here," Isa said, her voice shaky. "Or it's a t-test. Not sure why he feels the need to t-test me. I'm here to bring Christmas cheer and bring him happiness. Who d-doesn't want to be happy?"

A gentle knock shook the door of the shed. "May I come in?" a deep masculine voice sounded. Isa recognized it right away to be Wyn, the suited gentleman who wore sexily studious glasses.

"Please," Isa called out, too cold to move and open the door.

The old shed's door jolted open, and winter wind infiltrated as he entered. Wyn hunched over to avoid hitting his head against the low ceiling of the kennel shed. Over his suit, he now wore a warm winter coat with a black-furred hood.

"Have the dogs hurt you?" Wyn asked her, kneeling beside where she sat in the corner. "They tend to bite—" He paused, contemplating. "—well, everyone."

"I just asked them really nicely not to," Isa said. Though the dogs had certainly flashed their sharp teeth at her.

"They must like you then," Wyn said gently.

"I wish. It seems no one here likes me, which is hard to understand because they don't even know me. I am very likable. I think if they took the time to know me—" Isa cut off when a shiver wracked her upper body. Gods, she was cold.

Kneeling close to her, Wyn still towered over her, but his face... Isa studied the beautiful, defined edges of his jawline and the thick lashes framing his brilliant blues. Why couldn't this seemingly level-headed, gorgeous Arctic shifter be the Arctic king?

What if my new master never loves me?

"We're not friends," Isa said about the dogs. "But I like to think it's a mutual respect. I fear them, and they fear me?" The pitch of her voice rose at the end as if she asked a question. Truly, she was so cold, her vocal cords played tricks on her.

Wyn grabbed a bundle of fabric he kept under his arm and unfolded it. He draped a large, black wool blanket around Isa's shoulders. The action caused a whiff of air scented like him to puff over her face. *He smells like sweet vanilla cookies.* Warm. Soft. Sentimental.

"Gods, you smell good," she admitted dreamily.

Wyn smirked. "Do I?"

"Mmmm, yes." Not thinking it through, she leaned in a little closer and took another breath of his scent. "You smell like warmth. My favorite sensation."

Amused and surprised, Wyn flashed her an alluring smile and tenderly stroked a finger over her chin. "Nothing smells better than you. Purple saxifrage. The first flower to bloom in Arctic spring."

"That sounds pretty," she said wistfully. She wanted to see flowers and the Northern lights and everything she missed while kept inside her tribe's shelter.

"You haven't seen it? But it grows all over..." Wyn's eyebrows furrowed as the ends of his lips curled down. "I truly know so little about where you came from."

Isa stiffened and hugged the blanket tighter around her. "I come from a place that would never keep a female outside to freeze."

"So, you were treated well?" Wyn's serious expression was just so *intense* whilst focused on her.

All that *caring*—about her—granted her more warmth than the blanket. Even her teachers, who had adored her in the tribe, never stared at her with such fervor. Wyn stared at her as if she were the most fascinating subject in the world.

I...like him. Maybe she could fill him with Christmas cheer, too.

Wyn nodded. "I am glad. There are many tales of prey shifter mistreatment."

"Mistreatment?" This time, it was Isa's turn to frown.

Her tribe taught her that female prey shifters were revered and desired by alphas. She had been shown how to be useful to predator shifters and gift them happiness and pleasure. *What happens to the females that my tribe cannot find and help?*

"Some alphas are cruel," Wyn said.

"Is...is he cruel?" she asked.

The Noctu shifter blinked in surprise and touched the frame of his glasses. "You are asking if the man who banished you outside is cruel?"

Isa tilted her head and stared at Wyn. He was so well put together. He appeared so calm in his highly fashionable and expensive clothing, kneeling on a clump of snow and ice inside the shed.

If she had to choose a word that came to mind when she looked at him, she was caught between *professional* and *moral*.

"He must not be cruel," she said. "Because I do not think you would be friends with a cruel person."

Her words seemed to spear through him. He swallowed, dropped his gaze from hers, and wiped a palm over the top left of his chest. "You do not know me."

CHAPTER 7

"*Y*ou do not know me," Wyn said gravely.

Not yet. "I see you," she replied softly. Tenderly. "You're like me."

Wyn's lips twitched at that. He probably wondered what she thought a prey pet and an Arctic predator shifter had in common. "Is that right?"

"Yes."

"And what are we like, little flower?" he asked it with such a *fondness*, her toes curled. Or maybe that was the sensation of budding frostbite?

Isa smiled, still shivering from the cold but excited to have this time with him. "We are helpers. We try to make things better. The king...he must not be cruel if you stand by him."

"You say that while shivering to death." Wyn

clenched his fingers at his side and again broke his gaze from hers. "I shouldn't have let him put you in here."

Isa shook her head. "I do not blame you. We follow orders."

"Orders?" Wyn repeated.

Wyn was the king's advisor, right? Thus, he served the king—like Isa would. "We can help those with power, but we do not have any power," Isa said, repeating one of her class's mantras.

Wyn's mouth pressed into a thin line as he scowled. "You think I have no power?" he asked coldly. His eyes darkened in the dim shed, acting as little black vortexes for her every thought.

Uh oh. She had not meant to offend him. "I—I…"

"If I wanted to, I could take you from here. I could take one of the trucks and drive us far, far away, and show you every purple saxifrage you wanted to see. I could stop standing by his side if he goes too far."

Wyn rubbed a hand over his lower jaw and sighed. "But…I'm still waiting. Watching. I have known Nic for a very long time. He may be in a rut at the moment; being back in this home…brings back bad memories for him. But he will adjust and be a better king than his father. I have hope."

"Because he isn't cruel," Isa whispered. "You have hope because you believe he isn't cruel."

Wyn fought back a smile. "Again, you defend him when all you have seen is the bad."

Isa shrugged. She had been prepared for the worst—for a Grinch. *It will make earning his love that much sweeter.*

A strange inner voice whispered back, *You shouldn't have to* earn *love.* Isa shook her head, shaking the stray thought away.

"He just needs some joy," she said.

Wyn released an amused scoffing sound. "I don't think he knows that word. Joy."

Isa wiggled under the heavy wool blanket and said definitively, "I will teach it to him."

Again, the Noctu shifter wore an expression of confounded amusement. "You are...very interesting to me," Wyn said gently as he stroked an index finger under her chin, down the center of her throat.

He fingered her collar and the little bell that hung there. Her lips parted at the delicate touch over such a sensitive area.

"I wish to know what Nic did to deserve such a mate," Wyn said. "Maybe I could be as lucky."

Isa wiggled again, blushing under Wyn's intense attention. *I want to kiss him.*

His stroking fingers sank back to the side of her neck, below her earlobes, then to the back of her scalp, where he tangled them in her hair. He did not pull; he left them there, connecting Isa to him.

"In fact, I have never known jealousy until the Hag said you were his," Wyn muttered lowly.

It was the…first nice thing to happen to Isa that day.

Maybe that was what explained her reaction. Her deep sigh, her body's exhalation of tension. Her brain blanked.

She leaned forward, eliminating the space between them, and pressed her lips to his cheek, *very* close to the edge of his lips.

The touch started out innocent, but…

His warm room-temperature skin brushing her frozen lips triggered something dark and powerful.

Desire. Thick, hot desire choked her, throttling her with the temptation to kiss him again—to move her mouth over his. To press her soft body to his and steal his warmth and beg for more.

Wyn let out a loud *whoosh* of exhalation at the slight touch of her lips. Suddenly, the reserved, calm man of self-control emitted a deep, dark, and virile sound. A sound that had Isa's freezing body finally shiver *not* from the cold.

"Ah, little tsvetok, you do not know who you touch," Wyn said in a low voice.

His fingers pinched the bottom of her chin, turning her face to force her gaze to connect with his. His eyes blazed like circular pits of hypnotic blue flame. He moved so close, eye contact became impossible.

"Tell me," he rasped against her cheek as her eyelashes fluttered.

He inched forward until his mouth hovered over

hers. Their breaths mingled; all she seemed to breathe was his heady vanilla scent. Was there even any oxygen left in the outdoor shed that wasn't touched by a hint of his intoxicating, sweet alpha scent?

Her body moved involuntarily, dragging her nose over the sharp edge of his cheekbone. *Want to touch him and be touched.* Pets thrived on pleasure.

Another dark sound came from him. "Do you enjoy playing with fire?" he asked.

She blinked a couple times, trying to clear her "*a little closer and we could kiss*" thoughts. "Huh?"

"You kiss my cheek innocently," he said, a low rumble vibrating his chest. "But you hesitated to pull back. Your breath caught. Your pupils dilated. Just now, you wet your lips."

Speechless, she licked her lips again and swallowed.

"I have never seen a woman so obviously in need of a good, hard…kiss."

But he said it like "*fuck.*"

I have never seen a woman so obviously in need of a good, hard…fuck.

Isa swallowed thickly again, feeling dizzy even though she sat. She had only ever watched videos or felt her own fingers. Gods, what would he feel like moving inside her? She wanted to *know.* "Hmm?"

"Your chest heaves up and down. Your blush travels up your throat. Your eyes…glassy with want," Wyn whispered, lowering his hands to grip the sides of the warm blanket he brought her and pull it tighter around her, cocooning her in sudden heat. "Your gaze keeps falling to my mouth like you want to taste me."

Taste him.

"Tell me, are you desperate to be kissed?"

The way he said it made it sound a lot more like: *are you desperate to be fucked?* The answer was *YES, HELL YES!*

Isa shuddered. She grew closer and closer to her first heat cycle every day. Who knew how soon it could be triggered each day she spent around the attractive, Arctic predator shifters?

"Cold, little flower?" he asked, teasing her after seeing her quiver.

He trailed his tempting lips down the side of her face. His breath against her skin caused erotic tingles to invade her bloodstream. Every one of her pores prickled with *awareness*.

He purred, "I came out here to help warm you."

"T-The blanket helps," she replied unsteadily. *More. I want more.* But what if the king found out? *A good pet is loyal to her master.*

"But is the blanket all you need?" he asked. This time, his slow, low voice reminded her of thick, sticky molasses. She wanted to lap it up and roll around in him.

"M-Maybe you c-could, um, hold me?" she squeaked, not knowing why she felt embarrassed.

Good pets learned to never be embarrassed about

wanting to be touched. *But I want to impress my master.* And if she accepted help and failed the Arctic king's test of her resolve, she would never forgive herself.

I was gifted to him for a reason. She wanted to prove she was strong. She *wanted* to help him. Even if he banished her to spend the night in the freezing cold.

"You wish to be held?" Wyn asked, but he did not pause to hear an answer as he swooped down and encircled her in his arms.

He tugged her over his lap, so her side pressed to his chest and the tops of her legs draped over his lap. The back of her thighs laid over his taut, thick muscle, a hard stomach, and a hard…

She gasped but made no move to shift off of him. In fact, upon feeling the forming erection poke into the side of her ass on his lap, she cuddled into him more. "That's…nice."

Wyn's fingers clenched the blanket around her. "Nice?" he echoed in a not-very-nice tone.

Like she had insulted him.

CHAPTER 8

*S*he wiggled over his burgeoning erection and mumbled, *"Mmhmm,"* growing distracted by the heat radiating from him. She had never felt an actual erection before.

His cock is pressed against me. Hard and warm.

She wanted to take it out and suck it. Stroke it. Play with it.

She loved the idea of playing with Wyn. Watching his serious façade melt to one of pure lust. Would he pant enough to fog up his own glasses?

Wyn hissed, "Is it 'nice' to feel my cock harden for you, even out in this weather? 'Nice' to feel what being near you does to me? To my body."

"Yes," she replied, her breath choppy.

Wyn sipped a breath at her response. "Answer me this, why have I never once been curious about kissing another? Why has a woman or male never caught my attention? My desire? And yet, the moment I saw you, I wanted to learn every inch of your body. Wanted to read you with my fingers like braille. Study your skin with my tongue."

Was Isa breathing? Someone needed to check her breathing. *Pretty sure my lungs don't want to make any noise to interrupt this beautiful man*, she thought.

"I have only ever wanted to waste my time with books and lose myself between pages," he admitted softly in her hair as he nuzzled his face into her neck. "So, tell me, why do I suddenly want to waste every morning losing myself between your legs? Sating my every curiosity deep into your wet, little pussy. Your scent...calls to me."

Her jaw clicked as it fell. Lust slammed through her. Her nipples tightened to stiff peaks at his words and velvety tone. A subtle pulsing began at the junction of her thighs, where her clit awoke and pleaded. Could he tell the way her hips rocked down on him, grinding lightly against his erection?

"You kiss my cheek innocently," he said. "But I can smell your arousal."

Embarrassing. And sexy?

"I can scent your need in the air," he continued. His hand trailed down the blanket. "Your sweet wetness...is all I can think about."

His arm wrapped around her, and he draped his

hand over her lower abdomen. His long fingers pet the fuzzy wool blanket as she peered down and imagined those lengthy digits petting her between her legs, just two inches further down from where his hand laid.

He suddenly grabbed the blanket and fisted the material right over her core. "And now it's right *there*," he growled. "Your wet pussy, separated from my cock by only thin fucking fabric."

"*Mmmm*." Isa bucked her hips and rubbed her ass firmly over his bulge.

"I cannot stop thinking about touching you in ways I know I shouldn't." Wyn exhaled through a tortured expression. "How no one would know. How easily I could slip a hand under this blanket and feel you. Drag a finger between your slick lips and discover how wet you are. Would I find you wet for me?" He groaned. "Gods, I can *smell* it."

"*Mmmm*," Isa moaned louder than before as she bounced softly over his lap, finding it impossible to get comfortable when she was so aroused.

"Nic might cut my hand off if he found out I touched you. Hell, he might axe off my arms for holding you like this." Still, Wyn held her tighter, letting his warmth infiltrate her. He kept a hand positioned just over her mound; any lower would have had her hyperventilating.

Breathless, Isa whispered, "You said you felt jealous when the Hag said I was his." Wyn's knuckles were white from how tightly he gripped the blanket. Isa added softly, "I…I had been excited when you came into the room, and I first thought you were the king. That you were, well…"

It was as if she had pulled the ring from a grenade and tossed it into his lap. Her words acted as an explosion.

Something happened to Wyn. The best way to describe it would be a dam breaking. Or a hidden iceberg slicing right through a ship, causing it to flood with water.

"You…wished it to be me?" he repeated slowly. "You wished…to be my mate?"

She blushed and was glad to not have eye contact with the strikingly handsome Noctu shifter as she admitted, "Yes. I…I liked the idea of fogging up your glasses and being handcuffed in your belt."

Another grenade. Another invisible explosion to Wyn's self-control.

"Handcuffed…in my belt," Wyn said.

Isa nodded and gyrated over his erection some more, losing focus on the conversation. "Restrained in leather…as you touched me."

"You are submissive, then." Wyn's fist unclenched and laid flat over her lower stomach through the blanket. "You wish to be controlled."

Isa did not reply. She was too busy overthinking how close Wyn's fingers laid from her pulsating clit and how he had just inched them further down, getting him closer but not close enough.

"You wish to be dominated?" Wyn asked.

Yes. Take me.

"The implication of handcuffs," Wyn began and sifted pieces of her hair through the slender fingers of his other hand, the one *not* over her core. "You wish to feel out of control. As if it's not entirely your choice. Overpowered. Vulnerable."

Before Isa knew what was happening, she was no longer on Wyn's lap. She was on the shed's floor, the blanket under her acting as a soft layer of cushion, as Wyn stretched over her and grabbed her chin.

"Like right now. Vulnerable. Delicate. All alone in this shed. I could do anything I want to you," he said. "If I started petting your pussy, you wouldn't be able to stop me, would you? It would feel too good. You could try to keep my hand away, but I would just restrain your wrists."

Her heart raced at the picture he painted for her as he dominantly held her face.

"I would weaken you with kisses down your throat as I rubbed your clit until you begged for more. No one could hear you scream for my cock out here."

Isa's lips separated as a desperate moan pealed from her.

"Really? That arouses you?" Wyn's eyes narrowed on her, and he hummed. "Fascinating."

Fascinating. As if she were the subject of a scientific study. But she liked it. She had never been "fascinating" to someone before.

Study me, she thought, tipping her head back and revealing her neck, a signal to shifters that one was completely vulnerable and at the mercy of the other—willingly.

Wyn exhaled choppily and lowered his hand from her chin to lay over her throat again. A light leash just over her collar. He did not squeeze, but he let the weight of his fingers be known.

"And what if I took you out here, huh? What if I'm not willing to wait another second to have you? I have not once in my lifetime been this hard. Never felt this pent-up. Do you know what it's like to have never touched another, never cared to, and suddenly, I want to touch you more than anything else? To claim you before Nic does. It is a desire that threatens rational thought."

Isa nodded and rocked her hips up. His knee settled between her legs, bunching the long fabric of her dress as his kneecap rested right below her pussy.

"I want to know what makes you wet. Want to know what makes you tick." Wyn cursed as he hovered above her, holding his weight with one arm since his other hand draped over her nape. "I do not understand it. I don't *have* feelings."

He stated, "An advisor must be strategic and unfeeling. If I advise him to take out an army, I cannot have empathy.

If I need to apply all of my focus on next steps, I cannot afford any distractions. Food, lust, I've grown up tapering all of my desires. I don't get what I want. I'm not a king."

"You don't have to be a king to *feel*. And…enjoy."

"But *why* do I feel this way?" he asked. "What makes you so special?"

She blinked, dumbfounded. Surely, deep questions and thoughts were illegal when a person was this turned on. "I…don't know."

"Do you truly not know? Or are you being modest?"

Why was she special? She worked hard in her classes. She valued her calling—bringing others happiness. But special? "I think everyone is special," she said.

Wyn's smile cracked again, like a sunset barely visible through clouds. "By that logic, no one is special." His kneecap ground over her pussy as he stroked her throat again in that sexily dominating way. "In the mere hours of knowing you, I have witnessed you hug a stranger, naively grin in the face of a glaring man, and defend the man who banished you out here. Even now, as you freeze, your eyes sparkle with excitement."

Wyn shook his head and told her, "You are special. People like you do not exist in the Arctic we live in." He leaned forward, and Isa's breath caught. He pressed his lips to her earlobe as he whispered, "Will you let me study you, little flower? I've never felt like this…"

Isa stiffened for a moment.

The Hag had said the magic bracelet was charmed to make the Arctic king think Isa was his mate, but what if it confused other predator shifters, too? *What if...he doesn't find me attractive, and it is just the spell?*

She wanted Wyn to want *her*. She could not stand the idea of a spell influencing someone. She wanted genuine adoration.

Will the Arctic king hate me even more if I touch one of his friends?

Isa clenched her eyelids shut, knowing it would be simpler, easier, not to admit her lust for Wyn. "I—I think we should stop."

Wyn frowned, not appearing angry or upset, just confused. "Is this where I am supposed to dominate you and seduce you until your reluctance fades?"

That *did* sound sexy to her. How would he try to "convince" her? With his fingers stroking over her clit? "No, I think if we... I do not wish to give the king an excuse to hate me."

"He hates everyone. He doesn't need excuses." Still, Wyn retracted his hand from Isa's neck and sat on his knees before her. "You should not fear him. If you wanted me, I would protect you—"

"I'm near maturation," Isa rushed the words out. "Nearing my first heat cycle." It was an excuse meant to soften the blow of stopping. Good pets were never supposed to leave a man aching, but Isa feared it was a spell making Wyn feel so strongly for her. *He hardly knows me.* "I got caught up in the moment."

The second her words infiltrated the air between them, the shed grew colder. For once, the big dogs, which had paced and fidgeted, laid completely still.

"Ah." Wyn pulled back entirely. He tilted back on the heels of his feet and stood in one swift motion. His face and scent suddenly seemed too far away. The stark loss of body heat startled Isa and...hurt.

"So, that is all it is," Wyn replied curtly, his voice no longer low and velvety. "Hormones." His clipped tone made it clear that she offended him.

CHAPTER 9

S *our sugar cookies. Pissing off the one man who has been nice to me all day.* "I—I didn't mean it like that," she said quickly.

"Nyet, please, do not rush to cater to my ego. I should apologize for becoming inappropriate." His back turned to her as he stepped toward the exit. "You are my king's mate. My future queen. And I...do not trigger lust."

Isa shivered again and hugged herself under the wool blanket. Good pets were not meant to be rejected and were not meant to reject. Hurt swirled inside her lower stomach, even though she had meant to push him away. She wanted to scream, *YOU DO TRIGGER LUST!* And spread her legs to show him.

The thought of hurting Wyn's or anyone's feelings ate her up inside. Isa was not built to hurt. She only ever wished to *please*. "I'm sorry," she whispered, a bit of pain shooting up her side.

He faced her once more—expression like a block of unchiseled ice. Numb. "You have nothing to apologize for. I am the one who misunderstood your hormones for attraction. Ignorant and pompous of me."

She held herself and shivered. "No..."

Wyn's lips parted as an expression of guilt claimed his face when he registered how cold she must be in the shed. The loss of his body heat made quite a difference. "You should not be here."

"What did I do to deserve this 'test?'" *Other than lie and wear a charm that tricks the Arctic shifter king into wanting me.* But Isa didn't feel that detail was valid amidst her current situation. "What can I do better next time? What will make him like me?"

Wyn spun around to face the exit again. "I will talk sense into him." Even though he spoke to her, he stared at the door as if the sight of her displeased him. *I am meant to bring joy, not displeasure.* "You will not stay in here all night," Wyn promised.

All she wanted was a chair, a warm fire, and maybe some hot cocoa. Maybe to sit in a room with real, insulated walls to keep the cold out. "No, I...I need to stay here."

Wyn turned his head to look back at her, eyebrows high in disbelief.

"Being out here is a test." Isa hated to admit it; her

toes felt numb. "I need to prove to him that I can pass. A good pet is obedient to her master."

Wyn scoffed. "Master? You are his mate. You do not have to prove anything to him." He beckoned for her to follow him out. "You will come back inside. I will deal with the consequences. Come."

"No."

"No?"

"I will not fail my test."

Wyn let out a frustrated exhale, his breath visible. "Stubborn."

"You don't think I can stay out here all night? I can. I will." She was willing to do anything to earn the king's respect.

"Stubborn and prideful. You really are his mate."

She huffed and hugged herself tighter under the blanket he brought her. "I thought Arctic wolf shifters worshipped matehood. Aren't werewolves known for being adoring and catering to their mates?"

Isa had studied different shifter species and their sexual habits as part of her tribe's teachings. Werewolves were known to often put more importance on sex than, say, a vampire who was tempted to fuck anytime he fed. It was rare for werewolves to adopt pleasure pets because they waited for companionship from matehood.

"Nic is...different," Wyn replied, again referring to his king by the first name. "He has been through several events in life that are severely impacting him now."

Isa sighed. "Haven't we all?" No. She had not meant to sound so judgmental just then. After all, a good pet would want to know her master's every wound and cover him in healing balms and bandages.

"Nyet, no, flower," Wyn said gravely. "Not like him."

She pursed her lips but remained silent. Internally, her mind spun with unusually harsh thoughts like: *How hard can the Arctic king have it in his warm castle full of magnificent chandeliers, art, and sweets?*

Because yes, she saw the tray of small desserts and chocolates in the parlor and was still disappointed they offered her none. Though they had not known she never had such delicacies before—only seen them in movies. Her tribe could not afford such expensive imports.

"I will try to talk some sense into him. In the meantime, do not attempt to befriend the dogs," Wyn told her. "I was not joking when I said they bite everyone. They are hunting dogs who hate the indoors. No matter how much they are fed, they are always hungry."

With that terrifying statement, Wyn left Isa in the kennel.

She glanced back at the large, furry dogs and commented, "You guys wouldn't eat me, right?"

They flashed their teeth and growled back.

"It's been four fucking hours," Wyn exclaimed to Nic. "Four hours she has been freezing with those blood-hungry hounds you call names like "Spot" and "Marshmallow" and whatever other unfitting, juvenile names you chose when you were younger—"

"Rude. Marshmallow is the name of a savage," Alban defended his king from where he laid, lounging on the plush dark rug in front of the fireplace.

"Thank you, graham cracker," Nic deadpanned.

"Damn." The fox shifter clutched at his heart. "You dare refer to me as the worst part of a s'more?"

Wyn pinched the bridge of his nose and continued, "While you laze in front of a crackling fire, your mate's lips are turning *blue*."

"Peeked in the window again, did you?" The fox shifter chuckled. "You stalker, you."

Nic ignored the creeping jealousy heating the back of his neck as he imagined Wyn staring into the shed at the Arctic prey female. *Isa.*

Wyn had never shown any interest in a woman. Why *her*? "Maybe next time, don't come back smelling like my mate," Nic said. "She is clearly trying to use her feminine wiles to influence you. Further proof of her being a spy if you ask me." Buddying up to Nic's trusted advisor.

"She is your mate, Nic. Stop denying it and let her inside."

"If she can't take the cold, she can leave my compound," Nic stated. "She's not *locked* in."

Frustrated, Wyn grabbed at some of his long white-blond hair. "She won't *leave*. She's stubborn and prideful, just like a king I know," the Arctic Noctu shifter said pointedly.

"Oh shit, called out," Alban mocked.

Nic scowled at his new glass of scotch in his hands. The golden flickering flames from the fire made the alcohol glow. Nic didn't even *like* scotch. *Another form of self-punishment?* He wondered to himself as he took another sip.

"Wyn, you are my advisor." Nic placed the scotch onto his dark mahogany side table. "Tell me, does it sound realistic that after rumors of an uprising started, the royals' Seer 'found' my mate, who just so 'happens' to be a *prey*. Thus, solidifying more regional royal shifters with prey queens in power?"

"Eh, we all saw your erection when you scented her for the first time, bro," Alban commented. "She can't 'fake' being your mate. It's a chemical reaction."

"It's more than chemicals," Wyn said. "She is the one being in this world who can make you feel whole. The one person who can make immortality suddenly *not* feel like a curse. And you've left her freezing to death in a kennel."

"A kennel doesn't have walls. She has walls," Nic replied. "She is a political move. The royals want the Arctic shifters to have a prey queen."

"So?"

"So, *I* could be overthrown for her. Don't you get that? The Arctic will never accept a prey queen. Don't you remember what happened to—"

"Just don't marry her," Alban commented nonchalantly.

Nic and Wyn's heads turned to stare at the lounging fox shifter. "What?"

"You don't *have* to give our people a prey queen. Just keep her as a mistress. Don't let anyone know she is your mate. Say she is a sexual plaything—other predator shifters do it all the time with prey. Bada bing bada boom. Simple as that."

Wyn shook his head as his expression scrunched with disgust. "You asshole."

Feigning innocence, Alban threw his hands up. "What? I'm not saying he should *treat* her like a plaything, just that he can have a mate and keep his crown. Just don't marry her or give her any power. I am offering *solutions*."

Nic rubbed a palm over his jaw as he stared into the crackling fire, contemplating it. He could not afford his people thinking he was mated to a prey.

"You can't seriously consider listening to this semi-alcoholic, frat bro fox," Wyn said.

"Wow, you hurt feelings I didn't even know I had," Alban remarked and turned to his king. "Nic, he hurt my feelings."

"No one would be allowed to know she is my mate—if she is," Nic said. "I'm still not convinced it isn't a spell of some sort."

"You would keep your mate as a dirty little secret?" Wyn asked in his *you-disappoint-me* tone, which Nic had become quite familiar with. "After everything you went through? After all you have preached? You will denounce her as queen, her rightful place?"

"Man, she's a bunny shifter. Everyone will just assume you have her here as a sexual pet. You know how those Zayka females get..." Alban lifted his eyebrows up and down and cracked a mischievous Cheshire smile. "I heard they can move their hips so fast that a man cannot help from coming in minutes."

Wyn threw a couch cushion at the fox shifter. Hard. Through the cushion came a muffled: *"Fuck!"*

"Fine, I'll go check to see if she is still alive," Nic said, standing from his Chesterfield wingback leather chair.

Wyn grumbled, "About damn time."

CHAPTER 10

The twisting and turning in Nic's stomach stopped the second he stepped in front of the doorway, where his mate shivered and froze to death.

Nic did not like the idea of his emotions and physical reactions being tied so strongly to another person. The first time he breathed in her scent, he had been near incapable of speech at the lust that drowned him and buzzed over his skin. The last four hours of leaving his "mate"—if she even was such—outside in the cold gave him a migraine and stomach pain.

Nic did not like the idea of anyone having control over him, not after his horrific childhood.

Now, he peered through the small, icy windowpane to look at her.

She was…being eaten by the dogs?

Nic burst through the door. The wooden door

slammed against the wall, and the howling wind made it shudder again and again as Nic stared inside the shed in horror.

At the loud noise and sudden rush of cold, Isa and each of the three dogs turned their heads to look at Nic standing in the doorway.

Nyet, Nic thought, not believing his eyes. *Impossible*.

The dogs were cuddling with his mate.

Vicious Spot, Marshmallow, and Penelope—feared by some of the six-foot-four predator shifter guards on the Russian compound—each stood around Isa, protecting her from all sides and offering the warmth of their fur.

Meanwhile, she had thrown a blanket around all of them, not just herself.

And Penelope—the one who had bitten off several hands of Nic's royal guards and servants—had her large tongue flexed out against Isa's cheek. Penelope appeared as if she had just been licking Isa with adoration when Nic came in and interrupted.

"What..." Nic stood with his mouth hanging open.

The three big Russian dogs, which Nic had taken care of since childhood, started ferociously barking at him. Growling and yapping as if he were a threat. Yet, they made no move to leave Isa's side.

The beautiful Arctic prey shifter, with a button nose and a blush from the cold coloring her cheeks, weakly muttered, "Close the door, would you?"

He did. Immediately. As if his damn body couldn't wait a single second to obey his mate's every command. *Fuck that.*

"Still alive, then?" he asked.

"S-So far." She softly glared at him like she actively tried *not* to show her apparent disdain. "Why do you keep these three out here? They deserve better." She petted Marshmallow, and the savage pet's tongue lolled to the side. His tail thumped happily against the wall.

What. The. Fuck. She had to be bespelled. "I've watched that dog you're petting bite the nose off a maid who fed him five minutes late."

Isa's face blanched, but she proceeded with petting Marshmallow and asked in a baby-talk voice, *"Aww, somebody was hangry, huh?"*

Nic ground his teeth and roughly crossed his arms. "They sleep here because they choose to. They do not like to be kept inside. They prefer the cold."

"Sounds like your emotions," she remarked and held up a hand for Marshmallow to high-five. Instead, the large dog butted his head into her palm, demanding more pets.

What did she do to my blood-thirsty monsters? They had only ever liked Nic.

Those traitors.

When Nic moved closer inside the shed, he held his breath, unwilling to breathe in her tantalizing scent again. *Citrus and cranberries.* The flavor of his favorite scones growing up. Reminding him of times when he didn't scowl at the ceiling every night in bed.

"You didn't put on a coat?" Isa asked Nic. He still wore the same black turtleneck as earlier.

"I am used to the most brutal, harshest cold you can imagine," he replied.

Isa stared at him, absorbing his words like she might take a test on them later. No one listened to Nic quite like that. *Now I know why Wyn likes her,* Nic thought. *She analyzes. Observes. Thinks.* Not quite the sex bunny Alban thought she was.

His body stepped a bit closer. A little more. More. *Don't inhale,* he reminded himself. But finally, from up close, he saw it.

Her lips were blue.

And when he listened… Her heartbeat was weak.

His own heart froze in his chest, and his mind screamed. His wolf, his inner instinct, roared through him, "*YOUR MATE SUFFERS. HEAL HER.*"

"Fuck," Nic cursed and shot forward to grab her.

The dogs hostilely barked at him; one even bit his arm when he bent over to pick Isa up from the ground. Blood leaked from the new wound on his forearm onto her chilled skin.

Holding her in his arms was like holding a stiff ice sculpture. "*Fuck.* I'm taking you inside."

"N-No… I n-need to finish…the test."

"You need to get warm," Nic said. "Your heartbeat…"

He trailed off as he heard the consistent thumps become less and less regular.

"I can...survive this."

Her words pierced his chest like an icicle, leaving frost-covered shrapnel. *I can survive this.* Wasn't that his life story? That was his constant mantra to all of the pain he endured over the years.

I made my mate nearly freeze to death, banished from a warm castle like I was.

He had given her a replica of his own wound.

Fuck. His inner wolf clamored inside him, *"CHERISH AND PROTECT."*

Nic ran.

Carrying Isa in his arms, he ran with the speed of an alpha werewolf. At his heels were the massive and deadly Spot, Marshmallow, and Penelope, running beside him to the side entrance of the estate.

"Open the door!" Nic roared as he raced up the steps.

The black door hesitantly creaked open. His housekeeper peeked around it to see her employer carrying a half-frozen woman in a red silk dress.

"Oh my," Miss Belsky mumbled.

"Hello," Isa tried to greet her, but her voice came out weak.

Nic used his shoulder and bleeding forearm to press the door open wider for him and Isa. And the dogs.

"They can't come in here," Miss Belsky shrieked. "The floors!"

"Tell them that, Belsky," Nic shot back as he strode Isa straight to the closest fireplace. "Pretty sure they're not leaving her side tonight." His inner wolf felt the same way.

See? Mates make you weak.

The closest fireplace was in a small dusty library, his grandmother's favorite room. Maybe Nic's favorite as well, considering all the times he hid from his father in it. Bookshelves lined the walls with old leather-bound books as the fire cast dancing shadows around the cozy room.

Nic had not dared enter his grandmother's library oasis since he took the throne.

Nic avoided certain rooms in the castle for a good reason. *Too many memories.*

There was also the fact that his grandmother was the one member of his family still alive. She treated Nic like he was the same tender kid he was before being banished from his family's estate at the age of nine.

Whenever she reminisced about the past, she opened the wounds he tried to forget existed. She spoke about him like she still thought there was *good* in him.

She was, of course, wrong.

Thankfully, his grandmother was not in her library at the moment, which worked out for Nic. He did not want his grandmother to learn of Isa's presence and try to befriend her.

He gently laid Isa down in front of the fire and

darted to grab any blankets he could find on the various reading chairs. He wrapped them around Isa until she resembled a layered burrito. He nudged her closer to the fire until she laid on her side in the shape of a crescent moon.

"Fuck, you feel like ice." Nic positioned himself at her back, mirroring her body as held her close. The dogs laid their heads, paws, or tails over the couple.

They want a claim on her too, Nic realized, wondering if she could hear the increasing rhythm of his heartbeat.

Those dogs saw through people. The ones they had used as chew toys were never *good* people. The maid who got her nose bitten off was the one who kicked Marshmallow in the side for pissing on the Siberian lilies.

Do these dogs already see Isa as their queen?

"Y-You don't n-need to hold me l-like this," Isa stuttered through blue-tinged lips.

Nic suddenly hated the color blue. Well, not the shade of Isa's eyes, but he could no longer stand the blue shade of her frostbitten lips.

"I—I'm fine."

"Be quiet," Nic whispered to her, hoping if she stopped talking, his body would stop feeling such gut-wrenching guilt.

"I d-don't need your body heat."

He scowled at the orange and yellow flames in the fireplace. "Don't you?" She despised him so much already that she would rather freeze to death? "The sooner you get warm and can speak without your teeth chattering, the sooner I will let you go."

She wiggled under the blanket and wiggled and... wiggled.

Nic frowned, eyebrows furrowing in confusion as he dipped his head under the blanket to see what she was doing. As if seeing it would mean understanding it.

And he saw. At the sight, he quit breathing.

"Are you..." He began speaking with his face under the warm, black-fur blanket. He had a clear view of her hands dipping toward her pussy through the dress. "Are you touching yourself right now?"

CHAPTER 11

"*A*re you touching yourself right now?" The image of it consumed Nic's mind as he watched her squirm and press her fingers to her sex. His heartbeat accelerated; his breath became choppy. "Why the fuck do you have your hands between your legs?"

His cock twitched behind his black slacks.

She wiggled. "My fingers feel frozen, so I'm trying to warm them against the warmest part of my body," she explained.

Of course. An understandable explanation. But now, Nic couldn't stop thinking about Isa touching herself. Rubbing her pussy for him and moaning. Whimpering for his cock…

"I could help," Nic offered in a low voice. "The warmest part of your body is still cold. If you…wiggled against me, I could heat you."

"I thought you wanted me to freeze to death," she muttered sassily.

Nic bit the inside of his cheek, fighting emotions that threatened to bubble up inside him. The soft woman had some bite in her. *I deserve to be bitten.*

He whispered against the back of her neck, his breath playing with tendrils of her hair, "Not right now."

She huffed. "I d-don't understand how you could keep me out-t there when all I w-wanted to do was make you f-feel good."

Yup. There's the guilt. Nic swallowed some of it down, but the flavor remained in his mouth.

"Why w-would someone treat someone l-like that? I w-wanted to bring you j-joy and pleasure."

If she was a spy, she sure knew how to guilt trip a man because Nic felt like scum. "Let me warm you," he said softly, wondering if any words had ever left his mouth so gently before.

"Y-You're not warm enough." She shivered violently and said her next word as if it were the harshest insult to be uttered, "Cold-hearted."

He snorted at her frank honesty. *I do not wish to have a mate,* Nic thought. *But she does not deserve to die.* She did not deserve to be punished the same way Nic had been punished as a child for being different from what his father wanted.

Nic peeled back the blankets that cocooned her until he wrapped them around both of them, so she felt his warmth and cashmere turtleneck press against her skin and thin dress.

Noting how she squirmed when his lips grazed her earlobe, he whispered into her ear, "Do I still feel cold to you, little plamya?" *Little flame.*

She wiggled, arching her back and pressing the sweet curve of her ass against him. His cock lengthened at the teasing touch.

Still, she deadpanned, "You feel like ice."

A half-scoff, half-snorting laugh sound caught in Nic's throat. "Do I?"

"How many women have you given hypothermia to?" she asked.

"Ah." Nic smiled against the crook of her neck. "Zero."

"A lie." Even as she insulted him, she wiggled her ass over his crotch. Could she feel the bulge forming behind his slacks?

He wanted to nibble and lick and kiss her neck, so close to his lips. He wanted to grab her hips, turn her, and grind his hardening dick over her as she moaned for more.

I could have...killed her. Commence additional self-loathing.

"Arctic wolves mate for life," Nic said, his voice a little scratchy as he struggled to suppress the desire to pleasure her. Touch her. Anything. "They save themselves for their mates."

Isa remained silent, subtly rocking her hips under the blanket.

"I have never been with a woman," Nic admitted. "Never been interested in one."

Isa absorbed his words as Nic suppressed the instinct to blush. "I t-thought...but alphas need to be pleasured."

He frowned at the way she worded that but waved it off as hypothermia-brain. *Got to get her warm.* "Any time my cock has throbbed for relief, I have taken my pleasure into my own hands and stroked myself. My cum has only ever painted my own skin. It's simplest that way. But right now..."

He inhaled her sweet cranberry scent and groaned. "I can't stop imagining painting your perfect little ass with my cum. Marking you with it."

*I*sa panted as her body warmed from its bone-chilling temperature. Hearing the Arctic king talk about touching himself, jerking off his own cock, and coming on her *did things* to her.

She could imagine it. The Hag had hinted at it—him rolling around in bed, wishing for a mate.

Nic laying in bed, frustrated breaths coming out in heavy inhales and exhales. His fingers wrapped around his large, dusky erection. Determined hand sliding up and down and up and down as his chest concaved with ecstasy. His lips parted and eyebrows furrowed as he approached climax. His thighs trembling as he grew more and more desperate...

"Do you touch yourself, Isa?" he asked in that deep, luscious voice as his mulled wine, spicy scent awoke every horny hormone inside of her.

She stared at the crackling fire, watching wooden logs disintegrate under hot flames. Would that be her? Turning to ash from just a touch? Gods, she wanted to feel someone *else's* hand between her legs for once. Wanted to know what it felt like to be entered by a man.

"Have you ever satisfied yourself?" he asked against a sensitive part of her neck. Her skin flushed. "Ever pet yourself between your legs?" *Dear Gods.* "Felt yourself in need of being touched? Tingling to be filled?"

"I-If you've never been with a woman, how would you know how to..."

Nic chuckled darkly, sounding like a sexy villain. "Oh, baby, I *read.*"

She swallowed and shivered as her stiffening nipples dragged against the heavy furry blanket.

"Have you ever woken up with a hand between your thighs the way you are right now? Have you ever ground the heel of your palm to the top of your slit, developing a rhythm against your pulsing clit?"

Isa choked on her exhale. "I—I...*yes.*" This time, she

pressed her palm harder between her legs, no longer just to get warmer but because she couldn't help herself.

At her admission, Nic inhaled roughly and tightened his hold around her, pressing his front more firmly to her back as he cuddled her.

She could feel him. That bulge poking her ass. *Master is hard.*

Good pets know just what to do when their master is hard.

She frowned at the thought. No. This was the same man who had just nearly frozen her to death by exiling her outside while he sat in front of a warm fire and drank luxurious alcohol and... He had relaxed while she froze. Alone.

Why did he do that to me? Isa had always loved the Grinch in the movie, but...*I may be in over my head.*

"Now, tell me, do I still feel ice cold?" he asked with an audible smirk.

He said he didn't want a mate, so was he just saying those things now to tease her? To prove he could make her feel hot?

I want my master to really want me. Still, she bit her lip, trying and failing to quit squirming against his warmth under the fabric.

"What do I feel like, Isa?" he purred in her ear.

She shot back, "Like a glacier." She really didn't like him.

He chuckled again, but it sounded like a dangerous

sound. As if a mouse had just amused a hungry lion. "Little *plamya…*"

Suddenly, his warmth was gone. He had moved away from her and…

His black turtleneck fell beside her head.

Oh. *Oh…*

The sound of a zipper lowering made Isa's heart beat harder in her chest.

He was stripping behind her. The Arctic king was stripping.

When a master removes his clothes, a pet should already be naked.

"Wolf shifters are known to run hotter than others," he said normally, as if he was not taking his clothes off as he spoke. "Arctic wolves even more so."

"You're…getting naked?" she squeaked out as his pants fell to the floor close to the fireplace. How was the *sound* of him stripping this sexy? Surely, the view of it would have sent her into her first heat cycle.

"Your skin is still chilled; your heartbeat is weak. We need to heat you up," he said, laying back down behind her and rustling with the blankets until his bare front pressed to every inch of her back.

Oh, Gods. Isa's hypersensitive skin trembled. What would it be like to touch him? To make him, such a cold and controlled man, moan?

"Ah, I can smell your wetness," the Arctic king rasped. "So slick for me."

She shivered, but this time due to rising lust.

"I think it is time for some interrogation," Nic said.

He slid a warm hand over her hip, down her abdomen, to settle just over the junction of her sex. His palm and fingers cupped her pussy. Possessively. Teasingly.

Isa had to repeat to herself, *Do not immediately grind against him* as her brain told her, *Surrender to your new master.*

"If you answer my questions honestly, I will help 'warm you up' in the way I can tell your body wants."

All she could manage was a *"Hmm?"* sound.

"Were you sent here by the royals to spy? As a political trick? Are you really my mate?"

Not good, she thought. From her limited experience around the Arctic king, Isa could tell he had trust issues. And maybe anger issues. So, if she dared reveal that she wore a charm to make him *think* she was his mate...

This could be...displeasing.

"I am not a spy," Isa replied shakily.

"Your voice trembled."

"I am freezing."

Nic released a contemplative sound. "Hmm." He pressed his fingers lightly over her most sensitive flesh. The junction of where her thighs quivered. "You must understand, the chances of my mate being a prey shifter are...very low."

"The strongest and most resilient predator shifters

tend to die around me," he said. "My father, my brother, my enemies. The harsh winters pale in comparison to the cutthroat world of Arctic shifters. And running the damn kingdom? It requires a queen just as cold."

Isa pressed her lips together. She had never thought of herself as cold. *Who wants a cold leader?* And why did Nic say "cold" like it was a synonym for "power?"

Nic stroked a thumb over her inner thigh, and she lost her train of thought. The *barely-there* touches over her erogenous zones were distracting during such a high-stakes interaction.

"You look like an ice princess, and I...am no prince. Just a boogie man given a crown." He went quiet for a moment, *still* palming her pussy as if it were normal. Maybe it felt normal to him? Because of the spell? "It is difficult to believe fate would match us."

Isa remained silent because...guilt knocked at her chest. *Pretending to be his mate...* She had not thought about what that meant for his *real* mate.

Her tribe had taught her that only predator shifters had fated mates. After all, prey shifters had to always be available to pleasure alphas, so why would fate give them a mate? Preys also went into heat, so to suggest that only one man could satisfy a prey in heat would be ridiculous.

I am only meant to be a pet. A lover. Not a queen. Not a soulmate.

Nic turned her, moving her weight easily with his

strength, until her back was to the fire, and they were face to face. With much effort and self-control, she did *not* look beneath the blanket to see, well, *all* of him.

"You see, even though my body aches to sink into yours, even though my wolf is roaring that I should mark you and make you mine..." His right palm slithered between her legs until the rigid heel rubbed directly over her pulsing clit. "I don't think I have a mate."

The second he said it, his left hand shot up to cup her throat.

He lightly squeezed, cutting off her breathing for just a moment, before loosening his fingers and leaving them there to grip her neck, just above the collar the Hag left on her. His hold could have been simply dominating, but it was also terrifying.

He left me for dead earlier. Will he finish the job?

He continued, his voice sounding more menacing and deadly as he spoke, "I think you are some prey shifter the royals picked up off the street to 'charm' me and put more of your kind in power. Did they think I'd be seduced by a horny prey about to go into heat? I think the Hag lied. I think you will start a war in my region. Spark the uprising that already lingers in the air."

Eyes wide with fear and fighting to breathe through his firm grip on her throat, Isa tried to shake her head.

"No? I think you need to become a better liar," Nic

suggested. From his mouth, it sounded like a threat. "Because your 'Hag' forgot something very important."

He squeezed her throat again, too tight, and Isa trembled in fear. "I was never meant to be king. I wasn't meant to live past fucking nine years old."

His blue and brown eyes flashed wildly as if he looked through her, blinded by something else as he spoke. "Fate has *never* smiled upon me. Why the fuck would it grant me a mate who smells like candy and *hope*?" He spat out the word as if it tasted wrong on his tongue.

Isa's frantic heartbeat scared her; it was as if the organ tried to escape her chest. Even when she felt close to freezing to death, Isa was not as scared as she was with her throat in the grip of this cold-hearted king.

She could practically see him contemplating snapping her neck. The brewing of doom swirled in his one dark brown eye. The hesitancy at possible regret shined in his light blue one.

To kill her or not to kill her. The decision of a king.

I've hardly lived. I am just now free; there is so much for me to see and experience. I don't want to die.

"I don't care what mind-warp lust spell she cast on you." He grated, "You won't be queen. You won't take from me the one thing I have left. I will never let myself be seen as weak again."

Isa scratched her red-painted nails down his bare arms, trying to free herself from his grasp. *More air.*

Even though he was not choking her, she fought to breathe.

Her body prickled with so much tension—like it was having an anxiety attack. His expression spewed so much murderous anger.

Surely, his scowl made others' souls leave their bodies before, too.

She grew dizzy; her chest hurt. *Please don't kill me.* Was this what happened when a woman tried to thaw an icy man?

More hyperventilation. More raging anxiety. There was something about his grip around her throat and the crazed look in his eyes that chilled her to the bone worse than any cold.

She really, truly felt like she could die.

"I don't have a mate. So, this little power play manipulation and lust spell…" Baring his sharp canine teeth, he leaned in to enunciate each word in her ear. "Not. Fucking. Appreciated."

His grip did not tighten or loosen around her throat.

But her heart stopped.

CHAPTER 12

*N*ic heard it as soon as it happened. Her little heartbeat stopped. Just fucking stopped.

And he hadn't even done anything. His grip was not that tight. He had never cut off her airways. He had meant to scare her into confessing, not…

"Little plamya?" he asked hoarsely, too confused and shocked at how she laid motionless, without a heartbeat in front of him.

Her vibrant eyes…dimmed. Dead.

DEAD? His wolf bellowed and raged inside him. MATE IS DEAD? His first instinct was to rip his own heart out and insert it into her chest.

"*FUUUUCCCCKKKKK*," Nic roared so loudly, the orange and yellow flames dancing in the fireplace flung themselves in the opposite direction, nearly going out altogether.

Thudding, racing footsteps sounded from both sides of the hall before the door to the little library banged against the wall as Alban and Wyn launched themselves into the room at their king's cry.

"What happened?" Wyn asked in a rush as he strode forward and dropped beside where she laid.

"Dude, what did you do?" Alban asked solemnly as if Nic made an irreversible mistake.

"I didn't do anything," Nic exclaimed, shaking a motionless Isa in his arms. "Her heart just fucking *stopped.*"

"Release her," Wyn demanded before stealing Isa's body from Nic. He took her *and* the blankets wrapped around her, revealing Nic's naked form on the floor.

"Did you fuck her to death? Why the hell are you naked?" Alban asked.

"I didn't do anything!" Nic repeated, more panicked than before. A hand shot up to pull at the lengths of his hair. *Yank.* Pain. *Yank.* "I just...scared her a little. I was just trying to see if—"

"Rabbits can die of fright, Nic," Wyn supplied a not-previously-known fact.

"Fucking *what?*"

"You probably gave her a heart attack. Hare shifters are known for them when encountering severely fearful moments. Some heart attacks can be fatal."

Nic gave his mate—his *fake* mate, it had to be a trick

—a heart attack? As in what human males, who didn't watch their cholesterol, sometimes had?

Alban cupped the sides of his face in his hands as he gaped. "You scared her to *death*?"

"She is not dead," Wyn snapped back and hastily removed his glasses.

"Her heartbeat stopped." Did Wyn not want to admit it to himself?

The Noctu owl shifter bent over Isa, cupped her chin, and blew breaths into her mouth. Wyn's hands then fell to her chest.

"Get the fuck off her!" Nic bellowed and charged for him, but Alban tackled Nic.

"He is trying to save her, you idiot," Alban said, keeping his arms locked around Nic as Nic heaved his breaths and fought to control his aggression. "I know your wolf is screaming at you for letting another man touch your mate, but he's trying to bring her back."

Nic's inner wolf shrieked for his mate.

As Wyn performed perfectly paced chest compressions and medical care, Nic wanted to burn the estate to the ground.

After what felt like the longest minute in Nic's life, Isa gasped and sat up, blinking several times and gazing around the room as if looking for a threat.

Me. I am the threat.

"Shhh," Wyn comforted her and guided her back to lying down on the rug. He tucked the blankets around her and gently cooed, "You're okay. You'll be okay. Just relax. You are safe."

Nic fell to his knees. Hard. The action emitted a loud *bang.*

"She's okay, Nic," Alban told him, clamping a hand on his king's shoulder. "Wyn fixed her."

Nic stared at his advisor and his possibly fake mate.

Had Nic really just *killed* her?

PROTECT, his inner wolf growled.

Wyn, acting like Isa and himself were the only people in the room—*asshole*—stroked the side of her beautiful face and whispered, "You had a little seizure, *tsvetok.*"

Flower. He called Nic's mate *flower?*

"A minor heart attack," Wyn continued. "You need to remain calm and get some rest, okay? Can you keep your heart rate nice and calm for me?"

Coughing, Isa rubbed at where Nic had held her neck.

"Is your throat sore?" Wyn asked. "Would you like some calming, hot tea?" The loyal Noctu turned his head to cast a scowl at Nic. "Leaving her outside probably gave her a cold, too."

Nic scoffed and crossed his arms, not bothering to block the view of his bare body. He had no qualms with standing naked in front of his closest confidantes. After all, it was their natural pre-shift state.

Isa narrowed her eyes at Nic, pointed to him, fake-choked herself, and then shot an innocent victim expression at Wyn. Wyn: her new self-proclaimed protector. Nic's hands fisted, but he hid them under where he crossed his arms.

Wyn's jaw dropped at Isa's show of charades. He stood to fully address his king. "You *choked* her?" he questioned accusingly. "Are you so far gone that you have no respect for matehood?"

"I did not choke her." *Little tattle tale.* "I was just trying to scare her. I didn't *squeeze*," Nic stressed, gesturing to where she smugly smirked at him from behind Wyn's protective stance. "She can die of fucking *fear*, Wyn. How could I be mated to a hare who can die of fright? This can't be real."

"You do not touch her," Wyn stated through clenched teeth. "Ever. Again."

KILL, his wolf urged. No one stood between a were-wolf and his mate.

"Excuse me?" Nic asked, his voice no longer sounding like his own.

"You don't come near her," Wyn said evenly, acting as if he did not recognize his oldest friend. "You don't touch her. She stays here, under my protection, from now on."

"*Your* protection?" Nic's brows shot up, and he remarked, "She is not yours."

"So, you admit she is yours?"

Nyet. "No, I...fuck." Nic growled, "She can't really be..."

She couldn't.

Because he had just almost frozen her to death and now scared her to death.

I'm a monster. An abomination. Nic gripped at his hair again, tugging for sanity. *Never good enough. Why the hell would fate gift me a mate?*

"It has to be a spell," Nic said.

Wyn no longer cared to address his emotionally damaged king. "Alban, go tell Miss Belsky to make some warm milk and cookies."

Nic had a front-row view of how Isa's expression *melted* at Wyn's words. Her shoulders dropped, and her eyes might as well have projectile-vomited little hearts.

Fuck that. "Warm milk and cookies? Are you serious? You're going to baby her?" SHE IS MINE TO CONSOLE, his wolf growled inside Nic's mind.

Wyn placed his glasses back on and pushed them up on his nose. "She just had a heart attack, so yes, I am going to do *all I can* to soothe her."

Nic did not like the way Wyn stressed certain words in that sentence. Like they carried innuendo. *All he could do* to soothe her? "What the fuck does that mean?"

"Little flower, would you like to warm up in a jacuzzi hot tub?" Wyn asked her in a much warmer voice than how he had just spoken to his king.

Nic watched more sickening invisible hearts pour from Isa's eyes toward Wyn. The Noctu shifter ate up the attention. Cold and detached, Wyn—the man who had never even glanced in the direction of a scantily clad woman—*liked* her.

Fuck, why did that make Nic's chest ache? Instead of another burst of rage, his wolf whimpered at how his mate looked at Wyn. *Fuck*.

Alban rubbed his hands together and took a step toward the door. "I'll bring the milk and cookies to the tub." Now the fox shifter was in cahoots with Wyn?

"Miss Belsky told you no more eating in the hot tub, Alban," Wyn commented.

Gaping, Alban asked, "Is it a crime to soak with crumbs?"

A soft, pitiful coughing sound came from Isa as her lips curled at Alban's words.

Alban had made Nic's mate laugh? KILL, his werewolf instinct told him again. OTHERS COVET YOUR FEMALE.

Not noticing his king's jealousy, Alban blinked, swallowed, and rubbed a palm over his chest as he wondered aloud, "You think I'm funny?"

"Do not give the privileged white man attention," Wyn told her and patted her head from where she sat up on the floor. "Laugh at one of his jokes; he will think he can do standup."

Alban dusted off his shoulder. "I mean, I *could*—"

"Fucking *traitors*," Nic exclaimed and stormed out of the room, slamming the door closed after him.

They were going to treat her as if she were his

queen? Comfort her even as Nic told them she was a spy. How many times did he have to say she was not his mate?

She can't be.

That which seems too good to be true is always a sweet lie.

From down the hall, Nic heard Alban say, "No cookies for him."

CHAPTER 13

"So..." Wyn began and awkwardly pushed his glasses further up on his nose. It was an instinctual action whenever he was uncomfortable.

"It was a simple mistake," Alban told Isa as the three of them stood in front of the large hot tub in the mansion's steam room. "Wyn is not smart enough to trick you into skinny dipping. He just literally didn't think about you not having a bathing suit when he offered hot tub time."

Of course, she did not have a bathing suit for the hot tub. Wyn, the king's advisor, a wise Noctu owl shifter, was better than that slip-up.

The Hag had dropped Isa off with only the gown she wore and a briefcase—did that have clothing? Wyn would have to check the contents later to see what else she needed to stay here.

"Dammit." Wyn pinched the bridge of his nose and attempted to ignore the enchanting mental image that Alban supplied. *Isa skinny dipping.* Her stripping off her dress and stepping into the steaming water completely naked, her curves on display… *"Der'mo."* Shit.

"He never curses, by the way," Alban informed her, gazing at Wyn like he was a new, compelling reality TV show. "This new, horny Wyn is fascinating to watch."

Wyn chose to address only Isa and not the annoying fox shifter. "I would offer to let you bathe in the tub alone, but you really should be monitored after your…incident."

"He means heart attack," Alban added. "Near-death experience."

Isa nibbled on a warm, pryaniki honey spice cookie and gazed up at them with big eyes.

I want to hold her and never let her go. Wyn tried to shake off the thought.

"You could borrow my swimsuit?" Alban offered Isa. "I mean, your tits would be out, but if you've seen one pair of tits, you've seen them all, am I right? Though, Wyn probably has seen zero tits. His first internet search was something *academic.*" Alban gagged.

Isa took a big bite of her cookie and grabbed another from the tray beside the tub.

Alban asked her in an amazed tone one might use to excite a child, "Did you know there are topless beaches in other regions of the world?"

"We are in the Arctic," Wyn reminded him.

Finishing off another cookie, Isa leaned over and twisted the knob on the jacuzzi tub. Bubbles immediately erupted from the bottom of the tub, causing a lush blanket of foam over the water.

She gaped, then she jumped up and down and grinned at it.

Wyn didn't realize how absorbed he was in her adorable reaction until Alban cleared his throat.

"Seriously, lusting after his mate is messed up," Alban commented under his breath, too low for the prey shifter to hear. "He's going to apologize, and they'll eventually live happily ever after. Manage your horny little crush, dude."

Wyn replied dryly, "You just suggested she go topless."

Alban scoffed. "Sorry I believe in female freedom."

While the men went back and forth, no one watched Isa. Not until the sound of her gown wafting to the floor reached their powerful paranormal ears. Their necks craned instantly.

At the loud splashing noise, both of their expressions were struck with fear at the thought of her accidentally drowning.

But Isa happily splashed in the tub and smiled up at the ceiling as she relaxed and sank into the hot bubbling water until it lapped at her chin. Her naked body remained hidden by a blanket of white, foaming bubbles.

She is naked in the tub. Wyn rubbed a hand over his mouth. When did he last want to study something as much as her body?

"Why do I get the feeling she has never been in a hot tub before?" Alban asked as they watched Isa cup bubbles in her hands and giggle as they popped.

"Arctic prey often live in tribes on the edges of the ice to avoid predator shifters. No real civilization, not many imports," Wyn said. "It is possible she hasn't seen much modern society. Prey females are especially isolated."

Alban turned to Isa and cooed, "Aww, little hot-tub virgin. Do we need to remind you not to pee in the pool—"

Hot water slapped Alban across the face, cutting him off.

Face dripping, Alban's mouth hung open as he stared at Isa. "Did you just—"

She splashed him again.

Isa was…having fun? Yes, she had a heart attack for the first time an hour earlier, but now she sat in her very first hot tub—even more glamorous than the ones she had seen in movies.

Now that the intense, confusing Arctic king was somewhere far from her, Isa relaxed and enjoyed herself. Cookies, warm milk, and a massive hot tub of frothing bubbles and massaging jets.

And...*them.*

Wyn, the tall, fully suited man in glasses, who had sworn to protect her in front of his king. The man who watched her constantly. Those gorgeous eyes took in every moment's detail, making her feel utterly safe and seen.

And Alban... Though he acted flippant, carefree, and emotionally distant, it was a façade. When she half-tripped on a fancy rug in the hallway on her way to the steam room, Alban kicked the piece of fabric like it personally aggravated him for disrupting her steps.

Alban was also the only one of the three men who tried to make her laugh. His attitude was not all doom and gloom or all serious. He reminded her of herself, always trying to find the light in the dark.

She...liked them. Or maybe it was loneliness. Or the lust.

Incredibly strong, overpowering lust. *My heat is a ticking time bomb.* But when it happened, would the Arctic king help satisfy her, or would she end up begging for the next closest alpha to fuck her until her heat broke?

Would the next closest alpha be one of the two men in front of her now?

Even though she had just had a near-death experience—or maybe partial death?—her body hummed for touch; her gaze raked over them as she lazed in the large tub.

Their height and broad shoulders made her feel tiny in comparison. Made her feel especially feminine and them especially virile and male. Alpha.

Everything about them was attractive. Their icy blond hair, their thick lips, their perfect bone structure. Their features made her think of words like *wispy* and *sharp*.

Her nipples stiffened under the hot water as bubbles from the jet burst up around her and blocked the men's view of her breasts. If she sat up a little higher, they would be able to see her taut nipples.

Being so close to her heat and after being teased by the king, she needed relief.

She had not received a treat in a few days ago. She had not made herself come the last few days, edging herself as instructed by her tribe before the adoption ceremony.

My body needs to come. Her tribe had taught her that there was nothing wrong with masturbation and encouraged it, actually. Still, she had never been allowed to touch a man since she had to be "pure" to be adopted by a master.

Her gaze licked over the men, taking its time to savor the two widely different flavors.

"You ogling us, bunny?" Alban asked through a sexy grin.

She pointed to her face, feigned innocence, and then shook her head.

"Oh, I must have been mistaken." Alban's hands fell to his belt, and Isa choked out a cough. "I hope you don't mind, but these are designer."

Alban grabbed the hem of his shirt and pulled it over his head, tossing it to the wood floor of the sauna steam room. *Hello, abs.* Alluring ridges of taut muscle lined his torso, gathering moisture and sexily glistening from the foggy steam.

Every breath Isa took felt too hot, as if her lungs were pure steam. Gods, she was just so horny.

"Can't get them in hot water." He pulled his belt off, held out his arm, and dropped the black accessory to the floor in a dramatic show of arrogant smugness.

The rattling *clang* of the belt hitting the wooden floor had a tangible effect on Isa. The sound echoed in her mind, and a pulsing began between her thighs to match the rhythm.

She watched in silent torment as Alban teased down the zipper of his pants. So slowly. Like he wanted her to beg him to go faster. He ran a hand over himself, where a bulge began to form at his crotch, and Isa choke-coughed again.

He is hard.

He grinned and undid the button on his pants, lowering them down narrow hips and lean, muscular legs. He dipped three fingers into the waistline of his boxers and stroked his thumb over his lower abdomen.

"Think I should take these off too?" Alban asked Isa.

Wyn pinched the bridge of his nose again. "Are you really trying to perform a strip show right now? For your king's mate? After instructing me that it's 'messed up' for me to like her?"

"Don't talk to me about honor and betrayal after you basically laid claim to his mate with the whole 'I vow to protect her' thing. Plus, she likes it." Alban nodded toward where Isa held back drool. "Don't you like watching me strip for you?"

Isa gaped. The men could not see the way her thighs opened wide under the bubbling water. They could not see her hand fall between her legs. *So horny.*

"Because I like it. I like your pretty eyes on me." Alban moved closer to the large, steaming tub as he rasped, "I'm getting so hard thinking about your naked little body in that hot tub right now."

Isa gasped and squirmed at how her body's reaction was a sudden wave of heat—even hotter than the steaming water—and desperate tingles. Gods, she was overheating. Melting into a pot of boiling lust. She needed to come.

Her fingers swirled over the top of her sex under the water.

The mantra floated through her head. *It feels good to touch yourself.*

"Fuck, your arousal is scenting the air," Wyn cursed. When would they find out she was actively masturbating in the hot tub?

But Isa could not look away from Alban's tantalizing, needy expression. She could not stop circling her fingers over herself. Would he take his briefs off already? She had seen videos of men's erections before but never one up close that she could *touch*.

Her pussy grew slicker in the tub.

"My cock is getting so full at the thought of you watching me and getting turned on," Alban whispered as if the words were meant for her ears only. "This compound hasn't seen a woman in two years. To say the men here are pent-up would be an understatement."

Isa bit her lip. She felt pent-up, too.

"And you are..." Alban purred, "So fucking pretty."

Wyn scoffed. "More than '*pretty*,' you asshole."

"I've heard stories about prey shifters going into heat," Alban said, pushing his boxers down his legs.

Isa's jaw hurt from hanging open.

Alban kicked off the boxers, and his cock smacked up against his hard stomach. Thick, mushroom-tipped, and lined with two dark veins, his shaft stood tall and erect.

What would he do if I took him into my mouth?

Isa floated forward, closer to where Alban stood at the edge of the massive hot tub. She was underwater from the neck down, so they still did not see her hand rubbing between her legs.

Alban's hand sank to the base of his cock and gave it one long stroke. Even with a sore throat, Isa released a small, weak moan. *I want to touch him. I want to feel a man inside me. For the first time.*

Would the Arctic king finish the job and kill her if she had sex with his friend?

She knew alphas could be jealous and possessive creatures, but her tribe taught her that pleasure was vital to survival.

She wanted fun and pleasure and Christmas cookies and next-to-the-crackling-fireplace cuddles.

"I wonder what it would take for you to go into heat…" Alban wondered aloud as he stepped closer to the tub. "Maybe if I teased you for long enough," Alban said. "Maybe if I made you come enough times."

Isa whimpered and rocked her hips under the water. Alban's surprising peppermint candy cane scent wafted over to her in the steam. It acted like an aphrodisiac along with his words.

"That's enough, Alban," Wyn grated.

No, not enough. More, she mentally begged him.

"I don't think it is enough. I think she has had a stressful day. We are supposed to be soothing her and helping her relax, right?" Alban grinned wickedly as he ran his hand over his hard cock once more. "What's more relaxing than an orgasm? Don't you want to help her feel nice and calm?"

Yes, please make me come. Isa's breasts heaved in the water with ragged breaths. At this point, the hot tub was feeling almost *too* hot.

Her fingers slipped and slid over her slickness. Her face had to be claimed entirely in a blush by now as she lost herself in the sensations of need.

"She doesn't look calm to me," Wyn said. "Listen to her breathing."

"She is just getting excited, huh, bunny?" Alban asked. "Do you need someone to massage that pussy until you feel fully relaxed?"

At that exact moment, the bubbles stopped. Isa jerked in alarm, her thighs clenched and clamped around her hand. She glanced around the water, which became still and see-through.

"Just a timer…" Wyn started to explain the change to her but trailed off.

As the last bubbles died, the men had a clear view of how she had been masturbating under the masking blanket of bubbles.

CHAPTER 14

"*H*oly shit," Alban muttered so lowly that Isa almost did not hear him.

"Little flower..." Wyn whispered into the steam filling up the room.

Isa panted but did not move her hand. She just... couldn't stop rocking against it. She couldn't stop touching herself as she gazed at Alban's fingers fisting his engorged shaft. *I want it. Give it to me.*

"Have you... Have you been touching yourself this whole time, baby?" Alban asked in a raspy tone that was free of any comedic or playful teasing. "Were you stroking that pussy when I took my cock out?"

Isa's head jerked up and down in a mindless nod as she continued to swirl tight circles over her swollen clit.

"Fuck, you're not stopping." Alban groaned and squeezed his hand over the tip of his dusky cock.

"That's a good little bunny," he praised her as he ever so slowly began stroking his thick length. "So needy.

His voice was a deep, masculine rumble by the end of his sentence, and it triggered a powerful burst of lust in Isa. "Watching me touch myself and rubbing that clit. Keep going; it'll feel so good when you come. You'll feel so...relaxed."

As her eyelids fluttered, lowering to half-mast, she heard the soft splashing sound of someone entering the hot tub. Naked, Alban glided into the tub, closer and closer to Isa.

Where Isa sat, Alban stood in the steaming water, the liquid lapped just above his knees. At the hot temperature, Alban hissed. His dick twitched, seeming to reach out to her.

"This does not seem the best way to relax someone after a heart attack," Wyn commented as he stood in his full suit beside the hot tub.

"Enthusiastically disagree," Alban said as he stroked his gorgeous dick right in front of her panting mouth. "Don't you think coming will make you feel *sooooo* relaxed?" he asked her.

She whimpered loudly.

"Her throat is sore," Wyn scolded. "It probably hurts her to make noises like that."

"Aww, does it hurt to moan?" he teased her. "You need to be quiet, bunny. If Nic hears me pleasuring his mate, he might kill me, and you don't want my blood on your pretty little hands, do you?"

Wide-eyed and open-mouthed, Isa stared at him.

Alban smirked. "Can you orgasm nice and quiet for me? Hold your lips together. Squeeze them nice and tight like I want to squeeze those perfect tits of yours."

At his dirty words, her mouth fell open wider.

Alban smirked. "Hmm, maybe I'll just have to gag you." He spoke each word contemplatively, "But—what —to—use." Alban lifted his free hand to pinch her jaw. He asked Wyn, "What should I use to fill up her pretty mouth, Wyn?"

"What part of 'she just had a heart attack' are you not absorbing?" Wyn deadpanned.

The men continued to speak in a calm, nonchalant manner as if Alban was not jerking off right in front of Isa as she fingered herself.

"I'm just saying, these pretty pink lips, this lush little mouth… It deserves some attention, don't you think?"

Just as Alban leaned closer to Isa, his cock at face-level from where she sat in the tub, the door to the sauna room creaked open.

"Un. Fucking. Believable," the king growled.

*N*ic had tried to mind his own business. He had downed four shots of vodka. He had tried to make a new move in the endless chess game with Wyn, which was really more like a chess board set up in Nic's study that Wyn occasionally glanced at and moved a black piece occasionally, stumping Nic.

Nic had even tried to spend some quality time with his dogs, but they seemed to be victims of the same distraction as him, wondering where *she* was.

What was Isa up to? How was she feeling? Did she hate him now? Did she need hot soup? Nic couldn't get the pretty prey out of his head.

The jealousy was especially brutal—the way Wyn and Alban, of all people, were *soothing* her right now.

And what the fuck does that mean?

With his superhuman shifter hearing, he could—if he wanted to—figure out where in the castle they were. Figure out what they were talking about. Were they trading *I hate what a grump Nic has become* stories? Had he already lost any chance with her?

It's a spell. She is not really my mate.

But what if she was?

Nic's legs moved him like he was nothing but a puppet. *She* pulled the strings, and that aggravated the fuck out of him. To be vulnerable to someone else's needs. To be a slave to them... Had he not already lived that hell when he was a weak teenager, abducted and worked as slave labor for those with more power?

"*Aw, a little wolf, all alone,*" the low voice crawled through his memories.

The man who had found Nic at rock bottom,

freezing to death after wandering for days around barren Arctic land, after his father had exiled him for not being "strong" or "tough" enough to be associated with the royal family due to his limp and smaller-sized wolf.

"Got a bum leg, boy? That limp will be the death of you. But you won't have to run from me; I'll be your friend."

A trick. Because it always was.

Every meal Nic had was after hours of free labor. His jaw would hurt on each chew after being pistol-whipped for not moving fast enough in the cold. His back bled from the whip that struck him when he stumbled.

Of course, that was where Nic had met Alban, who was a child like him and the son of one of the town's prostitutes. Nic's abductor had frequented Alban's mom's bed.

That was when the two of them hatched a plan. For escape. For redemption.

Alban's childhood was as brutally stained as Nic's. Alban knew why Nic would fear a mate.

Mates were fated. Mates triggered the deep animal spirit in male shifters.

Having a mate meant no more free will. Was Nic really to be chained to someone again, unable to stop from doing their bidding? *I promised myself to never be so weak again.*

Even worse, to lose any independence and...cold indifference—a medical numbness that had served him well over the many years—because now there was *more* in his life.

Dangerous. Too dangerous.

Where the fuck is she?

His inner wolf located her instantly. Wyn and Alban's voices were prominent, but her breathing was a sound he felt so mystically attuned to, he could find anywhere. After all, what noise would ever be more important?

Splash.

They were in the sauna. Nic strode to the corridor where the steam room and hot tub resided.

Her breathing…was heavy.

Hurt? In danger?

Nic ran.

His limp made itself known most when he moved quickly, but he had never felt so unconcerned with anyone seeing it as he blurred down the hallway.

GET TO HER, his wolf howled.

Just before he ripped the door off its hinges, his body jolted to a stop. He froze as his nostrils flared and inhaled her scent of arousal.

Thick arousal.

Wet heaven.

MATE NEEDS US, his inner wolf growled. TAKE HER.

He burst into the room.

There she was. Masturbating in his hot tub while his

advisor stood in the corner with a bulge filling out the crotch of his dress pants and his fox shifter friend stood naked and jerking off in front of Nic's mate's face.

"Un. Fucking. Believable."

Everyone in the room turned to face Nic with big, fearful eyes. He wanted to rip Alban in half, but... He knew not to scare Isa again.

He would have to gently kill Alban. Maybe not in front of her. Maybe give her a hot cup of Chamomile tea and point out a window so she wasn't looking when Nic pulled a pistol with a silencer on Alban.

"It's not what it looks like," Alban said, moving his hand off his cock.

"It looks like you're trying to masturbate on my mate's face."

"So, it is what it looks like—Ha!" Alban pointed. "So, she *is* your mate."

Remains to be seen. But Nic's body and his wolf reacted like she was his mate, so...he would experiment with it. Maybe. Every spell faded with time. "Wyn, tell me honestly, was Alban trying to get her to suck him off?"

Alban shot Wyn a *help-me* expression as he pressed himself against the wall of the tub, as far away from Isa as he could be—*still* with a raging hard-on.

Wyn pursed his lips and shrugged. "Not entirely sure what direction it was headed in."

"And you..." Nic directed all of his attention onto Isa

as he strode to the edge of the hot tub. In his black turtleneck and goddamn expensive pants, he stepped into the tub.

As his costly clothing grew more and more soaked, Nic remained indifferent to it. As if he walked through air instead of hot water, only caring that he moved closer to her.

"You think you are allowed to get wet in front of anyone other than your goddamn king?"

CHAPTER 15

*B*ad pet.

Isa shivered in the tub, practically vibrating at the sight of the king's black clothing drenched and sticking to him like a second skin. This was her master, the man she was supposed to please. Sexy, handsome, magnetic.

But then he had to go and ruin it by trying to kill her.

Nic caged her to the wall of the hot tub. Stretching an arm out on either side of her, he whispered against her chin, "You think you're allowed to fill the room with your erotic as hell pheromones, messing with my men's brains?"

"I…" She couldn't help her arousal. Going into heat wouldn't be something she *tried* to do.

"I think we need to establish some rules," Nic said in

her ear, nibbling the lobe for a split second. "You're not allowed to be wet in front of my men."

He grabbed her hips and launched her out of the hot water. Outside of the water, she gasped as her naked body was now on complete display for the three men.

Droplets of liquid caressed down her bare breasts, getting caught on her nipples or dipping into her belly button as Nic sat her onto the ledge of the tub.

He wrenched her thighs open, and her heart rate accelerated again. Her clit ached to be touched, and she could hardly catch her breath as she watched the icy king lower himself.

His face hovered an inch from her pink, pliant flesh.

Eyes clenched shut, he breathed in her pussy and physically shook. When he opened his eyes to look up at her, his pupils were big circles of black, eating up his blue and brown irises. As if his arousal turned him into an animalistic monster.

She...liked it.

"See how her pussy glistens in the light?" Nic asked a question, though it seemed unclear who he expected to answer. "So wet." He tsked. "But that is not allowed. I will have to clean it away."

He leaned forward and dragged his large tongue from the bottom of her folds to the top of her sex, flicking against the hood of her clit. Her hips bucked as a rushed exhale escaped her lips.

After the first sensual lick, Nic reluctantly pulled

back. His tantalizing gaze skimmed over her pussy, analyzing it. "Hmm, still wet. That will not do." He leaned forward again and…

Lick.

"More?" Nic grunted.

Lick. Lap. Suckle.

Her moan broke out through the room, bouncing off the wooden planks.

"Uh, uh, uh," Nic tsked her as he placed small kisses directly over her swollen clit. "You need to *stop* getting wet in front of my men."

His tongue gave another leisurely lick, and some of her brain cells seemed to die. His touch was as impactful as hard drugs.

"You want to know why you shouldn't get wet around them?" Nic gently nipped at her inner thigh. "Because your scent floods the fucking air, and it tells every shifter around you just how horny you are. Just how bad you need to be touched. It gives them *ideas*."

Isa wailed again, trembling with need as Nic delivered soft kisses and licks over her needy pussy.

Nic added, "They will breathe you in and think they can touch you. But you're mine. Aren't you?" He slapped a palm over her thigh and massaged the area just as quickly, resulting in only tingles and heat, no pain. "Do you get it now?"

"I…"

"You need to stop being wet," Nic whispered against

the top of her sex as he planted kisses over it. Making eye contact from his position between her legs, he said, "I won't stop until I've licked this pussy clean."

And he...dove in.

She could *hear* it. Gods, she had gotten so slick, the sounds of his tongue lapping at her were audible. He *buried* his face between her legs like he planned to be there, feasting, for hours.

She swore his tongue was engraved for female pleasure because the friction of his tastebuds over the smooth pink of her most vulnerable flesh was too incredible to be natural.

His thumb moved up and gently pulled back the hood of her clit to reveal the sensitive nub. He smiled to himself just before flicking his tongue over the throbbing bud.

Then, he parted his lips, wrapped them around her clit, and sucked—

"*Oh Gods*," she yelled out, her voice scratchy and hoarse as the sensations overwhelmed her senses.

"My little mate doesn't know how to listen," Nic told Alban and Wyn. "She just keeps getting wetter."

Reminded that they were in the room too, Isa glanced up and saw Alban's hand had resumed its work of stroking his hard erection. Another rush of wetness and need gushed between her quivering legs at the realization that the fox shifter was jerking off while watching his king eat the hell out of her pussy.

There was a tortured expression on Alban's face like he just couldn't help but watch and stroke. Like he *tried* not to. Like he knew he shouldn't.

"*Please*," Isa begged.

"You beg so nicely," Nic grunted onto her overheating skin. "If only you knew how to obey when I gave you an order." He nipped at her clit.

She yelped and screamed out, "*More!*"

"Maybe you need to stop the wetness at the source, Nic," Alban said in a husky voice from behind his king. His hand slowly slid up and down his flushed cock.

"Where is my advisor with the good ideas?" Nic asked.

Wyn stood frozen, completely still, as he watched the scene play out before him. Isa saw the large bulge tenting his dress pants, but the glasses-wearing man made no move to touch himself. Which...disappointed Isa.

I want him to feel good, too.

Looking right at Wyn, Isa reached up to cup her own breasts. Her fingers played with her tight pink nipples as his blue eyes burned through her. *All that heat in one pent-up man.* She wanted to watch him explode.

"Ahh, now she thinks she can take her pleasure into her own hands?" Nic shook his head. "You are not in control here, little spy." Nic dragged his tongue over her pulsing clit before instructing, "Wyn, come over here and keep her from playing with those perfect goddamn tits."

Wyn moved. Fast. From a frozen statue to a man on a mission, Wyn strode around the tub and bent down to grab Isa's wrists. He tore her fingers from her breasts and moved her arms over her head.

Wyn trapped her arms behind his neck so that Wyn's mouth balanced beside her neck and earlobe. His warm breaths puffed against the tender skin of her neck, and Isa's brain blanked.

Held and dominated by two alphas.

"The whole lesson for you to learn is to *stop* being turned on," Nic reminded Isa. "You're not allowed to play with your own nipples when my men are in the room. They'll start thinking *they* can cup your pretty breasts in their hands. Like, Alban, are you thinking about how suckable my mate's needy nipples are while you jerk yourself off?"

The fox shifter cursed as he stroked his cock faster while watching them, not even pretending to stop. "Nic, I'm sorry, but I haven't been with a woman in so long, and I can't stop—"

"Answer the question."

"Fuck, yes, I want to taste those pink nipples. I want to suck them and bite them and thrust my dick between those tits. She's so fucking perfect, man."

Nic shook his head again and shot a disapproving

expression at Isa. "See what your horniness is doing to my men?"

"I—I'm sorry?"

"Shhhh." Nick quieted her apology the second it poured from her lips. "Shhh, we're going to fix the problem."

What did that mean?

Nic said, "I think Alban is right. We need to stop the wetness from the source."

He slid a long finger down, down, down, and pressed against her entrance.

CHAPTER 16

The Arctic king had never felt so hot. He was volcanic lava. He was the summer sun.

With each lick of his tongue against her warm, silken wetness, his inner wolf clamored to mark her. To claim her and bite her thigh so that she wore a mark forever more that proved she was his and his alone.

Yes, Nic still thought she could be a spy. He still thought it could be a trick, but…

I never want to stop this. He growled onto her pussy, and she moaned at the vibration. *When have I ever experienced such pleasure?* Yet, all he did was pleasure *her*.

"Just need to stop the wetness, and maybe then I'll be able to fucking *think*." So overcome by lust, he wondered if his eyes were becoming wolf-like. If his fangs would start to break through his gums.

Because nothing had ever made him feel more like an out-of-control animal than her taste.

His middle finger pressed against her slick, tight entrance and pushed forward, breaching her.

"Oh, *fuck*," Nic grated, more on edge than ever. His cock was so full, he was seconds from dripping pre-cum onto his briefs.

YOUR MATE IS WET. FUCK HER, his wolf raged inside him. MAKE HER CUM AROUND YOUR COCK. FILL HER UP. BREED HER.

"Gods...damn it." Nic's finger shoved inside her, harsher than he meant to thrust it.

He fought back his wolf's primal desire to turn her over and take her roughly from behind; it took a lot of mental energy.

WANT TO EXPERIENCE MY MATE, his inner wolf growled.

"So...soft," Nic grated as his finger curled and explored the hot, silky sheath he had spent endless nights imagining.

Finally...a mate. He never thought he would be so lucky. Shoving back the instinct to question any moment of happiness or again doubt her motives or authenticity, Nic decided to simply enjoy this. For once. *Enjoy.*

"You have no idea..." He trailed off as he inched his finger out and slowly moved it back inside her.

At the insertion, her jaw dropped, and a loud sexual

noise shook her throat. Her eyes rolled back in ecstasy, but he had not even gotten started.

He said darkly, "You have no idea what you've just unleashed."

He laid his mouth over her swollen clit and went to work.

His finger pistoned in and out of her as he licked and sucked. Tongue flicking. Teeth grazing. He curled his digit, and her slick inner walls clamped around him when he rubbed against a spot of ribbed flesh deep inside her.

"You like that?" he asked.

"Please," she gasped out and churned her hips for more as if she wanted to fuck herself on his finger.

"Mmm, you wet my finger so good." His own hips rocked forward as if his cock wanted to rip through his pants and somehow "accidentally" slip inside her to replace his finger.

"Bunny, tell us how good his finger feels," Alban weakly called over to her, like he held back his orgasm to continue watching for as long as it took. "Does it fill you up so good?"

"Mmmm," she moaned out. "So...full."

Nic added another finger. The more he felt her perfect pussy's grip, the more his body demanded he thrust himself inside her. *Really* fill her up.

TAKE HER, his wolf growled.

"Hare shifters are known to be fuck bunnies, right? I bet she likes it rough," Alban said.

Nic added another finger. *Got to get her ready for me.*

He watched her face scrunch up for a moment from the newly added sensation stretching her, but when Nic fastened his lips around her clit and sucked, pleasure burst through her expression.

"*Yes,*" she yelled.

He speared his fingers inside her, keeping a steady rhythm as he ate her like his last meal before a month's exploration of barren Arctic tundra.

"More," she begged.

What more? Did she want… Nic held his breath as he continued pleasuring the fuck out of her. Could she really want him—inside her? Gods, Nic had only ever imagined.

TAKE HER. FUCK HER. CLAIM HER. MY MATE. MINE.

His cock was heavy with seed, pent-up for years, waiting to be given to only one woman.

"More, please."

Did she mean it? Nic moved a hand down to shove at his pants.

"Still so wet. Do I need a bigger plug to keep the wetness in your pussy and away from my men, pet?"

She spread her thighs open wider and tugged at his head.

In the hot tub water, Nic ripped open his soaked

underwear. Once freed, his cock flopped up to his stomach and painted it with glistening pre-cum. He grabbed it and squeezed. "Do you need something big to fill you up?"

"*Please*," she moaned.

Alban groaned. "Damn, this sex bunny knows exactly what she wants."

Wyn released a low moan against Isa's shoulder from where he still held her arms above her, around his neck.

"I bet she knows just how to ride you to make you explode, Nic. Is our little sex bunny dripping to be filled with some thick, virgin king cock? Because the king has been waiting a loooong time—"

In a flash, Nic stood from the water, and Isa nearly toppled back into Wyn in surprise. Nic grabbed her hips and pulled her forward to the edge of the hot tub, so her calves sank into the water once more, and their hips were flush against each other.

Gripping his hard-as-rock erection, he aligned the head to her entrance, ready to replace his fingers. "She is so wet; she's fucking slippery," Nic groaned out in a tone of sheer tortured need.

He was really going to feel it for the first time—feel the wet, tight grip of his mate's pussy around his virgin cock.

"*Please*," she cried.

He ever so slowly pressed inside. Alban wasn't kidding when he described his king's girth as "thick."

The cock head was squeezed in a vice-like grip as he entered her. *Nothing else feels like this.* Her lush wet heat seemed to suck him in further.

"Oh fuck, I... My wolf is rising." A menacing growl shot out of Nic as he gnashed his teeth and shoved forward, fully impaling her on his cock. "I'm losing...control."

"Haha, ice king," Alban said and rolled his eyes. The fox shifter did not believe Nic was capable of losing control.

But Wyn saw it.

He saw the way his king's eyes flashed.

Nic pulled back to forcefully thrust inside her again. "Trying to go slow, but my wolf demands his...turn." Nic grunted the words through clenched teeth, "He wants to...take her."

Isa released a crazed, mindless moan. Her head fell back as he continued steadily fucking her.

"Hold it back, Nic," Wyn advised. "She is too delicate." To Wyn, Nic's wolf was a vicious monster. To many, his wolf was the unfeeling boogie man.

If his wolf took over his actions, there was no telling what he might do to Isa. Hell, his wolf wanted to kill Wyn due to his earlier promise to protect *Nic's* mate.

There was the inner wolf instinct, and then there was the wolf spirit that lurked in the shadows of Nic's mind, only taking over during a shift on a full moon. But now...it wanted out. It wanted to play.

THRUST. FUCK. SPILL CUM INSIDE MATE. BREED. FILL HER.

He couldn't stop thrusting.

Even as the wolf's control over him grew stronger with each moment Nic relished in the pleasure of Isa's body, Nic couldn't stop.

Couldn't stop dipping his throbbing cock inside her hot, wet pussy.

Couldn't stop watching a blush travel over her pretty face and chest.

Her breasts smashed up against his muscular chest as he thrust and thrust and thrust.

"Hold it back," Wyn warned again.

"I...I *can't*," Nic whispered in awe and surprise and... fear.

Fear for what it would do to his mate.

Isa wrapped her arms around Nic and undulated over him, where he thrust inside her. She bit his earlobe and whispered, "*More*."

And it was over.

"FUCK," he bellowed as his wolf overcame him.

His eyes flashed. His body...grew and became more robust.

Though he did not shift into a wolf, his inner wolf taking over caused a physical change. Shifted eyes and fangs and a bigger...*size*.

His cock lengthened and thickened even more inside

her as Nic's consciousness was pushed into the backseat as his wolf took the reins.

His wolf gripped her upper arms tight, wrenched her from him, and spun her around.

He clasped her wrists in one large hand and held her back to his front as he bent her over and thrust inside her from behind.

After so many years without ever knowing this kind of pleasure, his wolf...let loose.

CHAPTER 17

*I*sa wasn't in heaven. She was in…somewhere else. Somewhere devious and naughty and hot. Had she truly been revived earlier, or was this all a coma dream?

She had never had sex, and this did not feel like something that could be summed up by a three-letter word. It was so overwhelming that she made noises she didn't know she could make—some high-pitched and squeal-y, and some low and guttural.

I might become addicted to this, she thought as Nic's front slapped against her ass and caused waves in the hot tub to splash over the edge and wet Alban and Wyn's feet.

"Nic," Wyn yelled out, but Isa could hardly hear anything over the sound of her racing heartbeat.

More, more, more, her brain chanted.

Nic moved their bodies until one of the hot tub jets shot out toward Isa's clit, caressing it with a constant, forceful stream.

"Oh my Gods," she screamed and felt her inner walls clamp around him as she approached her first real orgasm—not caused by herself.

Then, the wolf...came.

A bellow of rapture sounded from behind her as she felt his stiff dick twitch and shoot ropes of his cum deep inside her. He kept thrusting, even after the last eruption; even as his cock began to soften, he thrust as if to push his cum even deeper.

Did he want to get her pregnant? Her teachings speared through her mind.

Pets should never get pregnant. An alpha predator's bloodline is sacred and must be preserved for the strongest and fastest offspring. Therefore, a pet may be a sexual plaything for her master, but she must never forget that she will only ever be a pet.

She had never questioned it before, but the words of her tribe felt almost *wrong* in that moment. The reminder to be a pet did not flood her with the usual dreamy sense of joy. It caused a twinge in her heart.

A pet is only good for sex.

"Well, man, how did pussy feel for the first time?" Alban asked in a jovial manner that grated Isa's nerves.

Her master came his brains out, and she was still horny as hell.

"Fuck," Nic cursed weakly in a deep voice, like he lost all energy to sound normal. He slid himself out of her and stepped back.

He did not cradle her. Or cuddle her.

I want more. Isa fought the urge to cry.

"Lucky your wolf was pent-up and came so fast, or he might have accidentally hurt her," Alban said.

"Fuck you," Nic remarked.

"Insecure cause of how fast you came and how you didn't get her off?"

Nic ignored his friend and touched Isa's hip, slightly turning her so he saw her face. His palm moved up to her cheek as his gaze scanned over her face, neck, and chest—taking an extra second to examine her breasts.

"Are you...okay?" he asked.

Like you care, a bitter voice whispered in Isa's head. It was a new voice, unlike her usual daisies, rainbows, and gumdrops voice. *Caused by withdrawal of treats?*

She shot back, "So, now you are nice to me? Because you have sampled what I'm good for?"

Nic's eyes and mouth opened wide in stunned silence at that. "*What?*"

"Now that you've come in me, does that mean you don't hate me anymore?"

Shame. It exploded over his expression like a snowball catapulted into a wall. Shame dripped from his eyelashes and clumped over his cheeks and lips like remnants of icy snow.

He blinked several times. "That's not..."

"I'm just a pet, here for your pleasure." Isa crossed her arms, hiding her breasts and her...heart. "I think I deserve a treat," she said adamantly.

The three men stared at her.

"I'm confused," Alban said. "Is she asking for a cookie or an orgasm? And what is this 'pet' kink that I've never heard of?"

Isa wanted one of her tribe's treats. The little blue pills were inside the briefcase Hag dropped her off with. Was the case still in the parlor?

She did not enjoy the withdrawal thoughts and feelings she was having. She wanted to be her usual positive and cheerful self. Not this hurt self who questioned being a pet to a predator shifter.

I should be happy the Arctic king is warming to me, right? Happy that I had sex for the first time...

"I...apologize," the king grated. "Clearly, I did not satisfy you—"

"Typical of a guy's first time," Alban commented.

The king flexed his jaw as a speck of anger gleamed in his blue and brown eyes. Hesitantly, Nic reached out for her again. His fingers grazed her arm, and she wondered how such a minuscule touch from him could leave her feeling so warm after he had treated her so coldly.

He started, "I want to—"

"I would like to retire to bed now, please," she said.

At least alone, Isa knew she could come. That was part of her nightly ritual: repeat her mantras before bed while touching herself. She was allowed to fall asleep after she orgasmed to the words, *I will always obey my master.*

Her desire for bed seemed to piss off the Arctic king. The vulnerable hand, which he reached out to her with, clenched into a fist and swung to his side. His invisible emotional walls shot right back up like they had never come down in the first place.

"Nic, do you want to show her to your—"

"She can sleep in one of the guest rooms," Nic growled. "Far the fuck away from me."

The temperamental wolf turned and climbed out of the hot tub, leaving his ripped pants and underwear floating in the water behind him.

He walked, butt-ass naked, out of the steamy room.

"I'm still up to giving you an orgasm, bunny," Alban offered, smiling.

Wyn launched a towel at the fox shifter's face. To Isa, Wyn said, "I will show you to your room."

"*I* will, um, grab you some clothes," Wyn stated, blushing fiercely, before leaving a naked—other than a wet towel—Isa in the hallway outside of his bedroom.

The three large, gray East European shepherds, who had patiently waited outside the hot tub sauna and trailed after her when she exited it, kept her company.

When Wyn reemerged, he handed her one of his favorite button-down shirts and a pair of pants. Already, he could imagine them on her—large, billowy, and slipping off her shoulders and down her perfect thighs. She really was tiny compared to the men.

"Your room will be down here." Wyn led her farther down the hall to a bedroom far from Nic's master suite.

Wyn did not know what he preferred to see: his king softening to Isa or Isa hardening against his king.

I...want her.

The treasonous thought hung itself in the corner of Wyn's brain, nailed and super-glued. It stayed there, along with the mental image of Isa's dripping, naked body as she stepped out of the hot tub and to where Wyn delicately wrapped her in a towel to dry her earlier.

There was no real explanation as to why Wyn was attracted to her when he had never been attracted to anyone else or felt any stirrings of lust in his many years of life. She was beautiful, yes, but there was something more behind those eyes.

A dichotomy of sunshine and rain that fascinated him to watch.

She was a puzzle. *What did she mean when she asked for a treat?*

Nic may have been dismissed by his mate after not making her come, but...Wyn could try. He had studied a few books in the past. He wanted to experiment and *learn* her.

Wyn opened the door, waiting for her to enter first, and showed her the spacious bedroom with a massive canopy bed. A large glass window took up most of one of the walls, displaying the harshly enchanting and beautifully brutal frozen landscape outside.

The three large dogs strode right inside, jumped, and laid at the foot of the bed. They watched Isa as if silently asking her when she would join them for some well-deserved sleep.

Wyn assumed she was in awe of the room as she stood there for a moment, completely still and taking in her surroundings. Then, she turned to face him, holding close her towel and the stack of clothing he supplied her.

Isa swallowed and commented softly, "I...can be good for more than just sex."

Wyn stiffened and blew out a choppy exhale at her soft words. "Isa," he stated. "We would never think otherwise."

Clearly, Isa had a past of being overly sexualized. What society was she used to? Wyn wondered as the horror pushed through his veins. What made her think…

Our society, Wyn bitterly admitted. The society built by powerful, alpha predator shifters who saw prey as food, servants, or toys. Hares and bunny shifters were often seen as sexual toys.

Hare shifters were known to have high sex drives and to reproduce in large numbers—partially due to wanting to have a strong, united front against hunters. Female hare shifters were notorious for going into heat easily.

Wyn had never had much interest in sex. However, he reviewed sexual manuals and manuscripts because he liked to know everything about everything.

Still… *Isa probably knows much more than I do on this topic.* He was not used to being the less knowledgeable in a room.

"Is it something Alban said?" Wyn asked. The fox shifter really was sounding more like a douchey asshole every day. "I know what you must think of us, but truly, we would never judge a woman for her sexual history," Wyn said. "Alban's careless nature and jokes… They are due to his own issues."

Wyn was not bothered by the fact that Isa was a hare shifter and had probably touched and been pleasured by multiple men before coming to the Arctic king's compound. He was bothered that he was less experienced than the first woman he was attracted to in his life.

And right now, she probably thinks we are all misogynist predators who don't make our women come.

"Alban says things that are, well—Alban is special," Wyn explained. "When he speaks of sex and women... Well, he grew up in a part of the Arctic that was not very civilized. Not many women and very male dominated by...not-good men."

Back when the Arctic was made up of many subsets of cultures and communities that mistreated each other. Back when Nic's father was king and only cared about money and power.

"His mother had a small home where she...uh, she was compensated for keeping men 'warm' during harsh winters." Wyn's pointed expression surely depicted the truth even though his words were cushioned.

Alban's mother was a fox shifter who became a hooker for the Arctic town where he grew up. As a boy, Alban had worn earplugs when his mother had her "visitors."

Wyn continued, "To Alban, sex was as normal as eating cereal in the morning. He became numb to it. Dabbled in it too much. Hit a rock bottom. Went two years without any." Wyn rubbed a palm over his jaw. "Alban's mother passed away before he was sixteen, and for money, he thought that he had to..."

Wyn swallowed and cleared his throat. "Nic got

Alban adopted by an American fox shifter pack, so Alban could attend high school and college in the United States. Nic thought sending him away meant saving him from the 'cold' here. But I don't know that Alban has ever felt warm anywhere."

Wyn sighed. "Trauma is not baggage he could leave here. Trauma is a shadow that follows until the light eliminates it or until it becomes unrecognizable in full darkness."

Isa listened, blinking those stunning blue eyes at him. *So damn pretty.*

Wyn had never *babbled* before. But he pursed his lips and added, "I guess young members of the pack Alban joined in America were expected to also join some kind of fraternity for shifters there. So, seven years later, when he popped back into the Russian Arctic to find Nic, he spoke like he had been brainwashed as an American 'frat bro.'"

Wyn snorted, fighting a smile. "He doesn't speak with his native accent anymore, and sometimes I think he does it on purpose. That if he hadn't reinvented himself, he would have…"

Wyn paused. *Too dark for the pretty woman.* "I say all this to tell you to be patient with us. We have not been around a woman in a long time, and some of us have… issues. Dark issues. We will not always say the right thing, but we will never *mean* to hurt you."

Wyn raised a hand to gently brush some of her hair

from the side of her face. "We do not view you as only good for sex. You are not some sexual slave or 'gift' Hag can leave here for Nic to 'enjoy.' You are here because the fates desire it; we just need to figure out why."

Isa blinked again, keeping her emotions hidden from Wyn. The man could read any book in any language, but at that moment, he could not read her.

Wyn's hand hesitantly fell from her face. "Tell me, flower, will you bring peace to us?" Wyn asked softly.

He reached for her hand and clasped it in his. So small. So perfect. She intertwined her fingers with his as if trusting him was easy. *A mistake?*

He asked, "Or are you here to start a war?"

Isa's breath caught in her throat, and Wyn analyzed everything and anything she displayed. She seemed to bite on the inside of her cheek. She blinked. But nothing screamed guilty.

"I just..." Wyn lifted her wrist and let her silver bracelet shine in the dim golden light of the bedroom. "I find it a bit odd for someone to wear a metal charm bracelet in a hot tub."

CHAPTER 18

Uh oh, Isa thought as Wyn examined the Seer's bracelet on Isa's wrist. The one that bespelled her to smell like the Arctic king's mate.

Isa typically did not wear jewelry; she did not know it was suspicious to take her clothes off but not a bracelet when entering a hot tub.

"I can think of a few reasons why you would keep it on," Wyn said.

His long fingers delicately stroked the pulse point of the inside of her wrist. Trying to monitor her heart rate for a lie?

"Maybe you are not used to wearing jewelry and forgot," he said. "In which case, it is new. But given to you by whom? Or maybe you wear the finest of metals and have no worry about hot water eroding any of its detail or shine. But to be wealthy and have never experienced a hot tub…"

Wyn fingered the little charm hanging from the bracelet. A silver Christmas tree.

"But my first thought is that you cannot remove the bracelet. Maybe because it is bespelled?"

Scrooge, she cursed in the privacy of her own thoughts again. *Control your facial expression*.

"Or because it was given to you by a treasured lover," Wyn said, but it came out more as a dark rumble.

The warmth from the fireplace in the bedroom became more noticeable as Wyn's demeanor took a turn. "That is the thought I cannot get past," he said. "That you have a lover you wish to get back to, that the Hag took you from. One who gives you lavish jewelry. One who wants other men to know you are taken."

Wyn's fingers closed over the charm bracelet and seemed to pinch it as if he wished to rip it from her. "Is that why you do not remove it? Because you have been claimed by another?" he asked.

Were her two options that she either wore a bespelled bracelet or had a lover? If the knowledge that she wore a bracelet to make Nic think she was his mate was revealed, she would be thrown out in the cold again. She would…most likely die. And she wanted to live.

I only have one choice.

Her choice: put her hand on his crotch.

Wyn's eyes shot wide open. His pursed lips separated to suck in a ragged breath.

"Wyn..." she said his name while dragging her fingers over the front zipper of his pants.

She watched with inner glee as his pupils dilated and his lips parted. She *wanted* to touch him, not just distract him from asking questions about her.

She asked, "Would you please make me come?"

He groaned and bit his bottom lip. "You have no idea how much I want that. How I won't be able to think of anything else tonight," Wyn replied huskily. "But... unlike Alban, I can maintain a semblance of control. And little flower, you have had a very long day."

She pouted, and he groaned and pressed a thumb to her bottom lip. "Maybe not after my king has left you needy and when you are not recovering from a heart attack," Wyn said tenderly.

She licked her lips and nodded, feeling that much warmer from how he chose her safety and recovery over his own pleasure. Still, she was left hornier than ever after the day she'd had.

Wyn tucked her in, under layers of the softest sheets she had ever felt on her skin, and the dogs rearranged themselves to settle around the foot of her bed.

Leaning his face so close to hers, he whispered, "It is entirely possible that Nic will take my touching you as an act of treason and war." He stroked a thumb over her cheekbone. "I would say war is inevitable now that you are here."

He gently kissed her forehead, and she again wished she was *his* pet. "Sleep well, little flower."

But she did not sleep well.

Because her survival depended on an emotionally disturbed man being filled with the holiday spirit.

Because she wore a charm that may or may not make her attractive to not only the king but his friends as well.

Because she inched closer to going into heat every day that passed around the predator shifters.

Because she wanted to live. She wanted to live a real life, free of the tribe, and have experiences. She wanted to experience joy from things that maybe were not all because she was a pet.

That night, she did not do her bedtime mantra routine. She did not think about how pleasuring her master gave her pleasure—which it did. *It does*, she admitted to herself.

But maybe I want to be more than a pet to him.

Maybe filling him with the Christmas spirit could involve real non-magic-induced love, too.

"So, no one else knows how she did it?" Alban asked the confused room—consisting of Alban, Wyn, Nic, and Miss Belsky—at the dining table for breakfast. "Even you, big brain?" he referred to Wyn, who frowned from where he stood at the opposite end of the table and poured himself a cup of coffee.

Miss Belsky shook her head. She stood against the dining room wall, holding a pitcher of freshly squeezed orange juice. "There's no explanation for it."

"Damn, she even left *you* a 'thank you' note?" Alban gawked at the household worker. "Does she know how much Nic pays you to do your job?"

Miss Belsky smoothed a spot on her skirt and replied in a heavy Russian accent, "She wrote, '*Thank you for the delicious cookies and for letting my dogs come inside.*'"

"*Her* dogs?" Nic repeated. They were *his* dogs.

Miss Belsky added, "She also promised to help me clean the floors if the dogs tracked in dirt."

"How'd she even find the pen and paper? Or have the time to write them?" Wyn speculated aloud.

"What did your thank you note say, Wyn?" Alban asked the Noctu shifter.

"I'd...prefer not to say," Wyn said after glancing at Nic.

Nic's hand fisted on the dining room table. Couldn't a man eat in peace without being consumed by jealousy first thing in the morning?

"What did yours say?" Wyn asked Alban.

"It said, '*Thank you for making me smile and laugh. But you don't have to do that all the time. I like your company when you forget to entertain everyone in the room. Sleep well.*'"

Smiling softly to himself, Alban's gaze glazed over as he stared at his cup of coffee. Alban blinked, looked up, and quickly added in a joking tone, "Don't know how the hell she slipped it into my pants pocket. Pretty sure she is a magician."

"What did your 'thank you' note say?" Wyn asked Nic, who glared an invisible hole into his advisor's head.

Nic grated out, "I didn't fucking get one."

Miss Belsky snorted and froze when she realized the alphas had perfect hearing.

Nic's back stiffened and remained tense as he said, "Miss Belsky, you are dismissed."

"Yes, my king." She bowed her head and speed-walked from the dining room.

"So, do you plan to say sorry to the pretty prey?" Alban asked his king in a baby-talk voice, poking and prodding at Nic's sensitive nerves.

Alban shoveled several bites of fried eggs into his mouth, chewing and asking, "You think that will make it okay? The whole almost killing her then coming inside her but not pushing her over the edge too, like a gentleman. A big 'I'm sorry?'"

"I didn't know about the heart attacks. I used an intimidation tactic because I needed information; I still need it," Nic replied coolly as he sat, stiff as a sheet of ice, in front of a bowl of porridge.

After such an eventful night, Nic had calmed. And drowned in guilt and shame. All last night, the image of her, cold and lifeless, haunted him. That, and the fact that he had sex and came inside a woman for the first time and hadn't made her come too.

Giving her more reasons to hate me. On purpose?

"I went about it the wrong way yesterday. Now that I know scaring her gives her a goddamn heart attack—" Nic cut off with a huff and crossed his arms. "I will be... softer."

"You haven't been soft since she walked in," Alban said. The fox shifter turned to wink at Wyn with a goofy grin. He held up a hand for a high-five. "I'm talking about his penis."

"The maturity level in this room continues to

concern me," Wyn commented, ignoring Alban's hanging high-five.

"I realize I've been in a bad mood lately," Nic admitted.

"Bad?" Wyn asked.

"Lately?" Alban joined in.

Nic rolled his eyes. "I am suspicious of the timing of her being dropped off here."

Were the men so blind to the coincidence? A prey shifter queen for Arctic shifters—right after a prey queen was appointed to all shifters and uprising rumors spread. *How could someone so delicate and pure and beautiful be my mate?*

Nic added, "But I can study her and get my information without using...force."

"*Study* her?" Alban questioned. "Now you sound like stuffy Wyn. I'd say what you *need* to study is how to be nice and make a girl come her brains out."

"I would have..." Nic fingers clenched into a fist on the dining table. He had been ready to lick and finger her pussy until she came. He would have happily done it for hours, but... "She wanted to go to bed." *She hates me.*

"She said she wanted a treat," Alban pointed out.

"That was odd, wasn't it?" Wyn posed the question to the men.

Nic closely watched his most loyal friend. The words Wyn shot at him last night still rang in his ears like offensive church bells. *"You don't come near her. You don't touch her. She stays here, under my protection, from now on."*

In that moment, his friend had chosen her—*a stranger*—over his king. Still, he had obeyed orders in the heat of the moment in the hot tub when Nic instructed him to hold Isa's arms.

Wyn placed the coffee pot down on the wooden table and lifted his cup to his mouth. "A treat implies she thinks of the behavior as something for which she deserves positive reinforcement."

"I mean, she deserved an orgasm," Alban said.

Nic ground his teeth. "I would have given her a—"

"Breakfast?" an enchanting feminine voice sounded from the dining room doorway. The men's heads turned immediately toward her.

Alban grinned, looking more actively happy than Nic could remember him being in…a while. "There's the little 'thank you' note bandit—er, secret writer."

Isa stood in a submissive—head lowered, legs crossed, and hands clasped in front of her—position. Her stunning icy-blond hair sat in poofy knots all around her head—the girl clearly needed quality time with some conditioner and a hairbrush.

Yet, to Nic, she was even more beautiful in the morning.

There were bags under her eyes, and Nic's first thought was, *"I hope she was up late thinking about me too."* Was he some kind of lovesick boy now?

This is what a mate does to a person. Weakens them. Nic internally chastised himself. Still, his wolf howled, MINE.

Then, he noticed what she was wearing.

CHAPTER 19

"Fuck. No," Nic stated, rather proud of how *not* aggressive he managed to sound. *She can die from fright. Dial it back,* Nic reminded himself.

"Hmm?" Isa blinked and looked at Nic after shooting a dreamy expression at the plate of silky, golden Syrniki stacks near Alban's elbow. Did the little bunny have a sweet tooth?

"Remember how the goal was to apologize," Alban reminded his king.

Nic ignored him. "Why the fuck is she wearing your clothes, Wyn?" Nic's voice was the equivalent of an icy gust of wind in the room. Still, he reined it back. To... protect her from another scare.

The long-sleeved white button-down shirt hung over Isa's body like a dress. Long enough to hit right above her knees. Black socks covered her feet up to mid-calf.

With the bedhead hair to go along with the ensemble, she looked like a woman who had been fucked so hard the night before that she couldn't find her clothes the following morning.

Her legs were on display. Her *fuck-me*, thick legs. *Goddamn it.*

He had not even breathed in her scent yet, and Nic had a raging hard-on. The smooth, bitable flesh was just right *there*. Front and center in his vision. He wanted to grip them, sink his fingers into that creamy, pliant skin, and spread her legs open until he could see where she was wet for him.

Because, damn it, the scent of her arousal was filling up the entire dining room. *I really should have made her come last night.*

"Can you try…not being so damn horny?" Nic bit out to Isa, trying his best to limit any intake of breath.

That mind-numbing scent. He had come harder than ever before in his life last night; he thought he might not be hard again for days. Yet, her aroused scent made his cock so full, so fast, he felt his mind slipping into animalistic instinct again.

Gods, to be inside her again…

Alban let out a whistle. "Rude."

"He just means…your scent is very distracting," Wyn told Isa. "And…strong today."

Nic glanced at Wyn's crotch. "Do not get hard for my mate."

"Her scent—"

"Then don't fucking *breathe*."

Alban snorted, "Bro, we have all gotten an erection from her at some point in the last twenty-four hours."

"What the fuck did you just say?" Nic knew they were both hard when Nic ate her out and claimed her naked body in the hot tub in front of them, but...

Warring thoughts fought inside his brain. A constant churn of: *she's mine, and no one else should even look at her* versus *she is a spy and not really my mate; I'd never be so lucky.*

Wyn pushed his glasses higher up the bridge of his nose and addressed his king. "She is wearing my shirt because she has no clothes."

"A Christmas miracle," Alban said.

Isa rolled her eyes, but a small smile curled her lips. Nic bit his inner cheek at how Alban's cocky façade *melted* into a charmed blush at knowing he amused her.

"She was brought here in a flimsy silk gown. She needs real clothing."

"Shopping spree montage," Alban cheered and pumped a fist in the air.

"She had nothing to wear, so you gave her *your* clothing?" Nic asked. *Why not my clothing? Her mate's clothing?* Nic's inner wolf screamed, MATE TO SMELL LIKE ANOTHER MAN? KILL.

"Correct."

Bored with the men's back and forth, Isa strode forward and snatched a Syrniki from a towering stack beside Alban. She brought it to her pretty lips and nibbled on the fluffy golden pancake.

"I do not want my mate wearing another man's clothes," Nic said.

Wyn seemed to experience disbelief at his king's possessive and somewhat immature reaction to Isa wearing another man's shirt. Wyn questioned, "What do you want her to do? Strip?"

See his mate's naked body again? Maybe claim it in front of his friends so they dismissed any fictional belief that she could ever be theirs instead of his?

"Yes," Nic replied.

*J*sa coughed on a bite of the buttery and soft Syrniki.

The king wanted her to strip out of the shirt Wyn gave her? As in, eat breakfast naked? In front of all three men?

Wasn't the king angry because he was jealous of seeing another man's clothing on her? How would her being naked in front of his friends improve the situation?

"You heard me, mate," Nic said. "The shirt comes off. Now."

His authoritative tone informed Isa of just how much the king was used to people obeying him. A cold self-assurance.

Blushing deeply, her instinct was to obey him. To be a good pet and compliment his domineering nature. She fought the instinct.

"That was impolite," she said, nearly surprising herself at her first act of plain disobedience. *My master asked something of me, and I denied him.* Part of her felt wrong, but another part...very right.

Her comment had the king blinking, dumbfounded at having his order questioned. Isa was going for a different attitude today.

"You may find different, more pleasing results from using the word 'please,'" she said.

After a good night's rest, she came to terms with the fact that, to survive, she needed to convince the king to care about her. Love her. The Hag thought filling him with the Christmas spirit was involved, but Isa knew the first thing she needed to do was earn his respect and trust.

So, she tipped her chin up, made daring eye contact, and said, "Or maybe we can strike a trade. It's a bit spoiled to receive what you want with no expectation to return the favor."

Her implication was clear. He came last night. She did not.

Nic blinked some more. His fisted hand loosened on the dining room table. He inched forward in his chair and finally asked, "Did you really just imply I am spoiled?"

"You *are* a king," Isa muttered after summoning the strength and mental fortitude to try to be sassy.

It did not work.

The men...laughed. They shed any air of superiority or coldness. They laughed in front of her as if she were a member of their inner circle.

They tipped their heads back when they laughed, something uncommon for a predator shifter to do since it left their jugulars vulnerable to attack. Isa supposed they did not see her as a threat.

"Please call him a spoiled brat king again, bunny," Alban begged through his laughs, wiping at his watery eyes.

"It was meant to be an insult. Not a joke," she said, vexed at their chuckling.

"And it would be funny to you, too, if you knew how Nic became king," Alban replied.

Even Nic smirked like he held back an amused expression. "I was not simply handed the throne," he said with a refreshing levity in his voice she had not heard from him before.

"Blood, sweat, tears, and frostbite, baby," Alban commented.

"I do not expect things because I was born to expect them," Nic said. "I expect things because everything I have done in life was to grant me the power to be the most fearsome creature you've ever beheld."

"And you believe ruling by fear gives you power. And that you can demand anything you want because of it?"

"Fear is the most powerful thing in this world," Nic said.

Isa tried to maintain a confident façade as she lied, "You are not so scary to me."

"Did the fear-induced heart attack erase your memory?"

"I think you are just like your dogs."

Alban guffawed again.

"And what makes you compare me to them?" Nic asked with a smirky little smile stretching his perfect lips.

"I think *you* think you are a cold, unfeeling monster, but some cuddling will prove you wrong."

"Cuddling?" Nic scoffed.

"Mutually holding each other and nuzzling into your chest and listening to each other's breathing and heartbeats."

"Sounds horrible." Nic repeated his original demand, "Take off Wyn's shirt."

"Say 'please.'"

"No."

"So, I am expected to eat breakfast naked in front of you all? While you remain fully dressed."

Nic quirked an eyebrow. "Would you like us to be naked too?"

Alban raised his hand and said, "I'm all for solidarity."

Nic pushed his chair back and stood. He brought his hands down to his belt buckle. His long fingers played with the metal clasp, and she held her breath as flames of lust licked down her limbs. She still remembered how perfect it felt—his tongue between her legs, his cock inside her...

He nodded at Isa, a silent command.

He would really strip with her?

"That is the agreed upon trade?" she asked in a shaky voice overridden with lust. Had the room temperature just jumped twenty degrees? "You will be naked if I am?"

"I'm pretty sure the second I see your bare body again, my cock will rip through these pants anyway." He unbuckled his belt and inched it slowly through the loops, pulling it from his dress pants' hooks.

Her hands trembled softly as she reached for the top button on the white shirt covering her torso and lower body. She was horny; he was right.

"Thinking you can wear another man's clothing..." Nic said in a low voice as she worked the first two buttons on the shirt loose.

Yes, he wore all black, but Isa could still make out the growing bulge at the crotch of his dark pants. The bracelet charm to make him believe she was his mate sure worked in *that* sense.

"I don't see how wearing another man's shirt is so bad," she commented as she undid the fourth button between her breasts and her bellybutton.

I am running out of buttons. She would be naked well before Nic at this rate. Thankfully, the shirt was long and hit her mid-thigh.

"Should I explain it to you?" Nic asked, cocking his head to the side and finally pulling off his belt. He sat it on the dining room table and strode closer to Isa.

His alpha scent wafted over her like an airborne drug. Spiced orange and cinnamon and mulled wine. *Damn, he smells so good.* Her cheeks pinkened. Her thighs clamped together. Wetness rushed between her legs like her body thought a lot more was happening than mutual stripping.

From a foot away, he stopped and watched her with icy blue eyes. "A woman with a mate should never wear another man's clothes. You have no idea how my inner wolf is clawing at me to rip that fabric to shreds. To fucking *bite* it off you. How it's howling to kill the male who dares to offer you gifts."

His scary admissions just turned her on more. Her nipples were tight peaks, poking through the thin button-down shirt. She said, "Your inner wolf sounds violent."

"Oh, little bunny, you have no idea." Nic's laugh rang out cold and without humor. "Wearing another man's shirt...letting the fabric rub against those hard little nipples. Letting it mess with your scent to make others think you are not *mine*," he bit out the word. "It feels like an act of fucking treason."

CHAPTER 20

She breathed more of his delicious, spicy scent and undid another button.

"You have no idea the dirty, wicked things my wolf wants me to do to you. To lay claim on you so no other man would dare look your way."

He pulled off his black turtleneck in one smooth move that flexed those muscular arms in front of her hungry eyes.

Without his warm fitted shirt, his defined abs and lickable happy trail were on complete display. Ridges and lines of muscle. And...scars. She had noticed them before but said nothing. They ran over his chest like war medals, begging to be acknowledged.

"Aw, does the little bunny not like my scars?" Nic asked mockingly, but a bit of raw, vulnerable anger slipped into his voice. He was clearly becoming defensive the longer she stared at the marked flesh.

One jagged scar sat directly over his heart. How did someone get close enough to death to have such a dangerous mark over his most vital organ?

"Not used to a marked man? Do the scars disgust you?" he asked the questions in such a low, angry tone that they sounded rhetorical. Like he already knew that there was only one believable answer.

"You wear them well," she shot back. "I…I like them."

He blinked again. She liked making him blink in surprise.

"A lie," he said.

"The truth. Your scars make me wet."

"You're not…lying," he stated. "I can smell your arousal."

Would he stop doing that already? There was wearing her emotions on her sleeve, then there were her pheromones drawing a big neon arrow to her lower body saying, *Open for business and eager to be serviced!*

His hands fell to his pants zipper.

And she forgot what they had been discussing.

"You know, I've never tasted anything like you," he rasped as he unzipped himself and smoothly stepped out of the pants.

His black briefs—because the man clearly had a style—bulged at the front, encasing his mouthwatering erection. "I thought about it all night. My mouth on that needy pussy. The sounds you made... I'm going to want more."

"And the king always gets what he wants?" Isa asked, unbuttoning the third to last button on her shirt.

"Never. But more of your taste, I will demand," he hissed as he removed his briefs and stood naked in front of her.

His large shaft lengthened into a thick, flushed erection. At the sight of the veins running through it, Isa thought about tracing them with her tongue.

He added, "Which reminds me...I'm hungry for my breakfast."

He grabbed her.

His big palms clamped around her hips, and he effortlessly lifted her and walked her to where his morning cup of coffee, bowl of porridge, and silverware were all set up at the head of the dining table. He brushed a spot on the table clean with his forearm, not caring about the glasses that trembled and threatened to fall from the table.

He planted her down, her ass pressed onto the cool wooden table. Nic's strong hands moved to the last two buttons of Wyn's shirt and ripped them off her. The little buttons fell to the floor with audible *pings*.

Wyn made a displeased noise at how his king ruined one of his shirts, but Isa was too entranced to look over at him.

Nic may have been the Arctic king, but he got Isa boiling hot.

Her body quivered and squirmed with desire at how he gifted her all of his intense, passionate, and dark, animalistic attention. It felt like a gift. Because something told her, Nic tried to maintain an air of indifference but couldn't around her.

Nic picked up his glass mug of coffee and sipped it. He licked his lips and quirked an eyebrow at her. She nodded, understanding the silent question.

He blew on the hot liquid and offered the coffee to her. The way he blew on it for her caused another rush of arousal to soak through her.

I've never had coffee before. She took a sip and flinched at the bitter taste. Not following proper etiquette, she spat it right out. The liquid dribbled down her chin and dripped onto her chest.

Nic snorted and commented, "No black coffee, then. My sweet mate needs something sweet."

She wondered if the smile he gifted her was the kind of smile he gave his enemies or if it was a special smile just for her.

He leaned forward, smothering her in his alluring mulled wine scent, and grazed his lips down the nape of her neck. "I require something sweet as well," he whispered.

He kicked back the royal high neck, wooden dining room chair to make room for him to kneel in front of her. He wrenched her thighs apart, revealing her bare sex once more.

It was odd, actually. Good pets were taught to give more than receive, and Isa was about to receive oral from her master twice in less than twenty-four hours without her asking or performing it on him.

He wishes to do it.

It made her want to do it as well. She had always loved those videos she watched in class. It transfixed her, the power the woman seemed to have when she sucked her master's hard-on. The faces of abandon and pure lust on the men. *Would Nic ever let go like that?*

"So, you are to feast while I go hungry?" she asked just as he planted a kiss on her inner thigh.

Nic looked up and quirked an eyebrow at her again. She swore the edges of his lips curled for a second. "You're right." He stood back up. "You require fuel before I make you come your brains out. Don't want you having an orgasm-induced heart attack."

He picked up a spoonful of porridge and lifted it to her mouth. She happily tried it and frowned. "Not as good as the Syrniki?" he asked.

"Pancakes trump cold oatmeal every time, dude," Alban offered a correct opinion.

"Pancakes offer her no protein. Certainly not the necessary nutrients to be fucked senseless."

"Is that what is about to happen?" she asked.

"Another bite, *zayka*," Nic said, lifting another spoon

of the porridge. Zayka meant *bunny* in Russian. A pet name?

She pursed her lips, hesitating, before realizing it could be fun to tease him.

After all, she had been a great student in her tribe. She knew tricks with her tongue. She had watched many informational videos of a pet on her knees.

She opened her mouth and closed her lips around the spoon.

Her eyelids fluttered shut. She moaned softly as she leaned forward and forward and forward until her lips touched the fingers with which he held the long spoon.

The tall metal shaft felt cool down her throat, and she reveled in the expression of shock and burning arousal on Nic's face when she opened her eyes.

"Fuck, no gag reflex?" Alban coughed out.

Isa leaned back, releasing the spoon but not without making a big show of caressing the spoon head with flicks of her talented tongue.

"What a naughty girl you are," Nic purred and scooped more porridge onto the spoon. He fed her again, and she again displayed her skillful mouth and tongue as she sucked and licked the utensil clean.

He took one spoonful to his mouth and leaned forward to kiss her.

He tasted like a healthy breakfast. Was it misleading? Nic had not been good for her health so far.

"You like to suck, zayka?" Nic rasped in her ear as he

loaded the spoon with another bite of porridge. "Watching that tongue and that pretty throat of yours is making me so hard."

She momentarily lost her mind to lust.

"Yes," she hissed as her hand landed on his chest and roamed, feeling the ridges of muscle. Her palm and fingers trailed down, down, and stopped on his abdomen, just above where his cockhead glistened and begged for her touch.

She wanted to try it. She wanted to try everything at least once.

"Ah," Nic looked down at where her hand laid on him. "Is my mate about to touch me?"

"Maybe we should leave you two alone," Wyn said and nodded to Alban.

"Nyet," Nic shot back, surprising them. "Watch." Ah. Territorial. "And hand me the fucking syrup. My sweet little mate is about to get even sweeter."

Wyn stiffly walked the small, teardrop-shaped glass pitcher of golden syrup to his king. Wyn hardly looked at Isa, his expression stoic and indifferent and...cold. Jealous? Why couldn't they just share Isa?

She liked Wyn, but right now, her body wanted Nic —the alpha Arctic king she felt such conflicting feelings toward.

Nic took the syrup and rubbed his thumb over the spout. "Would you like to touch me, Isa?"

She wanted to do more than touch him. She wanted

to explore his body. Explore how to make the icy man melt. Explore her own sexuality.

Maybe it was his alpha scent or her prey pheromones going wonky as she approached her first heat cycle with every passing day, but she ached to try out some of what her tribe taught her.

I want him to respect me...but I also want to be his—the one woman he got hard for.

She wanted him to choose her. She could see it... Could see him softening to her. Could see a future of them cuddling in front of the fireplace. Maybe she was delusional, but she had hope.

With every interaction, she felt more and more that Nic was a man who had never been held, and she wanted to hold him.

"Yes, I want to touch you," she whispered as if too shy and nervous to give the statement full volume.

He reached up and twirled a lock of her icy blond hair around his finger. "How do you want to touch me?" he asked.

"I want to suck you like a candy cane until your eyes roll back and you come in my mouth," she replied, dragging her fingers side to side on his lower abdomen, hardly grazing his cockhead.

The three men simultaneously cursed, "Fuck."

CHAPTER 21

"*I* *want to suck you like a candy cane until your eyes roll back and you come in my mouth,*" she said.

As Nic's dick throbbed to come, alarm bells rang through his head. *Too good to be true. Spy. Seductress.*

How was he supposed to believe fate gifted him a beautiful mate who wanted to suck him off?

Has to be a lie.

Isa sank down from the table and onto her knees before Nic.

I do love a good lie, his brain decided as it turned off and let his body's desire run the show.

"He has never had a blowjob before," Alban commented, and Nic regretted not sending his men away. "Might come in your mouth from just a lick."

"Shut the fuck up," Nic said. He wanted this to go

perfectly. He wanted her to like it. *I want her to like* me.

Isa tilted her head and leaned forward. She used one hand to grip the base of his shaft as she pointed his cock to her lips.

Nic poured a thin line of sticky syrup down his cock, just for her. "A little sweetness for my sweet," he whispered, feeling mesmerized by the excitement in her eyes as she opened her mouth and licked her lips.

"Did he really just say 'my sweet?'"

"Alban, you're allowed to jerk off while watching my naked mate suck me off if you shut the fuck up."

Alban pretended to sew his lips shut and throw away the needle.

The line of golden syrup shined on Nic's dick as Isa lovingly caressed it with her eyes.

"Do you like this cock, baby?" Nic asked. "I bet it felt so good inside you last night. You took it so well."

Isa's breath hitched, and her free hand lowered to between her legs. Her fingers sunk down to run over her pussy.

Nic groaned out, "Fuck, are you going to touch yourself while you suck me? Going to get yourself nice and wet while you take my cock in your mouth? Treat that clit nice and good for me. I'm going to be sucking on it for breakfast the second after you swallow, baby."

Mmm. Isa took her time as she aligned her tongue to where the trail of syrup began and dragged it up to where it ended. She released a huffy little moan at the sweetness as she licked him and rubbed herself.

Her tongue. He grabbed the edge of the dining table and felt the wood crack in his grip. *Better to break the table than pull too hard on her hair, right?*

But his dark side wanted to pull on her hair. Wanted to guide her. Wanted to thrust his cock so he fucked her mouth.

"Suck me down that pretty throat, pet," he said.

She obeyed. Instantly. She inched forward, moving her mouth down his shaft until her lips reached the base of him. She swallowed, and the tight muscles of her throat and the hot wetness of her mouth had him groaning in delight.

"Fuck, yes."

She slowly bobbed her head back and forth, up and down his cock, while applying the perfect amount of suction and squeezing the root of his dick in her hand.

"Faster, baby. Please." Had the king just begged? *I never fucking beg.*

She did move faster, and he learned it was possible for his cock to grow even larger with pent-up cum and not immediately explode. He just kept getting harder. He kept listening to the sound of his cock hitting the back of her throat with each movement and getting harder.

"Your mouth feels like heaven. Wet, hot heaven."

Nic's wolf demanded, THRUST. FUCK. TAKE. CLAIM.

"I want to own your pretty mouth," Nic grated as he held back his instinct to ravage her. "I want to listen to it speak and feed it sweet treats and fuck it…"

Isa moaned around his dick and shot him those big, innocent blue eyes.

"Would you let me fuck your pretty mouth, zayka?"

She rocked her hips and gyrated onto the hand she had between her legs. Was she turned on by the idea of him taking her roughly? He did not want to hurt her, but…

"Do you like the idea of being my little slut bunny? Letting me do whatever I want to you? Even if it's rough?"

"Nic," Wyn muttered as a warning. Trying to remind him how delicate his mate was?

"Breathe through your nose for me," Nic said. "And tap my thigh if it's ever too much."

Isa nodded and pulled back. She held her mouth open and welcomed him to take the lead.

Where did she come from? How many other men had she done this to? *I want to be special to her. I want her to forget everyone else.*

"I don't care how many cocks have been in this mouth," Nic said gruffly as he fisted his dick and tapped the tip to her lips. *Tap. Tap.* "This is the last one you'll ever have filling you up, angel."

He thrust forward, and she took him and flicked her tongue around him. *Yes.*

"I want you to keep playing with that clit as you imagine I'm fucking your pussy right now. Every thrust you feel in your mouth, I want you to feel hitting right against your G-spot."

"*Mmmm.*"

"I love when you moan around this dick." He thrust harder. Faster. Her wet mouth sucked around him. Sweat dampened the back of his neck.

Her lush scent of cranberries and arousal filled every air molecule inside the dining room. Nic knew his friends would be affected, knew they would be hard for her.

"Does it turn you on to know they are watching you be such a good girl for me? Taking this cock so well. So deep. Fuck, you feel so good." Nic's head fell back as he thrust and thrust. "*Fuck.*"

His hand tangled in her hair and fisted it.

And he let loose.

He couldn't think. Could only feel. Feel how good she was with that tongue. Feel how hard his heartbeat banged in his chest. Feel…dizzy.

He frowned and thrust faster into her mouth.

Why did he feel dizzy? It wasn't like she was a succubus sucking bits of his soul and life essence through his dick.

He glanced back down at her and recognized a

similar hazy fog consuming her face. Her eyes started to glaze over.

What was happening—

Nic fell forward. Avoiding falling onto Isa, he caught himself on the table. "Something is...wrong," he murmured as his sense of balance tilted on its axis.

Isa slumped over as well, grabbing at Nic's thighs as his hard cock slipped from her lips, and they both blinked and blinked and...

"Poison," Nic whispered as his knees went weak, and he sank beside Isa to the floor.

He circled his arm around her before he lost the feeling of control in his limbs.

Isa gasped for breath, and Nic weakly tried to get his fingers to her mouth to make her gag whatever the substance was.

He forced a finger between her lips and stabbed at the back of her throat. But then he couldn't...move...

"Shit," Wyn and Alban rushed over to them.

They moved to help their king first, but Nic turned his face away. He nuzzled the crook of Isa's neck and made it clear.

Save her first.

Always.

As death, which he had managed to avoid over so many cold and harsh years, rose up to take him, he held his mate.

Even if she isn't really mine...

CHAPTER 22

*I*sa weakly blinked her eyes open and saw that she now occupied an entirely different room of the house. The parlor.

She had no memory of getting there. She had been excitedly performing fellatio for the first time when things got hazy.

"*Poison,*" Nic had said.

She jolted awake.

"Shhh, it's okay, bunny," Alban's calming voice came from close by.

She rubbed at her eyes and glanced around to where Alban sat with his elbows on his knees on a chair across from where Isa laid on a sofa.

"Water?" Wyn asked her and kneeled to lift a cup to her lips.

A heavy, warm male arm hung around her waist; a body pressed to her back. Nic? Was he okay?

The arm tightened around her as she wiggled to her other side to face him. His eyes were clenched shut, as if in pain, as he held her close yet appeared in a deep sleep.

"Is he okay?" she asked.

"Stubborn guy had the poison in his system longer than you, bunny. Wouldn't accept help till you were okay. He'll be in pain for a bit."

She remembered how his instinct when they fell was to use his last bit of strength to try to get her to gag and get the poison from her system.

He...chose me.

"It wasn't just any poison," Wyn stated in a voice that leaked with concern. "It was rattle basilisk venom. That stuff...it's lethal to even the strongest immortals."

She stroked a thumb over Nic's cheek as his eyes moved back and forth under his lids like he was having a nightmare.

The icy king had wanted to save her before himself. *Maybe I* can *get him to love me.*

She leaned forward, cuddling closer to him, and kissed his cheek.

Her lips to his warm skin caused his eyes to open wide.

For a moment, he stared at her. One blue and one brown eye beamed through her.

He grabbed her face and turned her head from side

to side. He threw the blanket off their naked bodies and inspected her from the neck down.

"She is okay, Nic," Wyn said.

A deadly growl rumbled from the king's chest. "They could have killed her."

"If it makes you feel any better, the poison was clearly for you. You're the only one who eats boring porridge," Alban said.

Nic moved around Isa's horizontal body and stood from the couch. "I want their goddamn heads on spikes. *Now.*"

"I've already had everyone who went near your breakfast locked in the...uh, basement," Wyn had changed his wording after glancing at Isa.

Did they have a dungeon or something? A torture chamber?

Nic spun around to glare at Isa and point a finger at her. For a second, she thought he was back to accusing her of being a spy. He told her, "You do not eat a single fucking thing without Alban tasting it first."

"Nic, the poison was meant for you—" Wyn started.

"I don't fucking care about ME," Nic roared, vibrating with rage. Isa could practically see waves of wrath rolling off him and into the atmosphere. "I want every fucking person who touched that bowl to..."

Isa zoned out his threats as the wheels of her mind spun. Could he really be so angry over the possibility of losing her?

Her body moved without her brain knowing what it was about to do.

She simply wrapped her arms around him and buried her face in his chest. She hugged him tightly and kissed the skin above his heart.

He stopped listing out death threats at her touch. His shaking calmed. A large palm settled onto the back of her head as he held her closer to his chest.

"You…" Nic said. "You will not leave this room. No one is to know you exist. You are a ghost. A ghost under confinement."

Wait, what? Isa shook her head at that. No. *No.*

She had gone from a controlling tribe to freedom for the first time, and he wanted to cage her?

She wanted to go out and have experiences. She wanted to cut down a Christmas tree and go ice skating and go Christmas shopping and caroling and *live*. She wanted to see the Northern lights. He wanted to confine her?

"If they dared to poison me, they would put a hit out on her immediately if they found out I have a prey mate," Nic spoke to the men, not to her. As if she were a child. As if she had no real choice in his decision-making. "No one can know about her. She stays in this room indefinitely."

Slack-jawed, Isa glanced to Wyn and Alban for help, but they nodded. They agreed?

No.

"Get her bed moved in here," Nic instructed. "She'll stay here. Curtains should stay closed. Have a talk with everyone on the grounds who has seen her already."

"We need a story," Wyn said. "If a rumor has already spread about a prey here—"

"Say she is a sexual plaything to get us through the cold winter," Nic offered. "If no one believes she is important to me, she shouldn't be targeted. Make her sound disposable."

A *plaything*? What happened to gaining his respect? What happened to them saying she was worth more than just sex?

"No," Isa said, but the men didn't listen. They had superhuman hearing, and they didn't listen. "No. I will be fine. Don't keep me in here."

Nic spun around and grabbed her roughly by the shoulders. A crazed intensity shone through his dark and bright eyes as he shook her and said, "You could have died. *Again*. You were not built for my world. If you're my mate, fate got it wrong. You don't belong here."

Her heart...broke.

"I'd send you away if I thought I could part from you, but the thought of not knowing where you are makes me want to burn the fucking world, do you understand?"

Isa's mouth hung open. "N-No."

"You can't be here, and I can't send you away. So, I

will hide you. You, Isa, are delicate. Precious and breakable. Weak. *Fear* can give you a goddamn heart attack."

She crossed her arms, hugging herself. "I'm stronger than you think." He thought she was *weak?* She wanted to cry. She wanted to eat a bowl of rusted nails to prove she was tougher than he thought. "I do not need to be hidden. I am strong enough to—"

"Nyet, little prey. You are not," Nic told her. "We will protect you, and this is the best way." Nic strode for the door, and Isa followed him at his heels.

"The best way for *you*. You can't just keep me in here." Her desperate voice raised in volume as she pleaded. "I want to go out. Let me outside."

"And risk an enemy Polaris bear shifter kidnapping you? Risk you falling through a sheet of icy ground and drowning in freezing water? Absolutely not. You stay in this room."

"No," she shouted at him.

Nic grabbed her by the throat.

She gasped and grabbed at his wrists. He did not squeeze his fingers. Still, he cupped her with a strong enough hold that it felt like a second collar.

"I am the Arctic king," Nic reminded her coldly. "You are a defenseless prey shifter, but you are *mine*. I will protect you." He pulled her forward to growl against her chin, "I will protect you *any way I see fit*."

But he did not know.

197

He did not know where she came from or all she had been through.

He did not know that she had dreamed for so many years to explore and see and experience things—after being kept inside for so long, in classes teaching her how to be the perfect pet.

And I was. She became the perfect pet for the promise of being adopted and being sent out into the world.

Gripping his wrist from where he held her throat, Isa whispered, "Please, do not do this to me." *You do not know what it will mean to me.* "Do not leave me in here. I —I cannot be left alone, locked in here. Do not do this."

"Little mate, you should learn this early. I do whatever the fuck I want."

CHAPTER 23

*J*sa broke out within the first two hours of her confinement. The men were distracted and elsewhere, probably off torturing possible poisoners or spreading the stories about how Isa was just a "sexual plaything" and didn't "mean anything" to the king.

Thankfully, the men had let her three large, canine friends into the parlor to keep her company. They helped in the escape plan.

As far as clothing, Isa only had the ripped button-down shirt from Wyn and some fuzzy blankets in one of the wardrobes she found in the parlor.

The most important thing she found in the parlor was the briefcase of treats Hag left that her tribe gave her.

Upset about being kept inside, Isa wanted to give

herself a treat. She deserved one after the morning she'd had. The little blue pill would have erased every bad feeling. It would have had her flying in the clouds.

She wanted it. But when she opened the case, a note sat on top of the contents and read:

Don't be a bad pet! Only a master is supposed to give out the treats. Don't wanna act like a little drug addict. By the way, you have seven days to bring the king Christmas cheer, or his castle gets taken over by a faction of Polaris bear shifters and the war begins. Maybe start with a tree? Here is a hand saw for your consideration. —The Hag, AKA Hot And Gorgeous Seer

How was Isa supposed to help Nic, prevent a war, and get a Christmas tree all from the confines of a spacious parlor? She wasn't.

Hence, the breaking out.

Pets always listen and obey their masters. Yeah...not this time.

Isa motioned for the three large dogs to follow her after she used the hand saw to cut the locked doorknob from the parlor door. It opened with a creak, and she tiptoed out and headed straight for the kitchen, where she knew there was a back door to the outside.

The dogs followed her, seeming to pick up on the fact that this was a stealth mission.

Once they made it outside, the dogs ran on either side of her, and she rushed to the lush, wooded area on the outskirts of the snowy terrain.

She had no shoes and had wrapped herself in as many blankets as she could handle to fight against the bitter cold. No one would see her shape moving outside and think it was her. Nope, they would just see a blob of colors trembling from the cold and sprinting to the tree line.

"He said I'm w-weak," Isa muttered to the dogs as she trudged and stomped through the freezing snow.

Squinting through the soft snowfall, she analyzed the trees. She needed a fir, a spruce, or a pine. Something big enough to feel like the centerpiece for the parlor, but not so big that she could not carry it through the door with the help of the dogs.

"He thinks I'm too delicate for his world," she said under her breath as she positioned her hand saw and began cutting down her very first tree.

Every gust of wind kicked up bits of ice and snow and chilled her to the bone, but she did not stop.

She sawed back and forth.

"I survived hypothermia."

Back and forth.

"I survived a heart attack."

Back and forth.

"I survived a poisoning."

Back and forth.

"I survived the Hag's driving!"

Keeping a steady rhythm, she worked at the tree, sawing the trunk. Eventually, some cracking noises occurred, and she took that as good news. Because she was always positive. That was the way to survive. Not through anger, emotional distance, or coldness like Nic thought.

He needs to let go and have some fun.

But right then, he needed to let *her* go so *she* could have some fun.

"I'll prove to him that I deserve to be here. That I'm tough and strong."

She sawed back and forth.

"I'm not delicate."

Back and forth.

"Not weak."

The trunk was beginning to tilt. She kept going. Kept pushing herself.

"I'm good for more than just sex. I am going to bring holiday cheer and conflict resolution and prevent a war."

The dogs howled like they agreed, and a loud cracking sound stole her attention.

"It's going to fall!" Excited, she jumped up and down. She clapped her hands and grinned until she noticed the direction the tree was about to fall.

"*Run,*" she yelled to the dogs, gesturing for them to scatter as she tried to move out of the way of the tree.

It was not massively high. It was not massively thick.

But it was coming down swinging, and Isa had no muscle to catch it.

It would hurt.

And it did.

The popping sound of bone. The gut-wrenching scream as pain sliced through her shoulder and collarbone.

The tree trapped her in the snow as the dogs yelped and yapped, running around to try to see where she was underneath it.

"Ow," she squeaked through the greenery.

*N*ic walked back to his study for a drink after an hour or two of peeling off fingernails and cutting off ears, trying to find the person who poisoned and nearly killed his mate. And, he supposed, nearly killed Nic, too.

One is more important than the other.

The big and frightening Marshmallow ran down the hallway so fast that he slid right into Nic and took the king down to the floor. Marshmallow barked viciously at Nic and turned and walked down the hall, then turned back to see Nic did not follow.

Marshmallow jumped back onto Nic, grabbed a bite of his shirt in his mouth, and *dragged* the king down the hall.

"What the hell has gotten into you?" Nic asked, ripping himself free. "Gods, weren't you supposed to be protecting her—" Nic froze and narrowed his eyes on Marshmallow. "How did you get out of the locked room?"

Marshmallow stared up at him with angry eyes that shouted, *"Stop asking useless questions and come with me."*

"Crap." Nic ran for the parlor, only to find the door had been *sawed* open. How the hell had she gotten a tool like that? "She *left?*" Nic exclaimed.

Marshmallow growled again, clearly annoyed that Nic wasted time asking the obvious.

She left. *Your mate left you. Did you really think a beautiful woman would stay with you? Someone so undeserving?*

His father's old words sliced through him, *"You really think I'd let a cripple like you be associated with this family? You will never be king."*

All because he had a fucking limp that limited his wolf's run. *Banished into the cold, meant to never return.* Until he took the fucking castle himself.

FIND HER, his wolf roared.

Had she run away? Because she was scared of being poisoned again? Did she not think about the hypothermia? *She is a prey; they have smaller brains.*

Fuck, what if she was out there freezing to death or being used as a chew toy by a Polaris shifter or...worse. Being used as a different kind of toy.

MINE.

"Where?" Nic shouted and raced after Marshmallow when the dog took off running.

CHAPTER 24

"*I*sa!" Nic's deep voice bellowed from a short distance as Isa laid in the snow, forced down by large, heavy tree limbs and spiky pine needles.

Oh boy.

She didn't want to call out for help. She didn't want to give him another reason to think she was too "delicate" for his world.

He will probably lock me up in an even smaller room next time.

So, she didn't call out for help or make any sound at all. She quieted her heavy breathing and kept her lips pressed together as she summoned the strength to stop crying. Even though she managed silence through the pain, it was no use.

Because Penelope barked again and again from beside her until Nic found them.

"Thanks," Isa muttered. The large canine barked again as if to say, *"You are very welcome."*

"How the fuck did you..." Nic trailed off as he stood beside where she was pinned by the medium-sized Christmas tree. "Are you alive?"

She sighed, "Yes."

"Are you okay?"

She replied in a feigned human-sunshine voice, "I wanted this to happen."

Nic sniffed the air and glowered down at where she was pinned. "Salt. I can smell your tears. Where is the pain?"

She cursed her salty cheeks. She didn't want him to view her as the crying damsel in distress. She had just wanted to bring some Christmas cheer and surprise him with how capable she was, gosh darn it.

"If you could help pick up the tree—"

"Maybe it should stay there, so you don't *run away into the dangerous Arctic where all of my enemies hide and await the perfect moment to strike me down.*"

She pursed her lips. "You stressed a lot of words in that sentence."

"Out of everything out here, how the hell did you manage to become the victim of a tree?"

"It didn't appreciate my hugs as much as you did," she replied, again not wanting to focus on the negative of the situation.

She just wanted a Christmas tree. And maybe some

pain medication for her injury. Maybe a treat.

Nic looked around and saw the hand saw. "And how did you find a tool like that in the parlor?"

"It was a Christmas miracle. Now, if you don't mind lifting the tree off me—"

He was already doing it. The man gripped the base and flipped it in a single move as if it weighed nothing. It rose from her body and tumbled to the opposite side, caught by other trees in the path.

His nostrils flared, and frustration shot out of his eyes like sharp icicle darts. "You ran away in *that*?" he asked.

"I didn't run away."

"What the hell are you wearing?"

"I don't have any clothes," she reminded him. "So, I made do."

"With blankets?"

"They are high-quality blankets."

"I buy nothing but the best." Nic made no move to help her up.

He crossed his arms and surveyed her. She laid there, feeling frozen to the bone in the snow, completely still to avoid the pain of what she was pretty sure was a broken or dislocated left arm and shoulder.

He told her, "You left the room. I specifically instructed you not to."

"I specifically told you not to leave me there," she replied.

Again, instead of helping her up, Nic kneeled and crawled over her. His hulking, muscular body covered hers. His hands fell to either side of her head, and his breath caressed her chin as he held himself above her.

It might have been a sexy position if she did not have throbbing pain in her shoulder and arm.

"You dare think you can run away from me, mate?" Nic asked darkly. His hands turned to fists on either side of her head. "You think there is a corner on this earth where I could not find you?"

Isa blew out a breath. "I wasn't running away. I was getting us a Christmas tree."

"Excuse me?"

"Christmas is in a week, and I've never celebrated it. And I want to do everything I've seen in movies, and I wanted to start with a Christmas tree."

Nic blinked at her when she finished babbling her run-on sentence. "You've never…"

"I've never made gingerbread houses or ice skated or wrapped gifts or had eggnog or baked cookies. I want to do it all."

"It's overrated and meaningless."

Isa rolled her eyes. "You're just saying that because you're a Grinch."

Nic scowled but did not debate that fact. "You cannot disobey me again. When I tell you to remain in a room, you do so."

Isa's expression scrunched into one of *"No, thank*

you." Still, she politely said, "I do not want to be confined."

He moved his weight onto one arm and lifted his free hand to pinch her chin, forcing her gaze to meet his penetrating one. "When I tell you to do something, you do it," he growled.

In sexy situations? Sure. But this? No.

"I have earned my freedom," she stated. She was a great student for her tribe. She had been an excellent pet to the king so far, even after the near-death experiences. "I will not be caged again."

*N*ic frowned down at his little mate. The way she said those words gave him pause. "*I have earned my freedom. I will not be caged again.*"

What did she mean by that? When had she been caged previously? Nic realized how little he knew of his mate's past.

He had learned a few new facts, however. She had an odd obsession with experiencing Christmas for the first time, and she was stubborn and determined enough to venture out into the cold without any real clothing to keep her warm and try to cut a tree down by herself.

It was…adorable. And admirable. And annoyingly endearing.

"Did you learn nothing from the poisoning this morning?" he asked. "Keeping you in one room is a method of keeping you safe."

Isa's eyes flashed with a spark of obstinacy. "I would rather be poisoned than locked away again. I want to go out and experience things. Go out and *live*."

"Go *out*? Where other shifters will want to hunt you? Where strangers in the street would stab you for a warm meal?"

Eyebrows furrowing, Isa frowned, confused. "They would not need to stab me. I would give them a warm meal, no questions asked."

"And what if they still threaten to stab you after they've eaten the warm meal you've given?"

Isa's adorable face scrunched up as she replied, "I would offer them dessert."

"You are too…nice," he spat the word. *Nice*. His brother had been nice. Now, his brother was nice, cold, and dead—buried in one of the ice caves around the perimeter of the estate.

"Bringing others happiness is my purpose," she said.

What the fuck did that mean? Nic's bright blue and dark brown eyes narrowed on her suspiciously as he held himself above her on the snow. "You cannot be real."

"There is blood on your shoe." She changed the subject.

"I have been interrogating potential poisoners."

"With torture?" Isa frowned. "You know, maybe it would be better to find out what made them angry and want to poison you—and fix it. Maybe you should try to bring them joy so they like you. Oh, I could sing Christmas carols to them!"

"Hmm." Nic nodded to himself. "Psychological torture. Maybe you are my mate."

"No, not to torture them," she exasperated. "I could sing Christmas carols to them to warm their hearts so they won't *want* to poison you."

"I am still not understanding the difference between that and psychological torture."

She sighed. "Will you show me how to ice skate?" She changed the subject again.

"Put you on bladed footwear and at risk of a concussion? No."

"*Pleaseeeeee,*" she whined in a breathy voice that spoke right to his dick. "Please," she whispered and lifted her head from the blanket of snow to skim her lips over his jaw. "Don't you want to ice skate with me?"

Her scent. It overrode his brain. It brought back the memory and feeling of being inside her for the first time. The unfamiliar freedom and ecstasy of it. The way her slick inner walls had gripped him...

He licked his lips, remembering the current topic of conversation. "Not particularly."

"I'd make it feel so good," she whispered, and the words again went straight to his crotch.

His cock lengthened behind his pants as she grazed her lips over his jaw and chin again, so close to his mouth.

TAKE HER. CLAIM HER.

Her right hand moved up and petted the skin just above the waistband of his pants. His stomach muscles jerked at the tease.

"I'm here to bring you happiness," she said in that breathy, seductive voice that stroked over his growing bulge. "Here to make every day feel so good." Her fingers dipped down and gently cupped his quickly forming erection.

A low growling noise rang from Nic's throat.

"I think you would like skating with me," she purred and squeezed the outline of his cock in her palm. "Don't you want to rail me against the railing?"

"*Fuck.*" His hips tilted forward to press his cock firmer into her hand. "You think you can tease me, little mate?"

"I think you will like it when I tease you." She smiled slyly, and he wanted to kiss the fuck out of that smug face.

"Hey!" Alban yelled, interrupting their moment.

Jolting at the shout, Isa tore her hand away from

Nic's crotch, but he grabbed her palm and placed it right back over his cock. *Let Alban see.*

"What happened?" Alban asked as he ran toward them from where the third large dog, Spot, led him. The crunching sounds of his steps pounding over the fresh snow slowed as he came to a stop. "Bunny, are you groping the king?"

Reluctantly, Nic grumbled under his breath, rolled off of her, and got to his feet. He offered her a hand to help her up, but she refused.

"Um, I think I might stay here for a bit," she said, remaining completely still and flat on the snow.

"How hurt are you?" Nic asked. After all, she had just been groping him and saying she could tease him.

"Hurt?"

Glancing at Alban's questioning expression, Nic added, "A tree fell on her."

Flippant, doesn't-give-a-fox, easy-going Alban transformed in front of Nic's eyes.

The fox shifter looked over to the fallen tree and glared at it like he planned to beat it up until it spat out a sappy apology and begged for forgiveness. Then, he turned the anger onto his king. "You let a tree fall on her?"

"I didn't 'let' anything." Nic pointed down at where she laid. "She ran away."

"Got a Christmas tree," she corrected from her horizontal position.

"She smartly cut a tree down—onto herself."

Isa pouted and scowled at him for the sarcastic "*smartly*." "You should be nicer to me."

"I don't do *nice*."

"You don't earn *naughty* time unless you are *nice*."

"What the hell is she wearing?" Alban asked.

Nic rolled his eyes and bent down to lift Isa into his arms. When he picked her up, a loud noise of pain spilled from her lips, and Nic nearly dropped her as his wolf howled inside him that she was hurting. Was it a more serious injury than she let on?

"Where?" he asked gruffly, reduced to few syllables at her screech of pain.

"I think my arm is broken," she said. "Or dislocated. But it'll be fine. No need to worry or become upset and lock me up in a room again."

Broken? BROKEN? His wolf clawed at him from the inside, pushing him to destroy the cause of her pain. "It'll be *fine*?" Nic repeated.

"Yeah, because you guys will carry the tree back," she said pleasantly as if the tortured sound of pain hadn't just come from her at the minor movement.

"You mean the tree that damaged my mate? Fuck no, baby. That's getting burned to ash."

"What?" She gasped. "No!"

"It hurt you; it's getting goddamn destroyed."

"But—"

Minutes later, Nic and Alban burned the tree.

Isa protested and whined, but she watched in defeat as the flames engulfed it.

After a few seconds of watching the dancing red and orange flames, Alban closed his flask, now empty of the flammable alcohol, and lit a cigarette from the burning tree.

"We are taking you inside," Nic told her, picking her up again. "Getting you healed, getting you real clothes —"

"Boo," Alban pouted.

"And getting a new tree?" she asked, nuzzling her face into his chest and making the cold-hearted king feel warm and sane for the first time in...

Had he ever felt as calm as when she touched him? Well, calm and hot.

"I will order a *real* tree to be delivered like a sane, wealthy person."

CHAPTER 25

"The internet says that when looking for clothes to try on over a cast, choose stretchy fabric—ahem, sexy—avoid buttons and zippers—easy considering we would just rip them off her anyway," Alban said, glancing up from his phone to add additional commentary.

They all waited for the boutique worker to come back with some clothing options for Isa.

"Also, wearing looser tops is a suggestion," Alban said. "We should make sure any tops we get for her are baggy in the front so that when she leans down, we can see those tits—I mean, for her arm's sake."

Isa fiddled with her cast on the couch with the rest of the men. She was just...so excited.

Her grin confused the men, but she ignored them.

She was in a shop. A real shop. With clothes and

workers and dressing rooms and mirrors. Isa had only ever seen mirrors in movies. She kept glancing at her reflection from where the couch curved in front of a three-way mirror.

The compound's medicine woman had given her a strong drink of pain medicine and performed a small spell to quicken the healing.

Wyn had also demanded to call a "real" doctor that "humans use" since "prey are basically as breakable and slow at healing as humans." Isa tried not to take offense. The "real" doctor had arrived and fitted Isa for a cast under the intensely watchful gaze of the three men.

Alban slid his phone into his pocket. "Remind me again why she shouldn't just stay constantly naked? I mean, for the sake of her arm and the cast—"

"Because we live in the Arctic, and she would die without clothing outside within a few minutes," Wyn remarked through an icy glare.

Nic grunted as if her freezing would be acceptable. "Could help convince her not to run away again."

"I didn't run away; I got a Christmas tree," Isa said while lifting her hand and watching her reflection in the mirror do the same.

"You've really never seen a *mirror*, bunny?" Alban asked, incredulous. "What kind of cult were you living in?" he joked.

Isa shrugged and continued playing with her reflection. She did not understand the meaning of the word "cult." Isa's tribe was one of simplicity. Mirrors might have distracted her from her important classes.

But since she had graduated and been gifted to a master, this was her first chance to *experience* things. Common day luxuries she had never had.

She supposed many preys did not experience such luxuries because when they had first entered the shop, and Isa hugged the worker hello, the worker had shoved her back.

When Nic instructed her to find Isa a wardrobe, the boutique worker gaped and appeared offended as she asked, "A *prey?*"

The heat behind Nic's glare at the worker for questioning him gave Isa little butterflies. Or maybe that was the raging getting-closer-to-her-heat-cycle hormones.

"I guess we have fully dropped the 'lay low' and 'hide her in secret' strategy," Wyn commented dryly. "Every person we walked by in the street took a photo when they thought you weren't looking."

Isa still felt a little hurt from the way she had tried to hold Nic's hand as they walked on the sidewalk, and he had roughly torn his hand away from her reach and hip-checked her toward Wyn.

"We should have ordered clothing to the estate. Going out into town like this..." Wyn added in a low voice, "Nic, if *they* find out you have a prey mate—"

"She's not my mate, remember?" Nic grated. "She's just a sexual plaything. That's the story."

"How long can you keep up the façade without your wolf marking her?"

His wolf wanted to mark her? Isa had only heard rumors about a claiming bite from a werewolf, how it was an invisible territorial mark that remained on the mate for all paranormals to see.

Pets were never taught to expect such a gift. *To be claimed forever.*

Nic rubbed his jaw and stared at Isa's reflection in the mirror as she moved her eyebrows around and watched herself. She paid attention to their words as she played with her reflection.

Nic told Wyn, "Maybe we say she is your mate; how about that?"

"Noctu shifters are not lucky enough to have mates."

"Too smart to fall in love with a woman?" Alban joked and raised his hand to high-five Isa.

She looked at his hand, leaned forward, and gently kissed his displayed palm.

"Damn," Alban murmured and rubbed the hand over his chest like he suddenly suffered heartburn.

"Noctu are to serve as advisors. The same way foxes serve—though I have no idea what you've been contributing lately, Alban, between all the vodkas and scotches." Wyn frowned at Isa, meeting her gaze in the mirror's reflection as he stated, "We 'lesser' shifters do not get fated mates. Or it is extremely rare."

There was a single drop of pain and loneliness in

Wyn's voice, hardly noticeable. Isa noticed. She had been trained to pick up on the feelings, needs, and emotions of predator shifters. Just like Wyn said about himself, she also was there to *serve*. Her purpose was to provide pleasure and happiness.

Prey shifters did not have fated mates. They were simply pets or strays. Sleeping warm in a bed where they opened their legs or cold on the street, on the run. That was what she was taught.

But I wish I could have a mate, Isa thought. A real one, not one caused by a bespelled bracelet. *Being more than a pet...sounds nice.*

The sadness in Wyn's electric blue eyes speared through her as he maintained eye contact in the mirror with her. She felt it in every molecule of her body.

Loneliness is the most painful, slow-acting poison.

So, being her generous, caring, and positive self, Isa patted Wyn's knee and offered, "I will be your mate, too."

The men blinked, absorbing her words.

Nic's hand landed on Isa's knee and possessively clenched it. Heat trickled through her at the claiming touch. "I know you did not just offer yourself to my advisor. I know my impeccable, god-like hearing must have failed me just now."

Alban snorted. "To be fair, Nic, you just said that she should pretend to be Wyn's mate so no one suspects her of being yours."

Nic's fingers dug into Isa's lower thigh. It made her feel *wanted*. She licked her lips and squeezed her legs together. Now that the pain in her arm was dulled by the pain medication, her horniness was back.

"She was being kind," Wyn said. "She didn't mean it. We all know who she belongs to."

"Don't fucking forget it."

Isa frowned at the way Wyn flinched and looked away. She told Nic, "You should be nicer to your friend."

Nic quirked an eyebrow. "Should I be, pet?"

"Yes," she said. "Or I will like him more than you."

"I have never been nor cared about being liked."

"Fine," she said. "Then, you should be nicer to him, or I will be nicer to him for you."

Alban coughed.

The Arctic king pursed his lips and tilted his head as he moved his face closer to hers. Her master liked intimidation. The domineering move caused his delicious scent to infiltrate her senses, and she decided that she liked intimidation from him, too.

He rasped, "That sounded like a threat." He spoke the words in a tone of hardened disbelief.

Isa raised her eyebrows and wore an innocent expression.

"How will you be 'nicer' to Wyn for me?" he asked. "What does *nicer* entail?"

Glancing around, Isa curled a finger toward Nic,

gesturing him to lean closer because she was about to share a secret.

He leaned in.

She inhaled deeply. *His spicy, citrus scent...*

"Focus, bunny," Nic said. "How will you be nice to him?"

I will kneel before him and offer my mouth for his pleasure.

"Okay, I put several pieces in the dressing room," the boutique worker said as she reappeared in front of the three-way mirrors. She gestured for Isa to get up from the couch and follow her. "Ready to try some things on?"

"You need help, bunny?" Alban asked. "With the injured arm. I could help you strip if you want. I promise not to *not* look—"

"I want Wyn to help me into the clothes," Isa said. *Ha.* She reveled in the expression of vexation on the king's face. The apparent jealousy was the first real sign that he cared.

Nic's eyes flashed and narrowed on her, but he remained silent in front of the boutique worker.

Wyn stood from the couch and reached out a hand for Isa to take. "It would be my pleasure."

The two of them took three steps toward the private dressing room before Nic spoke up in a rushed, gravelly voice. "She will be trying on the clothing out here," Nic told the worker. "Move the clothing out here."

The boutique worker blinked several times in

uncomfortable confusion. "My king, this is a common area—"

"This is my advisor's...mate," Nic said through clenched teeth. "I need to...ensure she is good enough for him. She strips out here, we choose the pieces, and we leave you a much wealthier business than when we arrived."

The boutique worker nodded hastily. Isa wondered what made Nic so scary to everyone. Other than the obvious bad attitude.

What has my master done in his life?

There was so much brutality in his eyes. There was so much intensity in the way he spoke and gazed at things. In the way he held a glass or silver utensil just a little too hard. In the way he watched every breath Isa took, like he counted them to ensure they were stable and consistent.

"Now, Wyn," Nic said as he leaned back and splayed his arms out over the length of the back of the couch. "Strip your 'mate.'"

CHAPTER 26

*W*yn was the chess player, not the pawn. He did not like to be ordered; he *advised* on orders.

He did not like to feel out of control.

So, when his king ordered Wyn to strip the beautiful woman he spent the night imagining beneath him, knowing she was forbidden to him, he was…vexed.

Moments ago, the sweet prey had whispered to him, *"I will be your mate too,"* and Wyn wondered what she meant by it.

To protect his reign, Nic could not let it be known that he had a prey mate. Not with his family's history. So, Nic suggested they pretend Isa was *Wyn's* mate for the sake of the town's curiosity. And without consulting his advisor, Nic told the shop worker the lie.

My king wishes me to act?

Fine.

Wyn's throat bobbed as he swallowed. He breathed in Isa's titillating prey scent and felt his body react.

If Wyn was allowed to pretend she was his, he would...work hard to please his king.

Wyn whispered into Isa's ear, "You're mine for the next hour, little flower. How does that make you feel?"

Isa smiled at him as he pulled back to see her face. "Happy," she replied.

His nails half-shifted to long, black talon claws. He had always been a brain-over-body man, but something about her tipped the scales. His instinct—often hushed by his logical brain—ruled him.

"Happy?" he echoed before running a talon over her neck.

She gasped at the cool, smooth, sharp nail. He skimmed it down, down, and sliced the middle of the shirt she wore from top to bottom. The fabric split and waved open, settling against her skin.

Wyn groaned at the sight of her bared, pert breasts and suckable pink nipples. "Maybe I agree with Alban. Maybe she does not need any clothing."

Alban dropped his jaw in a show of dramatics. "Did I just witness, for the first time, the self-righteous, I'm-a-genius owl shifter think with his *dick*?"

"My blood flow does seem to be changing course from my brain," Wyn commented and stepped closer to where Isa stood with her shirt gaping open and her soft curves on display.

"Did he just make a *joke?*" Alban shrieked in shock again.

"I think he was just narrating his body's reaction, with no intention of humor," Nic remarked.

"We will not need any bras," Wyn told the worker who wheeled a small rack of clothing into the space. "I don't want anything obscuring the view of my mate's hard little nipples saluting me."

The worker glanced at the king, who nodded. Even when shopping for Wyn's "mate," Nic had the power of approval or denial. *Or maybe it was just the assumption that the king was paying the bill.*

"Are there any specific colors you like?" the worker asked.

Isa was too busy staring at Wyn's lips and licking her own to answer.

"Mate," Wyn said. "She was asking you."

Isa blinked. Her brows furrowed as she shook her head and replied, "A good pet wears what makes her master happy."

Nic and Wyn met gazes and frowned at her odd words.

"Is anyone else a little confused about her whole 'pet and master' kink thing?" Alban asked. "I mean, exploring it further with some handcuffs and a collar would help *me* better understand. Visual learner over here."

"Isa, you choose what you want," Wyn told her.

"We will tell you if we approve," Nic added, agitating Wyn.

A toxic thought ran through Wyn's mind, *I would be a better mate to her.*

"Do you have a favorite color, perhaps?" the worker asked Isa, clearing her throat and glancing at Nic.

She was clearly uncomfortable with having a prey in her high-end store. Still, the king's presence silenced her from showing outward judgment.

Maybe the worker worried Isa would go into heat and cause any alpha in a one-mile radius to burst through the glass windows and have an orgy on top of the expensive clothing.

Isa's smile was a beam of light, causing everyone in the room to blink and fight the urge to rub their eyes. People in this area of the Arctic, where hunger was a familiar emotion and violence a common occurrence, did not smile like that.

Who is she really?

Isa said, "I love every color."

The worker bit her lip and anxiously glanced at Nic. She clearly felt pressure to be the best boutique attendant in town. Maybe she had heard the rumors of Nic leaving a door covered in the owner's blood after he used some colorful language when referring to Nic's family history.

The worker nervously flipped through items

hanging on the portable rack she brought over. "Okay…"

Sensing the worker's anxiety, Isa added, "But maybe red and green for Christmas?"

Nic quietly snorted, amusement sparkling in his eyes. He lifted a hand to hide a quick smile—a rare facial feature on the king—as he said, "There she goes again."

Witnessing Nic's small display of amusement and fondness, Wyn begrudgingly admitted to himself, *She really is his mate.*

For some reason, a part of Wyn still wished that maybe…maybe Nic would push her away and into Wyn's arms instead.

"Your obsession with Christmas landed you in a cast," Nic reminded her.

"I like my cast," Isa said, tipping her chin up defiantly. "You're just mad because I wouldn't let you sign it." The boutique worker gaped at how the prey shifter nonchalantly addressed the Arctic king.

"You won't like the cast once the pain meds wear off and it gets itchy."

"I've never broken a bone before. It's a new experience," Isa said positively.

"Well, I've broken every bone in my body," Nic said. "And I can tell you right now, there's nothing fun about the experience."

Isa blew out an adorable little breath. "Experiences don't have to be fun; they are not called *fun*-iences."

Alban's hand shot up in the air. "Petition to put that on a T-shirt."

"Name one positive thing about breaking your arm, zayka," Nic challenged her.

Isa grinned at him. "Now, you'll *have* to help me build a gingerbread house."

Nic bit the inside of his cheek and flicked his gaze over Isa from head to toe again. Like Wyn, Nic kept reassessing the peculiar woman with each new bit of data he received.

It was odd for a prey shifter to have such a positive, sunshine perspective on life. *Prey have it...hard.*

In that way, Wyn and Alban could especially relate to Isa. Not all predator shifters were big, strong bears, or werewolves, or basilisks with a deadly stare. Noctu were advisors known for their big brains and amazing memories. Fox shifters were often foot soldiers or talented thieves.

We are all seen as pawns for the stronger species.

To have a use was to be protected. *But maybe that is not the way it should be.*

Shifting in his seat, Nic snapped, "Would you start fitting her in something already?"

*I*sa loved clothing shopping. But she was getting zero clothes so far. Every time Wyn helped her out of an outfit, his sharp claws slit through the material and ruined it. The fabric flitted apart and flashed her bare breasts, abdomen, upper thighs, etc.

"Wyn, you need to be more careful," Isa told him, not realizing he did it repeatedly on purpose.

"Sorry," Wyn said in a hungry tone that suggested he was not sorry but was, in fact, horny.

"I don't know; I think Wyn cutting her clothes off is important to test out the strength of the fabric. Seems vital for any wardrobe choice," Alban said. "Flash some tit again, Wyn."

The king nodded and deadpanned, "Finally, my advisor does something useful."

Wyn snorted, and a small smirking smile curled the edges of his lips. When was the last time the three of them had smiled and joked like this?

Wyn pushed his glasses higher up the bridge of his nose and tried to hide the small show of emotion. Isa found herself swooning.

Maybe it was the pheromones or the hormones or how he smelled like sweet vanilla cookies.

But, with no real explanation, Isa wanted to lick him. She wanted to run her tongue over his throat, and his chin, and the side of his face.

No idea why.

Wyn helped her into a red and green flannel shirt, and she leaned into him to breathe in more of his sweet, wholesome scent. Her tongue nearly lolled out of her mouth.

"Mmm, do you like this one, flower?" Wyn asked her.

She stutter-stepped closer, and he caught her waist like he thought she was tripping and accidentally falling onto him.

Not an accident, she thought. *I just need to nuzzle that chest.*

"Makes her look like a sexy lumberjack elf," Alban said. "Coming to ax down trees before she jacks off some real wood."

She licked Wyn.

His breath caught in his throat at her sudden attack of affection.

She had pressed her chest to his, nuzzled her face into his collarbone and neck area, and dragged her tongue from the bottom of his neck to his earlobe, which she gave a playful nip.

"Did she just…"

"You licked me," Wyn murmured, dumbfounded.

She liked reducing the braniac to a few words. "You taste good," she whispered.

The sound of a glass breaking stole their attention. Chards of glass dropped from Nic's hand, blood dripping onto the table by the couch. He had gripped his drink so hard that it broke in his palm.

The Arctic king sat in a tense, upright position as if his upper leg muscles were readying to launch him into a standing position at any moment.

The boutique worker rushed to clean up the glass on the table. "Do you need a bandage, my king?"

Nic's expression remained stoic as he sat in complete silence and stared at Isa. His hand dripped blood onto his pants.

"Are you okay, Nic?" Wyn asked solemnly.

"I read that hares and bunnies nuzzle and lick their owners to show affection. I think it's common for her kind to be...affectionate with their mouths," Alban said in a serious voice, this time not being cheeky. Instead, he sounded a bit...jealous.

Snapping out of his fit of silence, Nic asked Alban, "Since when do you *read?*"

Alban shrugged, and a dusting of pink covered his cheeks. "Last night, I looked up a few things."

Isa slipped out of Wyn's arms and stepped down from the elevated stage in front of the three-way mirror. She ambled over to Alban, bent over, and flicked her tongue over the slight blush on his cheeks. A little lick of affection, like he said.

Nic ground his teeth and glared at Isa.

"You do not need to be jealous," she told him and stepped in front of his knees.

He opened his muscular legs, and she inched between them to get closer. Odd how it felt like a chore-ographed dance whenever their bodies gravitated toward each other, even though neither of them had any practice or knowledge of the upcoming moves.

He closed his thick legs and trapped her to stand against him, her upper thighs pressed firmly against his inviting crotch. "Why would I be jealous?" he grated in a jealous tone. "My advisor's mate licks everyone but her king."

"Oh no." Isa leaned forward, placed her right hand on the back of the couch, and lowered her face toward his ear. "Does the king want to be licked?" Isa asked gingerly.

"A king deserves affection from his subjects," Nic replied in a clipped tone.

"Why does he deserve it?" she asked.

He exhaled in a rush, shock slapping across his expression.

Isa's head flung back when Nic grabbed a handful of her hair from the back of her neck and pulled. He nipped at her ear and whispered, "What did you say?"

"Huh?" She forgot what she said when he pressed his lips to the spot just below her ear.

Her hair being pulled was a trigger for her. In her classes, she rubbed between her legs and watched as men fisted women's hair and pulled their heads back so they could bite and lick and suck at their throats as they thrust and sated themselves between the woman's quivering thighs.

Isa was beginning to realize that she liked some things rough, but she wanted kindness behind the roughness.

"You were asking why I deserve affection," Nic reminded her.

"Why do you?" She thought back to his bad attitude and how he repeatedly pushed her away.

Every time she thought she might be growing on him, he pulled back. *Why?* She had been the perfect pet for him so far—other than her body being aroused by his friends.

"Because I'm the king."

"Why are you a good king?" Isa asked, wanting to tease him into nicely asking for a kiss or lick.

But he took her question poorly. Like it challenged him. Like it left a bad, poisonous taste in his mouth.

Nic's grip tightened in her hair, and she squeaked at the pinch of pain. "You think someone else would do a better fucking job, pet?" he rasped. "Maybe you'll get your wish. Maybe someone will replace me and fill the place with Christmas trees and throw my severed head into a warm, roaring fire where you can make s'mores."

Frustrated, she said, "I didn't mean—"

"My worthiness has been questioned my entire goddamn life," he growled viciously. His pupils grew into larger, animalistic black circles. Darker and darker. "You think I'm not good enough to rule? Because I don't preach sunshine and rainbows like you? You think a king should be positive and spout lessons like a fucking Christmas special? Someone dignified and *kind*," he spat out the word. "You've clearly been living under a rock because that's not how people survive the Arctic."

Isa held her breath as Nic's crazed eyes scanned over her face. His dark brown eye burned, and his light blue eye froze. To maintain eye contact was as terrifying as it was enthralling.

"After everything I've been through to get me here, you think I am low enough to take judgment from a weak, submissive prey?" he asked.

Isa's mouth fell open.

Her king, her master, really was ice cold, trying to award frostbite to anyone who got too close to him. Could she keep trying to melt him when she risked her own warmth to do so?

Nic extracted himself from her entirely. He hastily shoved her off of him. She would have fallen to the ground if Alban had not moved fast enough to catch her.

"I am leaving," Nic said. He looked at Alban and Wyn as he instructed, "Stay with her. I will see you all at dinner."

"You're running away?" Isa asked.

Nic's jaw ticked as he laid his enraged eyes on her. Always enraged. She was getting tired of it. "I do not run from anything."

"Then, why do you keep pulling away from me?" She reached forward, her body still drawn to him. Her hand flattened over his chest, and she swore his heart beat harder than the snowfall outside. "Why are you trying so hard not to like me?"

Nic grabbed the tops of her arms, his grip so tight it hurt. "Because you're going to fucking die, don't you get that?" he snarled at her.

For the first time, she saw the emotion behind the anger.

And it was fear.

CHAPTER 27

*S*he didn't fucking get it. Nic knew how this all played out. Fuck prophecies, he had been cursed. How else could someone explain his youth?

The second son, born with a limp. The black sheep, exiled to the uncivilized Arctic by a cruel father and a weak mother who never questioned her husband's decisions, even when they meant sending her nine-year-old son out alone in the harshest conditions.

His older brother, the "heir," got to stay warm in the castle as the "spare," Nic, wandered the icy terrain alone. The first few bits of frostbite were a blur. His skin had turned blue, purple, black, and cracked.

The first friend Nic made out in the cold had tried to sell him to an organ-harvesting cult. The second stranger Nic ran into tried to get him to shift so he could skin Nic and auction off his coat of white were-wolf fur to the highest bidder.

Finally, when Nic was starving and tired of tracking through the frozen terrain, an underworld business owner stole him and promised him a warm meal after hard labor.

Child slavery never seemed off to the child, thinking work was just how adults ate at night, too. *But the whip...*

Covered in scars, by the age of thirteen, even the word "trust" left Nic suspicious.

And then there was what happened to his brother...

By the time his brother passed away two years ago, Nic had already grown up to run the most powerful mafia in Russia.

After rising in his teenage years and killing the man who used the whip on him, Nic made his own power by visiting local towns with corrupt business owners or political leaders like the one he had experienced. He had delighted in overturning them in graphically violent ways to advise others against following suit.

If Nic had run a campaign for his shifter mafia Underworld Lord spot, the slogan would have been: *"If you think taking advantage of those who are weaker than you is how to rise, I will cut you down and burn you to death."*

Ruling through fear and violence was all Nic knew.

After all, wasn't valuing power over love, displaying numbness over feeling, the reason why Nic now had more power than he knew what to do with? Valuing love over power was why Nic's brother was dead.

Nic knew better than anyone that to be strong was to feel numb.

"What do you mean I'm going to die?" Isa whispered back as Nic continued holding the tops of her arms at her sides.

He probably held her too tightly. *She is a delicate prey. She will never survive this.*

"You really think you have what it takes to survive out here? You don't," he replied. *I will not relive my brother's mistakes.*

She shook her head. A bit of the light, which constantly lit up her blue eyes, dimmed. "You hardly know me."

His voice boomed and filled every nook and cranny of the shop, seeming to bounce off the three-way mirror as Nic exclaimed, "I will be damned if I let history repeat itself, trying to teach me a lesson I've *already* learned."

Everything I love gets taken from me.

Stunned for a moment at the show of emotion, Isa swallowed and blinked at him.

"If I let myself care for you, do you know what's going to happen?" he asked. "Because I do."

Isa bit her lip, staring up at him with those big, sweet eyes.

"You're going to be poisoned or taken hostage or killed or wander outside and freeze to death. If I care for you, if I claim you, then you will be a walking death sentence."

"Then, protect me," she shot back.

"First rule to survival in the Arctic: Protect and look out only for yourself."

Isa's eyebrows furrowed as she sputtered, "You're a king. You are supposed to be protecting all of your subjects."

"I don't *care* about being king."

"What *do* you care about?"

Ah, a question without an answer. "Second rule to survival: To be strong is to be numb. Care about nothing," he told her.

He finally let go of her arms to clench and unclench his fingers at his sides. The bones of the digits were so used to being fisted that stretching his fingers straight now felt like an exercise in itself. Like correcting a slumped spine.

"No," Isa said and stepped closer to him again. He stepped back.

Distance. Emotional and physical. It was what he was good at.

"Being cold and numb is not how to live. That's not being strong," Isa said, reaching out and flinging her palms onto his pectoral muscles where she glued herself to him. Where he didn't *want* to escape her touch. "To survive, we need each other. We need kindness and compassion and pleasure—"

"That's living, bunny," Nic said gravely. "Not surviving. Kings don't get to *live*."

"You can have a good life," she said, lowering her head to kiss his chest. "You don't have to be numb. Let me warm you," she whispered between tender kisses over his shirt. "Have fun with me today. Just try it, please. For one day, will you let yourself feel? Please."

MATE BEGS? GIVE HER EVERYTHING, his inner wolf demanded.

Nic tried to steel himself. He attempted to put up his tried and trusted walls. He imagined himself as a block of ice.

But she kept planting sweet, soft kisses over his chest and collarbone while his wolf roared to give her everything she wanted.

Funny how Nic hated strangers—his first instinct now when meeting anyone was that they were out to get him. Dark ulterior motives.

But this woman, whom he had known for a day, had him wanting to spoil her with expensive jewelry, feed her little fancy desserts, and cuddle her until she fell asleep.

"Please," she whispered, still kissing over his chest.

HOLD MATE. KISS MATE. CHERISH MATE, his wolfish instinct growled.

I don't want it to be a trick. Please, Gods, let this not be a spell. He placed a hand over one of hers on his chest. She bit her bottom lip like she expected him to rip her palm away from him.

And he did take her hand away. He clasped it in his, removed it from his chest, and lifted it to his mouth.

He kissed her open palm.

Widening, her bright blue eyes shot out beams of excitement and joy, spearing through him. There was a sense of renewed hope—hope in him—pouring from her pores. Like all it took was one kiss.

Nic felt...overwhelmed.

She is so delicate. How can I not break her?

Maybe that was what he had to do.

He did not need a prophecy to tell him what would happen between them. He knew.

If he allowed himself to fall in love with his mate, one of them would end up broken. And he didn't know yet which one he would prefer.

Maybe all he could do was enjoy her while he had her. Revel in her until she was taken away from him.

My kingdom will make me choose. His power or his prey mate.

And I've been through too much to give up what I have worked my life to achieve.

CHAPTER 28

Finally, Isa thought as the excitement bubbled inside her. *This is my shot.*

The Hag had been clear: Isa's life depended on her getting Nic to enjoy Christmas.

She was a woman on a mission.

"If I give you one day, what do you want to do?" he asked her, still holding her hand in his.

She grinned at him, breathing in his spiced, mulled wine scent and wanting to dive into his shirt collar. "I want to go in every shop on this street and look at every item and maybe do some Christmas caroling. And then, I want to go home and build a gingerbread house."

Nic's expression was...distressed. "I could buy you a gingerbread house right now," he stated. "Made and decorated by the best baker in Russia. It would be the most beautiful thing you've ever seen."

Isa rolled her eyes. "No, the whole point is to make it together."

Nic's brows furrowed, and he pursed his lips in reluctance. "You expect me to make a gingerbread house like a child?"

"It will be fun."

"You…wish this to be edible?"

She giggled.

"I can't imagine watching the terrifying king of the Arctic decorate a gingerbread house," Alban said. "This should be televised."

"Shall we leave?" Wyn asked. "Get started on seeing 'every item' in every shop?"

Isa bristled at the speck of disappointment in his tone. *Once we leave, Wyn can no longer pretend I am his mate.*

Well, Isa had a plan. As far as she could tell, it was not *just* Nic who needed the Christmas spirit. Each of the three men needed to open up. Needed to relax and feel valued.

She also needed to, ahem, relax.

Her body thrummed from all of the sexual tension and teasing and non-orgasming. Being left so horny, without satisfaction, was sure to push her closer to her heat.

She needed release.

I'm going to fill them up with holiday joy, she thought with a sly smile. *And so much pleasure.*

"*Y*our shop is so beautiful," Isa told the owner. The older man blushed and placed a hand over his heart, thanking her.

"Bunny, this is a general store," Alban scoffed.

"You just have so many items," Isa said to the owner, wandering through the aisles. "It's incredible. So many *colors*."

"She acts as if a convenience store is an art gallery," Wyn commented, amused.

She shrieked excitedly, and Nic rushed to the aisle where she was. "Snowballs! But they do not look like in the movies." She ripped open the plastic packaging and gripped the soft, pliant light pink and white ball. "How do they make them not cold?"

Holding it, she leaned back. With her good arm, she threw the snowball—actually a sugary baked good item of the same name—at Nic's face.

Shocked, the Arctic king's jaw dropped as mushy coconut-dusted marshmallow, cake, and cream stuck to the side of his face.

Alban ran to see the consequence of the commotion and misunderstanding. "Did she just...?" Seeing his king covered in coconut shavings and sticky frosting, Alban bent over and guffawed.

"S-N-O ball. It is a dessert cake, little *tsvetok*," Wyn explained, striding down the aisle toward them. "A snowball fight is often with balls made of snow from outside."

Isa's bottom lip pouted. "Why is it called a snowball, then?"

"When the company first created the snack cakes, they looked like poorly made snowballs—simple domes covered with shredded coconut and white marshmallow frosting."

Nic cleared his throat. Loudly.

Isa slinked to where Nic silently fumed, his cheek covered in snack cake debris. She whispered, "I'm sorry. I was having fun."

Apparently, those were the magic words. Nic took a deep breath, exhaled, and lowered his face to be closer to hers. She smiled and licked the icing from his cheek until he was clean.

"Snowball fights are fun," she muttered before getting distracted by something else she saw in the store. And something else. And something else.

"How has she never heard of this stuff?" Alban whispered to Nic and Wyn. "Some of these brands are everywhere."

"She is proving to be very sheltered."

"And trusting," Nic sighed as Isa walked around the counter and hugged the store owner.

Mid-hug, she told the stranger, "Thank you for

allowing me to peruse!"

"Isa, stop hugging strangers." Nic waved for her to return to his side.

She waddled back in an adorable, excited walk like a little penguin shifter. "But you never know who needs a hug," she shot back.

"It's called physical boundaries, bunny," Alban explained. "Of which I have none—get over here." Alban pulled her into a hug until Nic released a low growl. "Next location?"

As they explored the next ten shops, Isa hugged every owner and gushed about their great shops and how important it was to provide things people needed.

Then, she started inviting people to the castle.

"We will have a large Christmas dinner celebration or party and have everyone in town come for a warm meal and some presents," she told a random man on the street.

"Isa, do not invite people to my home," Nic remarked sourly.

"*This* is the king." Isa gestured to Nic as she spoke to the man. "And he is so good and worthy, and I think more people need to see how much he cares about his people. What other king invites a whole *town* to Christmas dinner?"

Wyn mumbled, "She is truly unstoppable, isn't she?"

Finally, at a jewelry shop, Nic expected her to *ohhhh*

and *ahhhh*. Instead, she walked right by the jewels and shiny gold and silver designs.

She strode right up to a fellow shopper.

Isa gushed to the woman, "You have such a magnificent scarf. I've never seen anything so beautifully perfect. So many shades of green…"

The shopper in the jewelry store sniffed the air, realized Isa was a prey shifter, and inched backward from Isa. It reminded Nic of how the townspeople had once acted when seeing his limp.

The shopper muttered, "Um, thank you."

"Look at all those stitches," Isa said dreamily, admiring it. "Someone really knitted that with love. What is it like to know you wear physical proof of being loved?"

"It's a Vaswechain designer scarf," the woman replied uneasily.

"Give it to her," Nic demanded coldly, walking up to stand behind Isa and stare down the random woman.

"What?" the shopper asked, gaping.

"Give her your scarf, and you can take whatever jewels you want from here."

Isa spun around and, instead of *thanking* Nic, chastised him. "You need to say *please*."

"Please hand it over," he said. "Or else."

"No." Isa shook her head. "That sounded like a threat."

Nic deadpanned, "It was a threat."

Alban snickered in the corner where Wyn hid a smile.

"I do not want *her* scarf. I want the *idea* of her scarf," Isa said.

Nic grunted. "Explain."

Isa reached forward and took Nic's cold, scarred hands in hers. "It was knit with so many stitches—by hands who knew the time and dedication required to finish such a long, thick scarf. That takes love."

The one thing Nic was incapable of giving her.

"I believe this was the last shop," Nic said. "Should we return back?"

"Yes." Isa smiled. "Let's go home to make a ginger-bread house and have orgasms."

"What?"

Isa blinked innocently. "What?"

Nic was caught on a specific detail.

She called it "home."

CHAPTER 29

"*I*t's falling!" Isa squealed.

"Fuck," Nic grunted and pushed the two walls of gingerbread back together, holding them so the icing would set and harden and keep the half-made gingerbread house together.

Considering the man's super strength, the two walls of cookies cracked and crumbled under his grip. "Fuck," he cursed again. "It won't fucking stay up."

She giggled at his frustration at failing such a small, unimportant act just because he knew it was important to her. With her left arm in the cast, she helped with her right hand as much as she could, but for some reason, that hand just wanted to grope Nic.

Hand on his chest. Back. Hip. Ass. Tight, muscular ass.

Okay, yes, she was very horny. Was it just her, or did

the smell of cinnamon, ginger, allspice, nutmeg, cloves, and pepper just get a girl ready for sex?

"Don't kids do this?" Alban asked from his spot at the end of the kitchen counter. His own gingerbread house masterpiece also had leaning walls. "This should not be this hard, right?"

"You both just need better focus," Wyn said.

They turned to glance at Wyn and gaped at the perfectly structured gingerbread house standing on a plate in front of where Wyn casually leaned against the sleek, black-painted kitchen cabinets.

"Damn, how'd you do that?" Alban asked.

"I'm good with my hands," Wyn replied smoothly, looking right at Isa.

Heat licked down her body. She could easily imagine it. With Wyn's talon claws retracted and his attention to detail, he could pull off some serious tricks with those fingers.

Her abdomen tightened as she thought about Wyn's hand sinking under the waistband of her new flannel pajama pants. How his expression would twist into one of pure, unrestrained lust when his fingers grazed her bare pussy, and he realized she was missing a pair of underwear.

Good pets never wear panties.

"Screw you," Alban said to Wyn. "I finger women to orgasm within a few minutes; you flip pages in books. Our fingers are not the same!"

"I think your issue is self-control," Wyn told the fox shifter.

Nic squeezed more icing onto the side of a new gingerbread panel and tried again. He held two walls together, his eyebrows scrunching in concentration.

Crack.

They broke in his hands, leaving a trail of icing coating his long fingers.

A low, guttural growl shook the king's chest.

Isa answered it with a soft feminine moan by his ear. "You're doing so good," she cooed.

He growled again. "Do not patronize me."

Her right hand wandered down his body. Arm, chest, hip...lower stomach. "It's so sexy how hard you're trying," she whispered onto his shoulder.

Due to his height, she could only touch her lips to his ears when he bent down, and she stood on the tips of her toes.

"When does the 'fun' you described begin?" he rasped.

She giggled to herself and gazed down at his fingers, now covered in white icing and little cookie crumbs.

She lifted one of his hands to her mouth and flicked her tongue over the icing stuck on his index finger.

"Now I am to be teased?" Nic asked.

"You will like my teasing," she promised, flicking her tongue over his finger again, licking away more sweet, addicting icing. "You liked my teasing this morning."

His eyes darkened, pupils growing larger as she caressed him with her tongue. "You think reminding me of you on your knees, sucking me off, is going to help me concentrate on building this goddamn cookie house?"

"Shh," she purred as she licked more sugary, sweet icing from his hand.

His scent infiltrated her every inhale, warring with her mind. Flooding her with need. Did any of the men notice how her hips undulated?

"The more you lick me, the harder my cock gets, and the less likely I will be to finish this."

"You taste so good," she whined, feeling herself slicken between her legs as she watched the lust roll over his expression.

"Your arousal is scenting the air," Nic said in a deep, rumbly voice that stroked over Isa's nerve endings.

Isa panted lightly, groping at his chest again. "Watching you do Christmas-y things must turn me on."

Nic's expression was dumbstruck before turning to one of determination as he picked up two new ginger-bread panels.

"Icing," he demanded from her.

She picked up the icing bag and squeezed a white trail over the lines as instructed. She then purposefully dragged the icing onto the back of his hand, so she *had to* lean over and lick it off his hot skin.

He grunted, "I see the fun now."

She smiled and leaned back down again to peel one of his fingers off the cookie structure. He loosely held it together as she guided the finger into her mouth.

She closed her lips around it and sucked as she continued taking more and more and more of him.

Once she had his entire index finger in her mouth, she licked and sucked as if it were his cock—which was the real thing she wanted in her mouth after seeing a new side to him today.

She wanted to crack away more of his walls, especially after learning he pushed her away because he was scared to care, not because he was incapable of caring.

My Grinch needs me to grow his heart.

But right now, she most wanted to grow his dick.

"Mmmm," she moaned around his finger as she licked and sucked and cleaned it of any icing.

"Fuck, I love that hot little mouth," Nic growled.

"Oh shit," Alban remarked, and they all looked over at him. His entire right hand was dripping with icing. "Whoops. Don't know how it happened. Could I also request this clean-up service?"

Nic rolled his eyes, and Isa giggled again. She may or may not have been hyped up on sugar and endorphins and just overall horniness.

"You have icing on your sleeve, too," Isa told Nic and pinched the fabric close to his wrist. She dragged her tongue over where the icing dried and commented, "Maybe you shouldn't be wearing this."

Nic's eyebrows shot up. "Does my mate wish me to strip?"

His chest was incredible. Why cover up such a view? She replied, "I just don't want you to be able to blame the gingerbread houses for damaging some of your clothing."

"Right." Nic smirked. His hands skimmed down his chest to the bottom of his black turtleneck and gripped it. "For the sake of the clothing."

Nic pulled the shirt up, revealing his breathtaking abs. The muscles quivered for a moment as he wrestled the fabric over his head and flung it to the floor. "Better?"

Isa's teeth sank into her lip as she nodded and traced a finger over the hard, chiseled lines and ridges of muscle. Heat and arousal trickled through her as her skin caressed his.

"Why do I feel like she wants to rub icing onto your chest and lick it off?" Alban asked.

Isa pointed an accusatory finger at him and said, "No wasting icing."

"But—"

"No." *But thank you for the future idea.*

"Okay, well then, separate request," Alban said with a crooked smile. "You take your nice new clothing off under your apron. We don't want that to be damaged. Nic paid good money for it."

Isa grinned at him, and Alban dramatically slapped a

hand over his chest like his heart tried to escape his ribs at seeing her smile.

"You do seem to be in a very cheery, cheeky, and horny mood," Nic commented, watching her every move with intense, hot eyes. "Does this Christmas shi—uh, stuff, really turn you on? Because that is all you had to tell us to get you a tree."

"So, will you take me ice skating then?" Isa asked.

"Nyet," Nic said adamantly. Desire faded from his face until the only emotion left could be described as *serious*. "I told you, too dangerous."

I am not delicate, Isa wanted to scream.

"Even mortal humans ice skate," Alban pointed out.

"Nyet," Nic repeated.

Isa pouted her bottom lip and groped Nic's chest some more with her good hand. His pectorals jerked at her soft touches. *Gods, nothing feels as good as his skin against mine.*

"But I'd be so turned on if you ice skated with me," she said huskily, trying to talk him into it.

"No."

"It'd make me so wet, holding your hand while we skate—"

"No."

"But my pussy would practically be dripping…"

"That's it," Nic snapped. He dropped his hands from the two gingerbread walls, which miraculously stayed standing upright this time.

The shirtless sex god of winter grabbed Isa around the waist and launched her at the counter.

"What—" she exhaled in a rush as he bent her over, face down, hands slamming onto the counter.

His foot kicked her legs apart, and she stumbled into a sexual stance, her ass in the air.

"You say you want to make gingerbread houses. You say you want to go ice skating," he said. "But I don't think you do."

One of his hands slid down her hip, down the side of her trembling thigh, to cup her ass. His fingers kneaded the curvy flesh. Slapped it. Massaged away the sting. *Slap. Massage.*

"You act like you want to do quirky holiday things, but I think you want to do something else more."

Smack. He slapped her ass again, and she gasped at how much she liked it. Her hips rocked, urging him for another.

He rasped, "I think what you really want to do is tease us and make us so hard that we lose all control and snap and fuck you senseless."

CHAPTER 30

*H*is lips at her ear, Nic asked, "Is that the game you are playing, zayka?" He wanted to bite and suck those earlobes.

The sweet cranberry scent of her arousal had his full dick throbbing behind his pants and stealing most of his capacity for thought. How could he think anything productive when his inner wolf growled, PIN HER. FUCK HER. CLAIM HER. LOVE HER.

It was a lot to ask for a werewolf to control his inner instinct. Still, he held back. Or at least, he tried not to grind his erection onto the heavenly curve of her backside.

Nic rasped, "I think you like the idea of making us so hard, we can't think straight."

"Mmm," she moaned weakly as he pinned her front to the counter.

"I think you like the idea of driving us mad with lust, don't you?" His palm came down on her ass again.

Smack. He reveled in her reaction and how she whimpered out a tortured moan. She writhed for more.

Delicate, he reminded himself. *Breakable.*

But every inhale he took of her pheromones... Fuck, they were practically airborne sex drugs. The aroused scent of a mate to a werewolf was like a lethal dose of Viagra.

PIN. FUCK. BREED. CLAIM. BITE.

He wrenched her flannel pajama pants down her legs. With the apron still secured around her waist and a T-shirt underneath, the backside of her lower half was bare, as if she wore a hospital gown.

"Admit it—what do you want," Nic demanded and slapped her ass.

The flesh jiggled at the assault of his palm. He massaged the pinkened skin, knowing the tingling warmth would travel between her legs and awaken her nerve endings.

"You," she squealed, gyrating her hips. She turned her face on the counter, and Nic saw her blushed cheeks and rosy lips as she repeated, *"You."*

"What do you want from me?"

"I want your..." she whined and kept humping the air as he caged her front against the counter. "I want your..."

Say it. Say my cock. Say you'll only ever want my *cock.*

260

"Your permission to go ice skating," she cried out. Then, she broke into a case of diabolical giggles.

"Un. Fucking. Believable." He scented her wetness and was harder than stone between his legs, and she was capable of laughter? *Hell no.* "You think you're allowed to giggle while making me so hard I can feel my goddamn heartbeat in my cock?"

Isa's breath hitched. Nic did not wait for a response.

In a swift move, he launched her over his shoulder, spun them around on his heel, and laid her on the long dining table that Nic's servants ate at before preparing breakfast for the king.

The kitchen table sat six people and was made of thick, high-quality wood. He was confident he could fuck her on it, and it would not break. The Arctic carpenters really deserved higher pay with the pieces they made to withstand Arctic shifter roughhousing.

Isa gasped as she flexed out on the long table and stared at Nic with those big, sparkling eyes.

"See how serious this is?" Nic asked, hands falling to unzip his pants and push them down his legs.

Isa gaped some more, possibly drooling, as Nic smirked and stripped out of his underwear as well.

His cock, enlarged, red, and leaking at the plump tip, stood tall, pointing up to the sky. He grabbed it from the base and jerked it up and down, slapping it against his stomach.

"See what you do to me? And you think you can *joke*

while I'm this hard?" He squeezed his erection, and Isa bit her lip and bucked her hips on the table.

"You think you can tease the most dangerous creature on the continent and get what you want?" he asked, cocking his head to the side.

"*Yes,*" she moaned.

Nic's dick twitched at the sound. "*Yes?*" he repeated in disbelief.

Isa's right hand, the one not captive in a cast, skimmed up her stomach and cupped her breast through the apron. She massaged it in circles as she said, "I've been a good girl." She spread her legs open wide. "And good girls get rewarded."

"And who the hell told you that you've been a good girl?" Nic asked roughly.

She blinked, and a bit of the dreamy lust dimmed in her gaze as she frowned. She still rubbed her breast with her good hand as she questioned, "What do you mean?"

"As far as I'm concerned, my mate was dropped off here, and she has proceeded to break my rules, disobey my orders, and lust after my friends. Not the traits of a good girl at all."

Isa's mouth dropped open again, and she sputtered.

"I don't think you've been a good girl," Nic told her. "I don't think you deserve to be rewarded."

She flinched and broke eye contact.

Her legs slowly started to close, but Nic caught both

of her ankles and kept them wide apart. His fingers clamped around her small ankles, and he leaned down to plant a warm kiss on her calf.

"I think you've been a naughty girl, Isa," he whispered, grazing his lips over the sensitive skin on her leg. "And so, we will treat you like a naughty girl."

She panted and glanced around at Nic, Wyn, and Alban, assessing the new situation. Her new lack of power.

The seductress becomes the seduced.

"You want to know why you are on the table, bunny?" Nic asked.

He returned to the kitchen counter and picked up one of the piping bags full of white icing. He twisted the bag, tightening it so that a bead of white icing formed at the end of the nozzle.

He said, "Because you're about to become a little art project."

*I*sa could not lay still. Her limbs twitched. Her hips bucked. Her chest heaved with little panting breaths as her arousal reached a new level.

There was something about being spread out on a

table, so vulnerable and open to anything the men wanted to do to her. The cool wood at her back did nothing to chill her warm skin.

The three men just looked so *hungry*.

Wyn's intelligent eyes blazed like hot, blue flames he could use to roast her. Alban bit his thumb like he readied his canines to give her a good *chomp*. Nic's lips curled like a sadistic animal about to feast on a prey.

What did he mean about her becoming an art project?

"You want to know what is about to happen?" Nic purred. "First, we're going to cover you in icing. Then, we are going to cover you in our cum."

Isa gasped and felt a rush of wetness between her legs. *Gods, I'm so slick; I'm going to leave a puddle on the table*. What would the king do then?

"Whoa, whoa," Alban said. "You're going to let us come on your mate?"

"If it is just me, others will scent it. This way, we keep up the story that she is just our...plaything," Nic replied.

Even through the lust, there was a slight ache of disappointment in Isa's chest at how the king refused to let anyone think he could have a prey mate.

Nic said, "She wants to be shared like the needy, horny girl she is. *Zayka* wanted us to decorate. So, we're going to decorate *her*."

Nic cupped her ankle again and tugged her forward until her calves dangled off the table's edge. "Come anywhere but on her face," he told the other men as he stroked a hand up her leg. Up. Up. Up. Closer and closer to where she ached for touch under the apron.

His fingers flicked under the hem of the cooking apron. The digits wandered for a moment then lightly traced the seam of her pussy lips.

He did not prod or enter to feel her wetness, but he delicately outlined the sensitive flesh and gathered her leaking juices. A rumbling groan sounded from deep in his throat.

"They can come on my face, too," Isa offered.

She was compassionate in that way. She was also mindlessly horny.

She wanted Nic to fuck her until he admitted he liked her—even just a little. She wanted to suck Alban until he could not feign an absentminded and jokey exterior. She wanted to suck Wyn until he could not maintain his cool, calm, and collected interior.

"Or in my mouth," she added. "They can come in my mouth, too."

"Hell, yes—"

Nic cut off Alban's cheer. The dominating Arctic king laid his large, possessive hand over her pussy. "Isa, you do not offer yourself to them. You are *mine*. I own your fucking body. Me. You understand?"

She panted at where his hand just barely applied pressure over her clit. More. *More.*

"Focus," Nic demanded, slapping his hand down on

her sex. She shrieked at the sudden throbbing in her clit. It felt...*good*. "I own you. Do you understand?"

"I understand," she muttered breathlessly and gyrated her hips to rub his hand over where she grew wetter and wetter by the second.

"Then, repeat it," he said. "Your body is mine."

"My body is yours," she echoed in a daze as she lifted her hips in little thrusts and worked herself onto his palm.

"*Good*," he cooed and rewarded her with a sharp grinding of the heel of his hand over her swollen, needy clit. "Say you understand that your pussy is mine to pleasure."

"My pussy is yours," she shouted back as he rubbed over her bundle of nerves.

"Mine to fill. Mine to come in," Nic grunted as he dipped his hand down to run his fingers through her glistening pussy lips and align the tips to her slippery entrance.

Yes. *Yes*. "Yours to come in," she whined. Her head thrashed from side to side as she undulated her hips and tried to force his finger inside her. "*Please.*"

"You want something, pet?" he teased.

Flushed and panting, she pleaded, "*Finger me.*"

"Say I will always own you. Say you'll always be mine."

"You own me," she relented. *But does he want me?* She

blinked open her sex-hazed eyes and added, "And you need to learn to share me."

CHAPTER 31

"Time to decorate. Wyn," Nic said. "Claws."

Wyn's nails shifted into talons in seconds as he strode to the table where Isa laid, spread eagle. He lined up his sharp claw to the top of her apron and undershirt.

"Apologies, flower," Wyn said. "We will buy you a new one."

Wyn easily tore through both fabrics, ripping them in half and letting the fabric fall to her sides and gape open on the table.

Licking their lips, the three men took their time examining her naked body on display.

"Alban, give her a leash," Nic commanded.

In a blur, Alban moved forward. He reappeared right behind where her head laid on the table. From upside down, she watched him lean over her and squeeze one of the icing piping bags.

Alban drew a steady line of sticky, white icing over her throat, a perfect edible collar.

"Very good. A leash for our good girl," Nic said. "What else does she need?"

"How about nipple pasties? For the sake of modesty," Alban commented.

"Yes. Go ahead," Nic told him.

Alban grinned, but Isa saw right through him. This was not his usual mischievous grin. It was one of real, genuine delight. Excitement. Joy.

Who knew getting naked was the best way to instill holiday cheer in these predator shifters?

Thick, white icing was piped over Isa's left nipple first. The pink peaks of her breasts were tight, hard, and tingling from her arousal. Alban painted her nipple with the bracing glaze, stiffening the tip and increasing her desire for more.

When Alban moved to cover her other un-frosted nipple, Nic clicked his tongue and admonished him. "Mmm, doesn't look right. You need to pipe it perfectly. She needs to know that we take this icing decorating seriously. Clean it up and do it again."

Alban clarified, "Clean it up?" His husky voice suggested he asked more than what he said.

After a silent, intense, and seemingly telepathic conversation with each other, Nic said simply, "*Yes.*"

Alban dipped his head. With his long tongue, he

laved Isa's breast from the bottom curve, over her icing-covered nipple, to the top of her cleavage.

"More," Nic said. "Create a clean canvas to start again."

Alban's tongue swirled around her nipple. Twisted and flicked.

Isa's eyelids fluttered shut at the feeling of stirring pleasure. *More.*

The flirty fox shifter's tongue danced over her stiffened peak until all icing remnants were gone.

Alban pulled back, bracing himself on one hand. His fingers spread out on the table beside her head. He licked his lips and muttered, "Delicious."

She shivered from her head to her curling toes.

"Again," Nic said. The king dragged a finger over his bottom lip as he ran his scorching gaze over Isa's naked and blushing body. "Decorate her better this time."

Alban smiled and held up his piping bag like it was a manly weapon that could take down an army. "I'm going to give her a nipple ring this time," he said excitedly.

"Very mature," Wyn commented from the corner of his mouth, which formed a judgmental line as he watched Alban pipe with a childish sense of glee.

"You don't think bunny should have a nipple ring?" Alban asked. "How else will people know what a bad, naughty girl she is?" Alban ran a finger down her chest, between her breasts, down her quivering stomach, and right above her core.

"*Please,*" Isa whined. Her hips rocked up, off the table again. Her clit pulsed for touch. Any touch. A swipe. A press. A rub.

"Wyn, do you want to give her some piercings too?" Nic asked calmly as if he was not watching Isa already spiral into an oblivion of lust. "I'm thinking a belly button ring."

Wyn rolled his eyes but played along and joined Alban around the table.

Isa's face scrunched into one of need as icing piped out over her nipples again, a delicate, heavy tease of cool, sticky white. Meanwhile, Wyn drew shapes and dots of icing on her lower stomach, just above where her pussy screamed for attention.

"Stop," Nic commanded. The men pulled back the piping bags. "She keeps bucking her hips and smearing the designs. Start again. Start *clean.*"

The men did not hesitate.

Alban's tongue scooped icing from her breasts. The wet, rough tongue flicked and laved her nipples, making them even stiffer peaks. He also kissed some of the icing away this time.

His lips closed over her left nipple and *sucked*, and she wailed out a desperate moan. He nibbled at the curves of her breasts and licked and sucked—

"*Yes,*" she cried out as Wyn's mouth settled on her lower abdomen and tasted her trembling skin.

She glanced down and made eye contact with the

fully suited man as his tongue danced and darted over her sensitive flesh.

There must have been secret portions of her stomach that were directly connected to nerve endings in her clit. The moisture his saliva left behind seemed to be absorbed instantly, resulting in more wetness between her legs.

He drew his tongue in a long, slow drag over the lowest part of what could still be called her stomach and not the top of her pussy.

His lids fell to half-mast as Wyn pressed his lips just above her slick mound.

And so, it began. Once they thoroughly and leisurely cleaned her, they covered Isa in icing, taking their time to pipe intricate details.

She almost told them to pipe on the gingerbread houses so their efforts could be kept and admired later, but her mouth didn't work for anything other than a few words and some gasps and moans.

Watching from the end of the table, where Isa's calves dangled, Nic smirked. "I have to say, this is the most I've ever enjoyed the holidays."

"Join in on the fun," Alban said.

"Any more attention and we might give her another heart attack," Nic replied, though he fingered the bag of icing he placed beside her thigh on the table.

"I'll be okay," she yelped as Alban purposefully

pressed the cool, hard nozzle of the icing bag to her tingling nipple and flicked it.

"See? She promises to stay nice and calm and not have a sex-induced heart attack. After all, you sexed her up in the hot tub post-heart attack, and she was fine."

Nic flexed his jaw and palmed her shaking thigh. "You think you could handle three mouths on you at the same time, zayka?"

"If she's getting nipple piercings and belly piercings made of icing, maybe she deserves a clit piercing, Nic," Alban said, just trying to be a helpful fox to his king.

"Bad girls *do* have clit piercings, huh?" Nic's voice stroked over her just like his fiery gaze. "But hmmm..." He slowly picked up the third piping bag. "I'll have to find the *mysterious* clitoris, a body part that has confused and confounded mortal men for millennia."

Alban snickered, Wyn smirked, and Isa frowned. She thought to herself, *He found it easily last night.* Why would he pretend to not know where it was now?

"Is this it?" Nic asked in a feigned inexpert tone as he brushed his thumb directly over her clit.

A loud moan pealed out of her, "YES!"

"Hmm, no, that must not be it." He removed his thumb and grazed the nozzle of his piping bag just to the left of where her clit swelled and throbbed with each heartbeat. "Maybe here?"

"That was it! That was it!"

"Mmm, I don't think so."

She panted.

As Nic touched and teased her pussy—intentionally granting *near* touches to her clit—Alban and Wyn smeared icing over her most sensitive spots and licked her clean with enthusiastic tongues.

"Fuck me," she authoritatively demanded in a deep, low voice that hardly sounded like her own. Her brain was breaking; maybe that was the explanation for the horny exorcist command that rose out of her. *"Fuck me."*

"You want us to stop?" Nic asked in an incredulous and sarcastically innocent voice. He trailed the nozzle between her pussy lips and aligned it to her puckering entrance. "But I thought you wanted us to decorate—"

Alban sucked *hard* on one of her nipples.

"FUCK ME," she shrieked. Her eyes rolled back, and she thrust her hips and tried to shove herself onto the damn nozzle of the piping bag. That was how bad she needed to feel something inside her. *Anything. Please.*

"Don't you want to fill us with Christmas joy and holiday lessons? Like being generous and nice..." Nic circled the piping bag over her swollen and distended clit. "Personally, I think you prefer when I'm naughty. Just look how *wet* you are."

"Please," she whined and thrashed her head from side to side.

He leaned forward and swept his tongue from the bottom of her pussy, up, up, over the icing that circled the perimeter of her clit. He pulled on her clit lightly as he sucked the icing from her.

"*Ughahudgjsofgbssugaj*," unintelligible noises leaked from her as the men teased and tongued her.

"No more lessons? Or judgy comments about how I need to learn to share?" Nic asked as he piped icing between her folds and piped a dot right over her tight entrance. His mouth followed suit.

She cried out for more as his warm, textured tongue slid over her slit, dipping and savoring and flicking and prodding against her damp tightness.

The tricks he did over her clit...

A hot tear fell down her cheek as the sexual frustration peaked inside her.

"Mmm, I think maybe this naughty girl should be taught a lesson about telling her king to share her," Nic rasped as he put down the icing bag and stood.

He grabbed the tender skin under her knees and yanked her further down the table until her ass sat right on the edge.

His wide palm stretched over her inner thigh and kept her legs wide apart as he stepped into the intimate space he created.

Nic's deep, rumbly voice wrapped around her like invisible velvet shackles. "Zayka, you're about to find out why you're better off *not* being shared."

CHAPTER 32

$\mathcal{N}$ic reached down and gripped his shaft. He stroked himself as he observed Alban and Wyn kiss over her breasts, one man on each side of her. *My mate.*

He was possessive. His wolf wanted to rip apart anyone who threatened his relationship with his mate.

But watching her dissolve into a puddle of wanton lust made his inner wolf *purr*. Her face and chest were pink with arousal. Her breasts shook as she panted and thrust her body into the touch of the three men.

The scent of her sweet, glistening pussy was a rope around Nic's neck, tugging him forward. If, for any reason, she got up and walked away from the table, Nic would have stumbled right after her.

She wears a collar, yet I wear her leash, he thought.

"Fuck me," she begged and dropped her hands

between her legs to pet herself as Nic took his time observing her. Her fingers dipped into her slit and swiped over her swollen bud.

"Nyet, no," Nic grabbed her hands and handed them to Alban and Wyn. Both men took a wrist and pinned it beside her head on the smooth table. "You think you can touch yourself?"

"*Please,*" she whined.

"I own this body, remember?" Nic smiled evilly. "*I decide when you come.*" After all, Nic craved control in every other aspect of his life. Why not during sex, too?

"Please, please."

Nic slipped a finger between her folds and drew patient circles over her weeping entrance. FUCK, his wolf demanded. "She just keeps getting wetter and wetter..."

"Give me your cock," she babbled nearly incoherently. Lucky for her, Nic's superhuman hearing helped him decipher her pivotal words. "I want it. Please. I need it inside me."

Nic pressed a finger inside her, testing out her tightness. The grip and sheer wet heat of her pussy dimmed his ability to think.

He tapped his dick against her clit and said, "You're making a little damp spot on the table."

Before she had time for a response, he aligned his cockhead and plunged his thick erection inside her. He shoved his entire length into the tight grip of her core, hitting her cervix. She cried out, *"Yesssss!"*

Fuck, he bit the inside of his cheek—anything to bring pain to numb some of the all-consuming pleasure. He wanted to mindlessly stroke himself inside her, rock his hips, and *thrust*.

He never wanted to leave her pussy. Two days ago, Nic had never had sex and had no interest in changing that fact. There were too many other, much more important things to do. Now, he felt like a brainless mortal man who wanted to walk around with his dick in his woman and carry her purse for her. Did he need to buy her a purse?

How was he supposed to give her up? *Feels like I was born to fuck her*. Meanwhile, he hadn't even been born to rule.

"Maybe I shouldn't let you come..." Nic said as he began leisurely pumping his cock inside her, keeping a languid, teasing pace. "I don't appreciate you begging me to share you like I'm *not fucking enough*," he growled viciously at the end.

He backed away. Rammed inside. Out. In. Out... Plunged back inside.

His every thrust was like a punishment. Like he wanted her to feel an ounce of the warring emotions that raged inside him every moment. The feelings that ate away at him.

His wolf railed and raged to pound her with impossibly fast thrusts. Wanted to bite and mark and hammer himself in her wetness. Fill her up with his cum and breed. Nic fought to hold his wolf at bay.

"I am going to fuck you nice and slow. So, so slow," Nic said. He wanted to control when she came. He wanted to draw it out and make her crazy for him. Only him.

Isa bit her lower lip as she stared up at him with pleading eyes. Her mouth opened like she was about to say something, but her gaze darted over to Alban's head as if he had just nipped at her breast and stolen her attention.

I want her attention.

Nic palmed her inner thighs and eased back, pulling out of her until just the fat tip of his length remained inside. Her slickness shined on his cock.

Want to be covered in her. Want to cover her. He surged forward, spearing her on his dick. He reared back, reveling in the feel of suction as her pussy fought his retreat. Groaning, he drove into her again.

"You don't get to orgasm after you stare at my men and bite your lip and bat your eyelashes for their attention. You should be batting your eyelashes at *me*. Am I not enough?"

"You are enough," she cried out like she *cared* about him. "You are everything."

Lies.

With every slow movement, he built more power

279

into his thrusts. At one point, he punched his hips forward so hard that his cock scraped the very back of her tight channel, causing her body to skid up the table. Alban and Wyn accidentally butted heads at her sudden shift in position.

"You don't get the privilege of coming when you spike the air with the scent of your arousal for *them* and not *me*."

"It *is* for you," she whined and tried to rock her hips and quicken the pace at which Nic thrust inside her.

"Is this thick cock not enough for you, huh?" Nic gave a brutal punch of his hips, yet Isa moaned and babbled incoherently like she...loved it. Shaking his head, Nic counted several seconds between each slow thrust. He cooed with a layer of sarcastic, chaotic evil baked into his seductive tone. "Doesn't it feel so good when I take you nice and slow?"

"No," she wailed and rolled her hips. "More. Faster."

"You were the tease earlier, pet," Nic rasped. "I am only returning the favor and showing you who is in control."

A lie. She could easily control him—that was part of the problem. Every time he told her, *"I own you,"* he inwardly whispered to himself, *"as you own me."*

But Nic knew better than anyone that where there was power over another, the seed for lies and manipulation and deep, deep pain was born.

His next thrust was particularly rough. She moaned

lustily at each of his merciless descents. Part of him wanted her to hurt, wanted her to realize he was too brutal for her.

Why can't she see already that I'm not good enough? His parents had seen it. The factions of conspirator Arctic shifters saw it.

But when he punched his hips forward and violently speared her with his cock, all she did was beg for more.

Who...is she?

He slammed into her harder, gripping her thighs so tightly there would be red marks if he lifted his hand.

"More, faster, *harder*," she pleaded.

"You think you could take any harder, pet?" he asked, disbelief bleeding from his voice and expression. "You want me to break your fucking pussy?"

"Yes," she squealed back with a complete lack of concern that Nic had paranormal strength, yet she was as delicate as a human. "Break me in! Make my pussy yield to your cock."

"Fuck." Nic pulled out of her and fisted his length, jerking it and delaying his orgasm. "You don't know what you're asking for."

"I *dooooo*," she whined.

I shouldn't fuck her when she begs like that. He could lose control. His wolf could take over and pound her with shattering thrusts. *If I hurt her...*

Nic chided, "You want a broken pelvis? Every second

I fuck you, I'm holding back. It's a miracle you haven't snapped in half yet."

"Yes, split me on your dick," she pleaded. "Come inside me."

Who the fuck is she? Nic wondered to himself as his hand ran over his length. "You should hate me for what I've done."

This was meant to be a punishment for her repeatedly telling him he needed to be nicer or share or just her overall desire to "fill him with the Christmas spirit" like he was a redeemable Scrooge and not a goddamn king of the most cold-hearted and terrifying shifters of the realm.

He added gruffly, "You don't know what you being here means... The danger... How fucking selfish I'm being by not shipping you off somewhere far, far away."

He shouldn't have been mated with a prey. The fates were too cruel.

After everything I have endured, to end up just like my dead, overthrown brother...

"You want to be split by alpha dick?" Nic asked, his tone turning sharp and almost mocking. "You want to be treated like a pet, like an alpha's personal slut?"

Because that's all you can be here. Mate or not, she would only ever be a sexual plaything—not a queen. Not his queen.

A prey queen was what got his brother killed.

Father is rolling in his grave.

"Yes," she squealed out, shocking him yet again.

"That's all you want? To be a shared pleasure pet?" It sounded wrong. It felt wrong. *Why is she okay with that?* It was a slap to the face.

"I will be whatever you need," she moaned out and undulated on his cock.

In a grave voice, Nic said, "You don't want to know what I need."

CHAPTER 33

*I*sa was pretty much too horny to think. She could see many emotions playing across Nic's face and light blue and dark brown eyes, but she had been teased...for too long.

She had not orgasmed in so long.

A prey shifter, approaching heat, around the most attractive predator shifters she had ever seen, being sexually tease-tortured without release...

She passed coherent thinking. Her brain was a repetitive chant of: *Want. Need. Fuck.* Come.

So, when Nic replied darkly, "You don't want to know what I need," her brain did not register the tonal change. Or the threatening, underlying tension peaking.

Her body merely registered: *take him.*

She easily broke free of Alban and Wyn's grip on her wrists, considering the men were distracted licking and sucking at her swollen nipples. Having studied every sexual position and every maneuver of the body, Isa snuck a leg around Nic's knee and shoved her right palm in precisely the right spot to use his body weight against him and tilt him over.

"Shit." Alban and Wyn backed away when Nic's back hit the edge of the table, and Isa climbed on top of him. "Did she just *overpower* him?"

Momentarily stunned, Nic blinked and flexed his jaw as he summoned his next statement to distract from the fact that she had just overturned him. "Is this what you think I need?" he asked hoarsely. "To be ridden?"

"*Shhhh.*" She reached down to squeeze the root of his cock and stroke it once with her hand. In a soft, lulling voice, Isa whispered, "All you need to do is lay down… and relax." She stroked him once more.

"I don't *relax,*" Nic grated.

"He would need hardcore drugs for that," Alban remarked.

"Just relax…and I'll take care of you." She sucked in a sharp breath as she pressed the wide tip of his dick to her soaked entrance. "Just…stop talking," she mumbled as she sank down onto his hard, thick length once more, feeling it stretch her from the inside out. "And *feel.*"

The shaft was so *warm.* More of her wetness rushed to coat around him until every downward thrust produced an audible, slick sound. She had never been this sexually pent-up. It felt…dangerous.

"Feel me, *mmm*, feel my pussy squeeze you nice and tight. Bury yourself in me and relax, and let me do all the work. Let me ride you," she whispered onto his neck. "Let me make you come your brains out, master."

Nic's mouth hung open.

"The king needs to relax and enjoy himself," she sighed out as she rose up on her hind leg muscles and lowered herself back onto him. *Gods, he feels so good.* "Need to stop being so anxious and angry and have some fun. You just need to *expel* all your negativity. *Leak out* all your worries."

Nic released a noise that resembled a half-snort, half-scoff hybrid. "You want me to *cum out* my bad attitude?"

Alban snickered and commented, "That is a magical pussy, bunny, but I don't think it can manage that."

"My pussy can do *anything*." Isa grinned and slowly rocked her hips.

Tilting her head back, she let her hair fall and sweep against her lower back with every movement. She laid her hands flat onto Nic's abdomen, finding her leverage and balance.

"Oh shit, are we about to see hare shifter speed?" Alban rubbed a hand over his erection and nudged Wyn. He knew her kind could move their hips at lightning speed.

Yes. Isa knew every erotic, tantalizing trick. Isa had been trained to be the perfect prey pet, after all.

Finally, her master was letting her serve her purpose. To bring pleasure and joy.

This needed to *matter*. *Because he needs me*, she thought after thinking back to his comments in the boutique clothing shop. He thought being strong and surviving meant being numb.

I'm going to make him come so deep inside me that he realizes it is better to feel than be numb.

"Master needs to let go of all his worries..." She rose up, then dropped herself down. Up. Down. "If you were cold and numb all the time, you wouldn't get to enjoy this."

She slammed her pussy onto his cock, and his eyelids clenched shut as he groaned and shuddered. He really did fill her up so well. "You need to get out of your head and stop thinking so much," she whispered.

Her thighs lifted, and she engaged her core and leg muscles. *Here we go.*

She began to *bounce*.

"Oh...*fuck*," Nic cursed. At her speedy pace, Nic's head fell back, hard, against the wooden table. She would have stopped to check if he injured himself, but his fingers dug into the sides of her thighs as he rasped, "Yes."

His eyes widened as he stared up at the ceiling. *Yes, let me show you heaven.*

She bounced with such speed that she blurred on top of him. She rode him with a fervor that suggested total abandon. Thighs shaking, head back, wispy ends of her long hair brushing against her ass. Her breasts swayed, a blur of jiggling motion in front of Nic, as she swiftly moved on him.

"How…" Nic trailed off as his hips jerked up and his knees bent. His body tensed underneath her—already fighting back an orgasm?

I'm that good.

"You're doing so well, holding back," Isa cooed to Nic.

After his teasing, she was now the one in charge, and something about that thrilled her. She loved being submissive; hearing she was a good girl always turned her on. But this…

It's like he is losing himself in me.

Nic glared at the ceiling even as she felt his cock twitch and inflate further at her words.

"So hungry for more but still holding back. Look at me," she said as she trailed her right hand down his chest. "Are you trying not to look at me because you know you will come?"

Grinding his teeth, Nic snapped, "I can't come in you again and risk a prey heir."

Don't let that hurt so much. A dark, hot desire blanketed her—one that made her want to break him.

She kept riding him.

"You're doing such a good job not coming so deep inside my tight, wet pussy," she whimpered. "It just keeps stroking you as your cock fills up with more and more cum, as you get harder and harder. You're doing so well keeping it in. Oh, gods, please don't stop. Please don't come and make this stop. Just keep letting it build and build. Just keep getting harder and harder."

"*Fuck*," he cursed again and clenched his eyelids shut as his hips jerked up, pinning her on his cock.

"No, no, open your eyes," Isa demanded as she rode him so fast, his thighs tremored with each hard slap of her ass hitting them. "Don't you want to see how good you're fucking me?"

Nic scowled but half-opened his eyes to peek.

"See how pink and stiff my nipples are for you?" she asked and reached up to cup her breasts. Her fingers fondled her smooth tits as she kept her rhythm. She lowered the soft curves over his face and let them jiggle above his eyes. "See how my breasts shake as you fuck me with that thick cock?"

"Goddamn it." Nic slammed his fisted hands down at his sides, rattling the wooden table they were on.

"Shhh, let yourself *relax*," she whispered. "Get lost in the feeling of the tight grip of my pussy. Get lost in the movement of my breasts. No more anger or worries. Let your cock fill up with every thought. Breathe deep. *Relax*."

In her tribe's trainings, Isa had ridden a chair with an "attachment" that she fed between her legs. It had stretched her and gotten her used to the idea of the "wild ride"—the act that every prey pet had to master before qualifying for adoption.

The tribe's women had been timed, and Isa was awarded the best record time for her fast hips. *This is what I know I'm good at.*

"You need to, *oh*, need to stop thinking..." she mumbled as she rapidly bounced on him. Each syllable jolted from her mouth with the speed of her hips. Up. Down. Up, down. *Updownupdownupdown.*

The rhythm she set was fast but stable. Consistent. Hypnotic. Her eyelids drooped a bit as she bounced and bounced and bounced...

"Pleasure is all that matters," she muttered. Her tone took on a faded, monotone manner as she kept the unbreakable rhythm.

Because these were her training mantras, seeping back into her mind as she kept a steady rhythm. Her mind reverted back to those classes where her teacher put headphones onto each of her classmates. They all listened to soft, melodic music and a low, mesmerizing voice as they slowly lowered themselves onto the built-in silicone toy fastened to the chairs.

Isa would always grip the back of the chair and *ride*. All that mattered was the ride.

The dildo-shaped attachment had a slight curve at the base that buzzed against her clit on every descent of her hips. It awarded her pleasure as the mantras played through the headphones and encouraged her to keep a speedy pace and perform a little *grind* on each downward roll of her hips.

Be a good girl and ride and repeat your mantras.

Ride and listen.

Listen and obey.

"Empty your mind and focus only on the pleasure," she said in that trance-like tone. *Pleasure is all that matters.* "A pet must make her master feel good. Feels... so good."

Nic frowned from underneath her, staring at her with a quirked eyebrow as her gaze turned hazy and her voice weakened to a feeble, hoarse whisper.

"Love to fill and be filled. Filled." Though Isa's hips moved at lightning speed, her words and voice came out slow, like thick, sticky molasses dripping from a mostly empty bottle into a bowl of gingerbread ingredients. Each word dragged on for an extra second than normal. Her body moved fast, but her brain slowed...

"Love being filled." She groped at her tits again, but this time, it was not to put on a show. Her right hand moved without her mind's instruction. "Pets have an endless desire to be filled and make their master come. I must make my master come. To be filled with cum is to feel pleasure. To serve is to feel pleasure."

"Um..." Alban muttered, but Isa ignored the confused expressions on the men.

She was in the zone. The zone of a perfect pet. More wetness gushed between her legs as her arousal spiked with her mantras. "My body is for master's pleasure. My body is a toy for your fucking. My mouth, my pussy, my ass—"

"Isa?" Wyn asked, sounding like he tried to wake her from a dream.

"This seems like more than a kink," Alban said.

She pinched and pulled at her nipples as her inner muscles squeezed and tightened around Nic's length. So close to orgasm. *So close.*

In a weak volume, Isa whispered, "Give into the pleasure. Give in. Don't think, just feel. Listen and *feel* and give in. I am a receptacle for master's pleasure. I want to be filled with his cum."

"It almost sounds like she's..."

Nic sipped in a breath as horror struck across his expression. He muttered, "Brainwashed."

Isa bounced down, hard, onto him as her pussy pulsed, hinting that she was moments away from an orgasm as she finished her mantra, "Obey and come. *Come.* I am here for your cum, master—"

Her loud wail cut off as Nic grabbed her hips and launched her off of him.

CHAPTER 34

*T*he men were yelling back and forth. And Isa's arm hurt.

She pouted in the corner of the parlor. Nic, Wyn, and Alban went back and forth, shouting things and speaking at high volumes as they ran anxious hands through their hair and took quick glances at Isa.

She had just narrowly managed to orgasm right as Nic threw her off of him earlier. However, orgasming around nothing was not satisfying when she knew the sensations she had built toward while riding him. *It would've been so good...*

But he had stopped her, and it had ruined her orgasm.

She wanted to cry, *Whyyyyyy?*

Her injured arm had also started throbbing with pain as the medication they gave her wore off.

Fresh off her mantras and still feeling needy, Isa bit her lip and clenched her thighs together, trying to sneakily provide pressure to her clit.

She knew what she wanted. A treat.

Isa scanned the parlor and saw clearly where her treats were. Sitting just beside the dark green velvet sofa was the briefcase the Seer left when she dropped Isa off at the castle.

Last night, Isa had fought the urge to tiptoe back to the parlor and grab one of the little pills. Now, with throbbing pain in her arm and annoyance at how Nic ruined her orgasm, she craved the peaceful, pleasant state her treats provided.

If the men keep talking intensely, I could probably slip right over and grab a treat without them noticing...

Isa had never felt pain from an injury before; her tribe had always ensured her safety—an easy feat when they kept her inside and monitored each day.

I deserve a treat to distract from the pain.

Isa inched toward the briefcase, watching the men and freezing whenever one glanced over at her.

Wyn pushed his black-framed glasses up his regal nose and stated lowly, thinking she could not hear, "It sounded like brainwashing. Her eyes glazed over, and she started reciting mantras in a goddamn monotone."

"Pleasure conditioning prey is forbidden," Nic shot back with hands fisted at his sides. His jaw ticked in frustration as he shot a glance at Isa.

Isa froze and attempted to look as innocent and unassuming as possible. She even offered him a little wave.

She knew stealing a treat was wrong. Pets were supposed to be *given* treats; it was wrong to take one without her master's approval. But her body itched and hurt and ached, and she missed that flying in the clouds, bubbly joy that the pills gave her.

Nic frowned at her wave and looked back to Wyn and Alban. "Who would be brainwashing prey shifters? They'd have to be fucking fools to break such a rule."

Without their attention on her, Isa side-stepped closer to the briefcase beside the sofa. Her foot grazed the black leather exterior, and she shivered at the rush of *need* for what lay inside. *It's been too long since I've had a treat.*

Wyn said, "They have clearly managed to remain under the radar if we have not heard of them."

Nic snarled, "Did you hear the shit she was saying? I want to know who the fuck is brainwashing women to think it's their purpose to fuck their 'masters.' I want an address."

"Mafia lord Nic is back," Alban commented—not jokingly.

"They made her think of herself as an *actual* pet. A sex slave... *My* mate." Nic released a sound of pure disgust and rage. "I've burned people alive for less."

Isa bent to open the briefcase. She worried the

clinking sound of opening the metal clasp would alert the men to her actions. Something told her they would disagree with her "treating" herself to a treat.

She shifted the briefcase onto the rug and slightly behind the sofa so the men could not see. Now, if she could just open it quietly...

Alban clucked his tongue at Nic's words. "Prey shifter sex slavery is an extremely lucrative business. No one would stop just because a king 'ordered' it."

Wyn added, "If Hag found Isa at one of those compounds, to buy an Arctic hare shifter...It would have been millions of dollars."

Nic slammed a fist against the wall, awarding Isa the perfect loud noise to cover up the sound of opening the briefcase's metal clasp. "My mate is NOT a sex slave," Nic roared.

Isa dipped a hand inside the briefcase and pulled out a packet of the little blue pills. She hastily placed one onto her tongue and swallowed. There, that would help with the pain in her arm and shoulder.

Alban cleared his throat and told Nic, "I mean, not *anymore*."

"Do you think they..." Wyn's throat bobbed on an uncomfortable swallow. "Do you think they touched her?"

"If they did, they will have their hands ripped off their bodies right before their dicks," Nic snarled. "Pet shops are forbidden. And brainwashing? We're not goddamn basilisks with hypnosis party tricks. I want their names and addresses now."

"We need to know where Isa came from," Wyn added.

"Think Hag got a receipt?" Alban asked.

"This isn't a fucking joke," Nic snapped at the fox shifter.

Alban threw his hands in the air and asked, "Really? Because as far as I can tell, you've been wasting away the last two years of being *king* of the Arctic shifters while prey women get brainwashed for alpha dick worship."

Surprised at Alban's outburst, Nic's mouth fell open. "You're blaming *me?*"

The tension chilled the air in the room, but Isa stepped closer to the crackling fireplace and waited for her treat to kick in.

"If you want to act like you have no idea that prey are being mistreated, hunted, and sold as slaves—"

"You think I knew? I would *never* allow—"

Alban continued, "It's happening everywhere. Not just in the Arctic. There are pet shops and prey farms, and just about any other kind of demeaning, lucrative way to abuse prey shifters in our world." The fox shifter stated, "You're a wolf, born into royalty and strength. You have no idea what weaker shifters go through to survive. You've never had to..."

Isa rubbed her eyes as the new trickle of warmth floated through her. *Those treats act fast.* Were these faster than the normal ones, or had she forgotten their potency?

"You don't think *I* get it?" Nic sneered. "Do you not remember the years of my childhood I lost to Aleks? Have you forgotten the scars on top of scars? How he would make us *both* kneel and kiss his feet—"

"Yes, but you killed him, Nic," Alban said. "In the end, you got out. Why? Because you are a predator shifter with the strength to kill your enemies. It took a few years for your wolf to rise to full power, but you did it. Prey don't ever get free. You want to know the survival skills they are taught? They're not told to fight; they are taught how to *please* their enemies. Taught how to appeal to the shifters who would mistreat them—use them."

Nic scowled at Alban; rather, he scowled at the truth.

Meanwhile, Isa felt her balance tip, and she stumbled and caught herself on the ottoman close to the fireplace. *Mmm, time to lie down.*

Alban added, "The same way humans become people pleasers due to trauma and the desire to avoid triggering a negative response—prey are born into roles where they need to cater to predator shifters to survive."

Nic replied, "You say all that like you know it well. You're a predator too, Alban."

Isa stumbled to the couch and laid on it, stretching out her legs and feeling tingles in her bloodstream. Pleasure seeped through her, from her head to her toes.

Alban solemnly pursed his lips with a sigh and said to Nic, "Being a fox shifter or a Noctu shifter does not include deadly, super strength. We serve roles; we serve a purpose to those with more power. That's how this warped society of paranormals works. You can only be granted protection if you are useful to those with power."

Nic's eyes widened. He opened his mouth and then closed it. Hesitating and absorbing. "You truly feel that way? That I only have you here for a 'use?'"

Alban shrugged, but the nonchalant action did not match his tense shoulders and expression. "Wyn is your advisor, and I am the entertaining comedic relief for when you want to break something during one of your temper tantrums—I mean, masculine and mature rages."

"You are my *friends*," Nic said adamantly. "And even if you weren't... Alban, even if you had never been kind to me, I would have freed you from Aleks. I would have offered you protection—without sworn allegiance. *Everyone* deserves to be protected—"

Isa moaned.

Loudly.

The pill hit her and hit her hard.

Suddenly, her heartbeat raced in her chest, her blood heated, and her skin prickled with awareness. *Sensitivity.* "*Soooft*," she whispered dreamily as she petted the extraordinarily fuzzy blanket folded over the couch.

"What the fuck?" The three men bolted to Isa.

Wyn bent to his knees to get close to where she sat, and Nic threw a hand onto the back of the couch and leaned over her. Alban stood just behind, peeking around Nic's shoulder. Confused, the men stared at her as she smiled at them.

"Hi," she giggled out. She just felt so *good*. So free.

Good girls are obedient, and obedient pets get treats.

"Treats? What the fuck is she talking about?" Nic asked.

Ooops, guess I said that mantra aloud, she thought before letting her full attention fall on how Nic's bare chest remained on display. Still slightly gleaming with sweat Nic worked up earlier. *He didn't come. I want to make him come.* Who knew, maybe he would give her another treat later.

"Her eyes..." Wyn commented. Nic grabbed her chin and forced it side to side so they could examine her eyes.

"Pupils like goddamn saucers," Alban said. "Is she... high right now?"

"Did you take something?" Nic asked her roughly, still pinching her chin in a dominating way that made her want to lick his thumb. "What did you do, pet—Isa?"

She frowned. She liked it when he called her 'pet.' It was a literal pet name.

"Did—you—take—something?" Nic bit out, grinding each word between his molars.

Guilt. It flooded her even though her body felt floaty and tingly. Her smile faded, and she sniffled. "I...I know you don't like me sometimes, but I've been a good pet, and my arm hurt, and I deserved a treat."

Wyn began, "We have no way of knowing what she was brainwashed to think is a treat, what the drug might do to her—"

Before Wyn could finish his statement, Nic had already pressed a long finger into her mouth, trying to gag her.

She coughed onto his fingers at first. Then, she remembered her lesson about how to keep the gag reflex dormant. She proudly sucked his fingers deeper into her mouth until the tip touched the back of her throat. She twirled her tongue around the fingers, and he pulled them out with a curse.

"What the fuck did you do?" Nic shouted at her.

"I deserved a treat for being a good pet—"

"You are NOT a pet." Nic palmed her shoulders and shook them, jostling her around. "You have no master. You don't have to 'give pleasure to feel pleasure.' FUCK that. Do you hear me, Isa? No more treats. No more collars—"

"But you said you own me."

"Yes, but I don't..." Nic growled. "I *want* to own you. I want your body and soul tied to mine because of how *you* own *me*. You are your own person. No one deserves to actually be fucking *owned*."

"But you don't want to share me."

"That's because I'm goddamn selfish."

A loud knock came at the door.

"Who the hell is it?" Nic shouted from where he leaned over Isa on the couch.

The door creaked open, and the housekeeper, Miss Belsky—who had nicely helped Isa make gingerbread house cookie blocks and icing—poked her head inside the parlor. "Sir, er, your majesty, you've got visitors."

"What?" Wyn stood; his spine went ramrod straight as he entered professional mode. "Who?"

"The Polaris heir is here...and he says he wants to meet your prey mate."

CHAPTER 35

$\mathcal{I}$f someone asked Nic, "What's the worst thing that can occur to you," it was a toss-up between: 1) Finding out his mate was brainwashed to be a sex slave and thus doubting every moment in the past where she expressed interest in him, and 2) the Polaris bear faction of Arctic shifters who threatened his rule as king finding out he had a prey shifter as a mate like Nic's overthrown and dead brother had.

"What the fuck do you mean 'prey mate?'" Nic asked Miss Belsky. "I don't have a prey mate," Nic said steely.

Miss Belsky's gaze pointedly moved to Isa, who waved good-naturedly at her.

Nic pointed and said, "She is not my mate."

Isa poked a finger into Nic's cheek. "Mean," she said and giggled, high off whatever drug she had taken.

"She is not his mate." Alban nodded. "Apparently, she is a sex slave."

Nic turned and grabbed the collar of Alban's shirt, yanking him forward to growl in his face, "I'll fucking skin you alive if you imply—" Nic cut himself off when he saw Alban's that-was-a-test-you-idiot expression.

"Yeah, you're going to need to keep your cool and convince the Polaris that she is not your mate," Alban said dryly. "You were the one who said she can only be known as a sexual plaything. A mistress. Not queen."

Nic grimaced. The fox shifter was right, of course. But that was before he knew she had been brainwashed to only think of herself as a "pet."

Was that why, no matter how many times he pushed her away, she came right back to him? Because she thought she had to? Because she was brainwashed to? Did she even like Nic?

The people who did this to her will drown in a pool of their own blood.

"He is right," Wyn said. "You must not let it be known that she is your mate."

"I know," Nic grated.

"*Mmmmm*," Isa moaned again.

The men focused back on her. Her right hand had slipped between her legs to pet her bare pussy.

"Fuck." Nic grabbed her wrist and tore her fingers from her pussy.

"Please touch me," she begged, huge black pupils eating up her beautiful irises. "Everything feels so good."

"Alban, get her clothed and...try to sober her up. Wyn and I will go 'greet' the guests."

"Nic, what if the drug she took..." Alban rubbed a hand over the back of his neck and blushed. The self-proclaimed sex expert *blushed*. *Isa is changing all of us.* "What if she goes into heat with them here? More alpha predator shifter pheromones can push a prey to go into heat."

Nic bent down to make direct eye contact with Isa's blown-out pupils. She blinked slowly and smiled coyly at him.

"Look at me," he demanded. He pinched her chin and held her face still as she watched him with glazed-over eyes. He dropped his free hand down to cup her pussy, and she emitted a high-pitched shriek of need.

"You are only allowed to be horny for *me*," he warned, *squeezing* her pussy in his palm. "If you breathe in their scents and get wet for them, I swear to the fucking ice gods—"

"Nic." Alban rolled his eyes. "What part of 'she is brainwashed for alpha dick' are you not absorbing?"

"I may not own you, but you own me, and you are *mine*," he growled into her face as she dreamily stared at him with a sleepy smile. "Alban will show you to a safe room. You will stay there until I get you, and we will both get out of this alive."

"What about them?" Wyn asked, referring to the Polaris shifters who had just walked in and requested an audience with the king.

"Whether they walk out of here alive remains to be seen."

"*D*amn it, hurry up and put these on," Alban fussed as he urged Isa to get dressed in one of her new outfits from the local boutique.

"I wanna *play*," she whined.

Her treat had her floating through the room and dancing without music. Her hips swayed and rolled, and she grinned when she noticed Alban check out the way her ass moved to the inaudible beat.

She asked, "Don't you want to play with me?"

"Baby, I wanna play the fuck out with you. But we can't right now. Cause some massive Polar bear shifters are meeting with Nic right now, and they need to be reassured that Nic does not have a prey shifter as a mate."

Isa pouted as Alban flung some knee socks at her to put on her feet. "Why would that be so bad?" she asked, bummed out that her treat was going to waste. She wanted to lay back and fade and touch herself and relax into the pleasure. "Why can't anyone know about me?"

"Because the last time an Arctic king made a prey shifter his queen, she was killed in an extremely graphic way and left under a Christmas tree for Nic's older brother to find."

That helped distract Isa from the tingles running up and down her limbs. "What?"

"To this day, no one knows who did it, but it could have been anyone. There were rumors about an uprising as soon as Nic's brother announced he had a prey mate. Predators do not react well to thinking a physically weaker species should be granted power over them. It's a fucked-up system, but Nic has slowly been trying to change it." Alban tossed another article of clothing at her. "Here, put this on."

A red velvet dress—she petted and swooned at the soft material.

"Focus and get dressed for me, bunny. We need to get you, not-naked, into the safe room, then I need to go help Nic convince the big, bad, traditional jackass bears that Nic is just keeping you as a sexual pet and nothing more."

Isa's heart hurt. Nic's yells still rang in her head. *"You are NOT a pet. You don't have to 'give pleasure to feel pleasure.' FUCK that."* He made it sound like he saw her as more than a pet. Like he could see her as his equal. As his mate.

But now, around others, he wishes me to act as a pet once more. How could the idea of it offend him so much in private, but he was fine with her being known as a pet in public?

She rubbed at her chest, the sensation of which distracted her again. *Even the lightest touch against my skin feels like...*

"Isa," Alban called her name softly. "You need to get dressed. Do I need to dress you myself?"

Isa pouted and lifted her right arm up; she struck a pose.

"Okay," Alban murmured through a gentle smirk and lifted the dress over her head, aligning the arm holes to best ease her cast through. "There."

He let the deep burgundy velvet fall around her, bouncing down to cover the tops of her thighs. He bent down to guide her feet into the white knee socks, and he yanked them up her calves.

"Okay." Stepping back, Alban nodded at her dressed state. "Let's go."

"Do you think he does see me as more than a plaything?" Isa asked, still swaying a bit. "Do you think he cares about me?"

"Isa..." Alban cupped her cheeks and lifted her face to stare her down with his bright blue eyes. Alban sighed and stroked his thumb over her cheekbone as he pressed his forehead to hers. "Isa, in my years of knowing Nic, I have never seen him care about anything

more than trying *not* to care about you. Do you understand that?"

Blinking, she replied, "No."

"Okay, let me try again. Yes. He cares about you. You
are one of the first things he has cared about in a long,
long time. He...he cannot afford to lose you. Not after
everything else he has lost in his life. Okay?"

Isa nodded slowly.

"So, can you please hide in Nic's secret room?"

CHAPTER 36

"*I* was sorry to hear about your brother," Nic said kind words even though his tone was as sharp and deadly as high-hanging icicles.

"I was not so sorry to hear about yours."

Nic held the butter knife a little *too* tightly in his fist.

Kendrick, the current heir of the clan of Polaris shifters, shrugged and tossed his long, icy blond locks over his shoulder. "I suppose we do have that in common. Second sons not born to rule and yet…" He smugly smirked and heavily sipped from the wine glass in front of him at the dining room table.

Polaris shifters really were massive. Kendrick's broad shoulders and wide build took up two dining set plates. *And his ego is even fucking bigger*, Nic thought to himself, grumbling under his breath.

Kendrick added, "Sending you off into a blizzard was

the best thing your father ever did. Hardened you. Made you ruthless. I don't know that any Polaris would have willingly taken direction from a wolf if you had not taken power."

"Yes, my ruthlessness is well known," Nic remarked, bored, and bit into a buttered bread roll. Maybe occupying his mouth with chewing would stop him from impulsively throwing out an insult or asking them to get the fuck out of his castle.

"I heard you once fed someone tomato soup that ended up being the blood of his—"

"Why are you here?" Nic asked coldly. Unfeelingly. This was the emotional state he was most familiar with. Isa was somewhere else in his home, and he slipped right back into his old demeanor without her present and staring at him with her big, innocent eyes.

"To meet your prey mate, obviously."

Nic's chest rumbled with a swallowed-down growl. "As I have already stated, the prey shifter is not my mate. She is a pet I am biding my time with. Indulging in."

"Truly?" Kendrick asked, sporting a suspiciously large grin. "I've never heard of a king buying thousands of dollars' worth of clothes for his sexual pet. I thought the whole point was to keep her naked at all times? Better access. Does spending money on her make her pussy feel more expensive?"

Do not stab his throat. Do not stab his throat, Nic repeated to himself. Wyn stared a hole into the side of

Nic's head, surely chanting the same sentence from where he sat a few chairs down at the long wooden table.

"The more clothing I buy for her, the more clothing I can rip from her delicious body any moment I desire," Nic said.

Kendrick snickered and nodded. "She must be a sexy little thing, then."

Nic did not know which word more made him want to scoop Kendrick's eyeballs out with a spoon: "sexy" or referring to Isa as a "thing."

"I never would've pegged you as a man to keep a prey pet," Kendrick said as he tipped back his glass and drained the rest of the wine. He motioned to Miss Belsky to fill his cup again. "Not just because your brother was a prey lover, but I just always heard you were ice cold. No interest in women or passion. I thought wolf shifters tended to stay pure for their mates." Kendrick lifted an eyebrow. "Why have a pet *now?*"

Nic plunged his butter knife into the glazed wooden table top, causing Miss Belsky to gasp and glare at the blade sticking through what had to be an antique.

Nic slammed a hand to the table and said, "You come here with no invitation, guzzle some of the finest wine in the region like it is fucking apple juice, and question why I've taken a lover? Since when does someone dare question whatever the fuck I choose to do?"

Kendrick sat up straighter in the high-back chair. Even though the Polaris bear stood at well over six and a half feet tall and his arm was as thick as the tree trunk Isa had sawed through, Nic was the king of all Arctic shifters. Polaris shifters were large and strong, but wolves were fast and vicious.

Nic would not accept any goddamn disrespect.

"I believe the real purpose of your visit was to assess if I have a new weakness," Nic stated to the three Polaris bears who sat at his dining room table and enjoyed wine from his mother's prized collection. "You planned to come here and what? Decide whether I had real feelings for a prey? See if I was a changed man? Weak like my brother and overthrow me?"

*I*sa pouted and played with her thumbs as she waited for Nic to send away the Polaris shifter and return to her. Alban had taken her to a hidden room full of bookshelves, candlelight, and dusty paintings. It appeared to be a lounge of some sort, but the space felt...tense. Lonely.

She sighed deeply and paced back and forth in front of the wide sofa.

The doorknob turned, and the door creaked open to

the room. *That was fast,* Isa thought, but she ran forward to hug her first intruder.

But it was not one of her men.

Isa's arms wrapped around an older woman.

"Hello!" the woman coughed out in cheery surprise. "And what is an elf doing in my library?"

An elf? Isa glanced down at herself. Alban had dressed her in a wine-red velvet dress and white knee-high socks. He had also stuck a candy cane to hang from her cleavage.

"I am not an elf," Isa told the woman who appeared in her early eighties. For a shifter with slow aging, she was…very old.

The woman smirked. "You don't say."

"I am Nic's, um, pet. Uh, plaything," Isa said, obeying the men's wishes. A plaything—was that all she would ever be to him?

"Plaything?" The older woman snorted. "My grandson does not have playthings. He never learned to *play* a day in his life."

Grandson? "You are…"

"Nicolas Sokolov's only living relative. His grand-mother, yes."

Unable to stop herself, Isa shot forward to hug the woman again. This time, she squeezed her even tighter. *Someone close to Nic.* "It is so nice to meet you."

The woman chuckled and patted Isa's back. "I am not used to hugs."

"I love giving hugs."

"So, why are you in my room, elf?" The woman extracted herself from Isa's arms and moved to the corner of the room where a rocking chair and a half-knitted scarf sat. She picked up knitting needles and a ball of yarn.

"I was told to hide in here," Isa told her. "Until the Polaris leaves."

"A visiting Polaris?" Nic's grandmother whistled. "That's not good. Those bears have never liked taking orders from a wolf."

"It's why they hid me in here," Isa said. Her distaste for being kept in small spaces was evident from her glum tone.

The grandmother shrugged and began knitting more yarn onto the scarf. Isa watched, fascinated. "Nicolas used to lock himself in here," the woman said.

"Lock himself...willingly?" Isa asked, confounded by the idea. "Why would anyone want to be locked in a room?" Isa had hated it at her tribe's compound when they kept her inside.

"To Nicolas, being trapped, alone, was to be safe. Though he did allow me to join him on occasion. I used to knit right here while he hid from his father."

"Hide? Like a game of hide and seek? I have never played that."

"More like a game of hide when his father drank scotch."

"It does not sound very fun." Isa's nose scrunched. "I would never like to be locked in a room."

Isa flinched when she realized Nic's grandmother *liked* this dusty room. She did not want to insult her, so she rushed to add, "Not that it is, uh, not a nice room. It is very...pretty. I like the stacks of paintings over there. I looked through them and, well, I don't understand why they would be leaning up against the wall in here when they could be where people could see them."

"That is something Nic inherited from his mother." Nic's grandmother's frown lines deepened. "He witnessed his mother put valuable items in a locked room or a safe or protective plastic. She cared more about protecting the things she loved than enjoying them."

"What about Christmas gifts?" Isa asked. "Surely, she enjoyed those."

Nic's grandmother's lips quirked at the edges as she knitted and stared at Isa with an amused expression. "There are some people who do not understand the *use* of gifts beyond protecting and preserving them."

"The use of gifts?" Isa asked.

"For happiness, dear." Nic's grandmother paused her knitting needles.

"Did Nic enjoy his gifts?"

The woman snorted and went back to knitting. "Nic has never received a nice thing in his life. I don't think he would know what to do with it."

"But...he received gifts on Christmas?"

The grandmother blinked several times, trying to tell whether Isa was real or not. "Nyet. Nic was not favored by his father, which made him not favored by his mother. He was... Nic was born with a damaged leg, which is worse when he shifts."

His grandmother frowned and added, "His father was unwilling to be associated with anything that could appear as a weakness. He sent Nic out in the cold when he was only nine years old."

Nine years old...wandering the frozen landscape alone...like Isa? Isa had her mother, but after she passed away, Isa had tried to survive on her own before her tribe took her in and housed and fed her.

What tribe had taken Nic in?

"Nic's father was a cold man. I pray every day that Nic does not become him."

"Why would he?" Isa asked.

"The wounds our parents give us, dear," Nic's grandmother muttered softly. "Nic's father taught Nic that weakness is death."

"Nic believes I am weak," Isa said. "He thinks that if I am around him, I will die."

"Men really learn the strangest things from trauma." His grandmother sighed. "He most likely does not think *you* are weak. He sees you as one of *his* weaknesses. Because he cares for you."

"He has not said that he does. He says that I am his and how much he loves my pussy—"

"Dear gods."

Isa continued, "But he has never said he *likes* me." After all, Isa was not really his mate. As far as the spell was concerned, all she triggered in him was lust.

But I want more.

"*Mealee.*" Russian for *darling*. His grandmother shook her head and asked, "Were you not listening? Nic only protects that which he loves. And for Nic, he believes protecting is locking something away from harm, even if it means he cannot enjoy it while it is being protected." His grandmother shot her a pointed look and lifted an eyebrow.

"Like...me?" Isa wondered aloud. "He keeps trying to lock me up, but...I don't want to be locked up."

"Sounds to me like you need to show him that he can *enjoy* his gifts instead of just 'keeping' them."

Isa grinned ear to ear and walked right up to the door to leave and find Nic. "I am going to go find him right now and tell him I like him too." She turned back to say, "Thank you, Nic's grandmother."

"You're welcome," she replied. "Nic's 'plaything.'"

CHAPTER 37

*I*sa walked right into the dining room, and Nic nearly had a heart attack. Had they not stressed enough that she was to remain hidden for her own safety?

Amid the peaking tension between Kendrick and Nic, Isa strode right inside and stole all of Nic's attention.

She wore white knee-high socks with a lace trim at the top that Nic wanted to peel off her using only his teeth. A wine-red velvet dress cinched her waist and fell over the tops of her thighs.

Nic had liked the dress at the boutique, but now, in front of Kendrick, it was too short. Too revealing. The velvet panels crossed over her chest and showed off lines of cleavage. Cleavage that if Nic caught Kendrick staring at, Nic was pretty sure he would murder the bear shifter with the slim, dull butter knife.

Isa also sucked on a candy cane. Lewdly. Her red lips —who the hell had put lipstick on her?—pursed and ran up and down the red and white striped candy. Her pink tongue flashed several times as she licked and sucked on it.

Kendrick blew out an impressed exhale as he said, "Wow. Got her dressed up like a Christmas present."

Isa followed Nic's orders and did not look at or speak to the Polaris bear shifters. She slinked over to Nic and slipped the candy cane from her mouth. She held the red and white candy out for him, offering him a lick, but he shook his head and clamped a hand over the back of her skull.

He was not putting on a show as he pulled her forward and smashed his lips to hers, tasting the minty sweetness. He just could not help himself.

Could the gods be cruel enough to gift him such a mate, only for him to learn she was conditioned to desire him? Nic knew all too well what it was like to not be wanted.

Abruptly ending the kiss, Nic wiped his sticky mouth with his forearm and smirked as Isa dazedly blinked like the kiss had put her in a trance.

"Huh," Kendrick muttered.

Isa's arousal scented the air, and Nic bit his tongue. His palm, as if magnetized to touch her, skimmed down the back of her dress and palmed her ass. He squeezed, and she mewled.

Lusty mate.

Nic's cock thickened behind his trousers, and he wracked his brain for how to act to ensure Kendrick and his men believed Isa was nothing but a sexual pet to him. He scooted his chair back, pissing off Miss Belsky by allowing the legs to scrape the hardwood floor.

Nic patted his lap for Isa to sit on him, and she immediately obeyed.

Does she obey me because she thinks she has to?

Then, Isa whispered to him, "I think you *liiiiiike* me."

Dear gods, she was still high on whatever drug she took.

"Bunny," Alban called to her. He gave her the universal *"hush"* signal. She pressed her lips together and pouted.

"As I was saying," Nic continued, addressing Kendrick. "I believe the real purpose of your visit was to assess if I have a new weakness," Nic stated to the three Polaris bears who sat at his dining room table and enjoyed wine from his mother's prized collection. "You planned to come here and what? Decide whether I had real feelings for a prey? See if I was a changed man?"

"Are you?" Isa whispered as she nuzzled her face into his neck. Nic's body stiffened at her comment. With alpha hearing, Kendrick could most definitely hear her.

Nic asked, "Did you come to assess if I was weak like my brother and overthrow me?"

Kendrick rolled his eyes. "You are so damn paranoid." Kendrick looked to Isa as he jokingly asked, "How does a man that jaded come? Tell me, pet, does he ever let his guard down?"

Nic held the back of Isa's head, cradling her as she nuzzled deeper into him, pressing small kisses over his neck. "Tell me that was not the purpose of your visit," Nic replied—as calmly as he could with his mate kissing his neck. "And do not speak directly to my pet again."

Kendrick whistled. "Very territorial."

"She is *my* pet." At the ownership in his tone, Isa moaned softly. But how could she be happy with only being referred to as a *pet*?

MATE, his wolf growled in his head.

Queen.

Kendrick sniffed the air. "She smells as if you've been sharing her."

"Do not get any ideas like she would be shared with you." Nic's fingers tangled in Isa's hair. *Mine.*

"I am a lonely clan leader, myself." Kendrick laid a palm over his heart. "Where could I find a pet so pretty and obedient? I thought pet shops were outlawed."

"Admit to why you visited," Nic demanded.

"We do not care if you have a prey mate, my king," Kendrick said. "Yes, I did wish to see her, but your father was the one who believed a prey queen would be your family's undoing. The Polaris care if you will start acting like the ruthless Underworld king you were before getting the 'official' crown through nepotism."

Nic's free hand—the one not mindlessly touching Isa —reached over to play with a new butter knife. The first knife still stood upright, stabbed into the table.

Wyn stepped in with an, "I believe you mean hereditary monarchy."

"Nepotism implies I ever had favor from my family —which I did not," Nic said.

At that statement, Isa planted her lips firmly onto Nic's neck and sucked hard. Like she wanted to suck his sad past right out of him.

I...care for her.

"Yes, of course," Kendrick said. "You used to paint doors of the town with the blood of Arctic shifters' enemies. To buy your 'pet' clothing was the first time you have been seen in town in...a while."

"Others run my errands for me."

"The vampires attacked our clan, destroyed my brother, and the Polaris have yet to see the icy, terrifying Nicolas Sokolov, mafia lord of all of Russia, now king of all Arctic shifters, do a fucking thing about it."

"You wish me to end all of the vampires in the Arctic? Some may be innocent."

"They are all goddamn leeches, and they are becoming more and more of a nuisance. They come to our region for the longer hours of darkness and feast. They leave blood-drained bodies out on the street."

"Do you know where they reside during the sunlight?" Nic asked.

"Somewhere none of us can fucking find," Kendrick muttered. "So, you can understand why, after learning our king had enough free time on his hands to adopt a prey fuck toy pet—"

The butter knife speared into Kendrick's eye before the man could blink. It flew from Nic's nimble fingers and hit with expert accuracy and aim.

Kendrick cried out and cupped his eye, not immediately removing the knife. The other two Polaris shifters Kendrick brought with him stood from their seats, ready for battle. They paused and hesitated when Nick picked up a fork and twirled it in his fingers.

Nic patted Isa's head and moved her off his lap as he stood.

He twirled the sharp silver fork in his fingers as blood ran down Kendrick's face from across the table. "My time away has clearly led to selective memory of how you are permitted to speak to your king," Nic said. "You should have sent a formal complaint. You should have asked me for help. Instead, you came in here acting like you have a speck of power—which you don't."

Nic tsked as he stepped around the table, moving closer to Kendrick. "My father exiling me out into a blizzard as a child did harden me; you were right about that. I learned a lot during my formative years. I learned that trust is a slow-acting poison. I learned that those who are stronger often believe they are better than others. I learned that families will kill each other for power."

I will never forget the way Father bragged about causing my brother's death or the sound of dear ole dad's neck cracking in my hands.

"You want to know how an exiled wolf prince rose to more power in the Arctic than any before—*not* a Polaris? Because you motherfuckers don't know how to fucking *think*." Nic shoved Kendrick's head down, breaking the man's nose on his mother's expensive porcelain.

"Fuck!" Bleeding, Kendrick cursed. "Do you wish for war?"

Nic released him and stared down the other two Polaris, who remained frozen in fear of losing an eye. "You bear shifters say whatever you want, no matter how stupid, because you believe your brawns give you power. But real power is learning to be everywhere. Real power is hearing and knowing everything. You would be surprised what a lone fox overhears, camouflaged in the white snow."

"You bring me a problem you created and ask me to fix it," Nic remarked. "You invited vampires here to kill your heir, your own brother, so you could step into power. And what was the next step? To come for my crown?"

Kendrick's eyes—or, rather, *eye*—widened, blood still dripping from his other. "I—"

"Wyn, have juniper and allicin essence put in the water supply and send nightshade to every household. That should immediately end the vamp feedings," Nic instructed without looking at his advisor. "And invite every vampire to a dinner party here. I would like to 'chat' with those who have stepped out of line."

"Yes, my king," the Noctu replied in a tone of pride like he was *proud* to serve his king. Nic forgot what that sounded like.

"As for you, Kendrick, I suggest you leave before I spread the word of how you inflicted pain onto our region to secure your own power. If I ever hear you use a term like 'fuck toy' to refer to a prey or female of any kind again, I will cut that tongue out and ensure it never grows back."

"We could overtake you. Easily," Kendrick spit out, along with some blood trailing over his lips. "You think others will choose to follow you once they hear you have a prey mate? I will—"

"See? A Polaris who doesn't fucking think before he speaks." Nic thrust the fork in his hand into Kendrick's other eye. The man shrieked, and Isa gasped at the violence.

She will think I am a monster, Nic thought.

Good. He had only been trying to tell her that since the beginning.

*I*sa finally saw it—the reason Nic believed he had to rule through coldness and cruelty. *Because that is all he has known.* Did she really have any chance at changing him? Did she *want* to change him? When the bulky stranger had referred to Isa as a "fuck toy," she had personally felt inclined to violence.

What if she was not just changing Nic, but he was changing her in return?

"I *hope* she isn't your mate," the burly stranger said, gurgling through the blood dripping into his mouth. "A prey would never survive you."

The comment struck Nic as if the words were a physical blow. Isa watched as Nic's lips parted, and he stumbled back a step behind the bleeding man's chair.

Isa moved forward and hugged Nic from behind. She burrowed her face into his back and whispered, "He is wrong."

Nic held her hands, keeping her arms wrapped around his stomach. "Nyet, he is not. Being with me is a death warrant." To Wyn and Alban, the king said, "Get them the hell out."

Isa hugged Nic harder as the men were ushered out of the room.

Once they were alone, she told him, "You were very

brave. Thank you for defending me. Thank you for… making me feel safe. I…I know I have not known you for very long, and you have not always been very nice to me…but I like you. I do."

Nic hung his head and groaned.

"I really do," she assured him. "It's not the, um, brain-washing, or whatever you guys called it. I like the way you care—you care so much, even when you pretend to care about nothing. You threatened that woman to give me her scarf because you knew I liked it."

"I threaten many people."

"You tried so hard to make that gingerbread house—for me. Because you knew I cared about it."

"Isa—"

She kept going. "I also like the way you blink at me when I surprise you, and I like how you smile like your lips are rusty at it. Like I'm one of the few things that amuse you and bring you joy. I love the way, when we were both dying of poison, you made them help me first. You were willing to die so I could live."

"Death is not a fear of mine."

"I know. Living is. But I can make it less scary. We'll live together and be happy, and I will show you how fun it is to write thank-you notes and to hug people. I know you've never gotten any gifts on Christmas before, and even though I don't have any money, I am going to *spoil* you with gifts. So many gifts, and you will have to enjoy them like you will enjoy me. And we will go ice skating—"

Nic squeezed her hands, and she paused. She flashed him an excited, innocent, and naïve smile.

In a tortured voice, Nic rasped, "I cannot keep you, Isa."

CHAPTER 38

"You...You are going to return me?" Isa asked, and her voice broke. Her voice broke just like her heart. The vital organ shattered into chards of icy, frosted arteries and tissue, just floating around like debris inside her ribcage.

A pet's greatest shame was to be returned. To be found inadequate. Unlovable.

Even worse, a pet in her tribe was only allowed one return in its life. Was that the future Hag saw for her: Isa not injecting Nic with enough holiday spirit for him to keep her?

"No," she mumbled through heaving breaths as her anxiety spiked.

Her frantic heart beat so fast in her chest—could he hear it? Would he keep her if he feared she might have another heart attack?

"Please don't take me back there. Please, no," she cried. "I deserve to be free; I was a good pet."

He pulled her face into his chest, clutched the back of her head, and stroked her back. "Nyet, no," Nic cooed to calm her. "I will not return you to...wherever you came from. In fact, I will burn those twisted fuckers to the ground. But Isa, it is not safe for you to be with me, and I cannot—" Nic cut off and sucked in a sharp breath. "I cannot let you die."

"I won't," she said, tears streaming down her face and dampening his shirt. "I am not delicate."

"Yes." Nic laughed. The sound was so hoarse and husky—like his rusted vocal cords had not performed such a thing in a long time. "Yes, you are. You are so delicate. So breakable. You are so pure and kindhearted and joyful. To watch that fade or be snuffed out... I cannot allow it."

"Then, tell everyone I am just a pet," she said.

Desperation flowed through her veins. The threat of going back into a cage. Of losing not just Nic but also Wyn and Alban. Her first...*friends.*

Friends she wanted to sex up and cuddle and stroke their hair as she listened to their dreams.

"That was the plan, right?" she asked. "As long as I'm not the queen. As long as they don't know I'm your mate."

"You wish to keep up a façade where you are treated like a common whore?"

"I want to *stay.*" *Anything to stay.*

"No." Nic palmed the back of her head and held her tighter. "It is not fair to you. You deserve better."

"Then, give me better!" she commanded. "You cannot make these choices for me. A dangerous life as a mate or a degrading life as a pet. I was prepared to be a pet my entire life—I had looked forward to it. *You* are the one saying I deserve more, yet you won't give it to me?"

Isa laid her palms over his pectoral muscles. Could she feel for evidence that he had a heart? She said, "Do not tell me I am worth more than a pet but not worthy of being a queen."

"Isa…"

"You are really just going to let me go? No." Isa fisted her hands and shoved them against his chest, hitting him with her pent-up frustration. "I am your mate."

But she wasn't. Not really.

The becharmed bracelet made him think she was. *But I want to be. I want to be the person who eases his tense shoulders and makes him smile.*

She told him, "You can't keep pulling me forward only to push me away. It's not fair. If you would just let us have fun and enjoy Christmas, everything will be fine."

"What is with your obsession with Christmas, huh?" he asked, pulling her head back by her hair so she had to look at him. "Why do you keep acting like it has some mystical powers to heal the past? It doesn't."

"When the Grinch realized—"

"I am not the Grinch," Nic exclaimed, exasperated. He removed his arms from her and moved over to where the bottle of wine sat on the table, keeping his back to her.

"Christmas is about forgiveness and kindness and giving," she said. "It's a time when a reindeer with a glowing red nose can feel useful. When people realize it's not important *what* you have in life but who you share it with. When Scrooges realize it's never too late to change. When—"

"Are you done?" Nic's fingers wrapped around the neck of the wine bottle and lifted it to his lips. After taking a few long sips, he wiped his mouth on his sleeve and scowled at her. "You know, I always thought mates were supposed to accept you exactly as you are, not want to change you and compare you to the Grinch."

Was that true? Isa knew so little of mates, but…even after such a short amount of time, she felt as if she knew Nic. "But you're not," she said. "You're not as you are."

"You're making no sense again, little prey."

"Wyn and Alban see it. I see it," she said. "You act as if you live in your own little snow globe of power and blizzards and self-destructive behaviors and hard decisions. But you're not alone. There are other people in the snow globe, there to help you and keep you company and love you—"

"Are you really trying to psychoanalyze me?"

"Do you wish me to 'convince' you that I should stay another way?" she asked in a harsh tone she was not previously capable of. She fingered the velvet material over her chest, peeling it back just an inch to flash him more of her breasts. "Is this how I am supposed to beg to stay? To prove my worthiness to you?"

It felt so new, this emotion. *Anger.*

Even as Nic scowled at her words, his gaze ate up the additional cleavage she showed him. "I had gone a lifetime without sex before. I can do so again," he stated.

"Oh?" she questioned and strode closer to where he leaned against the table.

She stole the wine bottle from his hands and flexed her tongue against the bottom of the glass neck of the bottle. She licked all the way up, tasting the drops of wine that had dripped to the side and clung there.

Nic watched the obscene and explicit way she ran her wicked tongue over the length and cursed, "Fuck."

"You really think that once you've tasted me, you can go without?" she asked him in a breathy, suggestive voice as she stepped closer.

She laid the bottle on the table behind him and let her wrist graze his ass as she returned her hand to her side.

She reached behind her neck and untied the red velvet straps holding up the top of the dress. She would need help with the zipper, but for now, the fabric fell just enough to reveal the full swells of her breasts and how they moved with her breaths.

"You are going to say goodbye to *these* after only feeling them and sucking them for a few days?" she purred onto his shoulder, wishing she were tall enough to reach his ear on her own. "If you send me away now, they will be like the ghosts of Christmas past and haunt you."

She leaned back and demonstrated petting the soft skin of her breasts. "You'll dream about them. How they moved while I rode you. How good they feel when you cup them. You'll wake up, hard and dripping pre-cum, at the idea of my tight nipples reaching out for your mouth..."

Nic's enthralled expression was so goddamn hot.

His half-lidded eyes were glued to her chest with no reluctance or hesitation. His lips were parted as his tongue darted out to wet them like he imagined licking the hard, stiff peaks of her nipples.

There was a hopeless fight playing out over his features as if he wished she had less power over him but could not help falling under the spell of lust she cast.

"Don't you want to touch them, even now?" she asked alluringly. "They are so heavy; don't you want to cup them and feel their weight in your warm palms?"

"I..."

"You love how good they feel in your hands. Don't you want to touch them?"

Nic growled deeply and snapped, "Fuck, I do."

"Then, do it. Touch them. Squeeze them. They are yours to play with. Play with them."

His large palms rose and sank just under the swells of her breasts. His warm skin settled under the curves and cupped.

"No, you want to do more than that," she whispered. "*Play* with them. Show my body who it belongs to."

CHAPTER 39

"*S*how my body who it belongs to."

Another guttural growl of weakening self-control poured from Nic. His fingers clamped down into the soft, pliable flesh of her breasts. His thumb pressed and pulled her nipple down, making her whimper.

What had started as a seduction of the king was now a seduction of herself. Her lower abdomen swirled with need as her pussy tingled between her legs.

"Look how hard you are," she purred as she stared down at the enlarged bulge tenting his pants. "Just from one touch of my breasts. So hard and thick. So much cum to give me and only me."

Nic released a vicious, provocative noise of frustration and lust.

"If you send me away, how are you going to deal with

all that cum? You're going to be thinking about how good my pussy wraps around your cock every hour. You're going to be constantly hard. You had gone without sex all your life, but now you know what it feels like when I ride you so fast that your eyes roll back in your head."

"FUCK." Nic gripped her by the waist and turned her onto the table.

He laid her back onto the cool wood and used his forearm to push away plates, silverware, and expensive, black smoke stem-wine glasses. He laid his face between her breasts and snarled.

She reached down to tenderly stroke her fingers over the bulging crotch of his pants.

His cock was a thick, warm length filling and stretching the fabric. She wanted him bare in her hands. She wanted to jerk him off and watch his face as he realized he could never give her up.

He ripped apart the front seam of his pants and shoved his underwear down to his knees, flashing his veined, stiff erection and full, seed-laden balls.

She lustily moaned for him, reaching for him, but he took her free hand and restrained it so she could not touch him. After all, with the cast, she was one-handed when it came to the seduction. *Losing power of the situation.*

"You are playing very dirty, *zayka*." Still, he dove his

mouth over her nipples and sucked like he had waited a millennium for the chance.

She gasped out as wetness leaked from between her legs, "You like me when I'm dirty."

"I like you—always," he admitted onto her breasts, laving and sucking and nipping at the sensitive skin.

Then, keep me, she wanted to shout at him. Instead, she asked, "How are you going to give this up, huh?" She bucked her hips to try to rub against his cock. "How are you going to go a day without my touch?"

He snarled, "I don't—fucking—know."

She panted and reached for him. "Let me touch you."

"*Nyet*," he bit out.

"Let me stroke your cock. *Please*."

"No."

A mixture of anger and desperate lust raged inside her as he pinned her down to the table. "You think you'll be able to just drop me off somewhere and not return immediately?" she asked. "You know how wet I am right now. You can scent it in the air. I'm so hot and wet for you, Nic."

Nic. Was that the first time she called him by his name?

She continued, "Do you think you'll be able to resist slipping that hard cock inside me right now?"

Every sexy word she said seemed to break more and more of his resolve. His gaze on her just grew hungrier and hungrier.

"You know how good it will feel," she said. "You know how my pussy will grip you and demand all of that cum. You know how I will drain you."

"Fucking stop talking," he commanded as he leaned back and gazed at where the skirt of her dress fell to flash her luscious, smooth legs.

"Are you going to send me away without looking at it one more time?"

He growled and tore the bottom fabric of her dress in half, all the way up to her stomach to reveal her little, white lace panties.

"Remember how good your cum filled me up? I could be pregnant and carrying your heir—"

"*Shut up.*" He snatched her panties down her legs, baring her pussy.

He wrenched open her thighs to get a better look. His eyelids fell to half-mast as he inhaled her scent.

"Mmm, how are you going to stay away from this?" she asked. "How will you stop yourself from sinking inside me right now? I'm so wet, you would slide right in. Think of how good it will feel to bury that hard cock inside me and feel the *squeeze*—"

"*Ugh,*" Nic grunted as he thrust inside her in one smooth move.

His body vibrated above hers. He clenched his eyes shut and flexed his jaw as his expression became one of struggling for self-control.

He stayed completely still, leaving his pulsing length

stretching her inner walls and scraping against a deep, ribbed spot inside her that caused a loud moan from her.

"*Yes*," she hissed and wiggled, trying to gyrate on his cock since he remained as still as a statue. "Feel how good we fit?"

"*Perfect*," he agreed.

"A perfect fit. Fuck, you fill me up so good."

"*My* pussy," he growled, sounding much more animal than man. Was his inner wolf rising up?

I want his claiming bite. Would he send her away then?

"Yes, your pussy," she said as she whimpered and rocked her hips. "Yours. Mark it so no one else thinks they can have it."

He glared, knowing exactly what she was trying to do.

S *he has no idea what she is trying to do*, Nic thought to himself as he grappled with holding back his inner wolf.

CLAIM. BITE. FUCK. KEEP. BREED.

His wolf had many demands, all of which Nic tried *not* to grant. Yes, he was currently cock-deep inside her, but that did not mean he *had* to fuck her. Did not mean he had to come inside her again and risk getting her pregnant.

"Please, you know I am yours," she said. "Don't you want to warn away other males? If you drop me off somewhere, someone else might try to claim me—"

"Stop it," he grated and pushed his hips forward, spearing her further onto his cock.

"It's the truth. An unmated female prey with a wet pussy, waiting to be sated. Others will covet me."

"Stop," Nic snapped and shoved inside her harder.

"Does a real alpha abandon his mate?" she asked.

Nic glared down at her and nipped her throat. "I know what you are trying to do. You are trying to talk to my wolf."

"Yes," she admitted plainly, looking so deeply into Nic's eyes that his wolf howled at the attention. "Mister Wolf, how can you let him abandon me? How can you give up your mate? Don't I make you feel so good when I…"

She clamped her inner muscles, causing her pussy to tighten into a fierce squeeze, leaving Nic breathless and his back bowing for a moment.

"Damn it, I am not 'abandoning' you. I am trying to keep you safe."

"By leaving me all alone?" She twisted her wrist free of his grip and palmed his muscular back. She let her nails dig into his lower spine. "Leaving me without any protection?"

PROTECT WITH LIFE, Nic's wolf roared.

"You won't need protection once you're far from me," Nic replied.

"How are you going to live without me?" she asked. "I have known you only a few days, and I can't imagine living without you and Alban and Wyn."

"Because you're fucking brainwashed," Nic shouted at her and slammed a fist onto the dining table.

He retreated, pulling himself out of her and stumbling back. He gazed at her in horror and shame—he could not believe he had started fucking her after trying to break things off entirely.

CUM IN MATE. BREED HER.

He ignored his wolf, creating distance between him and Isa, and told her, "You have been brainwashed by some goddamn cult to think that you are a sex pet. You do not care for me, Isa. You couldn't. In so little time? With how coldly I have acted toward you? In no real moment have I redeemed myself in your eyes. You just… you just don't know what life has to offer you. You think this—being with me—is it."

"That's not true, don't tell me what I think." She sat up from the table and pulled up the velvet straps of her neckline to cover her breasts. She crossed her arms and said, "Don't act like you know."

"It may hurt at first, but maybe that will help you snap out of your…training. I will find a nice village for you to live in."

"Abandoning a pet seems worse than returning her."

Nic sighed as he tucked away his erection. "Isa."

"All you seem to want is loyalty and for people to accept you as king. Loyalty, trust, and acceptance. Well, you cannot expect to receive something you do not give. Being cold and numb does not breed devotion."

"Devotion," Nic snorted. "You think I need love?"

"I think you need it more than your next breath."

"Zayka..."

"Okay, the riffraff is gone," Alban announced as he reentered the living room, dusting off and clapping his hands for a job well done. Alban paused when he noticed Nic's ripped fly and Isa's torn dress. "Wow, a quickie after such a tense moment? Does eyeball blood turn you on, bunny?"

Nic did not address the situation. Instead, he requested, "We need the town's witch here. Now."

"What for?"

"A locator spell for Isa's pet shop. I feel inclined to violence tonight."

CHAPTER 40

*I*sa glared at Nic. Alban and Wyn glared at Nic, too. It was a glare-at-Nic party.

As soon as Nic explained the plan to his men—the plan to ship Isa off somewhere for her to de-program and "be safe" without them—Wyn and Alban stared at their king like they had never heard a worse plan in their entire lives.

Now, they all sat in the back of a large, black arctic truck-van, with seats facing each other in parallel lines against the van walls like a SWAT team. The van sped over ninety miles an hour as the witch finished her locator spell.

The witch was a local sorcerer in the town where Nic bought Isa clothing. Her fingertips had black and gray lines running up her hands and arms. Like the magic she used had created new dark veins that rose to the surface of her skin.

"Instead of buying a protection spell for her, maybe we should just, I don't know, *protect her ourselves*," Alban suggested. "And *not* leave her somewhere."

Isa nodded at that idea. It had merit.

"Kendrick will always threaten war. He wants power —doesn't know what to do with it, but he wants it. But once the other Polaris find out that Kendrick was responsible for his brother's demise, they will never stand by him," Wyn said. "Keeping her...it *is* possible, Nic."

"Not as a queen," Nic stated solemnly. "And she deserves more than to be known as a mistress."

"The *king* of the shifters—as in king of *all of us*—has taken a prey mate and made her queen," Alban reminded him. "Times are changing."

"It will never last. There will be riots."

"Against Daxton Dragomir and Bastille mother-fucking basilisk snake king of the dark shifters?" Alban asked in disbelief and raised both white-blond eyebrows. "I think not. No chance anyone goes after Bastille's mate. Dude can kill through eye contact."

A prey with multiple alpha mates? Isa wondered to herself as she listened to the men. So maybe wishful thinking was not impossible. *Though, he is currently driving me to my new "home."*

"It's odd," the witch commented, frowning at Isa

under a beautiful set of wrinkles and thick black eyeliner.

Nic turned to face the witch as they all jostled in the van when it hit a rather large chunk of snow on the road. "Hmm?"

From the other side of the van, where seats lined the parallel walls, the witch touched Isa's chin and examined her. She turned Isa's face from left to right. Pulled Isa's chin up and down.

"Hmm," the witch made a contemplative sound again. She was much more calm-headed and civilized than the Hag. "The protection spell is not sticking," she said.

Nic squinted at their side of the dim van and asked, "What the hell does that mean?"

"When I try to perform the protection spell, it bounces off as if she already has one. As if she is already bespelled." The witch frowned at Isa. "It's very odd."

Oh...Oh no. If Isa thought there was still a chance Nic would come to his senses and not abandon her, that hope would disintegrate the second he learned about the Hag's spell to make him think Isa was his mate.

But I want to be his mate. Did not matter. Nic would see the whole thing as a charade, question their time together, and never trust her again. He would view it as a betrayal.

He cannot know.

"What do you mean already 'bespelled?'" Nic asked,

confirming he did pick up on the detail Isa wished he would not.

"The only reason magic bounces off and does not stick is if a spell is already sticking to that person. Put someone under a love spell, and you can't also bespell him to chew less loudly at the dinner table. Magic is pick and choose. You can never have everything you want."

Nic remarked darkly, "Don't I fucking know it."

"Can you tell what other spell is cast on her?" Wyn asked.

"It is very strong—"

"The Hag," Nic said simply. "The mother fucking Hag." He slapped his knee—nearly too hard. "I *knew* it."

"The Hag bespelled her?" The witch released Isa's chin as if it could have poisoned her from prolonged skin-to-skin contact. She held her hands up and shifted away from Isa on the long horizontal seat against the side of the van. "I cannot undo it," the witch said.

The van jostled them again as it drove over some uneven terrain.

"Yes, you goddamn can," Nic told her. He pointed at Isa and instructed the witch, "Undo it."

"Witches do not betray the Hag," Wyn commented dryly as the witch shook her head. "The Hag is the oldest and most infamous witch; she will know. She knows everything."

The witch added, "To undo her magic is to commit the pivotal witches' sin."

Nic rubbed his hands over his knees as if he tried to stay calm inside the moving vehicle. Still, his expression was anything but calm as he grated, "If you don't undo the spell right the fuck now—"

"What did we say about threats?" Isa cooed to Nic from her seat across from him in the van. "People respond best to positive reinforcement."

"Should I offer her a cookie, zayka?" Nic deadpanned.

"I love cookies," Isa replied. Maybe the witch did, too. Was the topic of cookies strong enough to change the subject?

The last thing Isa wanted was for the witch to undo the matehood love spell the Hag placed on her. Isa did not want to watch as Nic lost all ties and feelings for her. She did not want proof that everything had been one-sided without a spell.

I care for the three men. I wish to remain with them.

"I will not undo the spell," the witch said. "I cannot. It is too powerful."

Yay. Isa grinned, which Nic noticed. It appeared to piss him off.

"What kind of spell is it?" Nic asked. "You can tell that, can't you?"

Oh no, oh no, no no no. Isa bit her lip.

"A spell this strong would need a talisman. Has she worn the collar the entire time you have known her?"

Without a moment's hesitation, Nic shot out from his seat and *blurred* to her side of the van.

He ripped the collar off Isa, causing her to squeak from both alarm and a painful pinching sensation. Isa's hands shot up to grab at her throat and neck, petting where it burned from the collar being pulled off so haphazardly.

"What the hell, Nic?" Alban cursed at his impulsive king. "You could have hurt her!"

"*Hurt* her? *Her*?" Nic asked in disbelief, as if *she* had hurt *him*. Chest heaving as he huffed frustrated breaths, Nic threw the collar to the floor of the van and said, "Well?"

"Well?" the witch echoed.

Nic's jaw ticked as he sniffed the air and patted a hand over his torso. He growled impatiently, "Nothing is different."

Isa glanced over to Wyn and Alban and froze in fear when she saw Wyn's intense gaze zeroed in on her silver charm bracelet. He had noticed that she had not removed it when she went in the hot tub that first night. He had even asked her about it, assuming an old lover gave it to her.

Wyn knows, Isa realized as he stared at the bracelet and blinked at her. Would he say something? Or did he fear Nic's reaction when—

"It's the bracelet," Wyn said.

The speedy response felt like a betrayal to Isa. Like he had just stabbed her with a sharpened thorn from a holly leaf.

She gasped and instinctively held her wrist to her chest, cradling the bracelet. Would Nic try to yank the hard metal off her tender wrist? Would he break her other good arm in the process?

When Nic reached for it and pinched the metal in his fingers, he yelped and jolted back.

"Sounds like it is bespelled not to be removed," the witch said.

Nic glared at her for stating the obvious, wiping his fingers down his black sweater like they still stung from the defensive magic.

Isa's eyes welled up with tears. Wyn gave her up within seconds. Nic turned on her the second a "spell" was mentioned.

"You cry now that your façade is over?" Nic asked mockingly. Cruelly.

I really didn't change him at all.

*a*fter so many years of pain and disappointment, Nic did not know he had enough of a heart left in his chest to feel it break. But there it was, actively being crushed like the car he once had compacted in a baling press. Just like the unlucky car, the windows of Nic's heart exploded; the exterior metal bent and snapped under the pressure until no one could identify its original shape.

Too good to be true. He had called it, that it was all a spell. *I have no mate.*

"Tell me," Nic said in a deep voice that spewed revulsion. Disgust. *At her or me?* He did not know. *This is why I do not hope.* "Did you find it funny how hard you made my cock? How crazy you drove me? Were you writing letters to the Hag and giggling about how the ice king loved eating you out more than inflicting violence—once his favorite pastime?"

Isa's eyes glistened with unspent tears.

An act.

"Enough. Isa, tell him he is wrong," Alban said. The fox shifter looked pointedly at her, awaiting some reasoning behind the enchanted bracelet. Did he really choose to ignore the obvious proof?

"The Hag put you up to it, didn't she?" Nic brainstormed aloud. "Swooped you up from some pleasure cult, slapped a lusty matehood spell on you, and told you to seduce me into making you the Arctic queen. Is that it? Another prey shifter queen to solidify the new royals' reign?"

The witch coughed lightly and commented, "Um, a spell to replicate matehood—"

"You've done your job here. No need to speak again," Nic silenced the witch.

Honestly, any voice but his own was overwhelming at the moment. His inner wolf roared to hold Isa, and his other inner voice wanted to shove her out of the moving van and leave her in the cold. Wasn't that how Arctic kings dealt with disappointing emotions? His dad had taught him so.

"Do not be rude to her," Isa said softly to Nic, having the goddamn *gall* to frown at him. *Judge* him for how he treated the witch who had just delivered him gut-wrenching news.

How dare she? "Oh, was that too harsh?"

"I'm fairly sure that if anyone told you 'no need to speak again,' you would need to buy a new set of silverware," Isa said, calling back the image of Kendrick's two utensil-impaled eyes.

Alban snorted and smirked at that. Even Wyn pursed his lips as if he fought back a smile.

She charms my men even now? "This witch is here to do my bidding; I pay her extremely generously. I can tell her when she is no longer needed."

"Yes, but you don't have to be *rude*," Isa stressed.

"You think *I* am rude?" Nic shot back, "You LIED TO ME."

"When? I recall no moment where I lied," she replied, crossing her arms and unknowingly flashing the bracelet again.

The fucking charmed charm bracelet. To think, he might have risked everything—his rule—over a bespelled prey.

"Was the mission to 'change me' to be 'nicer' also from the Seer?" Nic questioned. "Will she be disappointed that you failed that part? If anything, you've made my attitude problem worse. Congratulations."

"How do you know I'm not your mate?" Isa asked, vulnerability ringing in her melodic tone.

Want to throttle her until she either tells me the truth or tells me she loves me. "You will pay for what you've done," Nic remarked icily.

"What I've—" Isa cut herself off on a scoffing and choking sound.

In a turn of events, Isa unbuckled her seatbelt and stood in the middle of the moving van. She was just short enough to not have to hunch over to avoid whacking her head against the metal ceiling.

"What *I* have done?" she asked loudly. Angrily. A brand-new side to her usual sunshine demeanor.

"Sit down," Wyn told her. "The van could hit a patch of ice—"

"What *I have done?*" she shrieked, seeming to have momentarily lost her mind.

"Isa, sit down and put that seat belt back on, baby," Alban requested, but she ignored him.

In fact, she seemed incapable of hearing anything but Nic's last sentence. *You will pay for what you've done.*

Standing and clearly fighting for balance as the large snow vehicle bounced and swayed, Isa said, "Ever since I met you, I have been threatened, growled at, scowled at, judged, ridiculed, nearly frozen to death, given a heart attack, lost my virginity without being given an orgasm—"

"Virginity? Another lie!"

"*Not* a lie. My tribe ensures the hymen is broken before our first times so there is no blood to 'bother' our alphas. You were my first." She continued, "I have been locked in a room like an animal, injured after trying to get you a Christmas tree—"

Nic interjected, "I did not *ask* for the Christmas tree."

"No, you do not *ask* for anything," she said. "You demand what you want and ignore what you need."

Nic rolled his eyes. What would she know about what he needed? "Did I 'need' a fake mate? You think I need a Christmas morning full of gifts and new beginnings?"

"You need exactly what you will never receive because you do not give it to others," Isa said as if *she* were becoming a poetic Seer.

"Patience?" Wyn suggested an answer to Isa's riddle on what Nic needed. "Trust?"

"Orgasms?" Alban guessed.

"Even when you believed I was your mate, you were going to drop me off in some random village." Isa accused him, "You were going to leave me."

"Yeah, I do my best thinking without my cock, clearly," Nic remarked, feeling no regret. "Considering you are *not* my mate. Gods, I could've made a prey my queen and lost everything for *nothing*."

"Hmmph," Isa grunted. "Then, you would have received what you gave: nothing."

She fooled with the bracelet, pulling on it, but seemed incapable of removing it herself. That was odd, right? Nic wondered. Odd if she was in cahoots with the Hag, yet she had no control over removing the bracelet.

"You know something?" Isa said, "I am glad to be

leaving you soon. I am tired of being subject to your warped mentality and mood swings."

"Warped—" Nic's hands lifted in the air like he wished to rip his hair out.

"All you want is to be accepted and valued, and I gave that to you. But you *never* gave that to me." Isa took a deep breath and exhaled for what felt like a full minute. She exhaled all of her anger as if it was that easy to just *release*. Calmly, she requested, "I would like to be dropped off at the nearest town or village, please."

Nic scoffed. "You do not get a choice."

"When have I ever had a choice?" Isa asked, her voice spiking in volume again and losing the temporary sense of calm.

The vehicle swayed to the right, and she stumbled over to where Alban sat, buckled in his seatbelt. Alban's hands shot out to stabilize her, and she gripped his wrists like they were lifelines.

"I should have known you are not my mate from how *forward* you are with my friends."

Isa let go of Alban and presented Nic with an expression that spewed anger. Was that a little glimmer of hatred in her eyes? Hatred for him, mirroring the deep-rooted hatred he had for himself the last few years.

"Does it hurt to know I like them more than you—because they are kind?" Isa tilted her head and asked the brutal question. "Imagine all you could have if you were nice."

"Instead of naughty?" Nic quirked an eyebrow and smirked. "For someone so obsessed with Christmas, you were a very naughty girl."

"I hope the memories keep you warm at night." Isa turned to address Wyn.

The stoic, suited, glasses-wearing man seemed to stare right through her. As a Noctu *and* a royal advisor, Wyn had to have taken the news hard on himself—that he did not see through the façade. The spell.

If there was one thing Wyn despised, it was feeling duped and being made out to be a fool.

Isa requested of Wyn, "I would like to be dropped off at the closest village."

"The king told you—you do not have a choice," Wyn spoke in a voice so much colder than he ever had to her before. He sounded like a different person entirely. *Good*, Nic thought.

"You hate me now, so just let me out." She turned to bang on the back doors of the van. "Let me out! Let me out!" *Bang. Bang.* She only had one good hand to hit against the metal as tears streamed down her face.

If she only needed to be my queen, why try to get that Christmas tree?

She could have simply focused on his lust for her; instead, she had snuck out and injured herself to get a tree to try to bring...joy. That confounded the Arctic king. Maybe it always would.

"I do not like to be *caged*," she screamed as she cried

and banged on the metal doors. "Let me out," she wailed between sniffling and wiping at her nose.

Alban knotted his fingers in his hair and lowered his face to his knees like he couldn't stand to watch the show.

"We are almost there."

Isa pressed her hand to the small back window, watching as they blurred forward through a snowy Arctic terrain. "All I want for Christmas is to never see you again."

CHAPTER 42

"*It was more than a spell,*" Alban whispered to Isa before they dropped her off in a small village. "*He will be back for you soon. Or I will,*" the fox shifter promised her.

Well, they should have done their research on the random town they dropped her off at as they drove on to find and burn down her old tribe's compound.

Because if Nic thought of Isa's old tribe as a "cult," she wondered what he would think of this one.

"Bless the king for bringing a sacrifice," the old woman with long white hair and a warm-looking fur coat spoke to the ceiling of the large igloo-styled center of worship.

A circle of the villagers, all strangers to Isa, chanted and drank a spiced hot cider rumored to help them better listen to the gods.

Watching the older woman dance in the center, Isa was both proud to see a female leading an Arctic town and terrified of what this ceremony entailed.

"The *skrumsli* will eat well tonight and avoid our village for many moons," she announced to the circle.

Skrumsli. That word sounded so familiar to Isa, but it was old. The old, Arctic language triggered a past memory of Isa and her mother sitting around a fire and eating fish.

Skrumsli meant "monster."

"The king is coming back for me," Isa said warily. Shakily. Basically, with no confidence or resolve because, regardless of Alban's promise, she believed herself as good as dead to Nic. *He will not be coming back for me.*

"Put her in the robes," the woman said. She lifted a silver goblet up above her head and chanted more old words Isa did not recognize.

Three women moved forward and forcibly stripped Isa's warm, green flannel shirt and matching pants from her body. The only thing Nic let her keep of her stay— gone. Isa tried to swing her shoulders back and forth to keep them back, but one of the men held a sharpened, walrus-tusk spear at her back and pressed the bone blade into her whenever she moved.

After everything I have been through, just to die now.

Isa swallowed back tears that would not help her.

She pushed her shoulders back and let the spear dig into her flesh.

The women pushed Isa's arms and legs into a short, red silk dress that did nothing to keep her warm. The fabric danced across her skin, flimsily lying and hardly covering her body.

The dress fell to her knees and dipped low in the front, displaying swells of cleavage. The thin silk also emphasized Isa's lack of a bra as her nipples stood from the chill in the air.

"Ready the sacrifice."

"I am *not*—" The spear dug into Isa harder, hushing her.

Once the women finished dressing Isa, they drew lines of dark coal over her eyelids and rubbed red berries over her lips, crushing and smearing them.

Even after being raised in a pet cult, Isa had never felt more like a piece of meat than at that moment. She half-expected the circle of chanting villagers to throw warm gravy on her. Anything to make her a more attractive sacrifice to the Arctic monster they referred to as the *skrumsli*.

The scant clothing had her wondering, *What kind of sacrifice am I?*

After earlier statements of the female village leader, Isa assumed that sacrifices were killed and…eaten by the monster. The leader had implied that Isa would serve as a gift from the king to protect the village from the mad Arctic creature and his brutal killings.

The *skrumsli* sounded like the boogie man or the ghost story told around a fire, detailing the rumors of the many bones littering his icy cave in the outskirts of the Arctic Tundra where no one dared venture.

Yet, as Isa fingered the dipping neckline of her dress, she felt like this sacrifice was not for her murder.

Will the creature...take me? In the sexual sense?

"Please, don't do this," Isa pleaded, but they all acted as if she had not said a word.

After more chanting, the leader nodded at the man with the spear behind Isa.

The spear jostled forward, sinking into her back shoulder. Isa cried out at the pain, but another man appeared on the other side of her with his own spear.

"We take you to him now," one of the men said in a heavy accent.

"No, the king will be pissed if you send me off to—"

"The king gave you to us," the female leader said. "Take her now. The *skrumsli* will be hungry."

"How can you *do this*? I have done nothing to you— why would you do this?" Isa shouted at her as she was ushered to the exit by the two men.

"Better you than us."

*B*orn an Arctic shifter, Isa was made for winter weather. But for the first time, staring out into the soft blizzard of dazzling snow and terrifying ice, staring out into the unknown danger, she felt unbearably cold.

Yes, she wore a skimpy red dress—against her will—that did not cover her shoulders or lower back. Yes, she was barefoot on the clump of frozen snow.

But the cold chill overpowering her came from the knowledge that she was now, officially, all alone.

Shunned by the man—maybe even men—who was supposed to love her. Sent off to be a sacrifice to an unknown monster lurking in the darkest, harshest parts of the Tundra.

Maybe it won't be so bad, Isa told herself, trying to stay positive.

An inner voice inside her deadpanned, *You are being sacrificed to a beast.*

Isa frowned at the two dueling inner voices. Maybe she was going crazy.

What if it's a Beauty and the Beast situation? Isa again tried to look for the silver lining. *What if he is a sexy beast?*

From what Isa gathered after listening to the group

who performed the ritual and sent two guards out with her, the rumors of the Arctic mystery Yeti monster were *not* sexualized. If it even *was* a Yeti. She bet few who came across the creature lived to spread the word about the monster's appearance.

This would not end up with Isa happily cuddling with a broad-shouldered furry man.

In a few moments, she could...die.

Think of it as a King Kong situation. Try to get the thing to like you, she thought to herself. After all, she was trained as a pleasure pet to appease alphas. *I have value to give.* And her value was...giving others pleasure. But would this be giving a monster pleasure at the expense of her own?

Dropped off in a random town only to be a pawn once again? Back to playing the role of the seducer to be guaranteed safety?

The two spear-carrying guards walked her out until she stood less than a mile from where the creature was rumored to live in an isolated, frozen cave. The bitter cold was harsh enough to kill a weak Arctic shifter—one *made* for the winter months in the frozen tundra.

Fear nipped her stomach. "You don't have to do this," she told the guards. "Please, if you let me, I can run to a different town."

"GO," one of them yelled from behind Isa, and she felt a prodding of the sharp walrus-tusk spear at her bare back.

"You couldn't have given me more clothes?" Isa snapped, yelling to them so they could hear her words through the whistling icy wind.

"The monster likes red," the second guard behind her replied. "You hare shifters prefer to be naked most of the time anyway, right? Little sluts."

A chill went down Isa's spine. Judged for what she was. Her species—something uncontrollable. *Again*.

"I am the Arctic *king's* little slut. He will come back for me and slaughter you all for this," Isa lied through clenched teeth as she shivered.

One of the two guards behind her shot back, "You think we can't tell when a man is done with his whore?"

Whore. Slut. Because that was all a prey shifter could be to a big, strong alpha, right? Not his mate. Not his queen.

Wrong. *Wrong.* She wanted to scream at the top of her lungs. Scream for Nic to come back. Scream that she hoped he died with regret of losing her.

"Seems a shame the king lost interest in a fuck bunny right before a heat cycle."

They could tell? She shivered again as the cold sliced through her.

"In a few days, practically panting for cock," the guard with the heavier accent said.

Asshole, Isa thought bitterly.

But...correct asshole. *Panting for cock.* To say she was horny was putting it mildly.

Every day, she slipped closer to her first heat cycle. *What happens to me if Nic misses it?* She didn't *want* to go into heat and lose herself to mind-numbing passion. Surely, there had to be methods to stop it.

"*Skrumsli* is in for a treat," the other man said as he forced her to walk further out on the snowy ground. "He has only ever fed from our virgins. You will be a different snack; add variety to his diet."

"We keep our females pure, no temptation, no pleasure."

"Sounds h-horrible," Isa stuttered in the cold. These were the types of clans, tribes, and villages that Nic ruled. Did he know what they were up to?

He was right when he said I do not fit into his world. She would not stand for girls being offered as sacrifices. She would not stand for women not being allowed to experience sexual pleasure. Their small tribe already had two strikes.

"Can't you give me a weapon to protect myself?" she asked. She just felt so…bare. Vulnerable. "Wouldn't you rather a sacrifice die while trying to eliminate the need for future sacrifices?"

The men behind her snorted, and a spear pressed harder to her back, pushing her forward a few more steps on the ice. "As if you could fight back against *it*."

"Be a good little sacrifice, and he will grant our tribe protection for several moons," the other man said.

Only two guards stood in her way of being set free.

A good little sacrifice? After everything, was she supposed to just stand in bright red fabrics, awaiting a monster to decide her future? Again.

Offered as a sacrifice to the most feared Arctic predator shifter in the Tundra. A rumored bloodthirsty Arctic predator shifter who had gone mad and left his clan.

If she ran, she would be caught.

If she fought, she would be killed.

"I can stay in your village; I am more valuable to you alive," she pleaded. "You don't have to do this. If the...the monster terrorizes your town, the Arctic king will kill it. If I die, he will kill *you*." Fear overruled her as the truth settled like the snow flurries to the frozen landscape under her feet.

A warm liquid splattered against the back of Isa's shoulder. Had the guard just *spit* on her?

He added, "As if our king cares about a prey slut like you."

Isa wanted to scream in frustration.

The spear sliced the back of her arm, and a warm trail of blood flowed down her pale skin. "Hard to imagine the king getting tired of all that soft skin. You really are a sexy little piece."

Fury and fright. Hurt and humiliation. It felt like her sense of self was melting, from a perfectionist people pleaser to something darker. Silent tears prickled Isa's eyes, blurring her vision.

"I wouldn't mind breedin' you," one of them said.

Bleeding and barely clothed, Isa staggered forward over the icy ground. Rage simmered in her blood. "You will regret this," she muttered.

"Only regrettable thing in this situation is sacrificing you before enjoying you during your heat."

Isa stiffened; her body went completely still—not even the slippery ice persuaded her to move.

"You smell...ripe."

From behind her, the tip of the guard's spear trailed down her back, down, down, to cut through the fabric at her hip and down to her thigh. A cold gust of wind split the pieces of red silk and allowed the guards a front-row view of her bare ass.

Isa ground her teeth, growing angrier by the second.

Angry at them. Angry at Nic.

Angry at her body for betraying her and heating at the idea of a man's touch. A prey's first heat cycle could make her fall to her knees and beg anyone to fuck her.

Isa swore to herself, *I will never let these guards touch me.*

"*Fokk,*" one of the guards cursed. "Look at that ass."

"Shiver again and show us how it moves."

Isa heard their boots shuffle and crunch on the thin layer of snow as they inched closer to her.

"Just one touch..." one of them said in a dazed, almost bewitched tone.

Isa held her breath in anticipation, wondering if she

could perform some kind of back kick in the ridiculous dress. Her tribe had never let the females learn fighting skills, but she had watched movies. Growing up in such an isolating and restrictive community, she loved movies.

"Seems unfair that the *skrumsli* should get the only taste of this prime prey pussy," one of the guards remarked.

When one of their cold fingers touched her skin, a loud, ferocious roar sounded off in the distance.

A deadly, bone-chilling roar.

CHAPTER 43

"**W**hat the fuck are you doing here?" Nic asked the Hag as Nic and his men climbed out of the back of the van. They had finally arrived in front of the entrance of Isa's old cult, where Nic's witch's locator spell led them.

In an absurdly puffy winter coat, the Hag laid in the snow and created snow angels by swinging her legs and arms up and down.

Hag paused and sat up to address Nic, Wyn, and Alban. "Ah, there you are. I am disappointed it took you so long."

"Took me so long to confirm you bespelled Isa's bracelet to make me think she was my mate?" Nic quirked an angry eyebrow.

"What spell?" Hag frowned. "No, I am disappointed it

took you so long to come to burn the cult to the ground and save all the prey inside."

"We didn't *know* she was from a brainwashed cult," Wyn said. "We found out hours ago."

Hag blinked. "Did you not listen when she spoke? Girl practically had Kool-Aid eyes."

Not understanding nor caring to understand Hag's statement, Nic walked past her toward the compound's main gate. No guards stood outside. The gate could easily be broken through with some predator shifter strength.

"Not much security," Nic commented.

"They probably thought no one would ever travel to this inhabitable edge of the Arctic," Alban said. "Even to steal their fucked up 'merchandise.'"

"They are prey shifters," the Hag said. "They do not think of violence."

"Not the prey victims, the cult leaders," Wyn clarified.

"Yes, the cult leaders," Hag said. "Prey."

Alban cracked his fingers and asked lowly, "Are you telling me that the people brainwashing and selling prey females as sex slaves *are* prey shifters?"

"Prey men often have pride issues because they'll never be real alphas. A man with hurt pride is a dangerous thing for women in this world. The males wish to rise up in the hierarchy of the Arctic, even if it means selling out their own kind," the Hag said. "They make almost as much money now as you did when you first started your little underworld business," she told Nic.

"Stealing and selling their own species...for power." Alban spit on the snow. "Fucking despicable."

"Will you be a spectator or a participant in the slaughter of the 'businessmen' and setting the prey free?"

"What do you plan to do with the prey once you free them?" Hag asked.

"They will be free to do as they wish." Nic's eyebrows furrowed like he didn't understand her question.

"Yes, but these are women who need to be deprogrammed. Protected from alphas who would take advantage of them."

"What are you suggesting?" Nic asked.

"Do you plan to house them in those fifty bedrooms at your estate?" The Hag suggested, "You have plenty of room. I am sure Isa would love to help them all adjust to normal life—"

"Isa will no longer be with us," Wyn said.

The Hag blinked again, her eyes flashing silver. "Oh...my."

"What?"

"This was the 'less great' future path. Poor girl."

Nic's head shot up as he turned from surveying the compound to staring at the Hag for clues of what she meant.

"Explain," Alban demanded, moving swiftly toward the Seer. The fox shifter did not care about Isa's ruse. Not like Nic did.

"She did not fill you with the Christmas spirit, then?" Hag asked Nic through pouted lips. "A shame."

"You bespelled her to smell like my mate," Nic accused with a pointed finger like he was in grade school. "Do not deny it."

"A spell? To 'fake' matehood?" The Hag cackled. She tossed her head back and laughed so hard that she wheezed her inhales. She shook her head at Nic's witch, and the two of them exchanged expressions of pure amusement.

"WHAT?" Nic growled.

"No such spell exists. I did tell Isa that a matehood spell was what her bracelet did, but sometimes a Seer has to tell some white lies for things to go according to plan."

"But you just said it didn't," Wyn pointed out. "That the 'less great future' was happening—"

"The bracelet was bespelled." Nic exclaimed, "My witch confirmed it."

"Yeah, it's called a 'delay the heat of a prey shifter' spell. You expected me to leave a brainwashed people-pleaser in your home full of predator shifters without giving her a few days there before dissolving into a puddle of lust?"

Nic's jaw fell.

"You really thought I would send you a fake mate? Who do you take me for? A warlock?" The Hag tipped her head back and cackled loudly again at her own joke.

Abruptly, Hag stopped laughing, glanced seriously at Nic's witch until that witch faked a laugh, and Hag went back to cackling at her own joke.

Frustrated, Nic told them, "Stop fucking laughing."

It could not be true. Even if it was, Nic had planned to drop Isa off somewhere else anyway. Planned to give away his mate. His inner wolf roared, RETURN TO HER. FIND. KEEP.

"So, the spell was not…" Wyn pushed his framed glasses up higher on his nose and opened and closed his mouth.

"Wow, a Noctu shifter speechless." Hag rolled her beady black eyes. "You powerful Arctic men are all the same. You think you know everything, and you think everyone is out to get you."

"They *are*," Nic shot back.

"Not her."

As Isa's back bled from the two guard's spears digging into her, a bellowing roar simultaneously shook the icy ground and made everything grow still.

The snow paused in its falling as if it were too frightened or maybe wise enough to avoid landing where a creature capable of that murderous sound resided.

"He's coming!" one of the guards yelled and shoved his spear forward, not realizing how deep the sharp tip punctured through Isa's back hip.

She choked out a tortured sound at the new burning pain from two open, bleeding wounds in the freezing cold.

"*RAAAAAAHHHHH*," the thunderous roar broke through the soft whispers of the wind again. This time, the beast, the monster—whatever it was—sounded closer.

"Has he ever sounded this angry at receiving a sacrifice before?" one of the guards asked the other.

"He has never *shown up* for a sacrifice before we leave them."

The hair on the back of Isa's neck stood up, bristling. Dread, anticipation, and pain swirled inside her as she stepped forward on the sheet of ice once more.

She did not know which was a worse fate: what the monster would do to her or what the guards had been about to try.

"Maybe we waited too long between sacrifices?"

A rumbling started under Isa's bare feet. *He is... running to us*. On all fours? There was something primal about how the Arctic ground itself shook with fear at the monster's approach.

The creature must be massive. No wonder the men laughed when Isa suggested giving her a weapon.

"There!" a guard shouted.

Isa peered over her shoulder to follow the direction of where the man pointed. There.

A blur of white fur and tan skin. Like a half man, half beast. He almost appeared in-between shifting as his body was too massive to be in human form but was not fully covered in fur.

"Is he coming *to us?*" one guard asked in disbelief. "He has only ever watched from the mountaintop."

"*Fokk*, he looks...violent."

A clear image of him was difficult to make out through the falling flurries of snow. He blended into the environment so well. *Unlike me*, Isa thought. Bright red dress. Two bleeding wounds. No way she could run and escape him.

Finally, he was just a few yards away, still moving at lightning speed, reminding her of a...bear.

Maybe the creature was not a fictional Yeti, but what if the monster was a Polaris bear shifter? And if so, why was he not in full bear or human form?

Is he stuck?

A loud, primitive growl came from the monster's broad chest.

"*Skitur*. Should we run? Leave her here for him?" The guard's voice dripped with fear.

"Run!"

Isa shivered and hugged herself as the guards ran from her. Left behind. Again. Would Nic feel as perfectly fine leaving her if he thought he would never see her again?

I want to live. I want Nic to regret abandoning me. I want...

She wanted to be queen.

She wanted to stop Arctic villages from performing violent, immoral practices like sacrifices. She wanted to prevent other prey shifters like her from feeling like they had to provide value—through sex or maid services or anything—to earn protection.

Everyone deserves protection.

It was why Nic and his men currently rode off to Isa's old tribe to "end the cult," as they had delicately put it.

Isa was tired of being told that she could only ever be a pet due to her species.

I want to be more.

And if she were to die, she would die worthy of being the Arctic queen.

CHAPTER 44

*P*ushing back her shoulders, Isa kept her chin high as the manly creature barreled toward her. Shoulder-length white-blond hair blew out in tresses around his face as he moved. Closer now, she could see the tan tone of his skin and the virile ridges of muscle outlining his arms and legs.

She could not see much else of him as he hunched, crouched, and ran on all fours. Still, her mind whispered wickedly that those muscles covered his entire massive build.

"Focus," she whispered to herself.

Just because she was nearing her heat did not mean she should lust after her murderer. Isa was already angry at herself for lusting after Nic when he was less than kind. *I will never let a cruel man touch me again—no matter how horny I am.*

But his rippling muscles...

She blinked, clearing her distracted mind long enough to realize the creature changed course. He charged past her in a blur of speed, heading for the guards who stumbled and ran through the snow.

One of the men glanced over his shoulder, noticed the monster chased after him, and let out an embarrassingly high-pitched scream.

The creature's speed... No one could outrun it—even hare shifters known for their speedy sprinting.

The broad-shouldered beast caught up to them in seconds.

Screams of pain rang out as the creature massacred the guards. Isa gasped and closed her eyes as the terrifying image of the creature *biting* the hand off one of the guards and blood *spraying* onto stark white snow haunted her vision.

Was she to die in such a violent manner? Couldn't he just snap a neck and make it easy?

Maybe all predator shifters like to play with their food.

"*No!* Please, no!" one of the guards shrieked.

More sounds of guttural, graphically horrific brutality.

When the screams stopped, a repetitive crunching thud occurred as the creature approached Isa once more in the snow. Maybe he found no reason to run to her because she stood perfectly still.

Instead, he walked slowly, with deadly purpose.

Something about that deliberate, unhurried descent was more terrifying than the primordial running.

Eyes still closed, Isa quivered with fear, internally chanting, *I don't want to die; I don't want to die.*

The thumping sounds of his steps finally stopped. He was right in front of her.

"*Mgahumnahu,*" the creature let out an animalistic, gibberish noise, but it felt like he attempted to speak to her. Did he not know the language? Could he not speak in his half-shifted, half-man state?

Heart racing, Isa opened her eyes to see a massively broad-shouldered beast of a man, maybe seven feet tall, covered in dark red blood, holding out a severed hand for her like it was a peace treaty.

Her scream of terror clawed its way from her throat.

The creature's bloody lips curved downward. "*Mmrunngahhnuu.*"

"*AHHHHHHHHHHHHH,*" she continued screaming.

He shook his head and tossed the bloody severed hand to her feet. "*Wuuhhyuue,*" he said. Again, gibberish.

"*AHHHHHHHHHHH.*"

Dripping with the guards' blood, he moved forward and grabbed her arm. His thick fingers wrapped around her tender skin, and a shocking heat slammed through her body. Sizzling tingles at the contact.

Her scream grew weaker at the touch, and as she ran out of air. Still, she shrieked in fear.

Gently turning her so he stood behind her, he moved

her bleeding backside to face him. He smoothed his fingers in a circle around the two areas where the guard had cut into her skin with the bone spear. A soft growl bubbled from his chest before he turned her back around to face him and pointed to the severed hand.

She stopped screaming.

He stared at her, a determination lighting up his intense gaze like he so deeply wanted to communicate with her.

She stared at him, a confounded confusion and slow understanding lighting up her expression.

"You...You killed them because they hurt me?" she asked slowly.

"*Mahgraddhur*," the beast mumbled back.

The shiny red blood covered his features, acting like a mask, but Isa could make out the bright, pale gray-blue of his eyes. Like the shadow of a blue Aurora hitting the snow. Pale cobalt moonlight.

No longer screaming, she inhaled his alpha scent, letting it seep into her lungs and leave surprising warmth. He smelled like spiced hot chocolate and roasted marshmallows. How could a crazed beast, covered in blood, smell deliciously wholesome?

Those brawny arms, broad shoulders, and intense territorial eyes are...getting to me.

Apparently, arousal and fear could be felt simultaneously. "Will you...hurt me?" she asked shakily.

"*Veettorahiya pohloeveenka*," he responded in a

different language again. His voice came out rough and gravel-like, yet it draped over her like soft satin.

She bit her lip. It didn't sound like a "*yes*." He spoke in a tone of pure, adamant certainty. She shook her head and hugged herself tighter as the cold winds speared through her thin dress. "I don't understand what you are saying."

His gaze fell to where she hugged herself. Specifically, his line of sight fell to her chest, where cleavage was on full display. Full. Display. Her right nipple threatened to pop out.

Uh oh. She blushed as his expression changed.

His nostrils flared, and he took ragged breaths, one after another. On every inhale and exhale, his lips remained parted as he stared at the swells of her breasts, partially exposed by the absurdly low-cut dress.

His pale blue eyes suddenly disappeared, swallowed up by the big black pupils taking over. Round saucers of darkness. Of unbridled need.

This monster lusted for her. He appeared ready to... pounce.

Blushing harder and feeling shockingly hot whilst out in the cold, she cleared her throat. Inching away ever so slowly, she started, "Listen—"

He pointed at her and slammed a fist to his chest, hard, in a possessive gesture. "*Veettorahiya pohloeveenka*," he repeated.

Thanks to her isolated tribe, Isa did not know much

about the different Arctic dialects or languages in the region. The one he spoke sounded...ancient.

"I appreciate you saving me from the guards and everything, but I don't know what you're saying, and I really must be going—" she cut off when she saw it.

A big *it*.

Between strong muscular thighs, it rested—if *"rested"* was even the right word for something so awake. Her jaw fell, leaving her gaping.

Below his dusted-with-white-blond-hair chest, below the breathtaking and tongue-tying pack of abs, was the largest, most erect cock Isa had ever seen.

In his half-shifted state, his girth... His length...

And it *grew*. The thick, dusky hardness twitched when her gaze focused on it. Liquid pebbled and glistened at the tip—as if his body was too pent-up to hold anything inside any longer.

He groaned huskily as she gazed at his thickening cock.

He was without clothing in his half-shifted state. Therefore, his bare erection raged for any bystander to see.

"Oh...my gods," Isa muttered, suddenly lightheaded.

"*Juueelett*," the creature growled.

His distended cock jerked toward her as it continued to grow.

Considering he had not killed her yet, she thought back to her King Kong plan of getting the creature to like her. Survival was her current biggest goal. Survival, first. Later, making Nic crawl back on his knees to her for forgiveness. After that, taking the throne from him to ensure the safety and happiness of all Arctic shifters.

She would not die today.

Suddenly, Isa's fate did not look so tragic because now she had a new option, a new path to travel. If this creature was attracted to her, she could...befriend it. Eventually, it would let its guard down, and she could escape.

Yes, escape, she thought to herself as her gaze devoured the blatantly sexual view of the man's dick. *I just have to pretend to be attracted to him, too.*

Even as she told herself it was pretend, her pheromones spiked, and the creature breathed in a strong gust of the scent of her obvious growing lust.

He was just so...big. Would he crush her?

When his eyes went entirely black, as if demonically possessed, Isa's instinct triggered her to turn and run.

She did not realize how much predator shifters loved the chase.

CHAPTER 45

"*I* see it now," Hag told the men as the three of them circled around her and lost their minds. "You were going to leave her when you thought she was your mate. Then, you thought she was not and left her still. *Sooooo*, how is your leaving her my fault?" Hag asked.

"Get back to the 'less great' future you mentioned for her," Alban ordered.

"I do not take orders, but I do give them. I would love a hot plate of gingerbread cookies with a spicy little kick to them—"

"Hag." Wyn pinched the bridge of his nose. "We were going to return to Isa. We were not going to leave her permanently."

"Yes, you were, once you believed your feelings were

manipulated by a spell," Hag said. "When you felt duped. Poor Mr. Smart Man felt played for a fool by a pretty woman. Congratulations, you are a normal man."

"Why not tell us about the charmed bracelet?" Nic asked.

"A Seer chooses what to say, so all things will go her way," she rhymed. "I suppose you wish her not to be bespelled at all? Fine." The Hag snapped her fingers, and bright white light shot out of her hands. "There. Happy now?"

"You undid the spell to delay her heat cycle?" Wyn questioned, gaping in horror at the impulsive Seer. "Why the fuck would you do that?"

"You men seem uncomfortable around spells on your mate, so *poof*. Happy now?"

"When will she go into heat now?" Alban asked urgently. When she did not reply within a second, he exclaimed, "What *the fuck* did you do?"

Hag shrugged. "She might have an hour before her heat is triggered."

"She is more than an hour's drive away!"

"Could be sooner if she is being sexually teased right now, which I can neither confirm nor deny."

"WHAT?" Nic felt a slight pain in his scalp as his clenched fingers came away with some of his hair. "Is someone touching her? *Already*? We have been gone a few hours!"

Hag's wrinkles deepened as she glared at Nic. "If you call her a whore, I will have to punch you in the jugular."

Nic scoffed and puffed out his chest. "I'd like to see you try—" Nic's airway cut off, and he choked and doubled over as he fought to breathe.

White light swirled around the Hag's hand after she sent a magical punch right to Nic's throat. "You really learned nothing from her about manners? You thought her lessons were unnatural, but it is usual to change from a mate. To learn and challenge each other to be better versions of yourselves."

Hag tsked Nic and said, "You think your torturous youth and successful ambitions gave you wisdom, but they gave you wounds. Maybe you do not deserve her. Maybe she is with someone right now who *will*."

"Who?" Wyn asked. "Who deserves her?" The jealousy in his tone gave him away.

"Maybe the real heir to the Arctic throne." Hag said pointedly to Nic, "Maybe you were right about not being worthy."

Nic rubbed his throat where she had hit him with a bolt of magic and scowled.

"Your twisted self-esteem, bad attitude, and inability to let go of the past have cost you your mate." Hag shrugged again. "I don't see how you will ever make it up to her. You *chose* to let her go."

Hag remarked, "A woman deserves a man who would rather die than leave his mate alone in a foreign town, with people who still believe in the Arctic gods and like to perform sacrifices to appease the weather—"

"WHAT?" This time, it was Alban who yelled. "What do you mean 'sacrifices?'" The fox shifter gripped at his chest.

My men care for her, Nic admitted to himself. *And maybe that is...a good thing.*

"Really, you should have done some research before dropping her off at a random village." Hag lifted a hand to the side of her mouth to dramatically whisper at Wyn, "That seems like a ball dropped by the king's advisor, to be honest."

"Where is she right now? What is happening to her?" Wyn asked, the anxiety and regret in his voice as apparent as the emerging blizzard and darkening sky.

"Without the spell, her heat quickly approaches."

"Fuck, Nic, we need to get to her. We left her all alone. No protection. Some bastards could—"

"Don't fucking say it," Nic warned.

Truthfully, he fully believed that if someone dared to suggest aloud that Isa would be taken against her will, his wolf would take over his entire body and *run* to her and rip anyone in his path to shreds without a second thought.

Already, his eyes and hands flashed between shifted and human state.

"There once was a brainwashed prey, who only wanted to be loved and obey. But given to a real-life, sexy Grinch, his heart didn't grow a cubic inch. So, she ended up given away, and now she will get a good lay—"

"Hag," Wyn stopped her. "Please. Where is she *now?*"

"She approaches her heat." The Hag eye's flashed bright white as she foresaw something. "She will be taken by the first alpha to find her."

Nic's wolf took him over, forced his head back, and let out a blood-thirsty roar.

*J*sa was a fast runner, but the beast caught her within seconds. Of course, he did. She was in human form, and he was...something else entirely. And by "catching her," it was more like he tackled her to the ground. *What if he is more animal than man?*

The fall took the breath from her lungs—a silent scream.

As cold as the ground was beneath her, an intense heat emanated from every inch of him as his body covered hers, protecting her from falling snow. His aroused cock, large and *full*, burned against her thigh.

The thin, red silk dress did nothing to limit the feeling of his dick rubbing over her sensitive, top inner thigh.

Again, oxygen failed her as she was left breathless by the overwhelming wave of erotic desire.

His spiced hot chocolate scent was surely legally registered as an aphrodisiac because even as she struggled to inhale, it infiltrated her senses and had her tingling.

"*Veettorahiya*," he continued huskily mumbling gibberish into her ear as he lowered his face to the crook of her neck and shoulder and rubbed his lips up and down her throat.

She sucked in a breath as those warm thick lips, still painted with the guards' blood, dragged over her earlobe and the sensitive erogenous zones of her neck that had never been explored before.

"Oh..." Her nipples hardened behind the thin red silk, deliciously scraping against the contoured ridges of his chest as he leaned over her. Her legs had fallen scandalously separated.

He pulled back to stare at her as his massive form loomed above. Dominating dark pupils still covered the beautiful blue irises she had seen earlier.

His hips rocked forward, thrusting his cock between them. The friction of it moving over her pulsing clit dumbfounded her—*awoke* something deep inside her.

The baritone, mindless sound of pleasure he emitted just from grinding against her almost made up for the spike of pain in Isa's back.

The motion of his thrust dug Isa firmly into the icy

ground, and she winced and yelped as her bleeding wounds pressed to the cold. Even as turned on as she felt, they were difficult to ignore.

He paused in his second thrust and blinked down at her. His pupils dilated a bit, revealing some of that pale gray-blue.

"M-Maybe we could get out of the s-snow?" she asked, shivering again.

He blinked once more, his dark pupils shrinking back to a more normal size. Isa laid in awe from gazing at his large eyes up close. *That stunning ice-blue color.*

"You are, um, surprisingly attractive?" She complimented him and then shook herself. *You didn't need to say that, Isa.* "But I'm just...currently bleeding. And cold. I know I'm an Arctic shifter, but this dress covers very little, and I'm used to indoor heating."

In a split second, Isa's world turned upside down.

Because the monster grabbed her and somehow got to his feet in one swift movement. He carried her over his shoulder in an odd manner that suggested he had never held a woman before.

His large, heavy palm cupped nearly her entire ass just behind his shoulder. He held her front to his front.

"Well, okay then," she said weakly, distracted by the view.

He moved her in a way so that her face rubbed against his hard, muscle-lined lower abdomen, very close to where the enormous monster-sized cock pointed to the sky. Or rather, due to how he held her, pointed to *her*.

"Gods, don't poke my eye out, am I right?" she tried to joke to his taut stomach. Alban surely would have appreciated her attempt at humor had he been there.

The monster's cock twitched as if nodding to her comment, as if confirming, *"I would never hurt you."*

CHAPTER 46

*a*s he marched forward, walking her toward the icy cave beyond the mountain, each jostling step caused her body to bob up and down. Her face—specifically her mouth—came very close to the aroused length rooted between his legs. It jerked and laid against his abdomen.

Being held firmly to him, she could not look away from how the tip darkened and glistened with pent-up need. With each step and each rhythmic squeeze of his palm on her ass, the tip of him leaked more precum.

Walking through the blizzard, his erection never waned. If anything, it became even harder and more desperate as he stomped through piles of snow, and her face bounced against his abdomen.

Maybe he knew what he was doing because a minute after the hot, wide palm on her backside began to knead her ass, making blood rush to a pesky spot between her legs, he dropped her just an inch.

From that readjustment came the soft brushing of her cheek against his feverish erection. Had that repositioning been intentional?

A chilling yet fiery growl came from the beast-man. His chest vibrated her with the ferocious, tantalizing sound.

She understood that she should tread lightly. This was possibly a Polaris bear shifter stuck between human and shifter form, who clearly did not have his full human-form brain activated to converse or be less... Arctic Tarzan.

This was a creature who just murdered two weapon-carrying men with utter ease and seemingly no remorse. She understood that, for the sake of self-preservation and future escape, she should remain submissive and take his lead and try to fade into the background as much as possible, but...

It was as if her mind blanked at the guttural, sexual sound he made from a touch as small as her cheek grazing his cock. Something overcame her. A piqued sensual interest. A dirty inclination.

Nic had never made such a tortured sound for her like that. His sound of sexual desperation and the intensity of the monstrous alpha, and the fact that he *stopped* when she yelped in pain after grinding against her, even though his cock was as full as a glass of milk left out for Santa...

He has already treated me nicer than the Arctic king did, Isa thought to herself. *I...want him.*

Lust and desire ruling her, she craned her neck, leaned ever so slightly, and tried to "accidentally" graze her lips across the tip of his arousal.

The monster stutter-stepped and paused. A deep breath shook his chest.

Trying to calm himself? She was thankful for the view of his abs and thankful that she could not see those intense silvery blue eyes burning through her.

This massive shifter had lost his footing just from *her.* After Nic's rejection, this creature's reaction stroked her pride and titillated her curiosity. *What would he do if I touched him more?*

"Uhguhm?" A deep, husky, inquisitive sound rumbled in his throat like he asked something. He wanted to know if the touch was innocent and unintended.

Not willing to admit the honest answer, she did it again. As if victim to the force of the cold wind, she tilted her chin, just barely swung the position of her head, and brushed her lips over the dark mushroom tip of his erection.

His skin tasted like her favorite tea flavor: cinnamon. Warm and spicy.

Was her lust for him a betrayal to Nic? *He betrayed me first.*

The beast's thighs trembled for a second after her lips' caress. His fingers dug into the curve of her ass cheeks.

This time, the sound he made was less mindless. The new dominating, raspy sound was one of warning—a sound that speared through her, echoing in the hilly expanse of harsh white winter around them.

She should have been terrified, but his threatening growl did not *feel* scary.

It warned her not to tease him. It warned her to let him take the lead. It warned her there might be hell to pay if she did not heed his instructions.

But the sound just turned her on more.

*M*y mate wishes to drive me wild? Baine thought to himself as he narrowed his eyes on her and let out another hungry growl. *Do not tease me. I could fuck you for hours on a sheet of ice and never cool.*

"No. More," he grated in a gravelly tone—hardly maintaining control of his inner beast. Still, he knew she did not understand him. Whatever language she spoke, it did not match the ancestral Polaris dialect that his risen beast understood.

Even if she could not understand his words, she needed to know the danger of teasing him. He barely held onto his self-control. Ever since getting stuck mid-shift, he was beholden to his most animalistic urges.

His current self-control to not take her on the ground in the middle of the soft snowfall was already a miracle. Baine was like a thin sheet of ice, cracked and ready to break under the slightest pressure from her.

The feel of her lips on him...made him want to fuck her against the closest icy structure available. He could smell her arousal. As shocking as it was that she was attracted to him in his current state, he had to focus on getting her to shelter and healing her wounds first.

"Don't. Tease." Every word was effort, even if she did not speak his language. Speaking felt foreign to Baine now. He had not needed *language* or words since his animalistic Polaris bear spirit overrode his brain and body.

Where others could shift back and forth, Baine's inner bear had refused to go away. The animal spirit in him never stopped sensing danger and threats. Witness enough tragedy, and the mind would always choose to remain a massive, deadly bear over a vulnerable man.

Right now, his mind ruled nothing.

MATE, his instinct screamed as his body burned for her.

His cock laid heavy and full, leaning flat against his

abdomen and aching with each step toward his cave. *Mate*.

When a Polaris bear shifter found his mate and breathed her scent for the first time, his body sparked with such desire, his cock expanded so quickly, hard and full for her and her only.

He could hardly think through the need to seek pleasure from her perfect body and pleasure her in return. He wanted to pinken her cheeks. Make her gasp. *Make her love a beast like me.*

Every gust of wind blew her beautiful white-blond locks and scent into his face like a cruel reminder that he finally had all he ever wanted—but she couldn't understand him.

She turned her head and craned her neck to peek at him from where he hauled her over his shoulder. Her eyes twinkled with naughty mischief. She *had* done it on purpose.

"Minx!" Cock throbbing harder, he swung her around so her face touched his back instead of his front.

He now had a better view of her bitable ass. *Gods, her curves, her legs…*

The woman muttered something in a breathless voice from her change of view from his front to his muscular backside. He would kill to understand her language.

MATE, his Polaris instinct growled.

He had to maintain some semblance of composure.

Don't want my mate to see me as a monster. He had already thrust his erection against her while her back bled into the snow. *Monster.*

His anger at himself for forgetting her injury still pierced his chest. But the feeling of her soft skin... He had been lost in her.

That lush, silky skin...

That *scent.*

The way she had lightly caressed his arousal...

Want her mouth on it again. Palm on her ass, he squeezed and breathed in more of her scent. Thoughts mixed with the animal urges. *Losing control.*

His pace picked up until he moved as a blur across the ice.

There was another pressing issue—more important than his bear's lust.

There was the fact that part of the reason he was stuck mid-shift was due to an untimely vampire bite and...turning. And the current smell of her blood drove him crazy. *Want her.*

It had been several months since Baine had consumed blood—often taken from the Arctic aquatic animals he fished out with his massive hands. Polaris bears were known to be able to fast and sustain themselves on little nutrients, but he was...hungry.

He really should have fed from the two men he had slaughtered. But they had hurt her, so they had bled *for fun.*

His fangs pulsed in time with his raging erection.

He needed to get her warm and healed.

This hunger for her...is unbearable. Possessive bear and virile vampiric instincts fought for what to taste first: her pussy or her blood.

Do not feed, Baine begged his animalistic instinct-ridden mind. *Could harm her. She has already bled out. No feeding.*

Able to hear the fast beating of her heart, the blood moving through her veins, Baine ran faster.

CHAPTER 47

*E*yelids growing heavy, Isa wondered what was happening to her as she watched the creature start a fire and roll rags of cloth out for her wounds. There were no bones or skeletons of past victims in his cave. As bulky as he was, once the blood was splashed from his features, Isa saw him as calm and...gentle.

Beautiful blue and white icicles covered the ceiling of his cave, thick and long and could-impale-and-kill-anyone if they fell. In a way, the eerie, stunning, yet dangerous décor fit the owner of the cave.

Maybe it was his spiced chocolate alpha scent, her approaching heat, or how Nic and Wyn broke her heart. Maybe it was how he killed the guards who had been ready to take advantage of her—so protective and ready to fight for her when no one else had.

Maybe it was how he had neglected his *obvious,*

painfully hard erection when she reminded him that she was hurt. He had even rushed to offer her a raggedy blanket and little bits of food he had stored in the corner of the cave.

When he wrapped the blanket around her, she thought, *I...don't mind this creature.*

But as she warmed to him, warmed by the fire, gazing at how the flickering flames cast shadows over his large form, he grew stiffer. Colder.

Ten minutes after getting to the cave, he had started turning his back to her as if wishing to breathe air that had not touched her yet.

"Did I...do something? Do I smell bad?" she asked, even though she knew he did not understand her words.

Did he used to understand? Or did the Polaris bears speak a different language from her region? She had understood the visiting Polaris stabbed by Nic.

I know so little about my own world. Isa frowned. If she could escape the Arctic entirely, what could be out there, waiting for her to explore?

The creature's erection still swung high, hard, and proud, but the new look of intensity in his eyes when the stark blues focused in her direction was different. Almost angry.

She swallowed thickly. "T-Thank you for the fire? I would write you a card, but I am all out of pen and paper. Also, I don't think you'd understand it..."

Drawn by the fire's warmth, she leaned closer to the

flames and winced when the wound in her back twinged with pain.

He growled loudly and raked a hand over his face, rubbing the bottom of his mouth. He strode forward and dropped down into a seated position beside her. The sudden act shook the ground beneath them. *Such raw power...*

He inhaled roughly again, and another charged rumbling sound came from his chest.

As on edge as the creature seemed, he slowly and calmly touched his mouth and gestured to the wounds on her back.

Okay... "I don't think kissing the boo-boo will make it go away," Isa remarked. "I know I'm sheltered, but even I know how modern medicine works." Well, she knew a little. The tribe had some pain relievers.

The creature's thick white-blond eyebrows furrowed as he pressed his lips together in displeasure and shook his head. He pointed to his mouth, flicked out a *long* tongue, and gestured to her back again.

She blinked, confused and distracted by the haunting, sensual image of that flash of tongue. "Um...what?"

Huffing in frustration, he lifted his wrist to his mouth and CHOMPED on it.

Isa screamed as the dark blood flowed down his arm. "Why?" she shrieked, shifting to her knees to grab at his arm. Red blood splattered onto the snowy white ground. "Why would you do that?" she yelled at him.

He leaned forward and licked the two huge puncture holes in his bleeding wrist.

The wound healed in a second; the skin connected back like it had never been sliced through.

In awe, she stared at it. "You… Your saliva heals?" she asked.

She had never heard of such a trait of Polaris shifters. Sure, some shifters had special abilities like basilisks, which could hypnotize, or Noctu owl shifters, who absorbed more knowledge than any world genius.

But healing saliva was a…vampiric trait, right? Isa tilted her head and studied the beast-man. "What are you?" she asked softly.

He ignored her question and positioned himself behind her. He lowered the blanket to bare her back.

His large palms, warm to the touch, gently flattened over the opposite sides of her back. The touch was not restraining. As his breath caressed her spine, she found his touch surprisingly comforting and sexually triggering.

Tingles ran over her back from the skin-to-skin contact. Her nerve endings lit up with a desire for *more*. More touches. More closeness. More of his toasty, spicy, and sweet scent.

What's wrong with me?

He was about to lick her wounds to heal them, about to press his tongue to her sensitive skin. Though surrounded by a winter wonderland of icicle-covered cave walls, she felt hot.

What if he was a Polaris shifter who was turned into a vampire whilst shifted? Is that why he looked half-man and half-beast?

"I—I've heard of vampire bites before," Isa commented weakly, voice cracking as his breath grew closer and hotter against the skin of her shoulder. "Some of the females from my tribe were, um, seduced by them."

Vampires were known to occasionally vacation and "hunt" in the Arctic due to the endless days of darkness found nowhere else in the world. With no fear of sunlight, vampires were known to be sloppy. Known to bite and drink and...have sex with their victims. Well, "victims" was not the right word. Maybe "addicts" or "thrill seekers."

"I've heard a vampire bite releases certain, uh, endor-phins," Isa rambled.

The truth was, she had heard and read about the bites before because they...intrigued her.

The first time a fellow prey whispered about the sexual release a vampire bite gave her, how it lasted almost ten minutes and vibrated through her entire body, Isa had clenched her thighs together and fanned her face. The dazed expression of the woman recounting her memory had haunted Isa late at night when she tossed and turned, seeking sleep.

Isa asked nervously, "But you just plan to lick me, not bite me, right?" Why did the way she asked that sound like she *wanted* the bite? Had he heard the slight disappointment in her voice?

The creature was silent behind her.

"Lack of response sure is a confidence builder," she joked.

That won her a low grunt from him.

One of his large, warm fingers brushed down her spine, and accompanying shivers wracked her. Thinking she shook due to cold, he let out another discontented huff and scooted her—lifting her by the hips and planting her back down—closer to the fire. He lifted her like she was a speck of snow.

Such strength…

Such…danger.

J *ust lick to heal her wounds. Do not taste. Do not bite. Do not suck.* Baine fought himself. *Maintain control.*

If Baine accidentally hurt his mate or drained her of blood, he would never forgive himself. It would be the end of him. And maybe that would be okay. The lonely life he had lived since being turned into a vampire half-turned monster was…cold.

To have a mate, that was a miracle. That was…everything.

I do not deserve her.

"Smell, uh, good," he grated. "So good."

Her sweet cranberry and lime scent mixed with the heady scent of her blood. Her presence, everything about her, drove him *wild*. His hands fisted at his sides, and he dug his knuckles into the snowy ground of the cave.

Do this. Heal her. Do not drink.

What made it worse was the evidence of her arousal. Each of her deep inhalations raised the tantalizing swells of her breasts in the thin, low constraints of her dress. Her nipples pointed through the front of the flimsy fabric. Her pussy, slick between her thighs, emitted more of that sweet scent.

"Do not move," he warned, hoping she would somehow understand his clipped, old language. "Stay. Still."

He bent to align his mouth to her first wound. He blew on it, and she trembled again. His tongue curled out and flattened over the injured skin. On the first taste, Baine fought to restrain his instinct to sink his throbbing fangs into her pliant flesh.

One lick, done. *Move away. Stop.* But his tongue

moved back to repeat the action once more. *Must make sure she fully heals.* An excuse.

"*Fokk,*" he cursed. *She tastes like pleasure.* How was a man supposed to stop at one taste?

Another lick, even though she was healed.

Another.

His fangs panged with need. *Could just sink into her and sate this raw hunger. Watch my cock sink into her wetness and then sink my fangs inside.* His pupils dilated once more into huge black circles as he licked her blood from his lips.

If he bit her, others would know she had been claimed. *And she tastes so good.*

More.

Before he could stop himself, he grabbed the back of her hair, wrapped it around his thick wrist like a leash, and pulled to tilt her head back. She gasped and let out a little whimper of desire. He tipped her forward, leaning her over the fire as he pulled her hair back, signifying he had utter control.

"Mine," he growled onto the back of her shoulder before his fangs pierced her.

Heaven.

Both of them moaned when the endorphins traveled through them at their joining. The flow of blood, each sip, occurred in waves like a sexual climax. The mystical properties of a vampire bite prevented any terror or scream from Isa.

Only pleasure.

He sucked and cupped her delicate throat. He grabbed the curve of her hip and pressed his front to her bare back. *More.*

His cock was so large, hard, and stiff it *lifted* her higher up in his lap, prodding her ass cheeks. She wiggled over him, rocking her hips seductively. *More.*

Her feminine plea and whine of ecstasy clouded Baine's mind even more.

The sounds she makes. He thrust from under her, grinding his rigid erection against her smooth skin. More of her sweet, tangy scent flooded his nostrils as she gyrated her hips to feel more of him.

My mate likes it when I feed from her?

A dream. It had to be. Decades of loneliness. Decades of cold.

She reached behind herself to pet her fingers over his thigh and the side of his full, aching shaft.

When the tell-tale scent of her arousal peaked in the air, Baine stiffened and realized, *She...*really *likes it.*

CHAPTER 48

"*Oh, gods.*" Isa's body shook as pleasure wrapped around her tighter and tighter like a rubber band, ready to snap as the broad-shouldered beast drank from her neck. "*It's so good.*"

A servant to her rising wicked inclinations, Isa reached for him behind her. Her ass slid back and forth over the hot, lengthy erection at her back. She wanted to touch him.

Her fingers stroked over the taut flesh of his arousal, and she moaned at the low groan he released. As Arctic shifters, their blood often ran colder than others. Yet, their bodies heated to a scorching level.

What if the icicles above us melt?

Gods, he was so *big*. Would something like that even fit inside her?

Still, she begged, "More."

When his fangs dug deeper into her skin, she felt like something was moving in and out of her, between her legs. It was as if an invisible dildo thrust inside her and teased those hidden spots that her fingers never seemed able to find.

This was what a vampire bite felt like? How did they ever stop? Why would they?

"Never stop," she whined.

He grunted as he jerked his hips to press her hand harder to his cock.

As he sucked from her, her mind turned to liquid. The only thoughts that floated above the surface were: *Yes, please, more, oh gods, yes.*

Her clit swelled under the hood, silently crying out for his touch.

He must have heard the noiseless cry because one of his meaty palms slipped low between her legs. His palm pressed to the top of her sex, where her clit pulsed. *Yes.* His big, heavy fingers settled right over it and *ground* up and down.

"*Yes.*" He was about to make her orgasm—hard.

Then, he stopped, lurching back from her.

"*Noooooo,*" she cried.

Releasing her, he staggered two steps behind her. She swayed to the side, catching herself and holding herself up with a palm against the ground of the cave lair.

She glanced over her shoulder at him and pouted her

lips as she whined, "Why?" Her own hand slinked down between her legs to rub herself. "It felt so good."

Her breathless voice of need had an immediate effect as the sexy, vampiric Arctic creature blurred back over to Isa, moving so fast she did not see him until his face was level with hers. He inhaled her scent and flashed his fangs. An inner battle shined in his bright blue eyes.

He was fighting *not* to bite her.

That will not do. She liked the high of her tribe's treats and now the high of the vampire's bite.

She wanted to forget her current circumstances and Nic's and Wyn's betrayal. She wanted more from the giant, warm creature who had so far treated her with kindness.

And she wanted to come.

Turning to fully face him, she fooled with the side sleeve of the red silk dress, pushing it more and more to the side until it slipped down and revealed her right breast. The nipple was hard and pink and poking straight toward the beast.

Fingering the nipple, she seductively asked, "Would you like to bite me here?" Even if he did not understand her language, he could put the pieces together to understand the meaning.

She palmed her breast, lifting it up like an offered treat. *Feed from me more.*

His nostrils flared, and his mouth opened to lick his thick lips.

"Please—"

His provocative mouth fastened onto her breast. His lips closed around her firm nipple and gave a little relishing suck. Then, he spat out her nipple and opened his mouth. He sank his mesmerizing fangs into the top of her tender breast.

"*Mmmmm*," she moaned, her head lolling back.

The insertion of the fangs spread that naughty, mindless feeling through her body again. Thoughts were not possible when her blood sang, and her skin howled, and her pussy screamed.

"Yes, yes, yes." Her hand again moved between her legs to grind against and touch herself.

With each long drag he sucked and each powerful sip he took, her toes curled. Her breathing quickened its pace. Her pussy drooled onto her hand through the thin red silk. The village had taken her panties when dressing her as a sacrifice.

With how good the beast made her feel, she wondered if she should send them a "thank you" card.

Then, he broke away again, removing his fangs from her flesh. She whined out in disappointment, and his thick white-blond eyebrows furrowed, his forehead creasing.

"Rahnumarah," he garbled out some primal noises that may have been another language and slammed a hand over his heart. He then slammed that hand into the icy floor of the cave, shaking the icicles above.

Isa licked her lips and rocked her hips as she kept grinding her needy pussy against the heel of her hand. "I need to come. Please. I can't think straight. It's like my body..." Was she close to going into heat? Could the creature trigger it?

"I—I can't stop touching myself," she admitted, surprising and scaring herself. "I—I don't know what's happening to me, but I can't s-stop, *ohhhh*." She gasped as her hips gyrated faster, rubbing her sex onto her hand.

Grinding against that tingling clit and feeling closer and closer to...something. Something powerful. "Please bite me again, please. Your fangs feel so good. When you suck—*oh gods*," she cried out.

The creature panted as he stared at her hungrily and licked her blood from his mouth.

"D-Don't I taste good? Please," she begged. "Take more." She leaned her head to the side to display her neck. "Please."

The creature's chest shook with a low, threatening rumble.

"P-Please, I'll taste so good." She rubbed her clit harder.

His stout, sturdy fingers shot out and wrapped around her wrist. He wrenched her hand away from herself and pinned it to her side.

Her chest heaved, one bare breast quivering on display, as she said, "No, please, let me come." She fought to get her hand back between her legs, but he held it down. She was no match for his strength. "Here, have some more blood." She tried to distract him by wiggling her chest and presenting her neck again for another bite.

She again tried to pull her hand free. Unsuccessfully. "Let go," she told him, blushing and struggling to match even a morsel of his strength. "I—I need…"

The beast growled and slid forward on his knees, closer to her. One of his palms still pinned hers to the ground, but his free hand jerked her knees apart. He dropped down to his stomach and lowered his face between her shaking thighs.

She held her breath, shocked at how the creature seemed to be readying to taste her *lower* than before.

He shoved his nose to her pussy and inhaled raggedly, letting his eyelids fall shut. His brows creased, and his lips curled back to show his white, sharp teeth again.

Another loud guttural sound came from him as he blinked open his eyes and stared up at her.

"Are you going to…"

The beast's tongue unfurled out of its mouth, and Isa's jaw hurt from falling so fast.

Her lungs sucked a large gulp of oxygen at the sight.

His bluish-black colored tongue was as thick as her wrist and stretched out almost eight inches, fully extended.

The massive appendage—because no other word could describe its sheer size; it was practically a human's limb—had clearly stayed in bear-shift state. Or was something in-between. Isa had never seen anything like it.

"Um, I don't know if," she started.

But the lengthy, broad tongue, textured with bumpy tastebuds, flicked out against her bare pussy.

It *dragged*, heavy and coarse and slippery, over her clit. The heat of it branded her.

And her thighs fell open.

And she screamed.

CHAPTER 49

*B*aine's eyes rolled back at the first taste of her sweetness. A deep groan hummed through his lips, vibrating them.

The loud scream of pleasure she emitted pierced his ears just before new wetness settled onto his tongue as he gave her sex a long, savoring lick.

Due to his shifted tongue's width and length, Baine could delve between her pussy lips and swipe up her entire bare slit with each stroke. He even grazed the back part of her ass cheeks with his broad, slippery tongue as he licked from the bottom of her folds to her clit.

He swirled the tip over both of her sensitive, puckered pink entrances, and she made guttural, primal sounds that he understood better than any of the words she had tried earlier.

This is how we will communicate, Baine decided as he lapped from her glistening entrance to her swollen clit and enjoyed her noises of mindless pleasure. *So very... sweet.*

He flattened his tongue over her clit and licked faster. Harder. His thundering heartbeat raced as he pleasured her. *More.* He wanted more. His mouth became more demanding, lips sucking and tongue grinding and licking.

"Give me more," he demanded. "Soak my tongue. I want my face covered in it. I will lick my lips hours after this."

"Ahhh!" she yelped and bucked her hips, shoving her pussy onto his face. *She likes it.* If he kept going, would she like *him*?

"Like this, mate?" he asked her in his familial language, even though she could not understand. "I *love it.*"

His tongue darted and swiped and worshipped. Meanwhile, his cock throbbed for relief. Stuck in his half-shifted form, there was nothing quite like an erection that was twice as big as his human state's *well-endowed* size.

In his current condition, he would never be able to thrust inside her. It would break her.

MATE. FUCK. TAKE.

In a half-shifted and blood-hungry state, he was bound to his bear instinct and beholden to the vampiric urges. They overpowered him easily—too much pent-up energy and strength.

Baine grabbed the swelling shaft in his hand and squeezed. "*Mmmm.*" He had not been hard in so long. Not even in his unshifted form had Baine experienced such a stiff, thought-eroding erection.

THRUST. TAKE HER. CLAIM HER BEFORE ANOTHER DOES.

"So hard. Aching for you," Baine mumbled onto her pussy lips as he licked out a detailed map over her clit with the agile appendage.

He feasted, repeatedly traveling his tongue in a steady and constant up and down. Her body produced more and more wetness, in an endless cycle, at his thorough passing over the length of her pussy as he tongued her again and again and again.

Baine doubled his efforts as he growled, "Waited so long for you."

Her fingers fisted his long, icy-white locks and held him firmly against her.

His large, heavy tongue plopped down hard, slapping over her clit, and she screamed again, howling for more.

"I love fucking you with my tongue," he hummed as he delivered faster licks and delved and dipped and explored her silky pink flesh. "Do not know what tastes better. Your blood or this."

She yanked hard on his hair when he skimmed the tip of his tongue down to her pouting entrance that grew slicker with each second he spent between her legs.

His eight-inch-long tongue stretched further from his mouth to graze the opening of her pussy. It fluttered against the tight passage, causing more slickness to gush from her. *Flick. Flick. Flick. Dip.*

He forced his thick tongue forward and dipped it inside her. She let out a noise of alarm, but he kept going.

The coarse and erotic appendage tunneled past her tight inner walls and slithered up her channel. It met pleasing resistance as her sex grew accustomed to the large size of his penetrating tongue. His tongue snaked and worked its way deeper and deeper inside her as she yelped and pushed at his head.

When he had several inches inside, he curled and rubbed his pillowy tongue against a wall of treasured ribbed flesh. Her G-spot.

His cock grew even harder in its already engorged state as his hot, satiny tongue performed thrusts and sweeps over her sensitive spots. His bulging erection leaked pre-cum and jealousy as his mouth explored her heavenly pussy, where a different part of him wanted to be.

He began to wiggle the tip of his tongue, making it seem to spin around inside her and hit the most electrifying spots.

His mate threw her head back and moaned loud

enough to vibrate the beautiful icicles above them in the Arctic cave. Her juices unashamedly ran down her sex and legs as he rushed to clean her of them with his mouth.

"Give it to me," he said, practically slurping her. "I want it." He wanted her to come.

He also wanted to come. His vampiric urges, drunk off her tart, sweet blood, commanded him to mark her with his teeth *and* his cum.

His right palm had fallen to no longer just squeeze but actively jerk off his cock. The massive dick had a mind of its own—or rather, it took over Baine's mind. As the majority of Baine's blood—and the heated blood he drank from her earlier—flooded his dick, it seemed to control more and more of his actions and thoughts until all that was left of him were dark urges.

TAKE HER.

His tongue stroked rougher. His fangs ached to bite into her pussy lips as his tongue flicked and curled deeper inside her, stretching her.

Her body stiffened more and more with each lick. Her muscles tensed, and her back arched.

Yes, I will make my mate come.

Her strained expression turned to one of ecstasy. Her eyes rolled back; she opened her mouth and shrieked as she convulsed and shuddered.

She orgasmed for a length of *minutes*, during which Baine continued lapping her up.

When she blinked open her radiant eyes, pupils dilated and glazed over with desire, she noticed his hand blurring up and down between his legs. She moaned lowly at the sight of him touching himself and opened her legs wider.

Did that mean... Did she want him inside her?

TAKE. CLAIM.

He knew he shouldn't. He knew the sheer size of his half-shifted cock could kill her.

But he no longer had control.

His inner beast had him withdrawing his tongue from her, and his large, furry hands gripped her thighs, shoving them open even further.

His hardness prodded her sopping sex, and she let out a cry.

*N*o, *no*. She could not fit that thing inside of her! What was he thinking?

He clearly was not thinking because his flushed cock was a girthy, long cylinder full of pent-up cum. She felt pent-up as well, even after coming.

How was a girl supposed to think after all that? *His tongue...* And the view of witnessing his awe-struck and hooded-eyed expression of dark satisfaction as he explored her wet pussy with his magical tongue.

The orgasm had hardly sated her. If anything, it had unlocked something even needier.

I am so horny, I could explode.

But that did not mean his absurdly massive cock would fit inside her.

"I think we should reassess—" She wiggled under him, trying to ease herself away and grant some distance.

Instead, her movement aligned her pussy to his hard length. The plump tip of his dick slipped between the outer folds of her pink sex, touching her wetness.

Noticing the dampness and heat of her against him, he jolted closer. As if touched with a live wire, his throat rumbled with the beginnings of a roar.

Isa watched in fascination as his pupils overtook his eyes again, turning them into pools of swirling black tar. His lips curled to flash his large canine teeth as he looked like an animal ready to rut. Ready to sate himself inside her.

Poking her entrance, he rolled his hips forward, and Isa squeaked at how the move forced his full, flushed member deeper. Even just the littlest bit inside her, with nothing more than the intense pressure of half of his bulky mushroom tip breaching her, she could not catch her breath.

Panting, she mumbled, "Maybe we should think this

through." His dick was so large that she wondered if it could kill her.

Death by sex. Had the Hag seen it that way for Isa?

Worse ways to go, Isa admitted to herself.

"Maybe we should—" She cut off on how he bowled his head and licked at her nipples. She bit her lip and relaxed her body as he pushed in deeper, his body weight pinning her to the ground. "Oh! *Yes.*"

A deep throaty rumbling sound came from the creature as he entered and settled the full, girthy head of his cock past the entrance of her pussy and circled his hips. He swirled his thick mushroom tip around inside her, stretching her inner walls in a way that hurt less than she thought it would.

"Okay," she said on an exhale of relief as he continued licking and flicking her nipples with his enormous tongue.

Her pussy had been so slick from coming that the tip just felt like intense pressure and not pain. "Okay, this is okay."

Maybe even better than okay? She had never felt anything like it, being stretched open so wide.

Hearing the surrender in her voice, he mistook the meaning of her words.

He must have assumed her yielding tone and exhale meant she was ready for more of him.

Because he reared his hips back and *thrust.*

CHAPTER 50

"*O*h," Isa squealed as he shoved inside her another inch of a cock as thick as her ankle. "Oh wow, that feels—"

"*UHGAHN*," the beast grunted loudly and flexed his hips forward again, piercing her with another inch.

The creature trembled above her as if struggling to hold back. Fighting to go slow. Even when losing control, he tried not to hurt her. But those full, dark eyes grew darker as his brows furrowed and his furry fingers dug into the snow beside her hip and head. Claws scraped into ice.

"Oh GODS," she cried out as he twisted his hips and swirled those three inches of his broad dick around inside her.

He kept performing that move to get her accustomed, before sinking deeper. The stirring sensation caused Isa's body to produce more wetness, which slicked his entry and path. It actually felt...good.

"Oh, oh." She did not understand how her body could take something as large as him, but her pussy just kept getting wetter as he pushed deeper. The little bits of pain were nothing compared to the achy, ravishing need to know if it was possible to feel more.

Her breathy pants and raspy voice preached succumbing to lust. Because the lust was powerful.

Overwhelming. Her back arched as he slipped a little deeper still. She could not tell where she ended and he began. "I don't know if I can take anymore."

Yes, you can, mate.

It was odd, the way she swore she heard a male voice in her head whisper that back as he grumbled broken syllables and gyrated his hips, breaching her with another inch.

"So...much," she moaned, but her hips bucked up to urge him deeper and change the angle.

What is happening to me? She couldn't help taking him. Her arm lifted; her hand clutched his upper arm. She dug her nails in and held.

She wasn't pushing him away.

So, he pushed deeper.

"AHHH, oh, my—UHH." Her sounds seemed to have no meaning other than a primal sexual hunger. Something really *was* happening to her.

A twisting sensation occurred in her abdomen

before an exploding ache shot out from her lower stomach and infiltrated her limbs. Waves of pain mixed with something else. Like going from holding her breath to breathing in the purest oxygen in the world. The sensation of anticipation and pleasure and need.

Primitive and carnal.

She inhaled sharply. It was as if his alpha predator scent injected her brain with hardcore drugs.

Electric shocks zapped through her when the pangs of pain stopped, and a new convulsion began. Titillating twinges. Gnawing need.

Whimpers poured from her lips as her lower abdomen rippled. Her inner muscles gripped the beast's girthy length, squeezed him, then submitted to his size. Wrung him, then yielded and made more room.

Her feverish body tensed and tensed. Her back bowed as she writhed from her position, pinned on his obscene length.

Wetness streamed from her, gathering around his sinful cock and causing him to slip forward, deeper again, until she felt as if his dick poked behind her stomach. He still was not fully inside her, yet he felt close to hitting her cervix.

"OH GODS," she screamed as the first round of crashing waves broke over her.

Her pussy walls rippled violently around him as her skin released invisible sensual airborne chemicals, tainting his breaths. Intoxicating pheromones perfumed from her like her pores each spurt out their own over-powering amount of hormonal narcotics.

Every cell in her body began to vibrate. Shaky and desperate and needy.

"*Mooooooooore*," she moaned as her pussy adjusted to his ample-sized alpha cock.

As he breathed in her heightened pheromones, any humanity or struggle that played across his features before, when he had rifled with his self-control, was swept away.

The dark eyes went blank and emotionless for a few seconds as his nostrils flared and his chest inflated with the newly pheromone-spiked air.

Her heart beat erratically in her throat as she watched his strong jaw tick to the side. His long, bluish-black tongue flashed out to lick his plump lips as his canines *lengthened* in his mouth. How the fangs grew longer, she had no idea, but she was incapable of thought anyway.

Because she had just gone into heat. After all the waiting and all the anticipation, it had finally happened —not around Nic, Wyn, or Alban, but in the presence of a half-shifted creature.

And every breath the beast took chipped away at his restraint and non-animalistic urges.

His body was so massive; he could easily hurt her. Now, her body released airborne drugs.

He slammed his fists into the icy ground below her,

shaking the icicle ceiling of the cave. *Bam, bam*. He pounded the ice, and it splintered beneath her.

Still half inside her pussy, the beast reared his head back and *roared*.

"*I*magine if others get to her first and rip her clothes off," the Hag said. "Prey are not immune from hypothermia, you know. They could fuck her to death out in the snow," the Seer mused as if she *wanted* Nic to throttle her.

"Wyn," Nic grated. "If she says another fucking hypothetical about Isa being harmed before we get to her—" Nic's claws dug into his own knees as he impatiently rocked in his seat in the van.

The driver sped over the hills of snow to get them back to the village where they dropped Isa off, earlier in the day.

"We are almost there, Nic," Wyn reminded him in a clear tone of: *Do not kill the Seer*. "And Hag, it might be wise to only share real prophecies and not worst-case scenario daydreams."

"But that is how the king of the Arctic likes to live, yes?" Hag questioned. "Believing only in worst-case scenario daydreams."

"It's called anxiety," Alban remarked. His tense shoulders and fisted hands revealed his anxiety as well.

Because he cares for my mate, Nic thought to himself.

The fox shifter added, "And you are making it worse."

"I believe I am making the *guilt* worse," Hag clarified. "The male guilt over abandoning a defenseless prey just because you worried about how your kingdom might react to her as queen."

"They would come after her," Nic muttered. "I know it." Just like his brother's wife—a prey shifter made a queen and slaughtered days later. "Am I to know love only to lose it?"

"So dramatic. They will not come after her," the Hag said plainly. "Your people will actually learn to love her. Make her queen, and there will be a great union and treaty. She will be celebrated every winter holiday season for bringing cheer and light to the Arctic kings. Bringing them out of the shadows."

"She won't be...killed?" Nic asked in a broken voice of pure relief.

His brain could not fully absorb the pivotal information the Seer just gave him. Her prophecies were infamous. Isa would be *embraced* by his people? *Was I that wrong?*

"What did you mean by 'them?'" Wyn asked. "Kings plural?"

Nic rubbed at his jaw and shook his head, still not

over the fact that he had treated Isa so poorly for no other reason but that he never chose to heal from his own past wounds.

Nic's one example of love was watching the joy on his brother's face around his mate. *Then, the blood...* All over the floors. From where the prey, Arctic queen had been murdered, and his brother had taken his own life in despair after finding her. *But I found and dealt with her killer.* His we-must-never-appear-weak father.

Nic's father never stood a chance against his son's strength and speed. *"I knew you would turn out to be a monster. And I am so proud,"* his father had told him just before Nic broke his neck *and* ripped his throat out with his shifted wolf teeth.

I was a monster to my mate. Why would Isa forgive him?

"What else do you see?" he asked the Seer as the van slowed to a stop. They were finally back. Now, where was Isa?

"I see...that it has happened," the Hag whispered after blinking away a flash of silver light emanating from her eyes. "You are too late."

"Too late?"

"*What* has happened?"

"She has started her heat cycle," Hag said.

Rage.

Nic broke through the van's back doors and jumped

onto the snowy field in front of the village. He howled brutally to the sky.

"*Goddamn* it," Alban cursed and joined Nic outside, followed by Wyn and the Hag.

"Where is she?" Nic yelled at the Seer as she stepped out of the van and onto the ground. His chest puffed up as he approached her; his face turned red. "Is she alone?" Nic asked. "Will we find her first?"

"She has started her heat and has already been found," the Hag replied.

"*Found?*" Wyn repeated.

"He's fucking dead," Nic snarled at the idea of another man taking advantage of Isa during her first heat, where she was vulnerable. The stories of the mindless lust... No one to protect her.

"Where is she—" Nic coughed. He choked on his next inhale, and his head shot to the side as his nose lifted to the air. "That scent."

"Oh shit," Alban muttered as he breathed it in as well. He rubbed a hand over his chest, and his pupils turned to black slits over crystal blue irises, matching a fox's. His body jerked in the direction where Nic faced, off into the soft blizzard. "Nic... It's strong."

"Fuck," Wyn, even the cool-as-a-cucumber Noctu shifter, stutter-stepped in the same direction like he lost authority over where his body took him.

"You're at least two miles away, yet her heat can affect

you all the way from here. Wild," Hag commented. "Must be several other shifters smelling her right now. Racing to her. I wonder if her heat will break before you get to her—"

Hag cut off and smiled at the backs of the men as they blurred forward in the snowstorm, running faster than most paranormal men were capable, to the mountains in the distance.

"I hope she forgives you," the Hag called out to their backs. "But I prefer grunt-y, Arctic Tarzan!"

CHAPTER 51

"*W*hat's h-happening to muh—" Isa's mouth hung open as the beast thrust forward. Hard.

In her heat, her pussy widened and adjusted to accommodate such a massive invasion. What should have been impossible turned…almost feasible. Still, she felt the stretch, but that pressure was turning to pure pleasure.

Eyes fully black and fangs distended, the beast appeared less human-hybrid than before. Her pheromones turned him into a hungry animal as he began a constant rhythm of slow thrusts, pushing more of himself inside her.

A low, gruff, grunting sound came from him after each punch of his hips, and she swore she could become addicted to the noises. Addicted to those growly groans that suggested he had never felt anything like her.

All Isa had ever wanted was to be craved that much.

Every pore of her hypersensitive skin tingled like any attention or touch would result in double the amount of typical sensation. His eight-inch long tongue unfurled from his mouth, and the tip flicked against her hard nipples, dancing around the needy peaks and teasing them as if the tongue had a mind of its own.

Her right hand slid down, and she dug her nails into his furry, plump ass as she exclaimed, "MORE."

He gave it to her. Brutal thrusts.

His large dick hit her cervix again and again, and she *loved it*. Every one of his movements was dominating and hard and nearly overwhelming; yet, still, her body twisted and burned and sweat and screamed. "MORE."

A prey shifter's heat was typically broken by *multiple* men—as none had the endurance to sate her alone. But what if this creature could?

He growled at her and gripped her hip tightly as he pounded her with his ravishing dick. Again and again and again.

"It's so *goooooood,*" she moaned, slurring the words. More invisible heat hormones flooded the air.

He bent his head forward to bring their faces close together as the beast growled out some syllables.

She swore his expression appeared almost...regretful. Like he was about to get rougher?

He dipped his head lower and sank his fangs into her neck.

"*Yessssss,*" she screamed.

With each drag and pull of her blood, she felt those invisible tongues all over her again, playing with her clit and every other erogenous zone as he drank and fucked her. Her body felt possessed. She swore she saw pink and orange streaks floating around in her vision.

This was erotic bliss. *Vampires are...wonderful.* No wonder there were rumors of so many members of her tribe leaving the Arctic to follow the parasitic para-normals.

He noisily slurped and grunted at her neck. She felt the suction on her clit, and she came around his cock again.

On a scream, she flung her head back and rolled her hips. Her pussy clamped down around him, rippling and seeming to *suck* him in deeper.

He roared and fucked through her orgasm, snarling at the squeezes of her inner walls. *Thrust, thrust, thrust.* His fangs never left her neck as his cock squelched through the wet, squeezing muscles.

Mouth agape at the pleasure, she couldn't form words. What were words?

Her bracelet began to sting; it warmed against her skin. When she glanced down, it briefly glowed before returning to normal. What...

"Can't stop..." the beast growled, and she understood him.

She understood him. Had her bracelet just been bespelled again?

He mumbled against her neck between grunts of pleasure, "Too—UGH—good. Can't—UGH—stop. Sorry, so sorry." His fangs penetrated her again as he fed from her and fucked her.

"It i-is so good," she agreed. "So good. Don't stop. Never stop."

Her pussy grew slicker for him and rippled again, trying to steal his cum from him. How long could this creature last?

"Don't want to hurt—but taste so good. Feel so good. Never known pleasure like *this*," the beast snarled as he shot his hips forward in such a powerful thrust that Isa skidded up the icy ground.

She would have been freezing if not for the fire beside them and his furry arms and legs brushing against her like the softest blanket in existence. It was an intoxicating sensation to feel as if she was overheating yet still facing the perfect chill from the cold air to cool her down.

"Can't control..." the beast grunted and thrust harder again.

So deep inside her, his mushroom tip bumped her cervix and seemed to inflate even larger. She choked out a sound as the tip ballooned and caused each of his new thrusts to drag heavily over and stimulate her G-spot.

"Need to stop," he rasped in her ear, yanking his fangs out of her once more. "Don't know...what's coming."

"Nooooo," she moaned and looped her legs around his waist as best she could with his massive size. Bucking her hips up, she kept his cock inside her as she reached to guide his mouth and fangs back to her neck. "Never stop. *More*. I need more." She felt close to coming again.

Just a little more.

He growled, "Losing...control."

"Give me *more*," she demanded and arched, sliding herself further onto his length.

He pounded his fists on the ground beside her, shaking the icicles above them. "WANT TO RUT."

"Do it," she challenged and jerked her hips. "Please. Gods, your body...so big and strong. I love your cock," she cried out even though—if she was not in heat—the size of it could maybe kill her. "It's *so good*."

His big, furry hands slid around the backs of her knees and lifted them to change the angle. He tilted her lower body to the side to get easier access to her neck. He cupped her ass cheeks in one of his warm palms as he settled back in to feed and thrust.

His heavy balls slapped up against her like a dominating hand with each hammering of his hips. As he sucked from her neck, the endorphins flowing through her took her over from head to toe.

"Yes, *yes*, YES." Out of nowhere, another orgasm slammed into her. Her pussy clenched so tightly around him that she swore he would roar and come inside her, but he kept going.

And going and going. And sucking. And pounding. And drinking her.

Her vision blurred, and she swore the cave moved up and down, as if traveling on an ocean wave.

"Uh..." She closed her eyes, trying to ignore the dizzying way the beautiful icicles on the cave ceiling blurred in her vision.

Was this a part of her heat cycle, or was he taking too much blood?

"*Uhhraahgahnnmm.*" The unintelligible noise she made did little to stop him. Her limbs grew weaker, and her fingers lost the tight grip she'd had on his ass cheek.

He moved her legs again, changing the angle and causing another orgasm to rip through her unexpectedly.

Her inner muscles continued trying to milk his cock even as her subconscious slipped.

*N*o, Baine shouted at himself. *No more.* But his body raged. MORE. TAKE EVERYTHING.

He wanted her blood, her orgasms, all she would give him.

But he could hear it. Her heartbeat slowed. Weakened.

Even as her pussy continued to wring his cock for more thrusts, for his cum, he heard her heartbeat slow. After her last orgasm, the intense pheromones had begun to recede. He had broken her heat by nearly breaking her, taking too much blood.

If my monster destroys the one bit of happiness I have had in years...

Summoning self-control the beast was not capable of, Baine somehow tore his fangs from her neck and stopped feeding. He licked her quickly, watching the puncture wounds heal.

Then, he launched himself away. Falling back onto his back legs and gasping for breaths, his large hand grabbed his beefy erection and jerked it in paranormally fast strokes.

Nearly hurt my mate.

Bad.

Monster.

He slammed his head into the icy wall of his cave, and the thundering sound of snow shifting on the mountain rumbled.

CHAPTER 52

"Her heat..." Alban muttered as the men ran toward where they scented her across the mountain. "It's over."

"Someone broke it," Wyn said, voice full of regret and unexpected anguish.

"I will slaughter any who touched her," Nic bellowed as they all continued to run in the direction of her scent. "Fucking rip them apart!"

A loud, strong, reverberating boom shook the ground, and the men looked up toward the closest mountain.

"Avalanche," Alban shouted.

"We need to get to high ground." Wyn pointed *not* in the direction of Isa.

"I get to *her*," Nic growled over the loud rumbling as

white snow began to roll down the mountain they ran toward.

"You cannot run through an avalanche! Nic, your leg—"

"I GET TO HER."

*I*sa huffed in breaths and tried to stay awake through the dizziness. "What…" Isa weakly muttered, unable to muster the energy to turn her head or move her neck as she stared up at the cave's ceiling.

"*Bad, bad, bad,*" the beast repeated as he banged his head against the cave wall.

Isa heard the rumbling avalanche effects and gathered the strength to blindly reach out for him with her right arm.

"Hey," she whispered feebly. "No…"

"Evil. Demon. Bad." *Bang, bang, bang.*

"Stop," she yelled in a hoarse voice.

The banging stopped, and a chilly silence floated through the cave.

Still staring at the ceiling, unable to move, she told him, "Come here."

"Hurt you," he grunted. "Never." He groaned angrily. "Did. Evil—" *Bang.*

"Stop, I'm okay," she said. "Come here."

There was a shuffling sound, but she still could not see him as she laid on her back and watched the ceiling.

"Come here. I'm cold."

He was instantly on her, turning her gently to her side to cuddle her from behind.

He curved her lower body to face the fire, so rays of heat warmed her along with his intense body heat. He nuzzled the back of her neck and breathed against her hair, his large breaths tussling the strands like gusts of wind.

"Sorry. So sorry. Monster."

"No." She wiggled, grateful for whatever new spell on her bracelet allowed them to understand each other. "You are not a—wow, you are still very hard," she commented, feeling his erection at her back.

He shifted and cuddled her tighter into him, his patches of fur and skin equally warm.

"You feel...good. And not just good in a sexy way," she said softly as she stared into the dancing flames. For the first time, she felt... "Safe. I feel safe with you."

Wasn't that crazy? A massive, monstrous beast who could kill her by squeezing her too hard made her feel safer than she felt in a while.

"Hurt you. Should've..."

"Hey, I have heard stories about heat cycles. They trigger the darkness in alphas, and...you fought it so hard. I didn't know alphas *could* fight their instincts like that."

"Would rather die than hurt you," the beast mumbled into her ear and pressed his oversized, plump lips to the lobe. "Mate."

"W-What did you say?" she asked. Her weakened heartbeat jumped a little faster, closer to normal pace.

"My mate." He held her tighter, but it was still gentle. Tender. Sweet. An opposite to how Nic did—tight, possessive, and almost angrily. So dominating and jealous. But this fanged beast held her like a delicate snowflake he wanted to carry around forever. "Waited. Here now. Never leave."

"You think I am your mate?" Isa asked.

Could the bracelet be affecting him by accident? It had heated up and glowed as if something were happening earlier. What if it was still the fake matehood spell and a translator spell now, too?

She mumbled, "It's probably the witch's spell."

Isa fooled with the bracelet, tugging at the metal charm and blinking away sudden, unexpected tears. "I just want someone to want *me*," she said. "Not because of a spell. I want someone to accept me as I am and love me and embrace me."

She backed into the beast's arms, so her back pressed flush against his muscular chest. He was just so *warm*.

She told him, "I don't just want someone to enjoy what I do for them. A relationship shouldn't be about the cheer I bring or the pleasure I give. I want someone who wants to match me. Who will take the time to do sweet things for me because I do the same for him."

Watching the flames dance in envy—because Isa wanted to dance too—Isa said, "I want someone who will bake cookies with me and not just eat them. I want someone to ice skate with, where we hold hands and accept that one of us falling means we both do."

She reached out toward the fire and held her palm over the haze of warmth it emitted. "I want to feel like a gift *and* a person," she said. "A partner."

"Protect. Cherish." The gravelly words vibrated from his chest as he grunted them.

"Would you be willing to brave the blizzard and get me a Christmas tree?" she asked him. "I've never gotten to celebrate it, and I really want—"

"You and your damn Christmas trees," a familiar voice grated, and the beast tensed at Isa's back.

*N*ic's mate—because it wasn't a fucking spell, it was fate—laid in shreds of a red silk dress, held close to a crackling fire by some kind of mutated, half-shifted Polaris bear abomination. One of his arms was entirely shifted and covered in white fur down to a half-paw half-hand.

The creature had the chest and abs of a man, if a man was three times larger than usual, and a partially snouted nose. A tussled mop of white hair and long fur sat on the top of his head and revealed the shifted white ears of a Polaris bear.

Faster than the others, Nic stood very still, alone, watching the half-shifted Polaris clutch Isa and growl. It looked as if the two were a loving couple, and *Nic* was the intruder.

Fuck. That.

"Isa, remain still," Nic warned, slowly stepping further into the cave. He moved cautiously, eyeing the shifter holding Isa and looking for any inkling of the beast's next move. KILL, his wolf roared.

"He won't hurt me," she said.

He would not hurt her now that the beast had sated himself inside her? KILL. KILL. KILL.

Nic's jaw ticked as his rage-filled voice gritted between his teeth, "He raped you."

Isa's eyebrows shot up, and she scoffed. "No. He did not."

Nic blinked and moved his gaze from the monster to focus on his mate. "I see the tattered clothing. I smell your scent all over him. I know he broke your heat."

"Yes. He did. He really, really did." She wiggled

happily in his embrace, wanting Nic to feel maximum pain. Goal achieved.

"You may *think* you wanted it, but a prey's heat can overcome the mind—"

"He was nice to me," she snapped at Nic from her sideways lounging position in between the fire and the half-shifted Polaris shifter.

"*Nice?*" Nic sneered. There she went with that word again. "He was nice while he raped you?"

The indomitable beast growled again, eyes narrowed on Nic.

"I will kill it and take you home," Nic promised.

"No," Isa told him, no longer the pleasing pet she had been in the past. "He did not take me against my will. He actually tried to resist me several times. He is nice and warm and cuddly." She smirked. "I like him."

"*What?*"

"In only two-ish hours of knowing him, he has helped save me from two men with spears, heal my wounds, cuddle me by a fire, make me orgasm multiple times while not doing so himself, and said he would protect and cherish me. Basically, he has treated me better than you have the entire time I have known you."

Nic shook his head. "Isa—"

"We were having a nice, touching moment before you walked in, so if you don't mind..." Isa waved her hand, gesturing for Nic to leave the cave. "Farewell. Safe travels."

"I came to save you."

"From what? A healthier relationship?"

Nic sputtered in shock as Wyn and Alban barreled into the cave from behind him.

The men skidded to a stop, sliding a bit on the icy ground, when they saw Isa and the half-shifted Polaris.

"Fucking hell…" Alban trailed off when the beast made direct eye contact with the fox shifter and let loose a rumbling growl.

CHAPTER 53

"*I*sa... Remain still," Wyn warned, saying the same thing Nic had.

Meanwhile, Alban...stared. And didn't know what to do or say.

Fox shifters were not as big or strong as wolf shifters, but this guy—a Polaris shifter stuck-mid-shift... *I stand no chance against him.* After all, Alban was only good for a joke, not a fight. He won battles by being liked by the real winners of battles.

How do I get this Yeti Polaris to like me so I can grab Isa from him? Alban wondered as his gaze took in every detail of the current situation.

"You *want* to be with him?" Nic asked her in complete shock. "A monster?"

"Better a monster on the outside than inside," Isa replied, and her words were like adrenaline shot into the side of Alban's neck. Isa had been just like him once, a people pleaser to those with power. And she had just called Nic a monster on the inside.

"Holy," Alban cursed, his head turning back and forth between Isa and Nic as if the invisible sparks and arrows flinging between their expressions were truly visible. "Isa—" Alban stepped forward, close to where she and the beast laid by the fire.

In a swift move, the beast jumped up and protectively moved his torso over Isa while he stood on all fours. The beast's hands planted firmly in front of her, caging her under him. Alban's upper body jolted back at the threat, but he stood his ground.

I want to get to Isa.

"No, he is okay." Isa patted the beast's arm from where she lay beneath his hulking form. "He can come closer."

I'm...okay? Alban thought.

Nic shot forward, but Isa glared right at the king and said, "Not you. Just Alban."

Alban's chest warmed like someone drizzled hot chicken noodle soup over it.

The fox shifter had never been chosen—not by anyone. Maybe by Nic, but Alban thought of that relationship more as an: *"I followed him around in childhood and cracked jokes until he liked me enough to keep me around."*

Alban would forever be grateful for the letter Nic

sent him when Alban left the Arctic for an American college in Alaska after his mother passed away.

"Tell me when you wish to return home, and it will happen," Nic had written him.

Home.

Alban's home used to be wherever Nic and Wyn were.

Until her.

There was something about Isa's eyes. A light blue, common in Arctic shifters, but they projected...joy. Constant happiness and excitement. He had seen her scared to literal death, yet hours later, she had splashed in a hot tub and grinned like it was the best day of her life.

Sometimes, she looks at me, and I feel like my whole life could change.

But she was his king's mate. Alban could joke and suck at her nipples and jerk himself off to watching Nic pleasure her pussy, but he would never *have* her. Not like Nic.

Fox shifters did not get mates. Foxes were not prey, but they were not strong enough to be a true predator— not up against wolves, bears, basilisks, and dragons. Foxes either became thieves, servants, or soldiers.

Fate did not favor him.

But at that moment, with the Polaris bear's protection, Isa *chose* to allow Alban close to her. Out of Nic and Wyn, Isa said *Alban* could come to her.

Not smirking or showing any smug humor in the situation, Alban approached Isa and the Polaris bear. Heavy emotion weighed down his chest. "Are you hurt?" Alban asked.

"I am fine," she said simply.

"You...You're not in heat anymore."

"He satisfied me."

Alban frowned and scanned his gaze over the beast. If the size of his arms were any sign, the Polaris bear was large *everywhere*. Surely, the fox shifter wondered the same as the others. *How?*

"My body, um, 'accommodated' during my heat," Isa explained. A light, rosy blush pinkened her pale cheeks.

"We want to take you home," Nic said.

"Why?"

Instead of rightfully explaining that Nic wanted *her*, the king snapped, "Would you rather live in a cave?"

Alban commented, "I believe what the frustrated and jealous king meant to say was that he wants you with him because you are his mate."

"But the matehood is a spell; you were right," Isa reminded them. She lifted her wrist so the bracelet sparkled in the firelight. "I could never be a 'mate to a king,' right? I could never be your equal because I am a 'weak' prey. Just a spell."

"The bracelet had only one charm on it until recently, little flower," Wyn murmured softly from several feet away. "It merely delayed your heat cycle." He pushed his glasses higher up the bridge of his nose. "There is no spell that can replicate matehood."

Isa shook her head. "But the Hag—"

"—is a lying bitch," Nic finished Isa's sentence.

"And by that, he means that the Seer likes to play by her own rules," Wyn said.

"I don't see how it *not* being a spell changes anything." Isa shot back, "You rejected me before that."

"I was keeping you *safe*," Nic exclaimed.

"By abandoning me in a random town?"

"Far from a kingdom full of enemies. Safe."

"Well, your safe town sacrificed me," she said pointedly.

"I will burn them to the ground. No need to reflect on such a hiccup."

Isa rolled her eyes and choke-laughed. *Bad sign*, Alban thought.

Isa said, "Ah, yes, your answer for everything. Violence. Burn it to the ground. Break it into pieces, and you can start again. It's what you did to me when you decided you didn't want me as a mate. Break me, abandon me, let me be sacrificed to a random beast, and now you think I will go home with you, no questions asked."

"You would rather stay in an ice cave?" Nic questioned. "You could be bundled up in the most expensive fucking blankets in the realm, drinking luxury hot chocolate while I feed you holiday cookies."

Isa blinked several times at that and twitched. The men saw right through her.

She *did* want that. But she was pissed. "Will I be locked in a room with no visitors? Will I be treated like a dirty-little-secret prey mistress?"

"Nyet," Nic said adamantly. "You will be a queen."

CHAPTER 54

Queen. Isa chewed on her inner cheek and narrowed her eyes suspiciously on the ruggedly handsome king. *This* was not what she expected. Regretting losing her, yes. But saying she could be queen?

What has changed?

"A prey queen? I thought your people would rebel."

"Only the ones who wish to die," Nic replied.

So violent. But this time, it was about protecting her, which kind of turned her on. "So, now you are willing to fight for me?"

"The Hag told him his people would embrace you as queen," Alban said, feeling the need to set the record straight and proving why Isa knew she could trust him.

Nic glared at him as Isa sighed.

"Ah, so you were told that making me queen would

help you," Isa said solemnly. "You are not choosing me despite of anything. Did you just expect to take me back to the castle, and everything would go back to how it was? Where I was there for *your* pleasure?"

Nic eyebrows furrowed as if he wondered why that was *not* a sound plan.

She told him, "You know, life isn't about always getting exactly what you want while giving nothing back."

Nic grumbled, "You're going to turn this into a Christmas lesson, aren't you?"

"Even kids know they need to leave milk and cookies out for Santa if they want gifts. You need to give to receive."

"You are my mate. You are *mine*."

Summoning her strength, Isa leaned up, supporting herself on her right hand so she could sit. Her lovely beast huffed and crouched beside her, ready for a fight or cuddles—whichever came first.

Isa thought to herself, *I wish to keep him.*

"Why? Why am I your mate?" Isa asked Nic. "Give me a reason."

She did not want him to want her because the Hag told him his people would embrace her as queen. She did not want him to want her because his wolfish instinct and fate told him she was the most attractive woman he would ever come across.

She was tired of feeling like a pawn for what others

needed—power, sex, happiness. Yes, she wanted to inspire happiness everywhere, but she also wanted someone focused on *her* happiness.

"*Why* are you my mate?" Nic repeated in confounded astonishment.

"Yes. Why?"

Irritated, Nic growled instead of replying with words.

"Express your emotions, ice king," Isa dared him.

Alban silently hooted her newfound confidence, grinning from ear to ear and shooting her two thumbs-up. Even Wyn smirked in amusement.

"You are my mate because..." Nic stepped forward, ignoring the deadly warning sounds the beast released with each inch Nic got closer to Isa. "You are nothing like what I wanted for a mate."

Nic knelt to be eye-to-eye with her, risking vulnerability at the viciously strong jaw of the Polaris bear. He said, "I always imagined my mate to be fearless and scarred and dark and violent and terrifying. And instead, fate gave me you."

Isa pursed her lips and swallowed down her rising emotion. It didn't sound like a compliment. "Disappointed?"

"No other being has ever had such a terrifying mate as I." Nic leaned his face down, below the bared, threatening teeth of the beast, so he could make closer eye contact with Isa where she knelt. "I have looked death in the eyes and smiled. Yet, you scare me more than anything."

He told her, "I fear losing you. I fear you waking up and realizing you want more than me. I fear you running off into the snow and trying to cut down a Christmas tree by yourself only to have it fall and crack your head open."

His intense eyes narrowed as he continued, "I fear sleeping in a home without the sound of your heartbeat. I fear you overexcitedly eating a holiday cookie, not taking proper time to chew, and choking to death. I fear you getting a papercut from one of your 'thank you' notes and bleeding out."

She remarked, "I am not fragile."

"Nyet, but that is what you make me." Nic reached forward and cupped Isa's cheek as the beast snarled at him.

Isa kept one hand on her half-shifted bear to calm him and tell him *not* to bite off Nic's head.

"You are nothing like what I wanted for a mate," Nic repeated, and his spicy, citrusy, mulled wine scent wafted over her face. "But you are everything I could ever fucking need."

*H*er eyes stared so deeply into Nic's that he was unsure if he was messing it up. He was not sure of anything, really. The Ice King did not apologize or make love declarations.

She had changed him. He *wanted* to change—for her.

"Arctic wolves live in the harshest of climates," Nic whispered to her. "We can spend half a year in twenty-four hours of darkness." He grazed his lips over the side of her cheek and breathed in her comforting scent of tart cranberries and *home*. "But know this, there is one brutal darkness I never wish to survive."

"One without me?" Isa murmured.

"*Yes.*"

"You abandoned me," she said, her voice cracking in pain. All of the men—including the beast—flinched at the sound.

"I was always going to come back for you. Even when I thought it was a spell. I would have always come back."

Isa turned her head away from Nic's palm, looking away from him. "Not good enough. You were prepared to ship me away because you didn't think I was worthy of you."

"Wrong," Nic snapped. "I am the one not worthy."

Her teeth sank into her bottom lip. "You were embarrassed to have a prey mate."

"No. I feared others would hurt you if you were near me."

"I want a man who would die for me—"

"Fuck that." Nic grabbed Isa's face with both hands,

forcing her gaze back onto him. "Anyone could die at any moment, and it just ends. What does dying for someone mean?"

Nic swore he felt her fingers in his chest, gripping his heart tightly as their gazes burned into each other. "I wouldn't die for you," he said. "I would live for you. *That's* what you mean to me. For years, I have moved like a zombie, half dead and gone, wishing to be left in misery and peace. Thinking peace was loneliness, knowing sorrow was inevitable, and believing that to be numb was to be strong."

He pressed his forehead to hers, wishing to get inside her brain and thoughts like she was always in his. "Not for a second of my existence did I dream of being worthy—of a mate, of happiness. But for you, I will try. For you, I will bake cookies even when I have workers who can do so. I will hold you on top of my shoulders and help you decorate a Christmas tree."

Nic swore, "I will take you ice skating and hold onto you the entire time. And if you dare to fall through the ice, I will warm you up by a fire with hot chocolate and slap your delicious goddamn ass until I feel you understand me."

Isa took deep, heaving breaths as if she kept forgetting to breathe during his speech.

"I was kept as the dirty little secret of my family—never good enough to rule. Seen as weak. Kept in small, locked rooms and eventually banished for my own 'safety.' It hardened me. And I realize now that I did the same to you. Fucking regretfully." He exhaled. "Hear me, I will dedicate the rest of my existence to softening you."

Did she get it? Could she see?

How he...loved her.

"My mate will be the most gracious, bright, *warm* queen the Arctic has ever seen. Her king, covered in scars, will bow to her."

Isa's mouth hung open for a moment. "A predator bowing to a prey?"

"Every goddamn morning," Nic promised, rasping, "How else will I enjoy my favorite breakfast?" He nodded down to her pussy, and she snorted.

"So, will you be returning with us?" Wyn asked from behind Nic, still standing near the cave's entrance. "We will have all of your old cult compound's female prey sent to the castle; they should be arriving in a few hours. They will need someone to...help deprogram them. Show them they do not have to be 'pets.' Make them feel safe and cared for."

Isa smiled, and Nic's heart twitched and ached like it had just grown an inch.

"I would like to help them," she said.

"And will...*he* be joining us?" Wyn nodded at the beast. "A vampiric Polaris shifter. I am assuming Kendrick's older brother, who was turned mid-shift? The rightful leader of the Polaris who Kendrick *thought* was destroyed by vampires?"

"That's what the Hag meant by plural kings. A wolf and a bear—" Alban was cut off by Nic.

"Him? Come with us?"

"Yes," Isa said. "He is also my mate."

Nic's heart shrunk again.

Isa rolled her eyes at Nic's displeased expression. "You will need to learn to share me. I have four mates, after all."

"Four?" Alban choked out. Wyn's expression suggested someone had just shockingly struck him across the face.

Isa smiled at Alban and Wyn as Nic ground his teeth. "Four."

CHAPTER 55

*I*sa liked being queen. She still wrote "thank you" notes, hugged strangers, and expressed an unwavering desire to check off every activity on her winter bucket list.

But she walked differently as a queen.

She lifted her head and made eye contact when she entered a room. She did not remain silent or submissive when she had something she wanted to say.

She no longer only wanted to *please*. In fact, she was actively *displeasing*.

"You cannot prove I stole all of the bread."

"Love," Nic said evenly. "Do you really think I do not have security cameras?"

She was a queen of mischief. A Robin Hood of stealing food from the castle and secretly gifting it to the townsfolk who could only afford to heat their homes.

"At least wear all black next time like a true thief," Alban told her. "Nic will forgive anything if you wear all black." It was his favorite color, after all.

Truthfully, Nic would forgive anything she did. She also did not steal for very long since he set up a food-bank, fully paid for by whatever underworld dealings he worked in the background.

Isa was doing what she wanted to—helping people.

Every day, she spent time helping the other prey females from her old tribe to relearn themselves and their capabilities. The other women did not understand how Isa was lucky enough to marry her master.

"There are no real masters," she told them as a group sat in the parlor and worked on their knitting with Nic's grandmother. "Only those you choose to give power and follow because you want to. But…any good alpha should be bowing to *you*."

All it took was realizing that a person did not have to be seen as "valuable" to be worthy of protection or shelter or love. A person did not have to say "thank you" to deserve a meal. A person did not have to smile to deserve a blanket warming them on a cold night.

And, at the moment, one day before Christmas, Isa reminded her sexy, strapping men that giving her orgasms did not mean they deserved to eat the many cookies she made for the castle workers and local townspeople.

"They are not for you," she warned, slapping their hands away.

"But I thought you were making them for 'everyone,'" Alban whined. "Am I not a person to you, bunny? Only a rock-hard dick and a chiseled set of abs?"

Baine, her vampiric half-shifted Polaris bear who only Isa could understand due to her charmed bracelet, huffed and nodded. He loved his mate's sweet treats, just like he loved her blood.

"You, mister," Isa pointed at Baine. "Have a cookie addiction."

He growled in his own language, "Hungry."

"For blood or just sugar?" she asked.

He stared intensely at her as if she asked a question that needed no reply.

"He will not be feeding off you," Nic said, suspiciously standing in the part of the kitchen where Isa had abandoned the bowl and mixers still covered in cookie batter dough.

"Don't get jealous." Isa sent him an air-kiss. "Sharing is a virtue, remember?"

Nic had done better with the idea of "sharing" than before. He finally stopped shooting glares at Alban every time Alban "mysteriously" located some mistletoe and exclaimed, "*Isa, it's Christmas law!*" After the fifth kiss between her and the fox shifter, Nic simply began "finding" mistletoe as well.

"Baine will have to feed from me eventually," she said.

"No. He nearly drained you last time," Nic responded. Nic pointed to Isa then pointed to his teeth as he told Baine, "No. Feeding."

Baine's bottom lip curled into a pout at that, flashing sharp bottom canine teeth.

Isa reached over to gently pet the white fur on Baine's partially bear-shifted arm. "He drank too much from me last time because he was hungry."

"We will find him a different blood bag," Wyn agreed with Nic.

Isa frowned at that, *wanting* to feel Baine's fangs in her again. She shivered and blushed just from thinking about how good it felt when he sucked on her neck.

Baine groaned huskily with a lusty expression as if he knew exactly what she thought about.

"Are you excited for Christmas morning tomorrow, bunny?" Alban asked her, moving his hands to her hips. The fox shifter always seemed to be touching her since she told Nic that they would all be mates, together. "I hear you will have *many* presents under the tree. And not all of them will be sex toys."

She grinned and hopped up and down. "I am so excited; I don't think I will be able to sleep at all tonight."

Wyn snorted, "What else is new?"

Ever since Isa demanded to sleep in a bedroom with

enough beds pushed together so the five of them could share a bedroom, she enjoyed every part of the sleep-overs but the *sleeping*.

If it was not Nic's teasing fingers, Alban's naughty mouth, or Wyn's exploring tongue, it was Baine's para-normally loud snoring.

But it was sexy snoring. Groaning, grunting sounds purred from his broad chest and resembled the noises he made during sex. Sex with Baine would only be during her heat—due to his, ahem, *size*—but she still reveled in pleasuring him.

In his half-shifted form, he was so...sensitive. When she had first licked over the slit of his plump cockhead, the men had to hold Baine down to ensure he did not accidentally hurt her by bucking his hips or making any sudden movements in his vast-sized state.

It had been so hot to tease him, knowing the other men restrained him. *The sounds he made when he finally erupted and came on my chest...*

"Uh, oh," Alban mumbled, smirking.

Baine let out a rumbling purr.

"I think our queen is getting horny again," Nic stated, sniffing the air and calling her out.

"You think other queens get this horny?" Alban asked.

"Only the ones with very lucky kings," Wyn said.

"You need to be tended to, love?" Nic asked, sidling closer to where Isa stirred the beginning ingredients of the frosting she planned to put on her currently-baking cookies.

"I—I shouldn't get distracted," Isa said in a strained, high-pitched voice as she stirred and turned her back to him.

She *wanted* to get distracted. But she had also planned to make cookies for everyone within driving distance of the castle. That was...many cookies.

Even though the Hag told Nic his people would accept Isa as queen, she wanted to be beloved. And nothing said starting-off-on-the-right-foot like delivering homemade baked goods on Christmas.

Okay, so she was still a bit of a people-pleaser.

"But wouldn't it be *more* distracting to keep going?" Nic rasped by her ear, and her blood heated. His breath caressed the back of her neck, where her skin tingled for touch.

"Wouldn't it be so distracting—" Nic stepped closer into her space. "—to keep making that sweet frosting when you can't stop imagining us licking it off your needy, shivering body? How good it would feel, our tongues on you..."

Isa shivered and swallowed loudly.

Alban snickered and approached Isa from the side as Nic caged her into the kitchen island counter. Nic stretched his legs on either side of her, trapping her in his sexy, dominating manner. His chiseled front pressed to her back.

Meanwhile, Alban slinked to the side and picked up a lock of Isa's pale hair to play with. "The king is right. Wouldn't it be more distracting to keep baking when your breathing is getting heavier, and you can feel your nipples poking your apron?" Alban asked in a sinful, low voice.

"Grazing against the material. Sensitive little peaks wanting to press *harder* and feel *more*." Alban asked, "Honestly, bunny, isn't it distracting to be clothed while you bake? Your panties firmly cupping your pussy. Your apron brushing against your nipples. Wouldn't it be less distracting to be naked?"

"Wyn," Isa sighed out, exasperated. She called out to the advisor for help in corralling the men. Mr. *Suit and Glasses* would surely assist.

"Yes, little flower?" Wyn strode to her other side and draped a hand on her overheating shoulder.

Wyn's nails shifted into owl's claws as he tore right through the top bands of her apron, causing the fabric to separate and flimsily fall to the kitchen floor.

"Wyn!" Isa exclaimed.

"Was that not helpful?" Wyn feigned ignorance.

At the sight of her breasts, bared at the elimination of the apron, Baine groaned and slammed a hand onto the kitchen counter. A large crack spread through the granite at the force and strength at which he hit it.

"Goddamn it," Nic cursed, but Baine ignored him. Nic had already cursed several times at minor damages that Baine's enormous body was prone to cause around the castle.

Baine grunted, "*Hungry.*"

Isa, the only one who understood him due to the spelled bracelet, kept the news to herself that Baine was hungry. The men had repeatedly made it clear that they did not want him feeding on her.

Baine opened his mouth and unfurled his eight-inch-long, bluish-black tongue, flicking it at her.

Isa gasped, remembering the talent of that tongue lapping over her clit and curling inside her. Her thighs clenched together at the sudden spike of arousal.

Okay, *now* she was getting distracted. "This isn't fair," she complained, topless without the kitchen apron to cover her.

She stood in nothing but a pair of panties, which was hardly any cover or armor against the tantalizing alpha scents filling the kitchen.

"Just have Miss Belsky make the cookies," Nic suggested in her ear between delicate kisses against her neck. "Let us take you to bed."

So, so tempting. "I have to make them. They are supposed to be homemade."

"They will be made in a home whether it is by you or the kitchen staff," Wyn pointed out, running his clawed fingers down to play with the side of her red lace panties.

"Hey, don't you dare—" Isa had no time to finish her

protest before Wyn cut right through the thin material and left her completely naked in the kitchen. "The cookies are meant to be a gift directly from the queen—" she cut off again.

Because Nic had just slipped his hand between her legs.

CHAPTER 56

"*N*ic," Isa gasped out as his fingers ever so softly glided over the top seam of her sex.

"You can keep baking, baby," he told her as he slowly inched his fingers up and down her slit. "We don't want to distract you."

She would have rolled her eyes if they had not already rolled to the back of her head when he pulled the hood of her clit back, so his touch settled against the bare, most hypersensitive part of her. "*Oh*," she moaned, her hips rocking forward into the touch.

"You can keep doing exactly what you're doing," he whispered onto her neck. "Just try not to get distracted." He pressed firm circles over her pulsing clit as he kissed a secret, thrilling spot under her earlobe.

Alban and Wyn joined in, kissing her shoulders and palming her breasts.

"*Hungry,*" Baine grunted loudly. The others did not understand him.

Nic's engorged erection heated Isa's lower back, and she moaned and rocked her ass against the provocative bulge as he slowed his fingers over her slickening pussy.

"Nyet, no, you cannot get distracted from your task," Nic teased as he slid his fingers down to her entrance. He prodded her tight pussy walls with his index finger.

He knew teasing could trigger an early heat cycle. She swore he wanted it to happen since he missed out on her first one.

"If you make me go into heat the night before Christmas, I'm going to…" Isa cut off with another gasp as Nic slammed two fingers deep inside her and curled them to rub her G-spot.

"Hmm?" He slowly withdrew his fingers, inch by inch, before delving them back inside her. "What would you do?"

She bit on her inner cheek and glared at the bowl of icing as her body begged for more. No amount of orgasms ever seemed enough around them.

Nic nipped at her earlobe. "If I made you go into heat…what would you do?"

Alban bent his head and lifted one of her nipples to his mouth so he could lick, and bite, and *suck.*

"*Oh,*" Isa whined, unable to control the needy sound.

"Would you…moan for me?" Nic asked in a husky voice that she felt right between her legs.

"*Mmmm,*" she moaned when Wyn began sucking at her other nipple in tandem with Alban.

"Would you get nice and wet for me?" Nic started a steady, thrusting rhythm of his fingers moving in and out of her.

"If we made you go into heat, would you take both of us at the same time?" Alban asked, purring it to her breast.

She stiffened before letting out a loud moan and flexing her hips to fuck herself faster on Nic's fingers. "*Please.*"

They had not taken her at the same time before. She wanted all of them at once. She was unsure how it would be possible, but she wanted it.

"See, now you're *distracting* her."

"*Hungry,*" Baine growled from behind them, but Isa was too focused on the fingers plunging inside her and the constant thumb strumming her clit while tongues played over her nipples.

"Share me," she begged. "Please."

"She thinks she can make the orders now that she is queen?" Nic whistled.

In a blur, Isa was transported by her fast, wolfish mate into one of the furnished living rooms of the castle, close to the kitchen. Beside a burning fireplace emitting perfect rays of warmth, Nic laid Isa on a fuzzy blanket on the floor.

Nic wrenched open her legs and pushed his pants

down his waist.

"Share me," she said again, this time pointedly glancing at Wyn and Alban.

"Giving me orders?"

"Yes," she shot back, chin high and queenly.

Nic smirked, rolled his eyes, and gestured for Alban and Wyn to come closer. Nic backed up and stood with his boxers around his knees. His long, thick length kissed his hard, muscular abdomen as Isa salivated over it.

"You heard your queen," he told Wyn and Alban. "She wants to be shared."

Alban raced forward before Nic finished his sentence.

From Alban's rather unorthodox childhood of growing up with a sex worker as a mother, he put little importance on sex. It was another form of currency, truly. People had sex for a warm meal, shelter, confirmation of feelings, pleasure…

Alban joked like he was the biggest manwhore in the Arctic, but truthfully, he had grown bored of sex. He had been fine going without sex for the last two years that Nic ruled from an all-male compound.

Until her.

"You and Wyn, show her how good it feels to get distracted," Nic said. "Meanwhile, I'm going to fuck that mouth until I like what comes out of it."

Nic moved forward and grabbed his dick to level it to Isa's face, where she knelt on the blanket. He muttered, "Giving me orders. Such a perfect fucking queen."

She moaned at his dominating words and licked her lips.

Alban's sudden rush of blood flow between his legs caused him to question his own hearing. Had his king really just given him permission to fuck her? *With* Wyn?

Nic petted Isa's bottom lip. Speaking to Alban and Wyn while staring at Isa, Nic added, "Be gentle with her."

Wyn blurred to kneel beside Isa on the blanket. Alban had never seen Wyn move so fast; he typically glided in smooth, patient steps everywhere he went. *Horny fucking owl.*

Wyn ran his fingers over Isa's wet slit and wore an expression of pure torture. For the first time in the genius's life, he probably did not know what to do.

Sex was one thing, but sharing one woman at the same time was a delicate science to achieve maximum pleasure.

"Wyn's never even been inside a woman before," Alban remarked. "I'll have to show him the right hole—"

"I've read books, asshole," Wyn shot back and fed Isa's pussy a long finger.

She slid onto it and gyrated her hips, whimpering. Nic's dick plopped against her mouth as he slapped it to her cheek, and she whimpered and opened her mouth to take him.

In sensual awe, the men watched her slow descent. She took Nic down her throat, displaying her apparent lack of a gag reflex, and *smiled* around his cock.

"Dear gods," Wyn muttered under his breath as he felt the damp depth of her sheath. "Like hot, wet silk."

"Much better than your hand," Alban said as he settled in on the other side of Isa. He pointed for Wyn to lie back. "Down, boy."

Wyn glared at the instruction.

Beasty Baine let out a loud snarl, but the men ignored it. Dude got to experience her first heat without them. He could sit this one out and watch.

Finally, Wyn relented and laid down on the floor, right behind where Isa knelt. Alban palmed Isa's hips and jerked his head at Nic to show how they needed to position her.

Alban asked the room, "How is Wyn going to fuck for the first time and not come in her instantly?"

"Fuck, you are so good at that," Nic hissed to Isa as she sucked.

Alban pulled her slightly away to position her on top of Wyn. Once she knelt with her legs open over Wyn,

Nic stepped forward again. He pumped his shaft in his fist and dabbed the head of his cock to her lips for an extra lick. She craned her neck farther to lick and kiss his length.

Wyn shifted his fingernails into talons again to rip through the front of his dress pants and boxers. He grabbed his erection and squeezed as he gazed at Isa's pretty, pink pussy and fumbled to align himself with her entrance.

I guess he did *read enough books to find the right hole,* Alban thought.

"Go slow," Nic warned Wyn. After all, his dick was in Isa's mouth.

"You can't tell a virgin to go slow for his first time," Alban commented. "He's going to come the second he slides inside her."

"Stop saying that. Unlike you, I have self-control," Wyn commented dryly and lifted his hips to rub his cock against her pussy lips.

Alban snorted. "Yeah, until you feel pussy for the first time. Do you even jerk off on the regular?"

"Would you both stop bitching and fuck my mate like she asked?" Nic snapped before turning his focus back on Isa as he stroked a thumb over her cheek. "Now...will you let me in that pretty mouth again, my queen?" Nic rubbed his cockhead over her lips. Isa obediently opened her mouth, and Nic's expression screamed gratefulness and lust.

"Let's get this done right," Alban muttered, rubbing his hands together as he moved behind Wyn. The fox shifter grabbed the root of Wyn's dick.

"What the hell are you doing?" Wyn yelped out as Alban squeezed his girth.

"I'm helping a virgin out," Alban grated and aligned Wyn's plump mushroom tip to Isa's slick entrance. "You'd probably shove inside her ass by mistake. And that ass is mine."

A blush darkened Wyn's cheeks, and he tried to slap away Alban's hands. Alban pulled Isa's hips down, which shoved Wyn's cock smoothly into Isa's sopping sex.

Isa howled out her pleasure around Nic's cock in her mouth.

"See? Aligned—"

"FUCK," Wyn growled.

His hands, which had been trying to push Alban away, slammed into the floor on either side of Isa's knees, where she straddled him. His long, sharp talons lengthened and pierced through the fuzzy blanket on the floor.

His pupils widened and grew into big, circular, owl-like eyes.

"Oh yeah, you have so much self-control," Alban snickered as Wyn's lower abdomen trembled and his hips jerked in small movements as if he was getting accustomed to the feeling of being inside her. "Now, thrust in and out." Alban tried to guide Wyn's hips, but the Noctu shifter steeled against his manipulations.

"I know what I'm doing." Wyn gritted his teeth.

Alban wondered if "directing" Wyn's first time was enough to turn his pacifist friend into a fox murderer. His talons *were* currently ripping up and clawing the blanket and flooring on either side of Isa as Wyn grappled with his control.

Nic released a husky groan as Isa bobbed her head on him. Nic's thick shaft moved in and out of Isa's sucking mouth, shining with more and more saliva with each thrust.

Beasty Baine again made a loud noise.

"Go slow," Alban said to Wyn. "Your instinct is going to be to rut."

"Would you back off?"

Isa let out a loud sound of discontentment at how Wyn had yet to begin truly fucking her.

"Yeah, I'm getting impatient too, bunny," Alban commented and maneuvered himself behind her. "This is going to take some shifting now, my queen."

Alban leaned Isa forward to see where her puckered back entrance waited for him, but a sound interrupted him.

A crooning sound came from Wyn as his body shivered from his head to his toes, and Alban frowned.

Then, Isa's eyes went as wide as snowballs and rolled

to the back of her head. Her mouth tightened around Nic's dick as she screamed onto it.

What the fuck just happened?

CHAPTER 57

*I*sa had never experimented much with feathers. In her classes to be a good pet, feathers were taught as a possible toy—that did not require batteries—to increase pleasure. Feathers were used in seduction and teasing, like ice cubes.

Isa never thought about how a Noctu owl shifter could shift body parts on command.

She had no idea what was happening until she let Nic's erection slip from her lips, and she peered down, between her legs.

Wyn had somehow "grown" three long feathers above his cock so that anytime he thrust into her and withdrew, the tips of the feathers grazed over her swollen clit. It acted as a tease-torture tuft.

The feeling of the light, feathery quills scraping her bundle of nerves blanked her every thought and lit her every pore on fire. The tantalizing sensation tightened every muscle inside her, building up her orgasm.

"Yes. Oh gods, it's so good," she begged. "Please make me come, Wyn."

"Will deny you nothing," Wyn gritted between clenched teeth as he jerked his hips up, allowing the feathers to stroke over Isa until her toes curled and her thighs shook.

Then, Isa felt Alban at her back, tilting her forward, changing the angle. The hot, thick tip of Alban's shaft prodded her tight, puckered entrance. The initial sensation shocked her. Her tribe had taught Isa about anal, but she had only ever tested it with tiny beads.

And Alban is large.

"Shhh," he cooed to her as he massaged her ass. His other hand dipped to gather some of her wetness and streak it over his cock.

"It's going to feel good, Isa," Alban said. Alban only ever called her by her name, and not "bunny," in very special situations. "I promise. But you need to stay relaxed for me. Don't fight it. Just relax those muscles for me."

Alban guided a finger inside her ass, and she puffed out air like she forgot how to properly exhale. "*Very* good," he said. "That's such a good girl."

"*Mmmmm.*"

"HUNGRY," Baine roared.

Isa gasped and turned her head but watched in helpless horror and lust as Baine sank his fangs into the closest person he could reach. Nic.

The king most against sharing—but doing his best to adjust—was now...getting shared.

Nic's shocked, wide eyes glazed over as Baine's fangs slid into his neck.

"Oh...fuck...you," Nic cursed out as if in slow motion as Baine took a strong and powerful gulp of blood from him in a toe-curling suck. *"Fuck."*

If only Nic saw how Baine, in a horny and bloodthirsty rage, jerked off behind Nic as he fed from him. Baine's intense black eyes burned into Isa as he masturbated his thick girth and gulped.

When she saw Nic's jaw tick, Isa quickly grabbed Nic's cock and sucked him to distract him, which perfectly distracted her and kept her muscles relaxed for Alban to fully enter her from behind as Wyn stayed inside her pussy from under her.

So much. All at once.

The sensation of Wyn's feather tuft scraping and massaging her clit with each of his thrusts inside her pussy. The taboo and new feeling of Alban's cock slinking in and out of her ass. Nic's mindless expression as she sucked him into the back of her throat. At the same time, he felt the endorphins and ecstasy-inducing vampire bite.

Her body quaked, shaking so bad that Wyn and Alban had to hold onto her as they drilled inside her.

Lust overload.

Pheromones shot out of her skin, and the men groaned and grunted as they breathed in her aroused scent.

"YES," she screamed. Her pussy contracted on Wyn's cock and a similar clamping occurred around Alban's length as he took her from behind in a steady rhythm to match Wyn's thrusts.

Her body's tremors got worse as the most powerful orgasm of her existence ripped through her.

She fell forward, pushing Nic's cock all the way down her throat until his balls slapped the bottom of her chin.

"Yes, take me." Nic tipped his head back as his hips shot forward. He filled Isa's mouth with jet after jet of cum; all the while, Baine sipped from his neck. The vampire bite must have added to the euphoria because Nic could not stop *coming.*

Isa moaned and swallowed as Alban and Wyn shouted from opposite sides of her as they filled her up as well. Baine's loud, long groan of satisfaction echoed around the room as he came on his hand.

"Dear gods..." Wyn muttered, holding himself up on his back elbows to try to sit, only to fall right back to the floor, searching for his bearings.

They had all come so hard, Isa thought she lost her sense of hearing.

She kept hearing a recurring wailing noise. Was it

her body screaming to stop being mercilessly fucked multiple times a day? She did not care to listen to such complaints.

Wait, no. A fire alarm was going off.

The cookies!

She had gotten distracted and burned the batch of cookies.

After running to the kitchen, taking the tray out with blackened treats, and witnessing Isa's eyes turn watery at the failure, each of the men devoured the burnt, charcoal-textured cookies until none were left.

Even as she told them they should just throw them away, they chewed what sounded like chunky rocks, crunched them into swallowable dust, and said they tasted perfect.

Because maybe the alpha men were people-pleasers too, but for a singular person.

For one woman, they would do anything.

The most fearsome Arctic shifters of the realm...Isa-pleasers.

EPILOGUE

Twas Christmas morning, when all through the castle,
not a shifter was stirring, not even to wrastle.
Five stockings were hung on the mantle full of love
in hopes that many gifts would fill thereof.
The mates snuggled in bed, pressed tight as a glove
when Isa jolted awake with a violently eager SHOVE.
She raced to the parlor, causing an unintended clatter.
Her mates quickly followed to see what was the matter.
She jumped with glee and rushed to open her very first gift.
The fox shifter had promised not to shoplift.
But the gift was from not-so-saintly Nic,
and what lay inside proved he was not just a dick.
The king, who always came across as cold and nonchalant,

had written a note in the box, promising, "Anything you ever
fucking want."
And with that vow, any doubts were swept out of sight—
Happy Christmas to all, and to all, a good night.

—The Hag (Hardly A Gloater)

ACKNOWLEDGMENTS

This Acknowledgments page is FOR YOU! Thank you for reading!! Thank you for picking this up and making it to the end! If you enjoyed it, I would LOVE if you would leave a review or help get the word out about this series to others who might enjoy it!

Also, thank you to my mom for not bringing up the smutty scenes after reading this. Love you!

If you have the time, please also leave a Goodreads Review ! Or on the platform where you purchased this book!

ABOUT THE AUTHOR

M. K. Kate decided to dabble in writing dark, edgy—and don't forget smutty!—paranormal reverse harem romance novels after watching too many spicy TikToks about monster romance. She seeks to put new spins on paranormal reverse harems and specializes in dirty-talking heroes and the sassy women who leave them tongue-tied. She also writes steamy romantic comedy romance novels under M. K. Hale. "M. K. Kate" is her alter-ego for all things filthy, kinky, and paranormal. "Pretty Little Prey" was her first reverse harem romance novel.

Follow her on social media: **@mkkateauthor**
    Join her newsletter:
    https://mkkate.weebly.com/contact.html

Also, if you enjoyed her writing, check out her steamy/spicy contemporary romantic comedy novels under the pen name "M. K. Hale!"
    Instagram: @mkhaleauthor
    Website: https://www.mkhale.com/

MORE BY M. K. KATE

PRETTY LITTLE PREY: Spicy Shifters Paranormal Reverse Harem Romance Novel

Some shifters might revel in their strength as werewolves or dragons, but Luna shifts into...a defenseless lamb.

HUNTED. ON THE RUN. THEN, HELD HOSTAGE BY HER MATES.

As a rare breed of *prey* shifter, Luna has been hunted most of her life for what she is. She learned not to trust predator shifters—especially of the alpha male variety—after losing her family to the claws of a wolf pack, led by her ex-boyfriend. *Hello, trust issues.*

So, when *multiple* deadly predator shifters claim she is their mate and try to keep her to themselves, she will do everything she can to escape them. Especially considering the men are enemies, and she is bound to be caught in their jealous crossfire.

HELD CAPTIVE BY FOUR OF THE MOST DANGEROUS PREDATOR SHIFTERS IN EXISTENCE.

A possessive, grunting alpha werewolf with an overactive sex drive.

A tattooed, black-leather-jacket-wearing basilisk with an attitude problem and a penchant for dominantly wrapping his fingers around her throat.

A seductive vampire with a drugging bite that makes her eyes roll back in her head.

A smirking, funny fox shifter who can tell when she is lying.

Being held hostage by these alpha men is one thing, but the more time an omega prey shifter spends in the presence of a predator, the more likely her heat is triggered. If she cannot escape them in time, her body will betray her—begging for their touch. Spoiler alert: it's already betraying her.

This is a full-novel length standalone reverse harem / why choose, high-heat shifter romance of almost 100,000 words. Readers 18+.

Warning: PRETTY LITTLE PREY *is an extremely spicy paranormal reverse harem romance that contains omega-verse heat, light bullying from one of the harem members (in the enemies-to-lovers sense), dominant and dirty-talking alpha men, and a deeply jealous love triangle between two of the harem members who are rivals not willing to share her affection. But, yay for happy endings full of group sex!*

MORE BY M. K. KATE

Coming Soon:

SUCCUBUS LESSONS: Smutty Paranormal Incubi Reverse Harem Romance Novel

INCUBI MATES—SUCCUBI—ARE EXTINCT. EXCEPT FOR HER...

CONTEMPORARY ROMCOM BY M.
K. HALE

The Drummer's Roommate: A Spicy Enemies to Lovers
Rockstar Rom-Com

He burns for her...but she can't hear him.

**"Unbelievably attractive male seeking roommate. Must be
able to tolerate loud drumming and even louder sex.
Serious inquiries only."**

That was the ad "delicate" wallflower Thea replied to. Stuck in
L.A.—jobless and homeless—after leaving her cheating ex,

Thea's best option is to move in with tattooed rocker and sex symbol Draven Maxwell. To Draven's dismay, Thea does not trip all over herself when Draven plays his sexy music—mostly because she cannot hear it.

A drummer living with a deaf woman sounds like a match made in roommate heaven, but the scorching attraction between the two utter opposites is hot as hell.

She thinks he is a smug playboy, but he only craves her.

When the heartthrob drummer reveals he is learning sign language to communicate with her, Thea's perception of bad boy Draven cracks. He's…nice? And funny. And puts subtitles on the TV without her asking.

Could the cocky rocker have a heart of gold behind his chiseled chest? And what's up with all those pining looks of agonized yearning every morning he sees her trudge around the apartment in modest pajamas and no makeup?

From enemy roommates to best friends, speaking different languages will not lessen their undeniable connection and sizzling chemistry. Through the thin walls, something becomes much louder than the nightly drum set, and it might sound like love.

NEXT STEPS...

To keep up to date for when a new smutty reverse harem novel comes available, make sure to follow me on social media:

Instagram: @mkkateauthor

Or join my newsletter: https://mkkate.weebly.com/contact.html

If you enjoyed my writing, check out my steamy/spicy contemporary romantic comedy novels under the pen name "M. K. Hale!"

Instagram: @mkhaleauthor

Website: https://www.mkhale.com/

Made in the USA
Columbia, SC
01 July 2025

59973559R00305